Backtalk

By: Jessica Terry

BACKTALK

First edition. September 9, 2022.

Copyright © 2022 Jessica Terry.

ISBN: 979-8986432151

Written by Jessica Terry.

I'm so grateful for everyone who has given me encouragement as I worked on this; my family, church family, friends; it means so much. And I always give huge thanks to my readers; your continued support over the years has been invaluable.

Chapter 1

· · · ·

"SYLVIA, COME ON!"

"I'm coming! I dropped my lipstick!"

"You gon' make us get caught! Hurry up!"

Sylvia stuffed the tube of Scarlett Red Fury lipstick that she had stolen from the local drug store back into her purse and ran to catch up with her friends. She wasn't about to leave it behind; the color was perfect and she had snagged the last one in the store. And since she was only fifteen and her mother had forbidden her to wear makeup for another two years, she snuck and wore the deep red shade every chance she got.

She and her friends Amelia, Moni, and Carol were skipping school again to go to hang out in their friend Jordanna's basement. Jordanna's parents were loaded and often out of town, foolishly leaving their daughter home alone way more than they should have. Sylvia loved going to Jordanna's, because she could pretend to be the grown-up that she longed to be. They drank, they smoked, they laid around doing absolutely nothing while eating all the food in Jordanna's refrigerator.

And on this particular day, Sylvia finally and officially met Deuce and Dub.

Deuce and Dub Parker were twins and by far the cutest and most popular boys in school. They were both tall, cinnamon-skinned hunks who looked older than their sixteen years. Sylvia had noticed them long ago but had never had the nerve to approach either of them. Deuce was known as the rougher, more aggressive one while Dub was more reserved. Sylvia had been nursing a crush on Dub for years, but he never really paid her any attention. If she had her way, all that was going to change today.

"Damn, he looks good," she mumbled to herself, her beer bottle against her lips. Lust overtook her young body.

"Girl, why you over here eyein' Dub like that?" Moni asked her, approaching with her own beer bottle in hand. "You might as well just go over there and suck his-"

"Shut up, Moni!" Sylvia interrupted, frowning at her friend briefly before turning her eyes back to Dub. She took a sip of her beer as she watched him dance with a big-booty girl nobody liked named Coco. "But to be real, I'd do it if he let me."

"You and me both."

Sylvia shoved her slightly. "Girl, you better back up! One threesome was enough."

"Please, I ain't tryin' to do no more of those, either!" Moni replied. She looked back at Dub. "Besides, Dub is not a boy you wanna share."

"Exactly. Which is why I ain't sharing."

"And what you gon' do? He hasn't even looked over here once."

"I'll *get* him to notice me," Sylvia proclaimed confidently, taking one last swig of her beer before plunking it down on a nearby table. She adjusted her tube top to reveal more of her ripe breasts and hiked up her skirt before placing her hands on her hips and beginning her strut over to where Dub was dancing. Her skin tingled in anticipation. She had always had a thing for Dub. Really, she wouldn't have minded getting with either twin, since they were both fine and gorgeous, but Deuce was a known player and not as nice as Dub. Deuce had never even given her a second look, while Dub had at least given her a polite nod once or twice when he passed by her in the school hallways.

Dub had just finished dancing with Coco and was starting to head to the other side of the room. Sylvia licked her lips and then called out "Dub!" before she lost her nerve.

Dub turned around and looked at her, but before she could say another word, Paula, who got around more than the city bus, stepped in front of her and grabbed Dub's arm.

"I know you're not going anywhere before you dance with me," she said seductively, looking up at him with tight eyes.

"I told you I would," Dub replied, subtly eyeing her curvy body.

"Well, I want it now," Paula insisted, taking his hand and leading him back to the middle of the room. She proceeded to dance seductively with him, winding her backside into his groin and putting his hands where she wanted them to be on her body. Everyone was watching them and she loved it. If she had her way, she and Dub would be going into one of the side rooms within the hour.

Sylvia just stood there fuming, her hands still on her hips. She couldn't believe Paula's nerve, blocking her like that. Part of her wanted to yank Paula by her wig, but she didn't want to get into another fight. She had gotten into enough trouble after the last one.

"Nice move," Moni mocked, coming to stand next to her.

"Shut up, Moni."

"Girl, please. You know Paula is a ho. Hell, 'ho' might be too nice a name for her."

"Hell, I'm a ho too, but she's the one over there grinding on him."

"Paula got you beat, girl. She'll sleep with anybody. Just talk to somebody else. There are a lot of cute boys down here."

"Yeah, you're right," Sylvia agreed, but her eyes stayed on Dub. And they stayed on him for the remainder of the night, as more girls kept getting in her way every time she tried to go talk to him. She was getting more and more agitated. She couldn't do anything but stand there and watch him dance with and talk to girl after girl after girl, oblivious to her desire for him. The more she watched him, the more she realized he seemed to have a type; he seemed to like the curvaceous and voluptuous, which Sylvia was not. She was rather thin, with a rather oddly-shaped body. Her breasts were small, her hips were narrow, but she had a decent-sized backside. She always hoped that she would grow to be a little more proportioned, but she was fifteen and it still hadn't happened yet. And she absolutely hated her legs; her thighs were rather toned but below the knees, they were spindly. Her face was average, and she knew it. No matter how much makeup she snuck and wore, she still couldn't make herself look as good as Paula and the other prettier girls in school. Sylvia wished she was as popular with the boys as they were, and any play she *did* get, she had to work extra hard for.

Figuring she wouldn't get any time with Dub anytime soon, Sylvia tried to concentrate on having a good time with the other boys and her friends. She danced and drank and smoked cigarettes and enjoyed herself, but before she knew it, just about all of her friends had hooked up with someone except for her. There was a lot more slow music being played over the stereo by then, and people were slow-winding in the middle of the floor or kissing and feeling each other up against the wall, or retreating to one of the side rooms to get busy. Sylvia heard the bedsprings and the screams of ecstasy and wished to high heaven that was her in one of those rooms. She was no virgin, having lost her virginity at age twelve, but her sexual romps were too few and far between, in her opinion. Boys liked girls who put out, and she wanted to give them what they wanted, but she was always one of the last ones picked due to her average looks. There were some sixteen and seventeen-year-old boys down there, too, and she was determined to get their attention that day if it was the last thing she did.

Putting down her fourth bottle of beer, she swayed to the middle of the room, slightly buzzed. As she watched Dub out of the corner of her eye slob Paula down, she began dancing seductively, winding her narrow hips as she slid her tube top down to reveal her black strapless bra.

"Oh shit!" she heard one boy exclaim.

Sylvia smiled, her eyes closed, that one exclamation all the fuel she needed to keep going. She could feel the eyes on her as she squeezed her small breasts in her hands before finally pulling down her bra and revealing them, awarding her more expletives of appreciation. When she put her hand between her legs and played with herself, something she had become a master at, it wasn't long before she felt hands encircle her waist from behind. She grinned. She didn't even know who it was that was now touching and grinding their hard groin into her backside; it didn't even matter. Someone was finally paying her some attention.

His hands were on her breasts. "Let's go in the room," they whispered in her ear.

Sylvia had hoped it was Dub, but that wasn't his voice. When she opened her eyes, he was still against the far wall with Paula, in their own little world. Jealousy flared in Sylvia but she was determined to not get upset. She would get her turn with him soon enough.

"Hell yeah, let's go," Sylvia concurred, taking his hand and leading the way, not even bothering to fix her bra. There were two bedrooms in Jordanna's basement, and Sylvia opened the door to the first one she came to. Her friend Amelia was already using one of the twin beds with Johnny, one of the guys on the basketball team, so Sylvia headed for the other bed, unfazed. Since there were so few rooms and always so many people at these parties, everyone was used to having to share a room. The semi-privacy was better than being completely out in the open in the main room, though that hadn't stopped some people in the past.

When Sylvia finally turned and looked at whose hand she was holding, she saw it was Hubert, a guy in her Algebra class that she had only spoken to once or twice. He wasn't all that attractive but he was available. Just like her.

Not wanting to waste time on foreplay with a boy she only found marginally attractive, she immediately started unbuckling his belt.

She had watched enough adult videos at her friends' houses to know that boys liked to be pleasured first; almost all of those films began with the woman going down on the man. She dropped to her knees and took Hubert into her mouth, just like she had practiced on the huge zucchinis at home, reveling in the immediate sounds of pleasure above her. She kept going until she had made him weak in the knees, then she grabbed a condom from the glass bowl on the nightstand and handed it to him. She hiked up her skirt and turned her back to him, opting for doggy style so she wouldn't have to look at him. Biting her lip as he entered her, she peeked over at her friend and Johnny in the next bed. They were doing it missionary style and not paying them any attention, completely into each other at that moment. Sylvia was already turned on, but watching them made her arousal triple, not to mention, Johnny was considerably better looking than Hubert. As she watched him pump in and out of her friend, Sylvia urged Hubert on, breathlessly ordering him to go harder and faster. And when he got his orgasm a few minutes later and wanted to go another round, she obliged him, loving the fact that he had enjoyed her so much that he didn't want to stop.

Sylvia had hoped that Dub would be finished with Paula by the time she was finished with Hubert, but when they emerged from the room about twenty minutes later, Dub was on one of the couches with his arm around yet another girl. Sylvia fumed inside, but tried not to show it. By then it was almost eight o'clock, and she knew her mother was probably wondering where she was. Sylvia had lied to her that morning and told her that she would be getting some after-school tutoring, but that would have been over with hours ago. She knew she was going to get a lecture and probably another punishment when she finally did get home, which is exactly why she was in no rush to get there. Her mother had no idea where she was and she was glad about that.

Her jealousy and arousal flared again when she saw the girl Dub was sitting with stand up, take his hand, and lead him to the room she had just recently vacated. Sylvia eyed Dub's retreating back, noting the absence of the crescent-shaped birthmark that adorned the neck of his twin brother. It was the only real way to tell him and Deuce apart, and Sylvia had imagined running her tongue over his smooth skin more times than she could count. She kept telling herself she would get her chance, although it didn't seem like it was going to be that night. And it wasn't. Sylvia ended up sexing three boys before the party was over, but none of them were Dub. The one quick look he had given her after she had called his name earlier had been the only attention he had paid to her. But she told herself that was just because all those other girls had beat her to him; she would just have to take a lesson from them and learn to be a little more aggressive. Or maybe get him somewhere where it wasn't so crowded. She smiled at the thought, already wondering what it would be like.

"What are you over here smiling about?" her friend Amelia asked her.

"Oh..." Sylvia blushed slightly. "Nothing."

"Don't lie."

"I ain't lyin'."

"Uh-huh. I see you takin' a break. Who all you been with tonight?"

"Hubert, Richard, and..." Sylvia looked at the ceiling, trying to remember the name of the last boy she had sex with.

"That's a damn shame."

"Ron! It was Ron."

"How was he? I've never kissed anybody with braces."

"Girl, we didn't kiss. We just had sex."

"What? Girl, kissing is the best part sometimes."

"I'm not all into him like that. We weren't like you and Johnny, acting like y'all were making love or some junk."

Amelia smiled, her dewy caramel cheeks blushing. "I don't know if I would say all that, but I surely enjoyed myself."

"I bet you did. Y'all were in there forever."

"Hell, he knows what he's doing. We'd still be in there now if he wasn't all worried about his curfew. He gave me his number, though."

"You gonna call him?"

"Hell yeah! Johnny is fine and he knows how to put it down! Plus he might even go to the pros after he graduates next year! I'd be stupid not to!"

"Can't blame you for that!" They slapped five.

"Did you get a chance to talk to Dub?"

Sylvia sighed. All of her friends were well aware of her crush on Dub, which had been in place since freshman year after the twins had transferred to Atlanta from Virginia. "Nope. But I will, though."

"He *was* looking fine tonight."

"He's *always* looking fine."

"Carol got with Deuce."

"Really? Oh well. Deuce might be an asshole but he's fine as hell, too."

"That he is." Amelia's eyes roamed around the basement, which was considerably emptier than it had been earlier. She checked her watch, stretched, then ran her hands through her brown bobbed hair. "I'm about to head home. It's starting to die down in here."

"Yeah," Sylvia reluctantly agreed, in no hurry to get home herself but knowing she would have to eventually. "Where are Moni and Carol now?"

"Moni left a while ago. Carol is still in one of the rooms, I think."

"Oh. Let me go change back into my other clothes; Mama is already gonna be trippin' enough about me coming in so late. Whose gonna take us home?"

"I'll get somebody to drop us off. Hurry up and go change."

Sylvia's mother, Sandra, was up waiting for her when she finally crept through the front door. Sylvia didn't even see her sitting in the dark living room, opting not to turn the lights on. When she accidentally bumped into the end table and cursed under her breath, Sandra turned on the lamp, startling her daughter to the point of screaming.

"Hush all that hollerin', child!" Sandra scolded.

"You scared me!"

"Well, then you know how it feels, then, 'cause I've been worried sick for hours! Where have you been? It's almost eleven o'clock!"

"I told you I was getting tutored after school," Sylvia lied.

"Tutoring doesn't take this long; don't even try that with me!"

"I needed a lot of help."

"You must think I'm some kinda stupid, huh? I can smell the cigarette smoke from here! Now I'm gonna ask you one more time; *where* have you been?"

Sylvia was just sure she had scrubbed any incriminating scents off of her when she had washed up in Jordanna's bathroom before leaving her house, but she apparently was mistaken. The nicotine smell had probably gotten into her hair.

"I'm goin' to bed. I've got school tomorrow," she announced, ignoring her mother's question. She headed for the stairs.

"You better stay your little yella behind where you are and answer my question!"

Sylvia sucked her teeth. "I was out with my friends, dang! Why you always worried about where I am?!"

"Because you're fifteen years old and no fifteen-year-old needs to be out in the streets this time of night!"

"It's not even that late!"

"It's too late for you to be coming in here from school! You missed your curfew *again*!"

"I don't even see why I have a stupid curfew! I'm too old to have to be in the house by some freakin' nine o'clock!"

"I don't care if you don't see it *or* don't like it, your curfew is nine and not a minute over!"

"Ugh!" Sylvia screamed in frustration. "This is so stupid! None of my friends have a curfew so early, if they have one at all! I look like a lame having to be home before everyone else!"

"Too bad!" Sandra crossed the room and got in her daughter's defiant face. "I don't really care *what* your friends do; they don't live here! Now you keep pushing me, little girl, and I'll move it to eight!"

"This is some bullshit!"

Sandra slapped her right in the mouth. "You better watch your mouth! Who do you think you're talking to??"

Sylvia held her hand over her stinging lips and glared at her mother. At that moment, she felt as if she hated her. But it wasn't the first time she had felt like that. "I wanna go live with my dad! He wouldn't treat me like a baby!"

"Well, you can't, 'cause he's too busy raising his *other* family up in Athens, so get over it!" Her voice softened only slightly, looking into Sylvia's wet and fuming eyes. "I make rules for your own good, child; you'll see one day when you have children of your own."

"When I do have kids, I'm not gonna be anything like you! I'm gonna be a *good* parent!"

Her words stung Sandra a bit, since she had been raising Sylvia alone for most of her life, after Sylvia's father Kelsey went and married somebody else when Sylvia was just six years old. Sandra knew she wasn't the best parent, but she was doing the best she could; working two or three jobs to support them and make sure Sylvia had everything she needed. The fact that this went unappreciated reignited Sandra's anger.

"I just know you better not come up in here late again," she warned, looking down at her. "Now you get your butt up those stairs! You are grounded!"

Even though Sylvia had been expecting to be punished, she still got upset. "Grounded??"

"Yes, *grounded*!"

"For how long?!"

"For as long as I feel like! And no phone, either! Now get!"

Sucking her teeth again, Sylvia stomped up the stairs to her room and slammed the door. Sandra started to yell at her for that, but suddenly realized how exhausted she was with the whole situation. She had been at work all day and she was tired; she'd just have to deal with Sylvia later.

She trudged to her bedroom, which was downstairs, and removed her bathrobe, not even bothering to turn on the light. She glanced at the clock on the side of the bed and felt her frustration flare upon seeing she would have to be up in just four hours, and knowing she had to work both of her jobs the next day. Sitting up waiting for Sylvia to come home had severely cut into her sleep time. Sighing, she knelt down at the side of her bed and clasped her hands together, her eyes focused upward.

"God," she began, "I'm gonna make this quick. Thank you for getting my child home safely. But I just don't know what I'm gonna do with her. She seems to be getting more and more hardheaded, and I'm doing the best I can but it doesn't seem to be doing any good. Please give me some guidance; I don't want my daughter to end up another statistic, pregnant or strung out because she doesn't know how to enjoy being a child and is tryin' to be too grown too fast. I pray that you show me what to do. Amen." She started to get up, then added, "Oh, and if she's thinking about sneaking out again tonight, please stop her 'cause I'm about to be dead to the world. Amen."

Sandra threw her tired body on top of her bed, not even bothering to get underneath the covers, and tried to savor her few hours of sleep while keeping one ear open.

• • • •

UPSTAIRS, SYLVIA WAS huddled underneath her covers, defiantly on the phone with her friend Carol, getting the dish about her romp with Deuce.

"How was he?" she asked in a hushed voice.

"Girrrl..." Carol hedged excitedly, "He was all that and then some! He banged my back out!"

"Did he have a big thing?"

"The biggest I've seen! You know, except for the ones in those nasty movies."

"I bet Dub probably has a big one too, then," Sylvia mused excitedly.

"Probably. According to Paula it's like a baseball bat."

"She told you that?"

"You know she loves to brag. I heard her saying it to somebody else. She practically went down on him in front of everybody."

Sylvia sucked her teeth. "Slut."

"You wouldn't be saying that 'cause she had him and you didn't, would you?"

"She blocked me! I know she saw me about to talk to him and she just got all in my way. He was looking at me and everything."

"If he wanted you, girl, she wouldn't have been able to block you. Not tryin' to be mean or anything; I'm just sayin'."

"Well, whatever," Sylvia sucked her teeth again, brushing off the idea that Dub just didn't want her. She couldn't bring herself to believe that. "I'm tellin' you, he likes me some kind of way."

"And what kind of way is that?"

"We're gonna be homie-lover-friends; watch what I tell you."

Carol hooted in laughter, causing Sylvia to frown.

"What's so damn funny?"

Carol calmed down, sensing she had hit a nerve. "I'm not makin' fun of you, girl. But I'm just sayin'...Dub can have any girl he wants. Hell, Dub *gets* any girl he wants. Damn near every girl in that school wants him. You'd have a better shot getting with Deuce."

"I don't *want* Deuce!"

"Do you think that maybe you think Dub likes you *some kind of way* because he's just a nice guy and has probably been polite to you at some point or another?"

Sylvia paused, then brushed off the suggestion. "Whatever, Carol. You ain't gotta believe me. But I'm tellin' you, one of these days, I'm gonna have Dub. Watch."

"Okay," Carol conceded, though it was clear she still wasn't convinced. "It's not like I can blame you for wanting him. I would have tried for him too if there wasn't already a line around the block. So I just settled for the next best thing with his twin brother. Once you're between those sheets you can pretend like he's Dub."

"I don't want to pretend; I want the real thing," Sylvia proclaimed, not even bothering to whisper anymore. She figured her mother was probably knocked out by then and anyway, she wanted to be sure her doubting friend knew how serious she was. "Dub is gonna be mine."

• • • •

AS MUCH AS SHE DIDN'T want to, Sylvia managed to get up on time for school the next day. She heard her mother downstairs in the kitchen fixing breakfast, but she didn't want to deal with her this morning. She was still mad at her mother for grounding her the night before. But Sylvia knew if she tried to leave without a word to her, it would just be more fussing later on that evening, so she just put on her simple white collared shirt, jeans, and sandals, rolled her eyes and trudged into the kitchen.

"Good morning," Sandra greeted her as she stirred some grits on the stove.

"Morning," Sylvia mumbled. "I thought you had to be at work early today."

Sandra eyed her. "They called me and told me I didn't have to come in until a little later. Which is good since I was up so late waiting for *someone* to get their behind home; I could get a little more sleep. Come on and sit down so you can eat."

"I'm gonna eat at school today," Sylvia said, making no move for one of the wooden dining chairs. She didn't want to sit there so her mother could fuss at her some more.

"No, you're not. You're eating here."

Sucking her teeth, Sylvia frowned. "Why I gotta eat here?"

"'Cause I said so! Now sit down!"

"I need to be at school early."

Sandra knew her daughter was lying. "Why?"

"I just do. A...project I need to work on before class."

"It can wait. Sit."

Sylvia stomped her foot. "I said I need to go! You're the one always nagging me about my grades!"

"Lil' girl, if you don't sit your butt down..." Sandra warned, glaring at her. She gripped the spatula she had been using to scramble the eggs in her hand.

With another suck of her teeth, Sylvia plopped down into a chair. She knew when her mother meant business, and she didn't need to get slapped across the face and risk having to walk around most of the day with a red cheek. So she just rolled her eyes and played with her nails, counting the minutes until she could be out the door.

They ate their grits, eggs, and biscuits with jelly in silence. Sylvia ate quickly, making sure to eat everything on her plate so her mother wouldn't have an excuse to keep her there longer. Sandra watched her out of the corner of her eye, not bothering to engage in small talk that would go one-sided. For the life of her, she didn't know why her daughter was always so angry; at least, when it came to her. When she was around or on the phone with her friends, she was practically jubilant. But when it was just the two of them, Sylvia didn't have much to say to her. Sandra knew Sylvia felt she was too strict with her, but it was for her own good. Sandra knew too many girls she had grown up with that ended up either strung out or saddled with multiple children before they were out of high school, or simply wasting their lives because they hadn't had any kind of structure or discipline growing up. Sandra wasn't trying to be Sylvia's friend; she was her mother. And she loved her enough to implement rules for her, even though it might not have been the 'cool' thing to do and caused her to fall out of favor with her daughter. She could only hope that one day Sylvia would grow to appreciate that.

As soon as Sylvia cleaned her plate, she grabbed her stuffed backpack and stood up.

"Why is that backpack so full?" Sandra asked.

Sucking her teeth at what she felt was a stupid question, Sylvia answered with attitude. "Books. I *do* go to school, you know."

"You better watch that attitude, Sylvia. I done told you I'm not one of your little friends, now."

"Damn sure ain't," Sylvia muttered under her breath, messing with her nails again.

"What was that?"

"Nothin," Sylvia headed towards the door. "I gotta go. See you later."

"You come straight home after school, you hear?" Sandra called after her.

"Uh-huh."

"I love you!"

Sylvia pretended not to hear her as she slammed the front door behind her.

Hurt, Sandra shook her head, said another quick prayer, and began cleaning up the breakfast dishes so she could get ready for work.

As soon as Sylvia made it to school, she ducked inside the nearest bathroom and began her daily transformation from ho-hum to hottie. She shed her boring clothes that she had left the house in and removed the halter top with padded inserts for her small breasts and mini skirt from her bookbag, quickly putting them on. Then she took out her makeup case and quickly applied the foundation and the eyeliner and the lipstick, trying to remember all the tips she had read about in Essence magazine. She took her dark brown hair from its ponytail and fluffed it out, rapidly raking her fingers through it to get rid of the slight dent her ponytail holder had left. She frustratingly tugged at it , hating that it wasn't any longer than it was. It was hovering just above her shoulders. Sucking her teeth and shaking her head, she stuffed all of her makeup and her perpetrating outfit back into her backpack and headed to homeroom.

She saw Dub and Deuce a few times in the halls; to her chagrin, Deuce paid her more attention than Dub did. Sylvia didn't know why he was looking at her so much today; he usually didn't pay her any mind at all. She wished Dub would have looked in her direction, but he was always preoccupied, either talking to someone or checking his pager or something else. Sylvia imagined grabbing him and pulling him into an empty classroom, being bold and aggressive and taking that first kiss she had fantasized about ever since she had first saw him, but she knew she didn't have the nerve to do that. It would be humiliating if he rebuffed her. That was something girls like Paula could get away with, not her. She would have to go about it another way; she just wasn't sure how yet.

When she got to her Spanish class, Mrs. Devera was waiting for her by the door.

"And where were you yesterday, young lady?" she asked.

"What are you talkin' about?"

"I saw you earlier in the day, yet you didn't come to my class."

Knowing full well she had ditched the class so she could go to Jordanna's house with her friends, she lied, "I had to go home. Got checked out early. I was sick."

Mrs. Devera eyed her, then checked her watch. Students milled past them, taking their seats. She looked at them then back at Sylvia. "I want to talk to you when class is over."

Sylvia groaned. She wasn't in the mood for another lecture. "For what?"

"You'll see after class. Now take your seat."

Trying to keep her anger in check, Sylvia stomped over to her desk and dropped down into it, already wishing she had ditched today, too. She hated Spanish class, having no plans or desire to learn the language. She only took it because it was required to take a foreign language. Plus, all of her friends were taking Spanish, so she figured it was the easiest of the three that were offered, the other two being French and Russian. In her opinion, she shouldn't have to learn a foreign language at all. This was America; if folks wanted to live here, they needed to learn how to speak English.

Sylvia didn't even bother paying attention during the fifty-minute class. She just looked like she was as she doodled Dub's name in her Spanish workbook, acting like she was following along with the lesson. Mrs. Devera kept eyeing her, and Sylvia wished she would stop. She hated that the mousy-haired teacher was paying her so much attention today, like she was the only one who ever missed one of her boring classes.

When the bell rang, Sylvia tried to ease out in the throng of exiting students, but Mrs. Devera caught her.

"Sylvia!"

"Dammit!" Sylvia muttered, turning around. She just looked at her teacher with her eyebrow raised, clearly already disinterested. "Yes?"

"Have a seat."

"You gon' make me late for my next class."

"Then you should probably go ahead and sit down so we can begin, wouldn't you say?"

Sighing, Sylvia sat down at the desk nearest her and crossed her arms over her chest. Mrs. Devera perched herself on her desk in front of Sylvia, looking down at her.

"That outfit is a little revealing, don't you think?"

"No."

"That's not really appropriate for school."

Sylvia sucked her teeth and dropped an arm on the desk. "Did you call me back in here for a fashion lesson?"

"No, I didn't," Mrs. Devera answered, removing her glasses. She sat them behind her on her desk then looked at Sylvia pointedly, her thin eyebrows drawn together in a slight frown. "I called you in here because I want an honest answer as to why you weren't in class yesterday."

"I told you already. I was sick. My mama came and got me."

"Sylvia, I checked with the office. You were not checked out yesterday. You didn't attend my class or any of the ones after it. So I'm going to ask you again; where were you?"

"Uh, last time I checked, you were my teacher, not my mama," Sylvia declared defiantly, not acknowledging being caught in a lie. "You don't have to be worried about where I was."

"But I am. I'm worried about you and where you're going if you continue with this kind of behavior."

Rolling her eyes, Sylvia tsked, "I don't know what you talking 'bout."

"Oh I'm sure you do, but I'll tell you anyway. If you don't start taking your education way more seriously, you're going to have a hard time graduating high school, let alone getting into any college or trade school. Then what are you going to do? Continue thinking that all there is to life is boys and makeup and acting older than you are?

Work a minimum wage job for the rest of your life, doing nothing significant with yourself? Have a bunch of babies you can't afford to take proper care of?"

Sylvia waved her off. "Please."

"I'm serious, Sylvia. Life is not a game, nor does it last forever. You might be just fifteen now and think you have all the time in the world, but you don't. Before you know it you'll be an adult with real responsibilities but no real skills to fall back on because you wasted so much time in your youth."

"Look, are you a Spanish teacher or you a counselor?"

"I'm just trying to help you because I can see where you're going if you keep this up."

"Yeah, well, I don't need your help. And just because I missed your ol' boring class one day don't mean I'm gon' be a failure. Matter of fact, I'm gon' tell my mama you said that!"

"I didn't call you a failure, but it might be a good idea to have a talk with your mother, anyway," Mrs. Devera suggested. "Maybe she can give some insight as to why you behave the way you do and what we can do to get you on the right track."

"My mama works two jobs; she ain't got time to be comin' in here for no conference. And it's not necessary, no way. I'm fine."

Mrs. Devera shook her head sadly, as if she pitied Sylvia. "You're not fine, *querida*."

Sylvia's face scrunched up. "What does that mean?? You trying to say I'm gay? I don't mess with no girls like that!"

Shaking her head again, Mrs. Devera clarified, "*Querida* means 'darling'. You would know that if you came to class."

"Oh." Sylvia looked at the clock on the wall. "Are we done?"

Sighing, Mrs. Devera put her glasses back on and stood up. She knew it would take a lot more to get through to Sylvia than the few minutes they had. "Yes, we're done. You may go."

Sylvia grabbed her backpack and sauntered out of the room without a word, already having forgotten her teacher's warnings.

In Sylvia's mind, she wasn't doing anything wrong. She felt she had plenty of time to get serious about life and all that; she was just fifteen years old. This was the time she was *supposed* to have fun. Boys and hanging out with her friends and trying new exciting things like drinking and smoking were on her priority list way above school and preparing for college. It was embarrassing that she was the only one in her clique to not have had a real boyfriend yet, but it certainly wasn't from lack of desire or trying. And since she knew her looks were just average, she had to try extra hard to get the attention from boys that she craved. Sure, they had sex with her, which she loved, but she wanted a boyfriend, too.

She made it to her next class just as the bell rang. Sylvia didn't look forward to Algebra any more than she had looked forward to Spanish, but at least her teacher didn't hound her about where she had been the day before. What she did say, though, was almost as bad:

"Put your books away; the test is about to begin."

Sylvia had forgotten all about that test. Of course she hadn't studied for it, and she knew she didn't remember hardly any of the material because she had only been copying her friend's homework. She thought Algebra was another useless subject, therefore she put no effort into learning it. But she knew if she flunked another test, her mother would probably ground her until the school year was out.

Thinking fast, she hurriedly scribbled a note on a sheet of notebook paper as the teacher handed out the test on the other side of the room. She quickly passed it to the boy in the desk next to her, glancing to make sure the teacher didn't see her.

The boy, whose name she thought was Leonard but she wasn't sure, glanced at her curiously before slowly sliding the folded scrap of paper in front of him and opening it. His eyebrows shot up in surprise and he looked over at her. She nodded emphatically with a smile, confirming what he had read. He nodded also, his demeanor now jittery and excited.

Sylvia sighed in relief. Crises averted. Leonard was going to let her cheat off his test, and all she had to do was suck his dick after school.

• • • •

"YO, UH...SYLVIA."

Sylvia turned around and looked at Deuce, wondering why he was calling her. "Yeah?"

"What you doin' after school?"

"Got an after-school thing, then going home," she answered, thinking about her promise to Leonard. "Why?"

"Was tryin' to see if you wanted to meet up. I done heard some stuff about you," he said, eying her from head to toe. He licked his lips lustfully.

"Stuff like what?" She wished he would stop looking at her like that.

"Don't worry about all that; just know it's *all* good stuff."

"Okay..."

"So you down or what?"

Sylvia didn't have to ask what it was he was asking if she was down for. And if it had been just about any other guy other than Dub's twin brother, she probably would have jumped at it. But even though she used to be willing to get with Deuce if she couldn't have Dub, and Deuce was sexy, he would have been considered some kind of consolation prize instead of what she really wanted. It was Dub or it was neither of them.

Not wanting to brush him off and risk him bad-mouthing her to his brother, though, she just said, "I definitely am, but I've gotta get on home today. My mama be trippin'. Maybe some other time, though." She started to walk off.

"How 'bout tonight?"

She stopped and looked back at him. "What's tonight?"

"Me and Dub are hittin' up a few spots and thought you might wanna roll."

Excitement shot through Sylvia like a rocket. Dub actually wanted her to hang out with them? Had he just sent his brother to invite her on his behalf? She figured Deuces' proposition might have been just to size her up for his brother. Was that something that twins did? Either way, there was no way she was going to pass up an opportunity to hang out with Dub; she didn't care what her mother said. She was already imagining what she would wear and how she was going to get out of the house.

"What time you gonna pick me up?"

Chapter 2

• • • •

SYLVIA'S EXCITEMENT about seeing Dub that night was halted upon finding her mother at home when she got there after school. She thought she would still be at work. It frustrated her that she didn't know her mother's schedule like her friends knew theirs'. She hated not ever knowing where Sandra was going to be.

She started to head on up the stairs and not say anything, but Sandra stopped her.

"Sylvia."

Groaning inwardly, Sylvia stopped and turned around. "Huh?"

"Excuse me?"

"I mean, *ma'am*?" Sylvia corrected herself with a roll of her eyes.

"Come here and sit down," Sandra said, choosing to ignore her daughter's attitude for the time being. It wasn't like it was anything new.

Sylvia started to protest and claim to have homework to do but she figured it wouldn't make any difference, so she dragged herself over to the couch where her mother sat and plopped down onto the opposite end of it.

"How was school today?" Sandra asked politely.

"It was aight."

"Anything interesting happen?"

Sylvia remembered her talk with Mrs. Devera, her meeting with Leonard under the football bleachers and most importantly to her, her invitation to hang out with Dub and Deuce. Deuce had said they would be by to pick her up around ten and she wanted to go upstairs so she could start getting everything ready, not sit down here having this boring conversation with her mother.

"Not really," she simply answered.

"Anything you want to talk about?"

"Nope."

"Sylvia," Sandra said with a sigh. "Why do you act like that?"

"Like what?"

"Like you're always mad at me. What have I done to make you so hateful towards your own mother?"

How 'bout giving me these average looks and this crazy-looking body? Sylvia thought to herself. She totally blamed her mother for passing her subpar looks on to her. Her dad was way better looking and Sylvia had always wondered why he ever got with her mother. Sylvia really believed that if she looked better, she would be a lot more popular and have a lot more fun than she had now. She would probably have a boyfriend by now, too. In her mind, the least her mother could do was lighten up on all these rules she always tried to lay on her and give her a little more freedom. Sylvia felt Sandra owed her that.

But she didn't feel like getting into all of this so she just shrugged and said, "I don't know what you're talking 'bout."

"Of course you don't." Sandra closed the newspaper that was laying in her lap and placed it on the couch between them. She thoughtfully eyed her daughter for a few moments before leaning forward and speaking again. "Do you think you know what you're doing?"

Sylvia looked at her, confused. "Huh?"

"Don't play dumb. You're so busy worrying about trying to be grown that you're missing your childhood. And yes, you *are* still a child at fifteen," she emphasized pointedly.

Sylvia sucked her teeth, but said nothing.

"You see how hard I have to work; being grown isn't all it's cracked up to be," Sandra continued. "I *wish* I was still a teenager with no responsibilities like you. All you have to worry about is going to school. Girl you just don't know how good you have it."

"Going to school ain't all that," Sylvia couldn't resist muttering.

"Yeah, well life isn't always about what's fun and hip or whatever it is you all say nowadays," Sandra retorted. "You've gotta learn how to handle your business. One day you're going to graduate from high school and then what? Have you even thought about that?"

"Man, I got plenty of time to worry about all that stuff. I ain't nothin' but a sophomore," Sylvia said dismissively.

"You'll be a senior before you know it. Assuming you pass all of your classes."

"What you tryin' to say?"

"I'm *saying* that I know you don't take school seriously and you are never going to get anywhere with just a high school diploma, if you even get that. The way you're going, I don't think you will, and it breaks my heart to even say that. School is not a joke or a punishment, Sylvia...it's important. And not just because there are boys there."

"If you say so."

Sandra shook her head, disappointed in her daughter's dismissive attitude. "I'm worried about you, Sylvia."

Glancing at her mother, Sylvia rolled her eyes. "You ain't gotta worry about me. I'm fine. And I *will* graduate high school, thank you."

"Not if you don't start taking it more seriously, you won't."

"You're being dramatic. Matter of fact, I just aced my Algebra test today," Sylvia said with a smirk.

"Really? That's excellent! Let me see it!"

"She won't give them back until tomorrow. But I *know* I aced it." *Thanks to Leonard*, she thought to herself.

"Well if that's true, then I'm really proud of you," Sandra said sincerely. "I always knew you were a smart girl. You could get a whole lot farther if you just applied yourself."

Sylvia certainly wasn't in the mood to hear the 'apply yourself' speech, though it was nice to get a compliment instead of the usual nagging. More than anything, she was anxious to get on upstairs and get ready to meet the twins. And of course she had to call her friends and brag about the invitation first. "Thanks. Can I go now?"

Pursing her lips, Sandra nodded. "Go ahead."

As she eyed her daughter run up the stairs with a smile threatening to stretch her lips, Sandra wondered if she had heard a word she had said.

Sylvia was all done up and ready for Dub and Deuce. She had spent the last few hours on the phone with her friends and getting ready, being careful to listen for her mother eavesdropping on her conversation from the other extension. She reminded herself to call her dad and ask him to buy her a cell phone. It was the least he could do, since he had abandoned her for his other family.

She poked her head out the door, listening for any signs of her mother. She hoped she was either gone to work or asleep so she could get out easily. Deuce had told her that he and Dub would be in a black Cutlass and would honk the horn and flash the lights once. She didn't want to run into her mother and risk them leaving without her; she could only figure they wouldn't be willing to wait on her for long. And there's no telling when or if they would invite her again so she wasn't trying to mess this up.

All was quiet downstairs. Sylvia closed the door and checked herself out in the mirror one more time, hoping she looked all right for wherever they would be going. She had flat-ironed her hair, took her time applying her makeup, adorned herself with big earrings and bracelets, and squeezed herself into the tightest pair of jeans and halter top she had. Wondering if Dub would like it, she twisted and turned in the mirror, admiring herself from every angle, making sure she looked as perfect as she could possibly look. Smiling, her skin tingled in anticipation of seeing Dub and finally getting close to him. She hoped that they hadn't invited a bunch of other people to go with them, namely other girls, because it would just be like any other time when she got pushed to the backburner. She wanted to be front and center so Dub wouldn't have any choice but to pay attention to her.

Finally, she heard the car horn outside and when she peeked out her window, sure enough, there was a black Cutlass just down the street, waiting on her. She had told Deuce that she might have to get past her mother first and for them not to leave her, but she had no guarantee that he would actually do it, so she knew she had to hurry up and get out there. Grabbing her purse, she eased her door open and began tiptoeing down the stairs, listening for any sounds from her mother. She figured she was there since she hadn't said anything about leaving, but Sylvia hoped she was sound asleep. But when she got to the bottom of the stairs, though, she realized she wasn't.

"Sylvia!" Sandra exclaimed, turning on the living room light and tightening her bathrobe around her. Her eyes widened upon seeing Sylvia's outfit. "Where do you think you're going??"

"Just out with my friends," Sylvia responded innocently, trying to contain her attitude. Her hand was on the doorknob.

"The hell you are! You are grounded, remember? But even if you weren't, there is no *way* you're leaving this house this time of night dressed like *that*!"

Sucking her teeth, Sylvia humphed, "Man, there is nothing wrong with how I'm dressed! You gotta quit treating me like a baby, dang!"

"I'm not treating you like a baby; I'm treating you like the fifteen-year-old child you are. You are not going anywhere! Now you get your behind back up those stairs and stay there!"

Knowing that Sandra wouldn't be able to get to her before she made it outside, Sylvia just said, "You can't stop me from going!" She opened the door.

"Sylvia!" Sandra yelled, starting towards her. "Sylvia! Close that door!"

"I'm out!" Sylvia quickly stepped outside, slamming the door behind her, and ran as fast as she could in her heels to Deuce and Dub's car. She ignored Sandra yelling her name from the doorway as she dove into the backseat. "Go!"

Sylvia watched her mother yelling at her to come back through the slightly tinted windows, coming to the end of the driveway in her bathrobe, a mix of anger and panic painted on her face. Sandra stood and watched them as they screeched off down the street. Shaking her head, Sylvia just told herself to not worry about her mother; she'd deal with her whenever she decided to come back. For now, all she wanted to focus on was Dub.

"I see why you say your mama be trippin'," Deuce said from the driver's seat, glancing back at her in the rearview mirror amusingly.

"Yeah." Sylvia waved a hand dismissively. "I ain't worried 'bout her. Hey, Dub," she greeted sweetly.

"Hey, wassup, Sylvia," Dub answered coolly. He glanced back at her, smiling politely. It was enough to send a fresh wave of tingles down her spine.

"So where are we going?" Sylvia asked. She inhaled the scent of cologne mixed with beer fumes and cigarette smoke.

"Some homies are having a little get-together, plus I know a bunch of other people are meeting up over at the skating rink," Deuce answered, smoothly driving with one hand while taking occasional swigs of beer with the other. Sylvia didn't even worry about him drinking and driving; for some reason, she trusted both twins that night. "But I gotta stop and pick up a package first."

"Sounds like fun," Sylvia commented. She would have been willing to go anywhere as long as Dub was there.

"Oh, we gon' have fun, all right," Deuce confirmed, glancing at her in the rearview mirror again. He reached over to put something in the glove compartment, and Sylvia could swear she saw a gun in there. Sylvia's nervousness as well as her intrigue shot to a hundred. What did they need with a gun??

"I hope you don't have no curfew 'cause we 'bout to do it up!" Deuce said to her, slamming the glove compartment door shut.

"Please," Sylvia scoffed, leaning back in the slightly worn leather seats and telling herself to chill out about the gun. If anything, she felt even better about being out with them because she knew the twins could protect her if they needed to. She tried to sit at an angle where Dub could readily see her, even out of his peripheral vision. "I can stay out as long as I want to!"

"That's good to hear, shorty. 'Cause we wasn't plannin' on takin' you back any time soon."

Dub glanced over at his brother, but didn't comment.

"I was gonna go scoop your girl Carol but she couldn't get out," Deuce continued. "That's too bad, too, 'cause she had some good stuff! I know she told you."

Sylvia didn't know if she really should tell Deuce that she and Carol had discussed their tryst. She didn't want Dub thinking that she was one to kiss and tell. "Yeah, she said a little bit about it."

"Uh-huh. I knew it."

"Well it's too bad she couldn't come. Guess I have y'all all to myself tonight," Sylvia commented flirtatiously, her eyes on Dub.

"Guess so," Deuce said, his voice tinged with amusement.

"You want a beer, Sylvia?" Dub offered.

She didn't, but she was willing to take whatever Dub wanted to give her. "Yeah, I'll take one. Thanks." She almost shivered when her fingers touched hers as he handed her the bottle. She licked her lips and smiled, absolutely giddy that she was in such close quarters with Dub, with no other girls to detract his attention. She didn't know if they were going to be picking up other people or not; she hoped not, but she knew she had to figure out a way to get Dub to open up to her. If he opened up to her, he might start liking her. And if he started liking her, he might kiss her and hold her and make love to her. He might even ask her to be his girlfriend. She knew all of her friends thought she was crazy for thinking this; they thought Dub was way out of her league. But there had to be a reason for the twins inviting her to ride out with them and nobody else. She took that as a good sign.

"Dub, you like my outfit?" she boldly asked, leaning forward in the backseat. None of them were wearing seatbelts.

Glancing back at her, Dub's eyes finally briefly met hers before sweeping up and down her frame. Treating her to a half-smile, he acknowledged, "Yeah, that's hot."

Sylvia grinned. Those three words of affirmation from Dub were more impactful and meaningful to her than all the years of obligated-compliments she had received from her mother. She actually felt beautiful. More than anything, she wanted to ask him to sit in the backseat with her, but she didn't quite have the nerve to ask.

"Why you ain't ask me what I think about it?" Deuce asked with a smirk.

Because I don't care what you think, she thought to herself. "You're driving; you can't look back here," Sylvia answered.

"Yeah, maybe, but please believe, I see everything," Deuce said, his eyes on hers again in the rearview. The amusement was still in his eyes and in his voice, and Sylvia wondered what was up with him. But she brushed it off; Deuce was known to be about the games at times and she didn't want to spend any time or energy playing with him. All she wanted to worry about was Dub. She didn't even notice that as hard as she was watching Dub, though, Deuce was watching her.

• • • •

SYLVIA ENDED UP NOT going home for three days.

She spent a lot of time with Dub and Deuce, hanging out, partying, and drinking. She stayed at friends' houses and borrowed their clothes so she wouldn't have to go home. She didn't want to deal with her mother and the impending lecture and punishment she was going to try to implement when Sylvia stepped through the front door. For once, Sylvia was having the time of her life and she wasn't ready for it to end yet. She hung out with the twins a lot and, in her mind, she and Dub were getting closer. He was nice to her and engaged in conversation, but didn't make any kinds of moves on her. Deuce, on the other hand, flirted incessantly, but Sylvia wasn't trying to hear him. They might have looked just alike, but she didn't want Deuce. She wanted Dub. And to her, it was just a matter of time before he warmed up to her even more and took their budding friendship to the next level. She just knew he would fall for her.

Especially since she had helped them on a couple of 'jobs' while she was with them, even having to drive Deuce's car once after he and Dub had gotten into a scuffle with a couple of roughnecks during a drop-off that ended in a gun being shot. Sylvia had been nervous and frightened, but also exhilarated; she saw a side of the twins' life that probably not many people knew about. It was an unspoken agreement between the three of them that the events of that night were not to be mentioned to anyone. Sylvia could only hope it showed them that she could be trusted, and that she was down for whatever.

"Hey Sylvia, you wanna come see somethin' in my room?" Deuce asked her. They were at their house, where Sylvia had been most of that day. Their mother Traci was there but she didn't care about them having girls over; her only rule was that they couldn't drink or smoke in the house. Sylvia thought this was the coolest thing ever. Her mother never would have let her have boys over like that. She didn't know why everyone else had cool parents but her.

"Not right now. Dub and I are playing cards, here," Sylvia said, glancing at Dub with a smile. They were playing a hand of Tonk on the blue ottoman, as they had been doing most of the afternoon. Deuce had gotten tired of playing after a few games.

"Y'all been playing all day. Come on," Deuce urged.

"I'm busy, Deuce."

"Yeah, okay. I'm gon' get you up there, though."

"Uh-huh. Is it my turn?" she asked Dub.

"Yeah."

Sylvia continued to play cards with Dub, not even paying any attention to Deuce, who always had his eye on her. He had been trying to get at her ever since they picked her up a couple of nights before. It wasn't that she was the most fly girl in school or anything, or even the cutest. What appealed to him was that she was easy. He had heard about her and how she was willing to give it up to just about anybody, and how she was actually really good at giving head. He wanted to test her out for himself. But it wasn't lost on him that she had a thing for his brother; any idiot could see that. But Dub wasn't into her like that, and Deuce knew his brother was too polite to tell her that, at least up front. Deuce was definitely the more outspoken twin, and some would say the least sensitive. He wasn't worried about Sylvia's feelings. He just wanted to bone her. And before it was all said and done, he knew he would.

· · · ·

IT WASN'T UNTIL SYLVIA'S friend Carol called Deuce and Dub's house to inform Sylvia that the police were looking for her that Sylvia decided to go back home. She didn't want to, but it was embarrassing enough that her mother had sent the police knocking on her friend's doors. She hated to leave Dub's company, but when he gave her a polite yet somewhat firm hug before they dropped her off, she felt reassured that their time together had only brought them closer to being together the way she always imagined they would be.

Sylvia tried to hang on to the high she was on from Dub's hug when she reluctantly and slowly trudged through the front door of her house, not knowing what to expect. Almost immediately Sandra was grabbing her and Sylvia initially tried to push her away until she realized she wasn't grabbing her in anger, but in relief.

"Thank God!" Sandra exclaimed, hugging Sylvia tightly. She rocked her daughter back and forth, repeatedly thanking God for bringing her home safely, and Sylvia could tell she was crying. Her arms feebly hugged her mother in return, but she knew it was only a matter of time before all this relief subsided and she would be getting yelled at for defying her and then staying gone for three days.

Finally, Sandra pulled back and looked at her daughter, her eyes examining her face and body to make sure nothing seemed wrong. She had been losing her mind ever since Sylvia had run out three days before, and she had no idea where she had gone. She had called all of her friends and none of them would really tell her anything, and she knew they were just covering for her. None of their nearby relatives had seen her. She hadn't gotten a good look at who it was that was driving the car that Sylvia had gotten into that night; all she could make out was that there were two boys in the front seat. Sandra had never been more worried in her life, and as angry as she was at her daughter, she was gladder to see her walk through that door, and unharmed.

After taking a few moments to gather herself, Sandra glared at her daughter before firmly grabbing her hand and pulling her to the couch. She pushed her down but didn't sit down to join her; she paced back and forth in front of her, her hands clasped together in front of her face. Sylvia pensively eyed her, just waiting on the explosion.

Then Sandra suddenly dropped to her knees in front of Sylvia, grabbed her hands in hers, and closed her eyes tightly. She bowed her head and launched into a fervent prayer, thanking God for keeping Sylvia safe and asking Him for guidance on how to deal with her, and also asking for Him to make her realize she needs to change her ways before she ruined her life. Sylvia just listened, not uttering a word or even knowing what to say, as her mother prayed over her:

"Lord, this is my only child, and I see her going down a path of destruction. I don't know what else to do, God...please, show me what to do!"

Sylvia shifted in her seat, her hands becoming clammy in her mother's tight grip.

"Please help her to realize that I give her rules because I love her so much; if I didn't care about her or what happened to her, I'd let her do whatever she wants. But you blessed me with his beautiful child and I'm trying to be the best mother I can to her."

Humph, we both know I am not beautiful, Sylvia thought silently. *Thanks to you.*

"Please reveal to her what she's doing to herself," Sandra continued fervently, "And I pray that if and when she ever has any children, she'll see everything I've been trying to tell her."

For some reason, her mother's words struck a chord with Sylvia, and she began to feel the tiniest inkling of guilt for making her mother worry like she had. It wasn't like she didn't love her mother; she just resented her for a lot of things. If Sandra would loosen up on her some, Sylvia felt they both could be a lot happier.

Eventually, Sandra lifted herself onto the couch and held her head in her hands. When she finally lifted her head, Sylvia could see how red her eyes were. Her eyes roamed her face; her mother looked tired. Lines that Sylvia had never noticed before marred her mother's light, applesauce-colored skin. Gray hairs popped up in between the black ones on her head, mostly around her temples. Sylvia briefly wondered how many hours her mother actually spent worrying about her.

"I just don't know what to do with you anymore," Sandra muttered, her head in her hands again. She sniffed. "I'm just so tired..."

Pursing her lips, Sylvia eyed her mother for a moment. She had enjoyed herself while she was with Dub and Deuce the past few days, but she wasn't trying to send her mother into an early grave. She knew she loved her. And as defiant as she always acted, Sylvia hated to see her mother always have to work so hard and never have any kind of fun or anything. It was like the only thing Sandra had to worry about was Sylvia. Sylvia hadn't even seen her mother with a man since her dad left.

Swallowing, Sylvia softly spoke up. "I'm sorry for making you worry."

Sandra looked over at her, dropping her hands. It wasn't often that Sylvia apologized for anything she did. "Really?"

"Yeah. I mean, yes, ma'am. I just wanted to have some fun with my friends and I knew you wouldn't let me go."

"That doesn't mean you just outright defy me and go anyway, Sylvia. Do you know the kinds of things that can happen to a young girl out on the streets at night? I was almost scared to watch the news 'cause I thought I'd see something about your body being found somewhere."

"I was fine. We weren't even all out in the streets like that. I stayed with my friends."

"That's not even the point. Their parents should have called me to let me know you were there. But I'm sure you told them I gave you permission, didn't you?"

Sylvia didn't want to tell her that her friends' parents hadn't even mentioned anything about whether Sylvia had permission to be there or not. They all knew her well enough to not make a big deal out of it when she came over. "No, I didn't tell them that."

Sandra shook her head. "Has it ever occurred to you that I might be a little more lenient towards you and let you do a little more if you were more obedient and applied yourself in school like you're supposed to?"

Sylvia paused, actually not having thought of that. She always thought her mother was making her life miserable just because she felt like she could.

"This isn't fun for me, Sylvia," Sandra said, seemingly reading her mind. "I don't *like* having to stay on you and keep you on punishment and always worrying about what you're doing when you leave this house. I get tired of fighting with you. But *you* have to understand, as your mother, it is my job to protect you and teach you and discipline you, and that's not always pleasant. I'm not here to be your friend, child. You need to get that through your head."

Sylvia just nodded, not trusting herself not to say anything disrespectful. It sure didn't seem like her mother didn't enjoy punishing her and making up rules. Sylvia had to be in the house by nine, she couldn't wear makeup until she was seventeen, she couldn't date until she was eighteen, she couldn't have company over when no one else was home, she had to be off the phone by ten, she couldn't wear anything too short or too tight or too revealing, she had a list of chores to do, and on and on and on. Sylvia didn't want her mother to be her friend; but she did want her to be cooler like her friends' parents were.

After a few moments of silence, Sandra blew out a long, tired breath. "Just go on up to your room," she said, her voice low. "I have to go to work tonight and I need to get on in here and cook dinner. I hope you know you're still grounded so you need to stay off that telephone and get in those books and do some studying. I wanna see more A's come outta you, like that Algebra test you brought home the other day."

Sylvia tried not to smirk, remembering what she had to do to get that A. "Sure."

Sandra waved a hand, dismissing her, and Sylvia got up and headed for the stairs, glad that things hadn't gone as bad as she expected. She of course had no intention of doing any studying, but she wasn't too upset about being confined to her room, at least for the time being. She was tired and just wanted to take a nap, anyway.

A couple of hours later, Sandra called her downstairs to eat. They ate their hamburger steak, rice, and mixed vegetables in a somewhat less tense silence than usual. Sylvia was savoring the memories of her time with Dub as much as she was the gravy covering her meat. She still couldn't believe she had gotten to spend so much time with him and that he had paid her so much attention; they had actually talked while they sat for hours playing cards. He asked her questions as if he was really interested in knowing the answers. She couldn't imagine he would do all of that unless he really wanted to. There hadn't been any intimacy and the only time she really got any contact with him was when they slapped the occasional five during their card game and when he hugged her good-bye (a hug he initiated, by the way) but Sylvia was still hopeful they were only going to get closer from here on out. She just knew Dub was going to be in her life for the long haul.

· · · ·

A LITTLE LATER, SANDRA went off to work and Sylvia immediately got on the phone with her friends.

"Did your mama trip when you got home?" Carol asked her.

"Not as much as I expected her to," Sylvia admitted, twirling her ankle in front of her as she lounged on her twin bed. "She actually just did more talking than fussing."

"Well, that's good."

"Yeah, she just left for work."

"I'm surprised she didn't try to take you with her so she could keep an eye on you," Carol joked.

"Don't even say that! I don't even want that out in the atmosphere where the idea can get in her head!"

Carol chuckled.

"So anyway, she'll be gone all night," Sylvia continued, now kicking her bare leg back and forth. She was wearing nothing but a t-shirt and some panties. "I love that I have the house to myself."

"I'm still surprised she left you there alone, given what you just did."

"Me too, really. She did say something about this being the first test as to whether she can trust me or not, or somethin'."

"Oh. I guess you wouldn't wanna get out tonight, then."

Sylvia sat up, her interest immediately piqued. "Get out where?"

"House party over at Moni's. Her folks went to some funeral in Tennessee and left her and her brother there."

"Oh..." Sylvia wanted to go, but remembered her mother's words about trusting her. As stubborn as Sylvia knew she was, she could admit to herself that she wanted that. And as much as she wanted to go to Moni's party, she figured she could sit this one out. Plopping back down onto the bed, she declined, "That's aight. I'm straight."

"For real?"

"Yeah. I'm just gonna chill."

"Okay," Carol sang. "But I thought you would have jumped at the chance to see Dub."

Sylvia sat up again. "Dub's gonna be there?"

"Yep. Deuce told me they were going."

Sylvia chewed her lip. This changed everything. She definitely didn't want to pass up any opportunity to see Dub, but she knew her mother would probably be calling to check in on her periodically through the night. *I can always say I dozed off early and didn't hear the phone*, she schemed to herself.

Grinning, she leapt off the bed and dashed across her small bedroom to the closet, digging towards the back where she kept some of the clothes her mother didn't approve of. "I'm down! What you wearin'?"

About an hour or so later, their friend Brandy, who was a junior, came and picked Sylvia up. Carol and Amelia were already in the car. Sylvia's skin tingled in anticipation, as it always did, knowing she was going to be seeing Dub. Her bare arms already had goosebumps.

"You don't think your mama is gonna trip, do you?" Amelia asked. She was usually the quietest out of the bunch.

"Hopefully not. She's already called once before y'all got here and I made it sound like I was real sleepy and about to go to bed. So she might not even call again tonight."

"I bet she will," Carol countered.

"Well, if she does, I'll just say I turned the ringer off or something so it wouldn't bother me."

"What if she asked one of the neighbors to watch you and make sure you didn't go nowhere?" Carol asked.

The thought had never occurred to Sylvia, but she quickly brushed it off. "I doubt she did all that."

"If you say so."

They arrived at Moni's house and there were already a bunch of teenagers there, dancing and drinking and partying. Sylvia's eyes immediately looked around for Dub, but he hadn't arrived yet. She hoped Carol hadn't been playing her when she said he would be there, because she could've stayed at home.

"You sure Dub is gonna be here?" she asked her friend.

"Yeah, girl; that's what Deuce said. You know they hardly miss a party."

Sylvia bit her lip anxiously, smoothing her hands over her short skirt.

"Chill out, girl. He'll be here. You look cute tonight, too."

"For real?" Sylvia looked down at her tight red tank top, black leather miniskirt and wedge sandals. "I appreciate it. Let's hope Dub thinks so."

"Well, let's just party 'til they get here...you up in the spot, you might as well go 'head and have some fun," Carol advised, grabbing her arm and pulling her out into the middle of the living room floor where everyone was dancing. Sylvia relaxed as she danced and drank with her friends, enjoying an occasional dance or two with random boys, all the while keeping her eye out for Dub.

After what seemed like forever, Dub and Deuce finally made their entrance, both sporting black leather jackets. As usual, there was a noticeable buzz that coursed through the room when they entered it. All eyes and attention went to them. Sylvia's goosebumps returned as she watched Dub make his way through the room, stopping to talk to someone seemingly every few steps, refusing girls' immediate invitations to dance. Her heart and insides jumped when she caught his eye and he smiled at her, waving. That was a first, and she wondered how many more firsts she would get to experience with Dub that night.

Eventually he made his way over to her and gave her a light hug. "How you doin'?" he asked her over the music.

"I'm good," Sylvia answered as casually as she could manage, even though she was ecstatic inside. He was actually *voluntarily* paying attention to her in the midst of all the other girls there. They were steady trying to get his attention, but his eyes were on her. Sylvia couldn't remember ever being so thrilled.

"Wasn't expecting to see you up in here tonight," Dub said. "Figured you'd be on lockdown or something."

He's been thinking about me! Sylvia gushed silently, trying to hold back the grin that wanted to explode on her face.

"Everything go okay with your moms?"

She shrugged lightly. "As okay as it could've gone, I guess."

"Cool," Dub said. His eyes briefly roamed the length of her before he gently grabbed her hand. "Come on; you wanna dance?"

She wanted to faint, but she managed to say, "Yeah, let's do it!"

They danced through a few songs and talked and laughed as if they were the only two people in the room. Sylvia was in heaven. Dub didn't grab or touch her too much; his hands only found their way to her waist a few times, but Sylvia didn't care. He was giving her all of his attention in a room with Paula and the other fly girls in school, and that meant the world to her. She wanted to get him alone, but there were no bedrooms they could retreat to like there were at Jordanna's house. Moni had already warned everybody which rooms were off limits and that included the bedrooms and master bath, and she was quick to put folks out. Sylvia would have to get creative if she wanted some alone time with Dub.

A while later, she went off to the guest bathroom to get some air and to check her hair and clothing to make sure she was still looking presentable. All those teenagers crammed together in the living room made things incredibly hot and sweaty.

She leaned forward to get a better look in the bathroom mirror, peering hard in the somewhat dim light. There was only one working light bulb along the vanity. As she turned to try to get a better look at herself, the door opened. Her heart surged when Dub stepped in, closing the door behind her. The collar on his jacket was pulled up.

"You good?" he asked her, looking down at her with something in his eyes she had never seen before. Everything in her wanted to believe it was desire.

"Yeah, I'm good. Just needed to check myself for a minute."

He grunted, his eyes lazily and lustfully trailing her body. "Everything looks good, from where I can see."

Sylvia's cheeks were on fire and her legs were shaking but she tried to maintain her composure. She didn't want to come off as some amateur. "The feeling is mutual," she responded boldly, treating herself to her own lustful stare.

"I like that. Come'ere," he growled, grabbing her waist and pulling her to him with way more force than he had ever used with her. Sylvia was immediately aroused to the hundredth power. She couldn't believe it was finally happening; she was actually about to have Dub!

When he pressed his lips against hers, she really thought her knees would give out. Her hands gripped his jacket with an eagerness she couldn't help. They were actually kissing, with tongue and everything. She had known it was only a matter of time, but she didn't think it would come this easily. She had expected to have to lure him somewhere and possibly even make the first move on him; she never expected him to follow her into the bathroom and seduce her. But she certainly wasn't complaining. Sylvia knew she would never forget how she felt at this moment for as long as she lived.

"Make sure that door is locked," he ordered in between kisses. Sylvia managed to reach a hand out and twist the lock on the door before returning it to its spot on his ass. Her other hand was clamped around the back of his neck. She held him to her, returning his kisses fervently, never wanting the moment to end but also highly anticipatory about what was sure to come next.

It didn't take long before clothes started coming off. He pushed her down to her knees and she eagerly took him into her mouth, wanting to perform the best head game she had ever performed in her life. She wanted him to remember her as the best he had ever had, so any other girl he got with afterward paled in comparison. But if she had her way, there would *be* no other girls after this because he would finally make her his. After several minutes and several satisfied screams later, he lifted her onto the sink and positioned himself between her trembling thighs. Folks were knocking on the door, trying to get in to use the bathroom, but they both ignored them. Sylvia literally shuddered when he slid inside of her for the first time. She gripped his shoulders as he proceeded to make love to her (as she considered it), closing her eyes in sheer ecstatic bliss. She simply couldn't believe this was finally happening.

"Why don't you take your jacket off?" she panted.

"I'm good," he grunted, his eyes on himself going in and out of her.

Sylvia left it alone. She didn't care if he was wearing a snow suit. He had come for her and was now making love to her. In a house full of people! This couldn't have turned out much better if she had planned it.

The banging on the door continued as they sexed on the bathroom sink, Sylvia's back braced against the cold mirror, her leg thrown over his shoulder, trying to make sure she was mentally recording every second of this. She looked at him in the dim lighting and wanted to ask if he was enjoying her and if it was good to him, but she didn't quite have the nerve. She figured the answers to both questions was yes, though, considering the fervency of his actions and the way he kept muttering how he knew it was gonna be good. It thrilled her to hear that he had been thinking about her the same way she had been thinking about him. He felt amazing inside of her, and she never wanted their time together to end.

Unfortunately, though, it had to. After he had gotten enough, he slowly backed off of her, lifted her off the sink, and cleaned himself. Planting one last lick to her neck, he left the bathroom first. Sylvia turned to the mirror, not being able to resist the grin that was causing every facial muscle she had to ache, and pinched herself. Had that really happened? Her knees were actually weak, and she held on to the sink for support. She had really just sexed Dub. And to think, she almost didn't even come to this party!

Everything in her wanted to give her friends the juicy details when she finally rejoined the party, but figured Dub wouldn't appreciate her kissing and telling, even though she was sure he probably figured she would tell her homegirls. It could wait until she got home, though she knew there was no way she was going to be able to think of anything else any time soon. And anyway, she was pretty sure her prolonged time in the bathroom, her flushed cheeks and unsteady walk gave her away.

"Girl, where the hell you been?" Moni asked her as soon as Sylvia re-entered the living room.

"I just...went out to get some air, that's all," Sylvia lied. Her eyes were looking around for Dub, but she didn't see him. She wondered if he had left.

"Some air? Then why do you look like you just got done exercising or something?"

"I mean, I walked around and stuff..."

"Hmph," Moni looked at her skeptically, then turned her own eyes to the party. "Well, I'm glad you're back. I'm about ready to get all these people up outta my house. Folks eating up all the food, breaking stuff, and somebody was getting busy in the bathroom."

Sylvia's eyes snapped to her. "What?"

"Yeah, girl! Folks were coming to me complaining that they couldn't get in there. I just told them to go use the one downstairs in the basement. I was trying to get my mack on with Arnold so I still don't know who it was. Do *you* know?"

"No," Sylvia responded a little too quickly. "I mean, I was outside, you know..."

Moni shot her a strange look, then shrugged. "Oh well. I don't really care. I hope whoever it was enjoyed themselves. But word is it was one of the twins. Not sure which one, though."

"Oh...girl it was probably Deuce. You know he's a freak and stuff."

"Yeah. You're right. Did they leave? I haven't seen him or Dub in a minute."

"I don't know," Sylvia answered, trying to sound nonchalant. She was wondering the same thing but didn't want to give herself away. She was already counting her blessings that no one spotted her coming out of the bathroom after Dub. She guessed Moni had already redirected them by then.

The party continued on for a while longer before Moni started putting folks out. She was known to throw a party every now and then but she was never one to have them last all night. After a while she got tired of all the people up in her space and then that was all she wrote.

After a while, there were just a few people left in the house. The music was still playing and Sylvia and her friends were just sitting around, drinking and watching the few people Moni hadn't put out dance in the middle of the room. Sylvia had been having so much fun tripping out with her friends that she had temporarily forgotten about where Dub might be. She figured maybe he had left after leaving her in the bathroom, but then she had seen him dancing a little while later. She tried not to let her jealousy get a hold of her; she figured it was too soon to expect him to claim her as his girl yet. They probably needed to talk about it first. She looked forward to that conversation; but in the meantime she could savor the memory of them in the bathroom, making love. There would be nothing that could erase the feeling of him inside of her.

"Y'all 'bout ready?" Brandy asked at around three in the morning, easing herself up off the couch where she had been reclining. She swung her long legs from the couch's arm and set her bare feet on the floor.

"I guess, yeah," Sylvia responded. She reluctantly set her empty bottle of beer on the end table that was cluttered with others and stood up.

"I am gonna sleep *so* good tonight!" Carol exclaimed, stretching.

"Y'all heffahs could stay here and help me clean up this mess," Moni grumbled.

"Your brother is here; he'll help you," Brandy joked.

"Plus these stragglers that don't seem to want to leave," Carol added, motioning towards the five or six people that were still hanging around.

"Oh yeah!" Moni said, as if realizing the option herself. She started ordering folks around as Sylvia, Carol, and Brandy filed out the front door. There were still a few people outside, and Sylvia's heart skipped when she saw Dub and Deuce standing out there talking to some of their friends. It was then that she noticed that they were dressed almost exactly alike; she had never known them to do that before. When Dub looked at her and winked, she felt a funny feeling course through her. He still had his collar up and there was something different about him; she couldn't quite put her finger on it.

"Sylvia, come on," Brandy rushed.

"Yeah, I'm coming," Sylvia hedged, hesitating. She wanted to stop and talk to Dub, but didn't have the nerve to approach him in front of his friends, even after what they had done in the bathroom. She figured they would talk soon enough, and just threw up her hand in a casual wave. He just lifted his chin in acknowledgement, his lips curled up in a small smile, as he followed her with his eyes for a few moments before turning his attention back to his friends.

Sylvia went home to an empty house, thankful that she wouldn't have to deal with her mother, and stripped down to her underwear. As she climbed into bed, she smiled to herself. She simply couldn't believe what had gone down that night. She had actually slept with Dub. The grin crept back onto her face and stayed there. As she turned over, pulling the sheets around her bare body, she just knew that from here on out, everything was gonna be different.

Chapter 3

• • • •

SYLVIA COULDN'T BELIEVE she was pregnant.

She knew it was Dub's. She had gotten her period before Moni's party and she hadn't slept with anyone else since. She hadn't even been able to think about anyone else since that night. It had been almost two months and while they hadn't been together or even talked about what happened, Sylvia was still over the moon. And now she was even more so, knowing that she was carrying Dub's baby. This was a way to ensure that she would be in his life forever, even though it certainly wasn't anything that she had planned. She never wanted to be a teenage mother, but if she had to have anyone's baby this soon, she was glad it was Dub's.

She wasn't sure how to break the news to her mother or even Dub yet, but Sylvia wasted no time bragging to her friends about Dub knocking her up.

"What?!?" Carol exclaimed.

"Girl, you lyin'!" Moni hissed. "How in the world..."

"I didn't even know y'all had gotten together like that," Amelia commented. "When did y'all have sex? And how come you didn't tell us about it??"

"It was at Moni's party," Sylvia somewhat hesitantly answered, glancing at Moni. "That was us in the bathroom."

"You heffah! How come you were acting like you didn't know what I was talking about?" Moni exclaimed, hitting her lightly in the arm.

"I didn't want to go blabbing about it right after it happened. It might've gotten back to Dub and he would've gotten mad at me for telling our business so soon. I was just trying to keep it to myself for a while."

"Girl, that was damn near two months ago!" Carol reminded her. "You could've told us by now!"

"I'm sorry! I've still kind of been in shock that it even happened."

"Well, you got what you wanted," Moni commented. "So what you gonna do now? You and Dub a couple now or something?"

"No. At least, not yet," Sylvia replied. Her hand lazily rubbed her stomach. "But I know we will be, especially after I tell him about the baby."

"You haven't told him yet??" Amelia asked incredulously.

"No...I just found out about it myself like, last week. It *did* kind of come as a shock, you know. I loved sexing Dub but I wasn't trying to make any babies. I'm not even sixteen yet."

"He wasn't wearing a rubber?" Carol asked.

When Sylvia thought about it, Dub *hadn't* worn any protection that night. It was the first time that had occurred to her. When she was in the moment, she hadn't even thought about protection or the fact that he wasn't wearing any. That didn't seem like something Dub would do; he was always considered the most responsible and level-headed of the twins. She figured maybe he had just gotten caught up in the moment himself, and so consumed with his want and lust for her that he wasn't thinking about any condoms. It made her absolutely giddy to think that he might have actually knocked her up on purpose.

"No," Sylvia answered.

"Girl, I don't even get down like that," Moni commented, shaking her head. "No glove, no love, baby."

"I didn't even think about it, and I guess he didn't, either," Sylvia defended. "We were all caught up in the moment. It's all good, though; I'm sure Dub doesn't have anything and I don't, either."

"Uh, yes you *do*," Carol countered, gently poking Sylvia's belly. "You have a baby."

"You're mama is gonna flip the hell *out*," Moni predicted.

"Yeah." Sylvia wouldn't say it, but she was actually a little nervous about telling her mother she was pregnant. She had been paranoid that she would somehow figure it out on her own just by looking at her, so Sylvia always came home and went straight to her room. She wondered how long she would be able to hide it under baggy clothes when she started showing. There had been a movie she had watched with her friends where a teenage girl who had gotten pregnant fooled her mother by wearing baggy clothes and getting rid of food in the refrigerator so her mother would think she had eaten it so when she started getting bigger, she would think she was just getting fat. Sylvia figured that wasn't a bad plan...what she would do after the baby was born, though, was another story. She didn't want to put it in the garbage like the girl in the movie had done.

"Yeah, well, I ain't worried about her," she lied. "I'm more worried about tellin' Dub. This is a big deal. So y'all gotta promise me that you're gonna keep this to yourself so Dub won't hear about it from anybody else but me."

"We promise," her friends chorused.

But despite her friends promise to keep their mouths shut, in no time at all word of Sylvia's pregnancy was all over the school. Everyone knew she was carrying Dub's baby, and she was sure they were probably wondering why in the world Dub would choose her to knock up instead of one of the prettier girls. Sylvia didn't care what they said. Dub had chosen her, and that's all that mattered. She wasn't even mad at her friends after a while; now that the word was out, all the other girls would know to step off. Dub was *her* man now.

When word got around to Dub, he immediately pulled Sylvia outside in between classes as soon as he saw her. The look on his face was not pleasant and Sylvia felt herself getting nervous.

"You wanna tell me why you're going around saying you're carrying my baby?"

"I only told my friends."

"That's not the point. Are you even really pregnant?" he asked, eyeing her stomach.

"Yeah, I'm pregnant. Why would I lie about something like that?"

"I don't know. You're lying about it being mine, so-"

"I'm *not* lying!" Sylvia exclaimed, immediately hurt. Why would he say such a thing to her?

"Sylvia," Dub said, trying to calm himself. He glanced around them, making sure no one was in earshot. "You and I both know we never got busy."

Sylvia's jaw dropped. Now he was denying what happened? "Are you serious? You're trying to act like we didn't get busy in the bathroom at Moni's party that night? Damn, Dub. I thought you were the good twin."

Dub frowned, taking a small step back. "Moni's party? What are you talking about? All we did was dance, Sylvia."

"Dub. You followed me into the bathroom and started kissing me and tearing my clothes off. Folks were banging on the door, trying to get in. You kept your jacket on with your collar pulled up. You tryin' to tell me you don't remember any of that? Really?"

It only took a few seconds for realization to wash over his face. "Oh, shit..."

"Look, maybe you were drunk or something. I don't know. But now you know, so what are we gonna do about it?"

Dub's expression had turned from angry to sympathetic, almost pained. He ran a hand down his face, resting it over his mouth for a few moments. "Sylvia..."

"We need to go ahead and be together, Dub," Sylvia interrupted boldly. She figured now was as good a time to say that as any, since they were finally talking and getting everything out on the table. "I don't want my baby to be without his father like I am mine." She ran a hand over her belly. "It deserves better than that."

Dub squeezed his eyes shut and momentarily turned his back to her, his fists against his lips. Sylvia figured he was just finally processing what was happening. It was only natural that he would be shocked; they were still in high school and she figured he had only meant for it to be a spontaneous quickie in the bathroom. But now they were joined for life, a thought that warmed Sylvia considerably.

After a few moments, Dub turned back to her and gently took her hands in his. It looked like he was searching for the right words to say.

"Sylvia," he began, his voice low. "I didn't have my collar up that night."

She frowned at him. "What?"

"I wasn't wearing the collar up on my jacket. I never wear mine like that."

"Yes, you did. It was like that when you came in the bathroom."

"*I* never went in the bathroom, Sylvia."

Sylvia looked confused, then she realized what he was trying to tell her. Her eyes widened in shock, then narrowed in anger.

"Look, if you wanna act like you don't like me now, fine!" she exclaimed, yanking her hands from his grasp. Tears were already blurring her eyes; she had never been so hurt in all her life. "But you ain't gotta try to play me like that, Dub. I thought we were cooler than that!"

"Sylvia, listen to me," Dub pleaded, grabbing her hands again. "Believe it or not, I *do* like you. Those couple days you spent at our house, I got to know how cool and sweet you are. But please believe, I would never lie about something like this and I don't play those kinds of games."

Sylvia looked into his eyes and could tell he was serious. Her heart started beating faster and faster with realization. "So you're saying..."

"That wasn't me in the bathroom with you, Sylvia. That was Deuce."

"*Shiiiiiiit!*" Sylvia screamed, grabbing her belly and doubling over. Dub immediately put his arms around her to keep her from falling to the ground. She couldn't believe it! All this time she had been riding high, thinking she had sexed Dub, when it had really been Deuce. He had tricked her! When she thought about it, he probably had worn his jacket collar up so she wouldn't see his birthmark on the back of his neck and know it was him. She felt sick to her stomach, not to mention incredibly played and stupid.

"I'm sorry, Sylvia," Dub said sincerely, holding her to him. "I don't know what to say, except I'm sorry he did that to you. I swear I didn't know anything about it."

This had to be some kind of bad dream. All the euphoric feelings Sylvia had been enjoying upon learning of her pregnancy were now replaced with a shame and embarrassment so intense it made her body tremble. She simply could not believe this was happening to her.

Of course, it didn't take long for word of this latest development to spread, thanks to Deuce. He of course had known all along that it was his baby she had been so happy about, not that he had any intentions of helping her with it. He knew as soon as Dub heard about supposedly being the father to her baby, he would set her straight and she would know what really happened. The whole thing was funny to him.

Sylvia was used to being talked about, both in good and bad ways, but now the rumor and gossip mills were going at full speed. Seemingly everyone was talking about how Deuce had tricked her and knocked her up, letting her think it was Dub. She was embarrassed about it at first, but then figured it could be a lot worse. At least it wasn't one of these other average boys she had slept with. After Dub, at least looks-wise, Deuce was obviously the next best thing. Hopefully the baby would look more like him and have an easier time in life than she was having.

And the bright side was, Dub would still be in her life, as the baby's uncle. It wasn't ideal or the way she had dreamed about, but there wasn't anything she could do about it. She couldn't very well ask Dub to claim the baby as his; everyone already knew the truth. So she would just have to roll with it.

• • • •

ANOTHER MONTH OR SO passed and Sylvia knew she would have to go ahead and tell her mother about her pregnancy. She didn't think she could pull off the plan like the girl in that movie, passing off her pregnancy as just regular weight gain. Sylvia had always been thin and didn't think her mother would buy her all of a sudden just getting bigger for no reason, especially since she had never been one to eat that much.

She removed the pillows from under her shirt that she had been using to try to estimate how she would look when she was further along and tossed them back onto her bed. Taking a deep breath, she opened her bedroom door and started down the steps, her nervousness increasing with every step. Sandra had just gotten home about a half hour before and was in the kitchen cooking dinner. Sylvia slowly walked into the kitchen, wondering just how she was going to break this news.

"Um, hey Mama," she greeted somewhat timidly.

Sandra glanced back at her as she slid her meat loaf into the oven. "Hey, child."

They had been getting along marginally better since the day Sylvia had come home after defiantly spending the weekend with friends. Sylvia's attitude had gone way down and she hadn't been sneaking around like she had been, other than the night she went to Moni's party. As far as she knew, Sandra still didn't know about that.

"I got something I need to tell you."

Sandra looked at her again, wiping her hands on a dingy dish towel. "What is it? You in trouble again?"

Sylvia bit her lip. She figured this was as good an opening as any. "Kinda but not really..."

"What does that mean?"

"I'm kind of...pregnant."

Sandra just looked at her, her expression unchanged. Her head shook slowly, her eyes dropping to look at her daughter's stomach, before turning to the counter to finish cutting up her vegetables. "All right."

Sylvia was dumbfounded. *All right?* That was all she had to say? Sylvia had been prepared to get reamed and cussed out until the baby came to term, but her mother was acting like she had just said it was raining outside. "Huh?"

"I said all right."

"That's all you gon' say?"

Sandra slammed her knife onto the scratched cutting board. "What am I supposed to say, Sylvia? It's not like I'm all that surprised. I prayed and prayed that it wouldn't happen, but apparently you were still out being fast and trying to act grown. I thought you had heard what I was trying to tell you about being a child and enjoying only having to worry about going to school, but I guess not."

"Mama, it's not like I did this on purpose..."

"You might as well have. You obviously went out and opened your legs for somebody without having the sense to make sure he had a condom on."

"It wasn't like that." Sylvia didn't want to admit that the thought had never even crossed her mind that night.

"Yeah, okay. Whatever."

Sylvia paused. "So you ain't mad?"

"Of course I'm mad. You're only fifteen and now you're knocked up. This is gonna affect *both* of us, child. But I guess you didn't think about that. I'm struggling just trying to keep a roof over *your* head and keep clothes on *your* back and food in *your* stomach; now I've gotta worry about a baby, too? You don't know the first thing about raising no babies."

"But I can learn," Sylvia declared, jutting her chin out with determination.

"Oh, you most certainly will," Sandra concurred emphatically, picking up her knife again. "I'll help you because it's just the right thing for me to do, but don't think that you're just gonna pass this baby off to me and go back to doing all the mess you used to do. That party is *over*, honey. You are going to get a job and take care of your *own* child."

Sylvia's eyes widened. "You want me to just drop out of school?"

"Absolutely not. You're going to go to school *and* go to work."

"What?? That's too much!"

"No it's not. People go to school and work all the time."

"But not when they're in *high school*!"

"Well, you probably should have thought about that *before* you went and got yourself knocked up." Sandra finished with the vegetables and headed out of the room, stopping when she got next to Sylvia. Leaning close to her ear, she said, "Be grateful I'm not putting your fast behind out. You wanted to be grown, so this is what grown folks get."

• • • •

"MAN, YOU GOTTA DO THE right thing," Dub said to his brother. They were home alone and Deuce was kicked back on the couch, puffing on a Black and Mild like he didn't have a care in the world. "You know good and well that baby is your responsibility."

"Bro, you can forget it. There is no way in hell I'm taking care of that thing."

"Why not?"

"You think I want to have a baby by somebody that looks like that?"

"Looks like what? You say that like Sylvia is ugly or something."

"Maybe not ugly but she sure as hell ain't fly. You know that just like I know it."

"Yeah but I ain't the one that chose to get busy with her; you did." Dub went to join his brother on the couch, shoving Deuce's feet to the ground.

"So I fucked her. I only did it 'cause I knew I could, not 'cause I liked her or some shit."

Dub shook his head. Sometimes it amazed him how different he and his brother were, considering they were identical twins. "You pretended to be me 'cause you knew she had a crush on me. That was some childish, messed up bullshit, Deuce. I thought we quit doing that kind of mess in elementary school."

"*You* did. I didn't."

"Well you need to. I'm 'bout tired of you perpetrating like you're me. Don't think I won't beat yo' ass, man."

Deuce sucked his teeth. "Man, this is not even that serious. Sylvia ain't the first chick to get pregnant. I ain't goin' around doggin' her; I just don't want nothin' to do with that baby."

"Like our dad didn't want nothin' to do with us, right?" Dub reminded him with a raised brow.

Deuce looked at his brother, then looked away. Their father had left their mother Traci as soon as he found out she was having twins. They had never laid eyes on him; hadn't even seen a picture. They wouldn't know him if they passed him on the street. That had always been something of a sore spot ever since Traci had told them the truth when they were about eight years old. Dub had always taken that better than Deuce had; he always suspected that was the reason his brother was the way he was.

After a few quiet moments, Deuce blew a long cloud of smoke from between his thick lips and stuck his Black into an empty soda can on the coffee table in front of him. He glanced at Dub briefly. "Okay, fine. I'll talk to her. But I ain't promising nothin'."

"That's all I ask," Dub said, satisfied for the moment. He knew that was probably the best commitment he was going to get out of his brother right then so he wasn't going to push him. He was just glad he wasn't being as stubborn as usual. Sylvia might not have been a dime, but she was a nice girl. And she didn't deserve to be left out in the cold like that.

* * * *

SYLVIA DIDN'T KNOW what to expect when Deuce followed her into the library the next day. She knew he was coming to talk to her 'cause the library was not a place he frequented; she just hoped he wasn't going to say anything crazy to her.

"Hey, lemme talk to you for a second," he said, sitting down in chair next to hers, facing her. She had just started pulling out her books for a report that she had been putting off for weeks.

She looked at him pensively. "Yeah?"

"So that baby you carryin'," he glanced towards her midsection, "It's...mine."

"I know that."

"Please don't think I'm 'bout to be your man or some shit."

Sylvia wanted to laugh. "I don't want you, Deuce. Trust."

"Yeah, we both know who you want."

Cutting her eyes at him, she slammed her pens down onto the table. "It was real messed up what you did, Deuce, tricking me like that."

"Yeah, well," Deuce shrugged, refusing to apologize. "Whatever. Ain't nothin' you can do to change it."

"Unfortunately."

"I ain't payin' no child support," Deuce informed her, looking right into her eyes. "I'm not doin' nothing but admitting it's mine. Aight?"

Sylvia just shook her head before flicking her wrist at him. "Whatever."

Deuce started to stand up to leave, but Sylvia stopped him. "Hold up a second, Deuce."

"What?"

"Just tell me why you did me like that. Why did you trick me?"

He sucked his teeth and looked at her like she should know better. "'Cause you a trick. And I could."

He walked off, leaving her there trying to fight off the tears that were stinging her eyes.

· · · ·

"EXCUSE ME?" SANDRA asked, folding her arms.

"I want to get an abortion," Sylvia repeated.

Ever since Deuce had insulted her in the library earlier that day, Sylvia's positive thoughts about her unborn baby had gone down the tubes. The rationale that being pregnant by the twin brother of the one she really wanted being almost as good didn't fly anymore. She knew Deuce could be an asshole, but she had never expected him to be so mean to her. And the fact that he wasn't going to help her in any way with the baby, acting like he was doing her some big favor just by claiming it as his, only helped to cement her decision. She wanted Dub's baby out of her.

Sandra looked at her daughter and could tell she had been crying, but she didn't ask what the source of the tears was. It could have been some petty teenage drama or hormones from the pregnancy. She was sure something had happened at school to bring on this sudden decision; maybe getting teased by her classmates or snubbed by whoever had knocked her up or even realizing that being a mother, especially a teen mother, was going to be way harder than she thought it would be. Either way, Sandra wasn't allowing her an easy way out.

"Absolutely not," Sandra said firmly.

Sylvia's eyed widened, actually surprised by her mother's refusal. She thought she would have jumped at the chance to get out of being a grandmother so early and having another mouth to feed. "Why not??"

"You are not about to kill this baby just because you don't want to deal with the consequences of your actions."

"It's not about that. I just...I don't want to have a baby with Deuce."

"Who?"

"That's whose baby this is."

"What kind of name is *Deuce*?"

"He's a twin. His brother is Dub." There was no way she was going to tell her mother how Deuce had tricked her and she had thought she was really sleeping with Dub. And that if this actually had been Dub's baby like she initially thought, there would be no way she'd be asking for any abortion. She would still be riding on cloud nine.

Sandra shook her head. "Well, that's too bad. You shouldn't have had unprotected sex with him, then."

"But I didn't mean to!"

"What do you mean you didn't *mean* to??"

"I'm sayin'...I didn't really think about it..."

"Well then you're even more stupid than I thought, 'cause if you're going to be bold enough to lay down with somebody I thought you'd at *least* have enough sense to make sure he had a condom on. You can't even say he wore one and it broke. But the fact that the thought never even occurred to you..."

"I was caught up in the moment."

"I bet you were."

Sylvia sucked her teeth. "You don't get it." She wanted to explain how much she loved Dub and had loved him since she first saw him, and how she had thought he was finally showing how much he wanted her back by making love to her. She wanted to tell her mother this not out of any desire to confide in her, but to give her perspective and justify her actions some. It wasn't like she had just been sleeping around with no protection; before Deuce, she had never slept with a boy without making sure he was wearing a condom.

But Sylvia knew her mother wouldn't cut her any slack if she told her all this, so she kept her mouth shut. All Sandra would do is say how she shouldn't have been having sex with *anybody*, and how even if you *do* use a condom that still doesn't guarantee anything, and so on. So if that meant Sandra continued to think of Sylvia as a stupid, irresponsible child, then so be it.

"No, I *don't* get how you could go and get yourself into this mess. But it doesn't matter. You are not getting an abortion. You made your bed, so now you've gotta lay in it." She dropped her arms and turned to leave the room. "You should be good at that."

• • • •

AS SYLVIA'S PREGNANCY continued, Sandra didn't let up on her at all. She helped her like she said she would, but she never missed an opportunity to remind her how she had screwed up her life and how disappointed she was in her. The words hurt for a while but eventually Sylvia became numb to it. One of Sandra's cousins owned a nearby store and Sylvia began working there after school and on weekends, and Sandra commandeered her paychecks to make sure she didn't blow them all on anything silly. All Sylvia was allowed to do was go to school and go to work at the store, and Sandra had *dared* her to bring home any bad grades, so Sylvia was finally taking her schoolwork seriously. She couldn't even remember the last time she hung out with her friends, not that they had time for her anymore, anyway. Ever since Sandra put her on lockdown, and especially since Sylvia started showing, they were always busy whenever she did get a minute to call any of them. They always had some excuse about why they hadn't called or come by to see her, and eventually, Sylvia got the message.

They didn't want to hang out with the pregnant girl.

And of course, Sylvia hadn't heard from Deuce. Not once during her pregnancy did he call to check on her and see how she or the baby was doing, not that she really expected him to. He had already told her he wasn't going to do anything other than claim the baby as his. The only one that kept up with her any was Dub. He would carry her books for her at school and walk her home and call occasionally to check on her and see how she was doing. When she told him she was having a girl, he actually got excited, already calling himself Uncle Dub. Sylvia was thrilled that he was so supportive and excited about her baby, especially since he seemed to be the only one that was, besides her. Her mother seemed like she was too busy punishing her for getting pregnant to be excited about her coming granddaughter.

But as happy as she was about having Dub's support, it only made her equally as sad that he wasn't the one who had actually fathered her baby like she had thought and hoped. It just seemed so unfair; why couldn't Dub have been the one who followed her into the bathroom that night? Why couldn't she be having *his* baby? Deuce didn't care anything about her, but Dub did. Dub was the only one who had her back.

The more Sylvia thought about how her friends left her and how her mother was treating her and how Deuce was ignoring her, it just made her more and more angry. Not even the fact that Dub was in her corner was enough to totally cheer her up. As she dragged herself up the stairs after another long day of school and work, her swollen ankles throbbing and her feet and back aching, she laid back on her bed, rubbing her big round belly and blowing out a long, tired breath. Staring up at the ceiling, she felt her eyes and her heart harden.

"Forget *all* them," she whispered, referring to her mother and her friends (but not Dub, of course). "Who needs 'em? My baby girl will be here in just a few more weeks, and she's gonna be all I need." She caressed her stomach mindlessly. "Yep. You're gonna be my best friend."

Chapter 4

Fifteen years later

"Sylvia, can you pull a double tonight?"

"I already told you no, Lance. I gotta get home to my kids."

"Kids? They're teenagers! They can fend for themselves!"

"I said no, Lance, damn!"

Lance just shook his head as he pulled out his cell phone, no doubt to call someone to come in and work the shift she refused to work. Lance was her cousin and ran the store after his father, the one who had initially hired Sylvia, passed away a few years prior. Sylvia was still working in the same store she worked in when her mother forced her to get a job after getting pregnant at fifteen. Sylvia had never meant for it to be a permanent thing; she figured she'd work there for a couple years, save her money, and when she was old enough, she'd move out of her mother's house and get her own place, then try to find something better. But that never happened. Sylvia had graduated from high school, but with only average grades. And seeing as how she had two kids by then, having gotten pregnant again two years after having her daughter, the last thing she was thinking about was applying to any colleges. She just wanted to be done with school for a while. And since she had no other kind of backup plan for what she wanted to do with her future, she just figured working at her cousin's store was better than nothing. So she stayed there. She didn't even remember when she had become complacent, but she had. She had a fifteen year old daughter, a thirteen year old son, and a job where she answered to her cousin who was three years younger than she was.

Sylvia's kids were as different as night and day. Her daughter, Candy, took after Sylvia in too many ways. She was way more focused on boys and clothes and having fun than school or anything productive. It actually kind of freaked Sylvia out, how alike they were. It was like watching herself grow up all over again right in front of her. They even looked alike; Candy had very few characteristics of her father, Deuce, who had kept his word from back in high school and hadn't been a part of Candy's life in any significant way.

But Sylvia's son, Valencio, was a well-mannered, respectful boy who did well in school and already had his top three colleges picked out. And while Sylvia and Candy were fair-skinned, Valencio was a rich chocolate brown, like his father, Bryce. Bryce Marks had been a transfer student Sylvia had met during the summer before her senior year. He had come into the store when she was working one day and struck up a conversation, his interest in her increasing after learning she was attending the same school he was going to. Sylvia liked him all right but wasn't as taken with him as he was with her; she figured he was just latching on to her until the school year started and he started meeting more people. Especially since he was actually cute, with his smooth dark skin, curly hair and thick lips. And plus, they didn't have a whole lot in common; she could immediately tell he was some kind of egg-head, already looking forward to going to college and possibly even grad school, while Sylvia just wanted to get her senior year over with so she could be done with school altogether. But she figured he was nice enough, and she wasn't getting the attention from boys that she used to since she had Candy, so when Bryce asked her out, she accepted. The last thing she expected was for them to end up having sex, but that's what happened. It was with Bryce that she first experienced getting busy outside, when he put her on his lap in the backyard of his parents' house late one night. It was probably that exciting encounter that impregnated her. And he had been wearing a condom.

Sylvia sighed as she looked at her watch. She was very tired all of a sudden. She still had almost an hour left on her shift, and she would have to stop and get something to eat before going home. She figured it would be KFC tonight; eating out was a somewhat regular occurrence in her house, as she didn't have the energy or the inclination to cook a lot. She just hoped her kids were satisfied with whatever she brought because she wasn't in the mood for any arguing tonight; Candy and Valencio were always at each other's throats. They just didn't get along very well at all. Sylvia knew Candy was the instigator most of the time, though. She was just so combative and often picked on her little brother for no reason at all. But Sylvia knew what the real deal was; Candy resented Valencio because of his looks. Candy, like Sylvia had when she was her age, yearned for the attention of boys and had to work harder to get it because her looks were just average. Valencio got all kinds of attention without even trying to, even from older kids, and Candy hated that. She also accused him many times of being a goody-two-shoes, because he cared about his grades and was respectful and didn't get into any trouble. Sylvia couldn't imagine two siblings being any more different.

A few things hadn't changed in fifteen years. Sylvia's mother, Sandra, was still tough on her, often giving unsolicited advice about how she was raising her children. Every time Sylvia turned around, Sandra was advising or criticizing something. And every time Sylvia heard one of these critiques, she put that much more effort into being as much the opposite of Sandra that she could. Sylvia was as lenient with Candy as Sandra has been strict with her. And while Sandra had constantly reminded Sylvia coming up that she wasn't trying to be her friend, Sylvia was trying to be exactly that to Candy. She often treated her more like a homegirl than a daughter, or at least, she tried to. Candy wasn't as receptive to this as Sylvia had thought she would be.

Another thing that hadn't changed was Deuce's involvement in Candy's life. He had kept true to his word that he wouldn't have anything to do with her. He had since had seven other kids and from what Sylvia had heard, he wasn't much more involved with any of them than he was with Candy. But thankfully Dub was there to pick up the slack for his brother; he would call or come by occasionally to check on them, and even gave them money from time to time, since Deuce certainly wasn't paying any child support. Every action Dub took to help them only bolstered the love Sylvia had for him, which hadn't wavered in all these years. She still yearned for him just as she had in high school, even though she had finally admitted to herself that she would most likely never have him. He hadn't made one move on her in all this time, but he obviously and sincerely cared about her and her children, and Sylvia had learned to be satisfied with that (even though she wouldn't hesitate if he suddenly decided he wanted her). He was the one friend she had been able to count on since high school, especially since she had long since fallen out of touch with Carol, Moni, and Amelia. She hadn't spoken to any of them in years.

• • • •

A COUPLE OF HOURS LATER, Sylvia finally trudged through the door of her apartment, tired and holding a bag full of KFC chicken and sides. She had worked a twelve hour shift and couldn't wait to get off her feet. The music from Candy's room was loud enough to vibrate the thin walls and Sylvia knew she and Valencio had probably been fussing about it already.

She kicked her shoes off and padded down the hallway, then banged on Candy's room with her fist.

"What?" Candy yelled out.

"Come eat!"

Sylvia continued on to Valencio's room and poked her head in. She smiled upon seeing him sitting on the bed, a book in his lap and headphones on his ears. He removed them when he saw her.

"Hey, Mama," he greeted her.

"Hey, baby. I got some chicken out here."

"Oh, cool. Here I come."

"Aight."

Sylvia went back to the kitchen and started taking the food containers out of the bag. Valencio entered shortly after and automatically started pulling out paper plates for them to eat on, and he got the soda from the refrigerator. Sylvia never had to ask him to help her; Bryce had always taught him to help her whenever and however he could.

A few minutes later, Candy dragged into the kitchen and immediately frowned upon seeing the chicken, coleslaw, and green beans. "What is this?" she asked with her nose turned up.

"What I done told you about asking stupid questions? What it look like?"

"I don't want no chicken. I wanted some pizza."

"Fine," Sylvia conceded quickly, digging into the pocket of her khaki pants. She pulled out her last ten dollar bill and handed it to her. "Go to the place around the corner and get it."

Candy snatched the money and sauntered back to her room without a 'thank you'. Sylvia, thinking nothing of it, took the top off the bucket of fried chicken. Valencio just looked at her and shook his head slightly, but said nothing.

Sylvia and Valencio sat down to eat. Shortly after, Candy rushed out, having changed clothes and taken her hair down, and slammed the door behind her. Valencio looked at her retreating back and then at Sylvia, but she was too focused on the chicken wing in her hand to pay attention to her daughter, who clearly was going out with the intention of more than just getting pizza. He didn't know if his mother was blind to that or if she just didn't care. Either way, he knew it wasn't good.

"You're just gonna let her go by herself, Mama?" he asked after several hesitant moments. He didn't want to be scolded for worrying about stuff that wasn't his business.

"Yeah, she'll be aight," Sylvia replied dismissively with a wave of her greasy fingertips. She tore into another wing. "She grew up around here."

Valencio left it alone, deciding not to continue with the questions.

"You had a good day?" Sylvia asked, looking at him as she chewed.

"Yes, ma'am. I got an A on my science test."

"Good! And what about girls?"

Valencio looked at her questioningly. "What *about* girls?"

"You got a girlfriend yet?"

"Um, no ma'am."

"Why not?"

Valencio wondered if this was a joke. "I'm just thirteen."

"So? Boy, do you know the kind of stuff I was doing at thirteen?"

He didn't, but he didn't really want to know. His grandma Sandra had alluded to enough stuff about how Sylvia used to be that he had a good enough idea. He could do without the details.

"My dad told me I don't need to worry about girls yet and just concentrate on school."

"Your daddy is just a big ol' goody-two-shoes," Sylvia scoffed with another wave of her hand. "And you're getting to be just like him."

Valencio felt a little pang at his mother's insult, but then remembered his father's warning about not letting what other people say worry you when you know you're doing the right thing. It wasn't like it was the first time he had been accused of being a square, but it was the first time his mother had said it about him.

"Yeah, well," he shrugged, trying to shake off the residual hurt from her comment, "That's what he said."

"Well, *I* say you need to get you a girlfriend. You spend way too much time with your head in them books."

"But I'm trying to be a doctor."

"And that's good, baby. I'm not trying to tell you not to be a doctor. I'm just saying that you gotta learn how to have fun, too. You're too young to be all serious and stuff like you are."

"But I don't want a girlfriend, Mama."

"Why not?" Sylvia asked sharply, looking at him. "Please, *please* don't tell me you're gay or something."

"No, I am not gay. The girls at my school are just stupid."

"Why you say that?"

"'Cause, all they care about is clothes and boys and makeup and all that kind of stuff. They're just trying to be popular. I don't care about that."

Sylvia didn't bother saying that he had pretty much described her exactly when she was his age. "Yeah, well. Still. You can't tell me that *every* girl in that school is like that. So you need to find you a girlfriend, a *cute* one, before this week is out."

Valencio's jaw dropped. "Are you serious?"

She looked at him with eyes that weren't playing. "I'm dead serious."

· · · ·

IT WAS ALMOST ELEVEN o'clock when Candy finally came home, nearly three hours after she had left. And of course, she didn't have any pizza. Sylvia was lounging on the couch watching a movie and smoking a cigarette when she came in.

"Where the hell you been?" she asked as soon as Candy walked through the door. She put her cigarette out in the ashtray on the end table.

Candy stopped walking. "There was a long wait at the pizza place, then my friend was up there and we just ate our food there and talked until it closed."

"You think I'm stupid? The pizza place closes at ten."

"Well, we sat outside...and I didn't realize what time it was."

"Girl, you can't pull that kind of mess with me. You can't *think* of nothing I haven't done, other than doing drugs. Well, other than weed. So you gon' have to come a little better with the excuses if you're trying to get one over on me. Now I'm gon' ask you again; where you been?"

Candy sucked her teeth. "Fine. I went to my friend's house."

"Whose house?"

"You don't know her."

"Try me."

"It was my friend, Montana."

"Montana? Is that that girl with the huge nose? She lives two streets over! I didn't tell you to go all the way over there!"

"But her brother is really cute, though!"

"Oh yeah?" Sylvia asked, immediately switching into girlfriend mode. She grinned and tucked her legs up under her. "He likes you or something?"

"Yep. Montana told me at school today. She said their dad was gonna be gone for a few hours and I should come over there and talk to him."

"Come sit down and tell me about him! What's his name? What happened when you went over there?"

Candy sighed. "I'm tired, Mama..."

"Girl, sit down!"

Candy flopped down onto the couch next to her mother. She hated when she made her dish about boys and stuff like she was one of her girlfriends or something.

"Now what happened?" Sylvia asked.

Rolling her eyes, Candy hurriedly answered. "His name is Roland. I went over there, we talked, we ate, we kissed and stuff, I dozed off for a minute, then I left."

"You kissed and stuff? What *stuff*?"

"I mean...he felt on me."

"Where?"

"Mama!"

"*Where!?*"

"Oh my *gosh*! Everywhere!" Candy replied, blushing slightly. "Between my legs, my tit-I mean, my breasts..."

"Felt good, didn't it?"

Blushing harder, Candy mumbled, "Yeah."

"Did you feel on him?"

"Yeah."

"You felt his dick?"

"Yeah." Candy's face was on fire.

"Y'all had sex?"

"No. We wanted to but he didn't have any condoms."

"Well that's good," Sylvia replied, referring to her abstaining for lack of protection and not the fact that she didn't have sex at all. "At least you have *some* sense."

"Uh-huh. Can I go now?"

"Yeah, go on."

Candy quickly stood and headed back to her bedroom. Remembering something, she stopped and turned. "Oh yeah, my friend Leelee is having a party next week. It's for her birthday. Can I go?"

"What day next week?"

"Thursday."

"Yeah, girl! Just make sure you're home by midnight."

"Midnight?"

"Okay, one o'clock. You're not getting any later than that so you might as well take it."

"Okay." Candy went to her room and closed the door, locking it.

Sylvia sat back against the back of the couch, grinning with pride. Her daughter was turning out just like she was. And they were talking like best friends, which was something that Sandra had never done with her. Sylvia was thrilled that her daughter was getting so much attention from boys and that she was so popular. She considered it a direct blow to Sandra that she gave Candy such a late curfew; she had *wished* Sandra had let her stay out until midnight or later when she was a teenager. Heck, Sandra had hardly let her go out at all; most of the time when Sylvia had gone out, it was because she snuck out. But things were different now; Sylvia had her own daughter and she could make her own rules.

• • • •

CANDY SIGHED AS SHE kicked her shoes off and threw herself onto her twin bed. She smiled, thinking about the past few hours. She had lied to her mother; she and Roland *had* actually had sex. And it was awesome. But they didn't use any condoms.

• • • •

A COUPLE OF DAYS LATER, Sylvia got a call from Bryce.

"Sylvia, why in the world did you tell our child to get a girlfriend??"

"Because he needs one. All he does is go to school and study."

"He's thirteen. That's what he's supposed to do, Sylvia."

"He can have fun, too, Bryce. I don't want him to have some boring childhood. Plus he's way too cute to not have a girlfriend."

Bryce couldn't believe his ears, but at the same time he could. He had long since figured out that he and Sylvia had drastically different values and ideals. Their parenting styles didn't match at all, and it worried him that it would confuse Valencio. Really, he wanted his son to live with him, but Sylvia insisted she wanted both of her kids with her. Bryce saw him pretty much every weekend and sometimes during the week, and he just prayed that Sylvia didn't start having too much of an influence on Valencio and have him start going in the wrong direction.

"He is too young to be worrying about girls. What, do you want him to start having sex, too? Give you a couple of grandkids?"

"Of course not! I never told him to do all that."

"You don't have to tell him. He might think that since you're pushing him into having a girlfriend, that he can just do whatever else, too. Once you get kids going on that kind of stuff, Sylvia, sometimes it's hard for them to stop."

Sylvia sucked her teeth. "How would you know, Bryce? Probably the worst thing you ever did coming up was go outside with your shirt untucked."

Bryce chuckled. "You don't think impregnating you when we were seventeen was bad?"

"It's not like you did that on purpose." Sylvia paused. "Did you?"

"No, Sylvia."

"I'm just askin'."

"Look, Valencio does not need a girlfriend, and that's that. He told you he didn't want one. And I really don't appreciate you accusing him of being gay."

"I didn't accuse him of anything. I just asked if he was."

"Because he doesn't want a girlfriend? Really?"

"Yes, really. Most boys his age are thinking about girls and sex and whatever else. He's a little behind, if you ask me."

"Well, if you ask *me*, he's right where he needs to be. He already knows what he wants to do with his life and he's taking his grades seriously so he can do it. I would think you would be proud of that."

"I am, but-"

"There shouldn't be any *but*. Why don't you try encouraging and appreciating him for that instead of pushing him to grow up faster than he needs to?"

"Bryce..."

"I'm not trying to talk about this with you anymore," he said with finality in his voice. "As far as I'm concerned, the case is closed."

Sylvia sucked her teeth, but said nothing. Bryce might have looked good but he sure was a stick in the mud.

They were quiet for a few moments before he spoke again. "Look, how about I take y'all out to dinner? Candy, too."

"Why?" Sylvia asked suspiciously.

"Why not? We can't all have dinner together?"

"I mean why do you want to bring Candy? She's not even your daughter."

"So what? It's just dinner, not a father-daughter dance. I wouldn't want to leave her out. Plus, I know you said her own father doesn't really pay much attention to her so I don't mind being there for her, if I can. I've told you that before."

"I know. But I already told you her uncle does what her daddy doesn't, so we're good."

Bryce sighed. "I'm not trying to be the girl's daddy, Sylvia. I just invited y'all out to dinner, that's all."

"Still. She doesn't have time to be hanging out with some man she's not even related to. Plus she's not here, anyway."

Bryce paused. "Where is she? If I may ask."

"At her friend's house."

"It's almost eight o'clock."

"I know what time it is."

"Hmm."

"What, Bryce?"

"Nothing. She's *your* child."

"Exactly. I'm making sure she actually enjoys her teenage years because she'll have plenty of time to worry about being responsible and all that kind of stuff when she's an adult. Look at me; I hardly ever have any fun anymore."

"That's your choice, Sylvia. You could if you wanted to."

"I work twelve hour shifts damn near every day. So no, I couldn't."

It was on the tip of Bryce's tongue to let her know that her life was the way it was because of her own actions, but he wasn't trying to start another argument. He just knew he wasn't about to let their son follow in her footsteps, as far as that.

"Well, anyway. The invitation stands, if you change your mind."

"I won't. Candy has a lot on her plate. She just started talking to this boy Roland around the way. He's a cute little thing, too. She's just like me," Sylvia declared proudly.

Bryce couldn't resist. "You sure that's such a good thing?"

Sylvia gasped. "What you tryin' to say?"

"Nothing at all," Bryce acquiesced. "You have a good evening and have Valencio call me before he goes to bed."

Chapter 5

• • • •

SYLVIA KNEW SHE WAS going to regret it when she picked up the phone at seven o'clock on a Sunday morning. Her mother was only calling this early for one reason.

"You and those children need to get up and come to church with me today," Sandra declared.

Sylvia groaned. She could hear the gospel music playing in the background. Sandra had always gone to church but in the past few years, Sandra had dove even deeper into her faith, and was always on Sylvia's back about how she lived and how she was raising her kids. While Sylvia believed in God, she didn't have the desire to get up and go to church every Sunday and sit in there for hours getting lectured by a preacher who was probably doing a lot of the same stuff she did when he wasn't in that pulpit. Every now and then she would watch TD Jakes on television, but that was about the extent of her effort.

"No, thank you," Sylvia responded simply, yawning.

"You need to."

"I'm good on that."

Sandra sighed. "I don't know why you're like that."

"Like what, Mama?" Sylvia asked, though she already knew.

"So bound and determined to do things your way. You're just stubborn, child. Think how much better your life could be if you had listened to me when you were younger. Now look at you. Thirty years old with two teenagers and still trying to act as young as them. You don't even realize the devil has a hold on you."

"Ain't nothing wrong with me. I'm fine and my kids are fine. They're not dead or in trouble so they're fine."

"None of you are fine. The only one of y'all that has any sense is Valencio and that's 'cause of his daddy. If you just had to have another child before you were even twenty years old, I'm thankful it was with somebody like Bryce. I still don't know why you two aren't together."

"Because he's boring, that's why."

"Boring? Child, you better be glad a man like that even wants your foolish behind."

Sylvia rolled her eyes. "Anyway, I need to go. This is my day off and I'm trying to get some sleep."

"I still say you need to be coming to church. There's one day you're gonna need the Lord and you're gonna remember how you're acting now. Mark my words. You're gonna regret everything you're doing."

"Yeah, I got it."

"You oughta be ashamed of the way you're over there raising those kids."

"I'm raising them the way I wish I was raised. My kids are my best friends. It's all good over here."

"See that's your problem right there. You're not there to be their friend; they need a mother."

"I *am* their mother."

"You just said you're best friends. It can't be both."

"Look," Sylvia said, tiring of the conversation, "I don't need your advice. You did things your way, I do things my way. So like I said, I need to go."

Sandra sighed again. "I'm gonna be praying for you, child."

"Thanks. Bye." Sylvia hung up the phone and pulled the covers back over her head, already erasing the conversation from her mind.

. . . .

A FEW HOURS LATER, after Sylvia finally got out of bed, she got up to fix herself a bowl of cereal. She passed by Candy's room, and the door was closed. Her music and television were both turned up loud. Valencio had already gotten up and fixed himself breakfast, as he usually did.

After Sylvia had herself a bowl of Fruity Pebbles, she flipped through the mail that was on the table. She just shook her head when she saw the bills. It looked like she would have to be working some more double shifts in order to be able to cover everything. She dropped the envelopes on the table and eyed the phone as she sipped her fruit punch, wondering if she should even bother making the phone call she was thinking about making. Figuring it might be different this time, she picked up the phone and dialed Deuce's number.

"Man, what she want?" Deuce asked, sucking his teeth, upon seeing Sylvia's name on his caller ID.

"Answer the phone and see," Dub replied. He had come over to watch the Falcons game with Deuce, who was still living in the house they had grown up in. Dub had moved out and gotten his own place when he was in college.

"All she gon' do is ask me for some money, like she always do."

"You need to give her some. It's not like she's asking you for it for no reason. She *does* have your daughter."

"Man, I told her before she had that kid that I wasn't paying no child support. I guess she thought I was playin'."

"What kind of man doesn't support his own children? You really wanna be that kind of dude?"

"It ain't like it's just her. I don't pay none for none of my kids. Except Dionne; I give her a few dollars from time to time."

"Why Dionne? What's so special about her?"

Deuce took a sip of his beer, clearly stalling. He shrugged. "Just do."

Dub eyed his brother. He knew Dionne was the woman that Deuce had actually had some feelings for, and probably the one he actually impregnated on purpose so he could keep having some kind of tie to her. But since Deuce wasn't one to be faithful to just one woman, she wouldn't have anything else to do with him outside of their daughter. Dub knew this hurt Deuce, but he also knew Deuce would never admit it.

The phone stopped ringing, then started right back up again. Deuce just looked at it and kept watching the game, but Dub grabbed it and hit the TALK button, putting it up to his brother's ear.

"Talk to her," he ordered in a low voice.

Deuce sucked his teeth and grabbed the phone in his own hand. "What, Sylvia?"

"Deuce, I know it's probably pointless to ask, but I gotta take Candy to the dentist next week. Can you give me the money for the co-pay?"

"Damn, ain't co-pays like ten dollars? You don't even have that? You work, don't you?"

"Yes, I work. But the procedure is gonna cost almost two-hundred dollars by itself. I just need a little help with it."

"Well I ain't got it so you're just gonna have to figure something else out." Deuce was lying. He had the money. He just didn't want to give any to Sylvia.

Sylvia sighed. "I should've known."

"Yeah, you should've 'cause I already told you not to ask me for any money. Get that through your head, dammit. Now bye." He hung up.

It was times like this that Dub really didn't like his brother. He just didn't understand how Deuce could be so heartless towards his own flesh and blood. He had seven children and hardly seemed to care what happened to any of them, outside of maybe the daughter he had with Dionne. Dub didn't have any children, but he knew that he would always take care of them when he did, even if he didn't necessarily care for the woman he made them with. But then again, he also had enough sense not to make babies with just anybody.

"You're a real asshole, Deuce."

Deuce glanced at him, then sucked his teeth again. "Man, whatever."

"I really hope one day you grow the hell up. You're going around making all these babies but not taking any kind of responsibility. Candy is your first child and I bet I know more about her than you do."

"I know all I need to know about her. She's fifteen, and has a stupid-ass mama who named her the same name as my favorite stripper over at Magic City."

"Why you gotta downtalk Sylvia like that all the time?"

"Why you always *worried* about me downtalking Sylvia all the time? You been on my back about her since high school."

"'Cause she doesn't deserve how you treat her."

"You act like you love her or something."

"I *do* love her, as a friend. And as the mother of my niece."

"Yeah, that's real sweet but whatever. You care about her so much, *you* get with her."

Dub just shook his head, not bothering to say any more. He knew it was pointless, but he tried to hold out *some* hope that his brother would wake up and realize what he was doing to his own kids. Deuce was doing to his kids what their father had done to them and he didn't even see it. Or he did and just didn't care.

Dub never told Deuce, but he actually knew who their father was. A few years back, he had been cleaning out the garage for his mother and he couldn't help looking through some of the boxes. He found some old papers and among them, his and Deuce's birth certificates. That's when he had seen his father's name for the first time. Jasper Campbell. Dub had just sat there, staring at the papers for a solid three minutes, not believing that he finally had some kind of information about his father. Upon further snooping, he had come across an old marriage license (he hadn't even known their mother Traci had been married to their father) and some other papers, all showing the same name of Jasper Campbell. He even found a picture of his mother and a man when they were apparently in their twenties. There was no name or anything on it identifying who the man was, but Dub knew it was Jasper. He knew it was his father. He and Deuce looked just like him.

Dub had gone to the local library and tried to find out what he could about Jasper Campbell, even looking him up on Facebook to see if he could find him on there. He didn't expect to, but he found him. And to his surprise, he was living right there in Atlanta.

Dub had dealt with the fact that their father had left them, but the more he sat there and stared at his father's profile, the angrier he became. All this time he had been a car ride away and he hadn't even bothered to check on them or come see them or anything, like they didn't mean anything to him. For the life of him, Dub just couldn't understand how anyone could just abandon their own children like that. The more he thought about it, the more he realized he didn't *want* to reach out to Jasper. Their father hadn't been concerned about him and Deuce all these years so Dub wasn't going to stir anything up now. He never said a word about what he found out to Deuce or their mother, Traci.

But knowing how it felt to be disregarded by your own parent, Dub hated for his niece Candy to go through that. He hated it for all of his nieces and nephews, but for some reason he felt a special affinity for Candy. Maybe because she was the first. Or maybe because she was conceived out of actual love, at least on Sylvia's part. He knew Sylvia probably never would have slept with Deuce if she had known it was really him in the bathroom with her at Moni's party that night. Dub hated that he couldn't give Sylvia what she wanted, which was a relationship, but he just never saw her that way. He wasn't lying, though, when he had told Deuce that he loved her as a friend. He genuinely cared about her and always tried to help her whenever he could.

It was because of this that he called Sylvia the next day to let her know he was going to bring over the money that she had asked for from Deuce.

"For real?" Sylvia asked incredulously.

"Of course, girl" Dub answered. "You know if I can help out, I will. You want me to just come by the store? What time do you get off?"

"I'll be here until about nine or ten. You can just come by here. I really, really appreciate this, Dub. I didn't know where I was gonna scrape this money up from."

"It's no problem. I just hate that my brother isn't doing it himself."

"Yeah, well," Sylvia sucked her teeth. "It ain't nothin' new."

"True. Hopefully one day he'll start acting right, though."

"I ain't holdin' my breath for that. Hey, you wanna come eat dinner with us this weekend? I'll be off Saturday night and you can come eat with me and the kids. I just wanna do something for you, since you're always helping me out."

"I appreciate it, Sylvia, but it's not necessary. I'm Candy's uncle; it's what I'm supposed to do. And anyway, I can't Saturday; I have some things planned already that I can't get out of. But thank you, though...maybe we can all hang out another time."

"Okay. Just let me know when. And thank you again, Dub."

"Don't mention it."

Dub ended the call, sighing. He didn't want to tell Sylvia that the reason he couldn't accept her dinner invitation was because he had plans with his girlfriend, Jelissa, who already wasn't crazy about how much attention he showed to Sylvia. If it wasn't for that, he wouldn't have had a problem going over to hang out with her and her kids.

"Only so much I can do," he mumbled to himself.

· · · ·

SYLVIA FELT MUCH OVERDUE for some grown girl talk and was glad to have her friend Delta over for some wine and gossip. She met Delta when Valencio was in elementary school; Delta had been there with the father of one of Valencio's classmates and they started talking after one of the little school plays. Delta was pretty much the only friend Sylvia had, and she appreciated her, though she sometimes did miss being part of a group of girlfriends like she had been with Moni, Carol, and Amelia back in high school. She might not have spoken to them in years, but she knew what was going on with them, for the most part. Facebook allowed her to be nosey. Carol was married with a couple of kids, Moni had gone into the military, and Amelia was a proud pro basketball girlfriend of Johnny, who she had gotten with in high school. Sylvia couldn't believe that them getting busy at a basement party would lead to them still being together more than fifteen years later, but judging by their pictures, they looked happy. Sylvia didn't even bother trying not to be jealous.

"Sometimes I still just can't believe it," she mused, sipping her red wine from her favorite pink plastic cup. She mindlessly raked her bare toes over the thin carpet. "Its like, it doesn't seem fair. How come Amelia can still be with Johnny but I couldn't ever get with Dub?"

Delta peered at her friend, having heard some variation of this question a million times. It amazed her that Sylvia still seemed stuck in her high school years. "Apparently they fell in love, Sylvia. I know you've heard of high school sweethearts staying together until they're dead and gone. It's kind of romantic, if you ask me."

"Yeah, but it just figures that Amelia's high school sweetheart turned out to be a rich pro ball player. She always did get the finest boys out of all of us."

"Just because they're still together doesn't mean they're happy. All those pictures you keep looking at on Facebook could just be them frontin'. And it's not like they're married. You'd think after this long they'd be married, right?"

"Hmph," Sylvia grunted, taking another sip of wine. "You think if I got plastic surgery, Dub would get with me?"

Delta rolled her eyes. "You can't be serious."

"Yeah, I'm serious. Maybe if I did something to my face to make myself more appealing, he'd quit looking at me like a sister and start looking at me like somebody he wants to get with."

"Girl, be glad that you two are as close as you are. I know it's not like you want, but at least you're friends. The man obviously cares about you. He's in your life 'cause he wants to be. That should count for something. You don't need any damn plastic surgery."

"Would he still care about me if I didn't have his niece, though?"

"Weren't y'all friends before you got pregnant?"

"Yeah..."

"Well, then. There's your answer."

"It still trips me out when I think about it, though," Sylvia said, gazing up at the ceiling. "How one little ten minute fuck-fest on the bathroom sink could change everything. As much as I was in love with Dub, how could I have not recognized that it was really Deuce that night?"

"I don't know, girl," Delta replied, having heard this question a million times, too. "Maybe you were just too caught up in the moment and high off the excitement of everything to really pay attention. And they *are* identical twins, don't forget."

"I still feel like I should've known, though."

"Sylvia, let it go, honey," Delta advised, although she knew it was falling on deaf ears. "That happened years ago. Deuce got you. There's nothing you can do to change it."

Sylvia sucked her teeth as she got up to refill her cup.

"Where are the kids?" Delta asked, reaching to get an oatmeal raisin cookie from the paper plate on the coffee table.

"Valencio is with his dad this weekend. Candy is...out somewhere."

Delta looked over at her in shock. "Out somewhere? You don't know where? You do know it's going on midnight, right?"

"Yeah, she'll be coming in soon enough," Sylvia replied dismissively, refilling her cup to the brim.

"When is her curfew?"

"She doesn't have a curfew."

"What?" Delta exclaimed. She and Sylvia had butted heads many times over the years about Sylvia's laid-back parenting style. "She's just fifteen!"

"Girl, don't start that with me tonight. My child knows how to handle herself; she's fine." Sylvia rejoined her on the couch, taking a long sip of her wine. "And anyway, I *wish* I had been able to go out without a curfew when I was Candy's age."

"So...because *you* couldn't do it back in the day, you let Candy do it?"

"Yep. I'm raising her the way I wish my mama had raised me. And keep the lecture, 'cause I don't need it," she added when Delta opened her mouth to respond.

Delta shook her head. "I'm not gonna lecture you, but I *will* tell you that you need to check yourself."

"I check myself everyday. I'm good."

Close to an hour later, Candy came home. Delta and Sylvia were still up watching one of their favorite movies, *School Daze*. Delta eyed Candy for any signs of being drunk or high, since Sylvia didn't seem concerned.

"Hey," Candy greeted, upon seeing them. Sylvia just waved in return, engrossed in the movie.

"Hey, Candy," Delta replied, sitting up. She noticed how giddy Candy seemed. "You all right?"

"Oh, I'm great!" Candy replied enthusiastically. Delta raised a curios brow.

Candy peered at the television. "Y'all watching this old movie again? Haven't y'all seen this, like, a million times?"

Sylvia looked up. "Girl, this a classic. Come sit down and watch it with us. Get you some wine."

"What?" Delta shrieked.

"Girl, calm down. It's just wine. If she can eat grapes, she can drink wine."

Delta's face screwed up in incredulousness. "That is *not* even the same th-"

"Yeah, I'll have a lil' bit," Candy said, grabbing Sylvia's half-full cup and downing it like it was Juicy Juice. Licking her lips, she plunked the empty cup back down onto the coffee table. Delta just looked back and forth between them in shock, not believing what she was seeing.

"Well, I'm goin' to my room," Candy announced, flipping her long hair. "See y'all later." She disappeared down the hall and a few seconds later, they heard the close of her door and the click of the lock.

"So..." Delta hedged, still trying to process what she just saw, "Your fifteen-year-old child comes home at damn near one in the morning dressed like she just came out of some kind of bad rap video, giggling when nothing's funny, and you actually *offer* her alcohol, then you let her go back there and lock her bedroom door??"

"What's wrong with that? She's always in her room with the door locked."

"And you don't see *anything* wrong with that? What is she back there doing?"

"There's no telling. Regular teenage stuff."

"Which is? I'm very interested in what *you* consider *regular* teenage stuff."

"Delta, girl, will you chill out? It's not like she's in there making bombs or anything."

"How do you know?"

"Because she ain't got enough sense to do nothing like that. The girl can barely pass gas. She's probably just talking on the phone and stuff."

"You should know that, Sylvia. She is under *your* roof."

"That's her business."

"What? You *do* at least go into her room after she's gone and check around to make sure nothing crazy is in there, though, right?"

"I can't be invading her privacy like that. Did you want your mama to be doing that to you when you were a teenager?"

"Maybe not but now that I'm an *adult*, I can understand it if she did. And anyway, my mama didn't care nothing about *invading my privacy* 'cause I didn't have any. She wasn't tryin' to hear that. Whatever was under the roof she paid the bills for, she could do whatever she wanted with. That's how you need to be."

"Who says? Just because I do stuff different than how everybody else does it doesn't mean its wrong," Sylvia stated stubbornly.

Delta looked at her friend pitifully. "You need to quit trying to be that child's homegirl and start being her mother. One of these days you're gonna wish you did and there won't be anything you can do about it."

Sylvia rolled her eyes and snuggled deeper into the corner of the couch, pulling her gray fleece blanket tighter around her. "I appreciate the parenting advice and everything, woman-who-doesn't-even-have-any-kids, but I know what I'm doing." She yawned. "And for the record, I can be both the mama *and* the homegirl. Watch."

Chapter 6

• • • •

"MS. JENNINGS, YOUR daughter Candy has been either tardy or absent a lot this past month. This is severely affecting her grades, which weren't too great to begin with. Is everything all right at home? Is there something we should know about?"

Sylvia didn't have time for this, but Candy's principle had been leaving messages for her all week so she figured she'd go ahead and talk to him and get it over with. "Yes, everything's fine and no, there ain't nothing you need to know about."

"Then why has she been missing so much school?"

"Don't worry about all that. But just know whatever work she's missed, she'll make up."

"She's behind in every one of her classes, Ms. Jennings. At this rate it's pretty much concluded that she'll have to repeat her freshman year."

"She won't have to repeat anything. Like I said, she'll get caught up. I'll get her a tutor if I have to." Sylvia was just telling the man what she figured he wanted to hear. What she really wanted to tell him was that what Candy did wasn't any of his business, but she didn't need him calling any authorities on her for being negligent.

"Would you be able to come in this week for a conference? We would really like to speak with you."

"You're speaking to me now."

"We'd like to speak with you in person."

"What's the difference? I work double shifts practically every day so I really don't have time to be coming up there. We're on the phone so say whatever it is you gotta say now."

"If you're working double shifts, who's supervising your children?"

Sylvia felt herself getting heated. "Excuse me?"

"Do your children have supervision while you're at work?"

"Look dammit, you don't need to be worryin' about who's watching my kids. I got that taken care of."

"Ms. Jennings, there's no need to get angry."

"Well maybe if you quit overstepping your boundaries, I won't get angry."

"Candy's education is well within my boundaries, and she's sinking fast. I think we need to talk about getting her some help."

"I already said I was gonna get her a damn tutor. Didn't you hear me when I said that?"

"I did, but I think she needs more than just academic help."

"What the hell you tryin' to say?"

"I'm saying I think she needs some counseling. And perhaps you do, also."

Sylvia was done trying to be nice. "Look, gotdammit, I done already told you what you need to know, but now you're pushing it. Ain't nothin' wrong with my child, ain't nothin' wrong with me, and you got a lot of damn nerve telling me that I need some damn counseling."

"Ms. Jennings-"

"Like I already said and will say again for the *last* time, Candy will make up the damn work she missed and pass her classes, and I'm gon' make *sure* she does it just to prove your ass wrong."

"We want nothing but the best for-"

"Don't try that! You done already pissed me off so don't try to be all nice now! You think you're gonna just call my phone insulting me and I'm just gonna take it?!"

"Ms. Jennings, I wasn't trying to insult you and I apologize if it seemed like I was."

"Uh-huh."

"But we are very concerned about Candy's education and we just want to get her the help that she needs so she can succeed."

"Yeah, well, thanks, but like I said, she'll be fine. I'll make sure that she is."

There was a brief pause. "I'm glad to hear that. Just know that we're all on the same side, here."

"If you say so. One more thing, though."

"Yes?"

"Don't call my damn house no more."

• • • •

SYLVIA MIGHT HAVE COME across like she wasn't concerned about how Candy was doing in school, but she was. She didn't want her daughter having to repeat her freshman year and possibly be the source of teasing and ridicule. That would be pretty embarrassing, for both Candy *and* for Sylvia.

So when Candy got home that day, Sylvia wasted no time getting onto her.

"You need to tighten up."

"What?"

"You heard me."

"Tighten up on what? What are you talking about?"

"On your schoolwork. Apparently your grades are dropping faster than your panties are."

Candy's face turned bright red. "Wh-what? I ain't-"

"Girl, don't even try it. I know you be out there fuckin'. But this ain't about that right now."

"What are you even doing home so early?"

"Don't worry about all that. Your principal been blowin' my phone up trying to let me know that your grades suck 'cause you hardly go to class."

"I go to class."

"Apparently you don't. I already know you gon' lie if I ask you where you be goin' so I'll just tell you that you need to get your ass in that classroom and get your grades back up so you can pass everything. And I'ma have to see about getting you a tutor."

Candy frowned. "I don't need no tutor!"

"The hell you don't. 'Cause even when you *were* going to class it's not like you were makin' A's. Hell, I was happy when you brought a C home. So you're getting one whether you like it or not. 'Cause you ain't finna be stupid."

Sucking her teeth, Candy started back towards her room. "*This* is stupid. Excuse me for wanting to have some fun. I got plenty of time to worry about my grades; I'm just a freshman."

Sylvia was hit with a strong sense of déjà vu. She had that same logic when she was Candy's age. "I know what grade you're in, and ain't nothin' wrong with having fun, but I'ma put it to you like this: if you don't get it together, you'll be a freshman again *next* year."

That stopped Candy in her tracks. She turned to look at Sylvia. "Is that what the principal said?"

"Yep."

"Dang," Candy whispered under her breath. Without another word, she stalked back to her room and closed the door.

With a heavy sigh, Sylvia rubbed her hands over her face and plopped down onto the couch. She was going against her natural instinct to not hound Candy by forcing her to get a tutor, but when it was all said and done, Sylvia didn't want Candy to end up like she was. She wanted her daughter to be better than her, even though the way she had chosen to raise her might have suggested otherwise. Sylvia wasn't worried about Valencio; she already knew he'd be greater than all of them put together. But Candy was another story.

• • • •

SYLVIA SMILED AS SHE got dressed, making sure to look extra cute. It was rare that she really got to go anywhere other than work so she was planning on taking full advantage of having an evening out, even if it was just to her son's basketball game.

She pulled her braids into a high ponytail and slipped into a tube top that bared her stretch mark-laced midriff, some skintight black skinny jeans that took her ten minutes to get into, and some sandals that she took from Candy's closet. She tried to remember what she read in Essence magazine about creating a smoky eye as she applied her makeup. When she finished, she sprayed on some perfume and stepped back from the mirror.

"Still got it," she mumbled, smiling at her reflection. She turned and admired her backside, which had always been her best feature. Over the years, her body had filled out a little more than when she was a teenager, but not as much as Sylvia would have liked. Her breasts were bigger, though, and in the right bra, they looked amazing. She was getting turned on just looking at herself.

It had been too long since she had gotten any, and Sylvia wasn't ashamed to admit she hoped to get lucky that night. Maybe she'd meet someone at the game, or if Bryce wasn't acting all choir boy-like, she wouldn't be above doing it with him. Of course, the number one person on her list was Dub, but she wasn't going to hold her breath for that. He had made it pretty evident in all these years that he wasn't interested in her like she was interested in him. Plus, she knew he had a girlfriend, and Dub wasn't a cheater like his brother. It was one of the things she loved about him, even though she didn't think she would ever like the idea of him being with anyone other than her.

When Sylvia arrived at the gym, she automatically looked around for Bryce. He usually sat a few rows behind the team bench. When she spotted him, wearing his usual green baseball cap that he wore to the games and eating the peanut M&M's he loved so much, Sylvia made her way over to him.

"Hey," she greeted somewhat breathlessly.

"Hey," Bryce replied. He was trying not to look at her strangely and turned his eyes back to the players warming up on the court.

"You gonna scoot over so I can sit down?"

Bryce didn't want to, but he slid over to make room for her. It wasn't that he didn't want to sit next to her; he just didn't want to sit next to her when she was dressed like she was a thirteen-year-old who was trying too hard. He chose not to comment on her outfit, though, because he knew she probably thought she was the finest thing walking.

Sylvia did think she had it going on, but stepping up onto the bleachers in the super-tight skinny jeans she had on was proving to be a task and was something she hadn't thought about when she was choosing her outfit. She grabbed Bryce's arm as she practically hopped up the bleachers and eased down next to him. Thankfully he was only sitting two rows up.

"What you lookin' at?" she snapped at the older white man who was sitting on the other side of her. He had been eying her ever since she walked over there.

"Sylvia, please don't start that mess tonight," Bryce said.

"Start what? He's the one sitting here staring at me like he got a problem. You see something you want or somethin'?" Sylvia asked the man, jutting her breasts out to him. The man's face turned bright red and he looked away.

"Sylvia!" Bryce admonished.

"What?"

He just shook his head and shoved some more M&Ms into his mouth. It was pointless to get onto her about her behavior, and he knew it. And anyway, it wasn't like she was his woman or anything so he wasn't about to worry about her.

"You seen Candy?" Sylvia asked, looking around the gym.

Bryce looked at her. "You don't know where she is?"

"I let her hang out with her friends after school but I told her to make sure she came to watch her brother play."

Choosing not to say what he was really thinking, Bryce just responded, "No, I haven't seen her."

When the teams finished warming up and started to head back to their benches to prepare for the starting lineups to be called, Sylvia stood and started clapping loudly.

"There go my baby!" she yelled. "Mama's proud of you, Valencioooo!"

Clearly embarrassed, Valencio hurriedly took a seat on the bench, his back to his mother, and ducked his head.

"Y'all ain't ready! Y'all ain't ready!" Sylvia chanted to the other team. "Y'all might as well pack it up and go on back to where y'all came from 'cause my baby 'bout to put it *on* ya!"

Valencio looked like he wanted to run out of the gym. Bryce felt for his son, but it certainly wasn't the first time Sylvia had embarrassed him. He once told Bryce that he wished Sylvia didn't come to the games because he always got clowned about how she dressed or how she acted (or both). Bryce understood, but he knew Sylvia wanted to be there to support him when she didn't have to work. And whenever he tried to broach the subject of how her behavior embarrassed their son, she got upset and defensive. So he just told Valencio to deal with it the best he could.

Sylvia didn't chill out until the second quarter. Valencio had scored six points, and after every basket, Sylvia had jumped up and screamed like he had won the game-winning championship shot.

Valencio wished he could just go back to the locker room and stay there.

"I didn't know he was this good!" Sylvia exclaimed to Bryce, grinning. "He might be able to go straight to the NBA after high school, if he keeps this up."

"He doesn't want to play pro ball; he wants to be a doctor. You know that," Bryce responded.

"What's wrong with playing pro ball? And it sure as hell doesn't take as long as being a doctor does. He can be getting *paid* before he's even twenty!"

"He's going to college," Bryce stated firmly. "Besides, they don't even let you go straight to the league from high school anymore."

"That's some bullshit," Sylvia muttered. "He could be taking care of both of us in just a few years. You know how much school and money and stuff it's gon' take before he's a full-fledged doctor? I watch *Grey's Anatomy*."

"That's what he wants to do. And he's willing to work for it so it really doesn't matter how long it's gonna take. Just be proud of that and quit thinking about yourself."

"I'm not!"

"Yes you are, Sylvia."

"Whatever." Sylvia braced her hand on his thigh as she pushed herself off the bleacher. "I'm going to the concession stand. Don't let nobody take my seat."

She made her way out to the lobby and fished down in her purse for a couple of singles so she could get herself a candy bar. When she looked up and saw Candy in line, she hurried over to her.

"What's up?" she greeted, eyeing the two girls Candy was with.

Candy looked at her mother's outfit and wished she could pretend like she didn't know her. But unfortunately, they looked too much alike for her to try to deny that she was Sylvia's daughter. "What do you mean, what's up? And why you wearin' my sandals??"

"You were supposed to call me," Sylvia said, ignoring the question.

"I forgot. I've been chillin' with my friends. We're going to a party after the game."

"What party?"

"Just a party. We're just gonna be hanging out."

"That's it, huh? Some boys gonna be there?"

Candy's face twisted. "Why would I wanna be at a party with nothing but a bunch of girls? I don't get down like that!"

"You better not," Sylvia mumbled. "That boy Roland gonna be there?"

"I don't know."

"Uh-huh. You got some condoms? 'Cause I know you probably gonna be fuckin' somebody tonight. If it ain't Roland it'll probably be somebody else."

Candy's face turned bright red and one of her friends slapped a hand over her mouth, stifling laughter. "Oh my god, really??"

"Really, what? Don't try to act like you some kind of virgin. I already know better than that. Just be sure you tell me all about it when you get home."

"I'm not gonna do anything!"

"I don't know why you keep tryin' to play me like I'm stupid. Everything you do, I've already done and got the trophy for it." She looked back at Candy's friends. "Who are y'all?"

"Why?" Candy challenged before either of them could answer.

"'Cause I wanna know. Now shut up and let them answer!" Sylvia looked at the two girls with a raised brow, waiting for the introductions.

"I'm Mya," the one on Candy's left spoke up, briefly lifting her hand.

"China," the other girl piped up. She had long blue weave that went almost down to her waist.

"Mya and China...aight, then. Well, nice meeting y'all. I'm Sylvia, Candy's mama."

"Hey," the girls chorused. They briefly exchanged a look.

"You can just call me Sylvia. I don't like that 'ma'am' mess. Makes me sound old."

They just nodded, looking slightly uncomfortable.

"Yeah, well...we gotta go," Candy said, anxious to get away from her mother. She had already told her friends how Sylvia often embarrassed her and now they had a first-hand example of it.

"Remember what I said, now," Sylvia reminded her before sauntering past them to get in the concession line. "And don't be trying to stay out all night, either. You got until two in the morning to get your party-on."

"I shouldn't have no curfew on the weekend!" Candy whined.

Sylvia, wanting to prove how much of a cool mom she was in front of Candy's friends, relented. "Okay, but if you stay out later than that, you need to text me and let me know. And I wasn't playing about you telling me all about what happens."

Rolling her eyes, Candy grabbed her friends' arms and quickly pulled them away, not even bothering to thank Sylvia for extending her curfew. Sylvia smiled with a strange sense of pride, glad that her daughter even had somewhere to go where she wanted to stay out late, and that she had friends to hang with. She was turning out to be just like Sylvia, after all, and Sylvia was thrilled about it.

After the game, Sylvia waited with Bryce for Valencio to come out of the locker room. They had won the game 56-41, and Valencio ended up with twelve points. Sylvia's loud cheering and taunting had continued throughout the second half, and any attempts Bryce had made to calm her down were futile. She just brushed him off and continued doing what she was doing. It was only after one of the security guards came to warn her to calm down that she chilled out, much to the delight of everyone around her.

When Valencio finally (and somewhat hesitantly) emerged from the locker room, Sylvia raised her arms and screamed happily, causing her breasts to almost spill out of her tube top and the other people still in the gym to look over at them all.

Bryce quickly stepped in front of her, shielding her from their onlookers. "Sylvia! Will you calm the hell down and fix your clothes?" he hissed.

"Folks act like they've never seen titties before," Sylvia mumbled, adjusting her tube top over her breasts. "Y'all need to lighten up."

"Your son doesn't need to see *yours*," Bryce responded harshly. "Haven't you embarrassed him enough for one night?"

"Embarrassed him? You trippin'." She stepped around him and went over to Valencio, embracing him in a proud hug. "I didn't embarrass you, did I, baby?"

Valencio glanced at his father. He didn't want to lie but he knew if he told the truth and said yes, Sylvia might go off and humiliate him more than she already had. "Umm..."

"See there? I didn't," Sylvia said, looking at Bryce haughtily.

"He didn't say you didn't. He's just scared to tell you the truth," Bryce informed her, his arms folded.

Sylvia's head snapped to her son. "Is that true?"

Valencio, clearly uncomfortable with being put on the spot, looked again to his father before shrugging lightly. "I don't know. Can we go, Dad? I'm hungry."

"You're supposed to be coming home with me. This isn't your dad's weekend," Sylvia protested.

"I wanna go with Dad, if that's okay," Valencio requested. He wasn't about to say that the main reason he wanted to go with Bryce was just so he could get away from Sylvia for a while. His teammates had teased him a lot in the locker room because of Sylvia's behavior during the game and he couldn't help but get upset about it. He just needed a break from her. "Can I?"

Sylvia glared at Bryce and wondered if he had put Valencio up to this, but then decided this was a good thing. She was still riled up and horny so this meant she could go out and try to find something to get into, especially since she was already looking cute.

"Fine, go ahead," she said, giving him a slight nudge towards his father. "Stay over there all weekend, if you want to. Good game."

"Bye, Mama," Valencio said, looking relieved. He led his dad out of the gym. "See you later."

"I'll call you," Bryce told her before following Valencio out of the gym.

"Hey," Sylvia called out before he reached the door. Valencio continued on out into the lobby.

Bryce paused and waited for her to come over to him.

"Hey," she said again when she got close to him, looking up at him lustfully. "You wanna hook up after he goes to sleep later?"

Bryce cocked a brow at her. "Are you serious?"

"Hell yeah, I'm serious. You lookin' real good tonight and I saw how you was looking at my titties a minute ago," Sylvia replied, lightly grabbing the waistband of his jeans.

Bryce peered down at her. Despite her off-putting behavior and the glaring differences between them, he actually still found her attractive. The only problem was, Sylvia wanted him when she felt like it and didn't want to pay him any attention the rest of the time.

She was still trying to be a teenager instead of the thirty-year-old woman she was, and Bryce couldn't get with that.

And yeah, he noticed her breasts. They looked great to him. He wouldn't have minded sleeping with her and releasing some of the frustration of the past week. But he wasn't about to have a booty call with their son in the next room, even though Valencio often slept like a rock, especially after a game.

"Maybe next time," he said, gently grabbing her hand and lifting it to his lips, planting a soft kiss on the inside of her wrist. "Be careful tonight." He walked out.

Sylvia looked after him and just shook her head. "Still acting like a damn square," she mumbled.

Sylvia sucked her teeth when her call to Dub went to voicemail.

"Damn," she whispered, pondering whether she should try again. She was sitting in her car, pondering where she should go and thought about Dub. It had been a little while since they had hung out and she would have loved his company. And truth be told, after the way Bryce was looking at her, she was feeling herself more than usual and had a little extra confidence running through her. She wanted the company of a fine man, and there was no finer man to her than Dub. But when she called him again and he still didn't answer, she figured he was busy, or out with his girlfriend. And she didn't want to make him upset with her for blowing his phone up so she left well enough alone.

When her stomach started growling, she remembered she hadn't eaten anything since that morning, other than the candy bar she had at the game. She only had about twenty dollars in cash that had to last until her next payday, and she knew she didn't have anything other than cereal and a bunch of canned goods at her house, none of which she wanted. She wanted some real food.

Her thoughts strayed to her mother, who she knew still cooked everyday like she had when Sylvia was younger. Sylvia debated if she wanted to be bothered with Sandra's lectures just to get some dinner, and figured she might as well go and deal with it, since she knew Sandra would get on to her sooner or later about not coming over there to see her.

Telling herself she would stay over there no more than thirty or forty-five minutes, she headed over to Sandra's. She still lived in the house Sylvia had grown up in and Sylvia still had a key, but she rarely used it. The last time she had, Sandra had fussed at her so Sylvia always just knocked on the door like everybody else.

"What are you doing over here?" Sandra asked when Sylvia arrived. "I didn't know you were coming by here tonight."

"I was over this way so I figured I'd stop by and see you," Sylvia responded, subtly sniffing the air for any aromas from the kitchen. She closed the door behind her. "What you doing?"

"Straightening up the kitchen." Sandra eyed Sylvia's outfit and shook her head.

"You cooked?" Sylvia asked, ignoring the look.

"I always cook. Why, you want something to eat?"

"Yeah, I'll take something, thanks," Sylvia replied as she headed towards the kitchen, as if that hadn't been her main reason for coming over in the first place.

"Make sure you clean up after yourself," Sandra called out after her, plopping down onto the couch.

Sylvia fixed herself a plate of meat loaf, pinto beans, and scalloped potatoes and reluctantly went out to join her mother in the living room. She really wanted to just stay in the kitchen but figured that wouldn't go over so well.

"So where you comin' from?" Sandra asked after a few minutes. She had been laying there with her eyes closed and Sylvia had thought she had gone to sleep.

"Oh, I went to Valencio's basketball game," Sylvia replied, wiping her mouth with a paper towel. "They won. My baby had twelve points!"

"You went to the game wearing that?"

"Yes...what's wrong with it?"

"You're thirty years old, Sylvia. With two children."

"And?"

"You shouldn't be running around looking like...that."

"There's nothing wrong with what I have on," Sylvia retorted, taking another bite of meat loaf. She started to eat a little faster since it seemed like her mother was getting her lecture-motor running.

"You look like you're supposed to be on a street corner somewhere."

Sylvia sucked her teeth. "Please. So I'm wearing something that shows my stomach. Big deal."

"It barely covers your breasts, Sylvia. And if you're gonna be showing your stomach you might wanna do some sit-ups or something."

"So you tryin' to say I got a muffin-top or something? Please. I look good."

Sandra shook her head. "I just can't believe you went to that boy's game dressed like that. I bet you probably embarrassed him."

"I did not," Sylvia insisted.

"Where is he now? Why didn't you bring him over here with you?"

"He's with Bryce."

"I thought this was your weekend."

"It is but he asked to go with him," Sylvia shrugged.

"Hmph," Sandra grunted. "I bet it was because of that outfit."

"Can you please get off my outfit? I like it so that's all that matters."

"Uh-huh. Still ain't learned anything, I see, thinking it's all about you. Where's Candy?"

"Out." Sylvia set her empty plate on the coffee table.

Sandra frowned. "Out where? And with who?"

"She's fine, Mama. She's with her friends; I already talked to her."

"So you let that fifteen-year-old child go out with her friends without any kind of adult supervision? Where did she go?"

Sylvia sighed, regretting ever coming over there. She could've just hit up the dollar menu at Wendy's. "To a friend's house."

"*What* friend?"

"Why you worried about it?" Sylvia exclaimed, exasperated. "Candy is *my* daughter and I know where she is and who she's with, so that's all you need to know."

"If she's anything like you were at her age - and sadly, she is - she probably told you one thing and did something else. There's no telling where that child is right now and you're too stupid and busy trying to be the 'cool mama' that you can't even see that."

Her temper flaring, Sylvia quickly grabbed her plate and stood, stalking into kitchen. "I don't have time for this," she muttered to herself, quickly washing her plate and fork. She re-entered the living room, heading straight for the door.

"I didn't come over here for no lecture so I'ma have to talk to you later," she said, grabbing her keys from where she had been sitting on the couch.

"You never did wanna hear the truth," Sandra said. "But one day, you gon' learn."

Ignoring her, Sylvia walked out.

Sylvia was still too riled up to go home and be there alone, so she headed to the first place with a bar that she came to. Thankful that there were some decent-looking men in there, she sauntered over to the bar and eased herself up onto a bar stool.

"What can I get you?" the bartender asked, placing a small napkin in front of her.

"Uh, just water for now. I'm still deciding what I'm in the mood for," Sylvia responded, praying someone would come and be willing to buy her a real drink.

She noticed a man eyeing her from the other side of the bar, and Sylvia smiled at him, wasting no time turning on the flirting. She breathed a sigh of relief when she saw him get up and head over to her.

"Mind if I join you?" he asked.

"Not at all," Sylvia responded, as the bartender set a glass of water in front of her. She held out her hand. "I'm Sylvia."

"Percy." He shook her hand before perching himself on the stool next to her. "You look like you've been somewhere having a good time."

Giggling, Sylvia causally shrugged a shoulder. "I don't know about all that. But I hope to have a good time later on tonight." She eyed him suggestively.

"Is that right?" He eyed her back as his sipped his beer. "What's up with the water? You tryin' to be a good girl tonight?"

"Being a good girl isn't any fun. And like I said, I wanna have a *good* time." She subtly jutted her breasts forward.

He noticed and licked his lips, 'causing an arousal rush to shoot through her that almost knocked her off the stool.

"We need to get you a real drink, then," Percy said, signaling to the bartender. "I *definitely* want to be sure you have the best time you can have tonight."

Sylvia grinned and ordered a Hennessey and Coke.

They continued to sit and talk and flirt with each other until Sylvia started feeling a good enough buzz and enough liquid courage to invite him home with her. As far as looks, he was somewhat average; not ugly at all but certainly not what she would call handsome. But he was dressed nice and smelled good and not stingy with the drinks so he would do. Above all, he was interested.

When they made it back to Sylvia's apartment, they wasted no time getting to what they both knew he was there for. As soon as the door was closed, Percy slid Sylvia's tube top down and helped himself to what he had been salivating over all night. Sylvia's eyes rolled back, feeling instant ecstasy. They kissed hungrily in the middle of the living room and Sylvia prayed that Candy didn't come home any time soon.

"You got any condoms?" Sylvia whispered, unbuttoning his shirt.

"I got all the protection you need, baby," Percy responded. He unbuttoned her jeans. "I got you."

"You got me?" Sylvia breathed.

"I *got* you." He sucked on her neck and grabbed her ample backside. "Where's your bedroom?"

A couple hours later, Sylvia rolled over, sweaty and satisfied. That was just what she needed.

"We gonna hook up again?" Percy asked, buttoning his shirt as he stood next to the bed. He smiled at her and Sylvia noticed for the first time that he had dimples.

"Most definitely. Make sure you leave me your number so I can call you when I need a fix."

"So I'm your fix, huh?" Percy smirked.

"You got a problem with that?" Sylvia smirked back.

"Not at all," he leaned over, bracing his fists on the squeaky mattress and gave her a quick peck on the lips. Before he could pull back, Sylvia grabbed his shirt and deepened the kiss, and before long she had pushed his jeans down and they were going at it again. Sylvia felt like she had been in withdrawal, the way she was binging on Percy. She couldn't get enough of him; it was like she wanted to stock up in case of another sex famine.

When Percy got dressed to leave again and Sylvia was walking him to the door, dressed in nothing but a big t-shirt, Candy walked in. When she saw Percy, she frowned immediately.

"Who are you?" she asked.

"This is your uncle. On your daddy's side," Sylvia spoke up quickly. She didn't want Candy knowing he was some guy she had just met in a bar a few hours before.

Percy glanced at Sylvia, but didn't comment. It was obvious from the resemblance that Candy was Sylvia's daughter.

Candy looked at him skeptically, but then shrugged her shoulders. "Yeah, okay. Whatever." She dropped her purse on the couch and headed to the kitchen.

"Sorry about that," Sylvia whispered to Percy, opening the front door.

"No sweat," Percy waved off her apology. "I get it."

"I'll talk to you later." Sylvia leaned up to give him a quick peck on the lips, glancing over her shoulder to make sure Candy wasn't watching. "And thanks for the workout."

"Anytime." Percy winked at her and then walked out.

Candy emerged from the kitchen as soon as Sylvia closed the door, sipping on a can of soda. "How come you're just wearing a t-shirt around my uncle?"

"I didn't know he was coming over here. It was a spur-of-the-moment thing and this is just what I threw on." Sylvia had honed her ability to think on her feet when she was young. And to her, it wasn't *technically* a lie.

"Okay. Well anyway, I got something to ask you," Candy said, going to sit on the couch with her feet tucked under her.

"What? And take those shoes off if you're gonna sit like that."

Lightly sucking her teeth, Candy kicked off her shoes and then resumed her position. "How old were you when you first had sex?"

Mildly surprised but greatly pleased by the question, Sylvia joined her daughter on the couch. "I was twelve. Got it in in the bathroom with some boy in my class during lunchtime. Nobody even noticed we were gone."

Intrigued, Candy leaned forward slightly. "Really?"

"Yeah! He was in a different class and he asked me if I'd let him do me. Really, I don't think he was expecting me to say yes, but he damn sure didn't complain."

"So...y'all went in the stall or something?"

"Yeah, we went in the stall in the boy's bathroom. Laid a whole bunch of toilet paper on the seat, then he sat down and I straddled him. It hurt like hell at first but after a while, I loved it."

"I thought you were supposed to do missionary the first time. That's the way I did-um...that's what I heard."

Sylvia rolled her eyes. She didn't know why Candy kept trying to front like she was still a virgin when Sylvia already knew better. "I don't know who told you that bullshit, but you can do it any way you want to. I rode him then he hit it from the back. And anyway, we were in a bathroom stall, not a hotel room. Only so much we could do in there."

"Did you go down on him?" Candy asked, enthralled.

"Not that day but I did eventually."

"Did you like it?"

"No. Not at first. At first I was only doing it 'cause the boys wanted me to. But I damn sure love it now."

"I have another question...how does it feel when a guy goes down on you?"

"Girl," Sylvia hedged, excitedly turning to face Candy. She was thrilled that Candy was practically hanging on her every word. "There is nothing like having your stuff eaten. I can't even really describe it...it's like...all these things swirl together on your insides and then you just explode! One of the best feelings in the world, for real."

"Mya told me it felt good."

"It does, as long as the guy knows what he's doing. All of 'em don't. But let me tell you this; if he won't eat southern cuisine, then you don't go to the South Pole."

"Huh?"

Sylvia sighed. "Read between the damn lines. If he won't go down on you, then you don't go down on him."

"Oh."

They continued to talk for another half hour or so before they both went to their rooms. Sylvia felt great that Candy had actually come to her and asked for advice on something; it really felt like they were two girlfriends talking. Or almost like Candy was her little protégé and Sylvia was providing some life-experienced coaching. It felt good to be able to pass along some knowledge to her daughter.

That night Sylvia went to bed with a huge smile on her face. Valencio had won his basketball game, she had gotten her boots knocked, and she and Candy had bonded.

"Finally, a good day," she yawned before drifting off to sleep.

• • • •

A COUPLE OF NIGHTS later, Sylvia dragged in from work. She immediately kicked off her sneakers and dropped her purse and jacket on the couch as she continued on to the kitchen to get her some wine. It had been a long day on her feet and she needed to unwind, especially since she would have to do it all over again tomorrow.

After downing a couple of cups of wine, Sylvia retrieved her purse and jacket and started to head back to her bedroom. She knew Valencio was still with Bryce, but Candy should have been home. She started to knock on the door when she thought she heard Candy moaning inside her room.

"What the hell?" Sylvia frowned, leaning in closer to the door. There was definite moaning and hissing, like someone was being seriously pleasured. Sylvia tried to open the door, but it was locked. She pounded on it with her fist.

"Candy!" she yelled. "Girl, what the hell you doing?? You better not have a boy up in there with you!"

There was whispering before Candy yelled back, "Mama, chill out! I don't have nobody in here! I'm just on Skype with Roland!"

"Oh," Sylvia responded, relieved. "Okay, then." She continued on to her room, not giving it another thought. She would much rather Candy and some boy video-freak than do it in person.

Chapter 7

· · · ·

"WHERE ARE WE GOING?" Jelissa, Dub's girlfriend asked. "I thought we were going to the restaurant."

"We are. I've just gotta drop this money off at Sylvia's first."

Sucking her teeth, Jelissa folded her arms in a huff. "For real? Why are *you* taking her money?"

"'Cause Deuce isn't gonna do it and his daughter needs it for something. And Candy *is* my niece, Jelissa."

"I just don't understand why Sylvia's always calling you when she needs something. You're not her man."

"I know that, baby," Dub said, trying to be patient. "And she didn't call me asking for anything; she called Deuce and I happened to be right there to hear him shut her down. It wouldn't be right knowing I could help out and I didn't."

"I'm just saying, though, Dub..."

"I need you to stop trippin' about this, baby," he said, reaching over to clamp a hand on her thigh. "I'm with *you*. I've *been* with you for over a year now and haven't stepped out on you once, so why are you acting jealous of my niece's mother?"

Jelissa sighed. She knew he was right; Dub was by far the best man she had ever been with. She didn't have anything to complain about, as far as how he treated her. And it wasn't like she was insecure; she had seen Sylvia before. Jelissa knew she looked better than Sylvia. But something just didn't sit right with her about Sylvia being so dependent on her man.

"It's not really about me being jealous, Dub. I don't think you're gonna leave me for her or anything. But you can't tell me that woman doesn't like you."

"Yeah, she likes me. I like her, too."

"You know what I'm talking about, Dub. She wants you."

Dub was quiet. Of course he knew Sylvia had a crush on him; she'd had it for years. But she didn't act on it, which he appreciated. He didn't want anything to happen to derail their friendship.

"Even if she does-"

"She does," Jelissa interjected.

"Okay, but so what? She knows by now that I'm not interested in her like that and she doesn't try anything with me, so what's the problem?"

"I just think you're encouraging her by being there for her so much."

"And I think you need to chill out," Dub said, returning his hand to the wheel. "I consider Sylvia family and I don't neglect my family. And you know why I don't."

Jelissa softened upon hearing that. She knew Dub and Deuce's father had abandoned them, and it was because of that that Dub had a fierce loyalty to his loved ones, especially since Deuce was almost exactly the opposite.

"Okay, I get it," Jelissa said softly after a few moments. She reached over a rubbed his leg. "I'm sorry."

Dub just nodded. It annoyed him that Jelissa often got an instant attitude every time he said anything about doing something for Sylvia or Candy, and it had been the cause of more than a couple of arguments between them. He just didn't get why she acted like she was so threatened by Sylvia. Surely she knew that Dub could have been with Sylvia if he wanted her like that. But he wasn't. He wished she would just be secure in what they had together.

They rode the rest of the way to Sylvia's in silence.

When they arrived at Sylvia's apartment building, Dub got out of the car without a word, leaving Jelissa in the front seat. He tried to clear his mind of the discussion they just had as he approached Sylvia's door and knocked on it.

The door swung open after a few moments and Candy stood there, looking at him.

"Hey, Candy," Dub greeted her.

"Hey," she responded. "Are you my daddy or the one that Mama wishes was my daddy?"

Dub couldn't help but blush at that. He knew Candy had always had trouble telling him and Deuce apart, but he wasn't aware that Candy knew about Sylvia's feelings for him. It made him wonder what else she knew about.

"I'm your uncle Dub, sweetie," Dub answered.

"Oh."

"How are you?"

"I'm okay. You want to see Mama?"

"Yeah, is she here?"

"Yeah, she just got home a few minutes ago. Hold on. Mama! Uncle Dub is here!" Candy yelled before leaving Dub standing in the doorway.

Dub stepped in but didn't close the door behind him so Jelissa would still be able to see him from the car. Sylvia appeared from down the hallway a few moments later.

"Hey, Dub," she greeted happily.

"What's up, Sylvia. I just wanted to stop by and bring you that money for Candy's dentist appointment."

"Thanks *so* much," Sylvia said appreciatively as Dub handed her two hundred dollar bills. "I'll get it back to you as soon as I can."

"Don't worry about paying me back. I'm glad to help."

"You're not just helping, you're saving me, 'cause I didn't know where I was going to get this money from. I've already been pulling double shifts six nights out of the week."

"You know you can call me if you need to. If I got it, you got it."

Sylvia's grin widened. "You're so good to me. You want something to drink? I have some pound cake, if you want some of that."

"I'm good."

"You sure? I know it's not much but I at least wanted to give you *something* for helping us out."

Dub relented, appreciative of her appreciation. "Okay, I'll take a slice, then. Thanks."

"Cool! You can come on in."

"Oh nah...Jelissa is out in the car so I can't stay too long," Dub said, pointing.

Sylvia looked and saw Dub's girlfriend sitting in the front seat of his car and forced a tight, polite smile on her face. She wasn't afraid to admit (to herself) that she was jealous of Jelissa. Not only because she had Dub, but because she was so much prettier than Sylvia was. Jelissa was a bow-legged beauty with honey-brown eyes and lips that even Sylvia wouldn't have minded kissing, they were so plump and perfect. And she had this really thick, jet black hair that stopped right above her shoulders and looked like it should be in Dark and Lovely advertisement. As for her body, nothing stood out more than anything else; everything was just nice and proportioned, which was something Sylvia was never able to say about her own body. Sylivia had never spoken to her directly but she didn't like her, for no other reason than she was with Dub. But Sylivia would never let Dub know this, because she didn't want him upset with her.

She quickly wrapped up a big hunk of the lemon pound cake in some foil and went over and handed it to Dub, along with a can of fruit punch.

"For you to snack on later," she smiled as he took them from her.

"Hey, thanks Sylvia," Dub said appreciatively, grinning. "You know how much of a sweet tooth I have."

"Yeah, I remember."

"I can't be eating too much of this kind of stuff, though. Trying to keep the physique," Dub joked, patting his flat stomach.

Sylvia swallowed, imagining the six-pack that she knew was under his shirt. Of the twins, Dub had always been the finest one, even though Deuce wasn't too far behind. But as they had gotten older, Dub had put more effort into keeping himself up while Deuce hadn't. Deuce still looked good, but he wasn't quite as firm as he used to be.

"Yeah, well," Sylvia said, hoping she wasn't blushing. "One piece of cake won't hurt you."

"You're right. Well let me get on outta here. I'll see you later, okay?"

"Okay."

Dub gave her a quick hug before trotting back to the car, with Jelissa eyeing them the entire time. Sylvia waved politely before closing the door.

"Bitch," she muttered.

· · · ·

THE NEXT NIGHT, SYLVIA had to work the overnight shift at the store to help do inventory, so Candy and Valencio were home alone. As usual, they were in their respective rooms; Valencio was doing homework and Candy was on her computer. Before Sylvia left, she had gone into Valencio's room and sat on the bed.

"I'm about to head out, baby."

"Okay. Have a good night at work."

"I doubt it but thanks. What are you planning on doing while I'm gone?"

Valencio shrugged. "Just finish my homework, maybe watch a little TV, then go to bed. Why?"

"You can invite a few friends over, if you want to."

"Really?"

"Yeah."

"I don't have anybody I want to invite over here, really."

"You don't know any girls?"

Valencio's eyebrows shot up. "I didn't know that's what you meant."

"Yeah, that's what I meant. It doesn't have to be *just* girls, but you can invite some of them, too. You remember what I said about you having a girlfriend."

"Yeah, but Dad said not to worry about that."

"I know," Sylvia grunted. "That doesn't mean you can't *hang out* with girls, though."

"Okay," Valencio replied, going back to his Algebra book. He hoped she would drop the subject, because he wasn't about to invite anybody over there.

Sylvia looked at her watch. "Shoot, I gotta go." She stood up. "But remember what I said."

"Yes, ma'am."

Sylvia gave him a quick kiss on the top of the head before leaving the room. On the way past Candy's room, she yelled out that she was leaving without bothering to stop.

• • • •

SYLVIA HADN'T BEEN at work a good hour before her first headache came.

"Hey Sylvia," her former nemesis, Coco, greeted her as she breezed through the front doors of the store. As usual, her clothing was too tight and she looked like she was about to burst out of everything, just like back in high school. They never liked each other back in the day and they didn't like each other now.

"What do you want, Coco?" Sylvia asked, cutting her eyes at her.

"Just had to pick up some goodies for my date tonight. What aisle is the whipped cream on?"

Rolling her eyes, Sylvia pointed. "It's in the dairy section, in the back."

Coco quickly headed in that direction without thanking her, switching her hips so hard Sylvia half expected her to pop something out of place. Sylvia just shook her head and went back to restocking the grocery bags.

She didn't recall exactly what it was that started the disdain that she and Coco had for one another. They just never got along. Coco seemed to think that just because she was more physically developed than most of the other girls, that she was somehow entitled to get everything she wanted; or namely, all the boys she wanted. There was more than one occasion where she and Sylvia had their eye on the same guy when they were at a party or something. Coco almost always got the guy, but she still resented Sylvia for even daring to try.

Sylvia knew, though, that a lot of the problem was that she was one of the few people that Coco didn't intimidate. Sylvia might not have been as attractive as she was, but one thing she never lacked was confidence, and that allowed her to stand up to Coco when a lot of other girls wouldn't. They almost got into a fight once, but a teacher came and broke it up before it could really get going. Sylvia always kind of hated that she didn't get the chance to beat Coco's ass and always waited for her to say just the right wrong thing to give her an excuse to do it now.

A little later, Coco came back with a shopping basket full of whipped cream, wine, chocolate syrup and assorted fruits.

"Got everything I need," she chirped.

"Good for you," Sylvia said dryly. "The registers are that way."

"And what are you gonna be doing tonight? Oh yeah, you'll be working in this grocery store just like you've been doing for the past twenty years."

Sylvia didn't even bother correcting her. It had only been fifteen years.

"I mean, damn, Sylvia. I thought you would have at least had a decent career, since you don't have much else. Are you at least a manager or something here?"

"You don't have to worry about what I am. Just go pay for your shit and leave me alone."

"Oooh, that's not very professional," Coco scolded mockingly. "I might have to tell on you."

"Go ahead." Sylvia knew that short of killing somebody right in the store, there wasn't anything she could do that would make her cousin Lance fire her.

Sucking her teeth and irritated that she couldn't get more of a rise out of Sylvia, Coco tired of the conversation. "Whatever. You're not even worth the time I'm giving you. I have to go get ready for my date tonight. When's the last time you had one of those?"

Sylvia threw her the deuces without even looking at her.

A few hours later, Sylvia's co-worker Toni rushed over to her.

"Sylvia, I need your help!"

"With what?"

"My dad just got rushed to the hospital; they think it might be a heart attack. I'm supposed to work until nine; can you *please* cover for me so I can go to the hospital?"

Sylvia didn't want to 'cause that would mean working four more hours, but saying no would seem heartless and insensitive. "Yeah, I got you."

"Thank you *so* much!" Toni gushed, throwing her arms around Sylvia's neck before rushing towards the back of the store.

Sylvia sighed. Her feet hurt, her stomach was growling, and she was dog tired. But she didn't mind helping Toni out, especially since Toni had covered for her a few times in the past.

Sylvia pulled out her cell phone and called home to let her kids know she would be coming home later than expected.

Candy answered the phone and Sylvia could immediately hear other voices in the background, none of which belonged to Valencio. She smiled at the fact that he seemed to have taken her advice and invited some of his friends over. It was a little late for them to be there, but Sylvia wasn't going to trip about it. She was just glad he was finally coming out of his shell.

Without even bothering to ask who all was over there (or to even verify if they were Valencio's guests or Candy's), she just told Candy that she would be coming home a little later and to make sure they didn't tear anything up and to stay out of her room.

Chapter 8

• • • •

SYLVIA KNEW IT WAS going to be something she probably didn't want to hear when Bryce called her and asked if he could come over when he got off work.

"What for?" Sylvia asked skeptically.

"I just have something I need to talk to you about."

"Can't we just talk about whatever it is now?"

"No, Sylvia, I'm about to head to a meeting so I don't have time right now. I wouldn't ask if it wasn't important. Can I come over there later or not?"

"I guess."

"Good, thanks. I'll let you know when I'm headed that way."

Sylvia tried to prepare herself for whatever it was that was so important that Bryce had to come and talk to her about it in person. No doubt it had something to do with Valencio. She wondered if Valencio had told him about her suggestion to invite some girls over while she was at work. If there was one thing about Valencio that got on Sylvia's nerves, it was that he told his dad too much about what went on in their house.

When Bryce arrived later on that evening, he wasted no time getting to the reason for his visit.

"I'm concerned about how you're raising our son."

Sylvia got an instant attitude. "Excuse me?"

"I'm sure you're probably getting ready to go off right now, but please just listen to me. I'm not here to insult you or place blame or anything else, but I wouldn't be much of a father if I didn't speak up about the things I've been seeing and hearing."

Folding her arms, Sylvia challenged, "Like what?"

"Well, the whole thing about telling Valencio to get a girlfriend and that he's too focused on schoolwork when he's just thirteen.

Encouraging him to have a party when you're not even home. I'm really not crazy about just him and Candy being here alone overnight when you have to be at work, but that's not my main concern. I feel like you're trying to make Valencio into the opposite kind of man I'm trying to teach him to be."

"Why do you say that? And for the record, I didn't tell him to have a party. I just told him he could invite a few people over here, that's all."

Bryce looked at her like she should know better. "Come on, Sylvia. We were both teenagers and we know how teenagers are. You give them a little leeway and more often than not, they take too much. A couple of friends come, then they tell some of *their* friends and they show up, and so on and so on, and before you can even blink its House Party up in here. It doesn't take long for things to spiral out of control."

"Why are you being such a stick in the mud all the time? Valencio knows better than to let that happen. Otherwise I wouldn't have told him he could do it in the first place. It's not like I told Candy she could do that; I know better than that."

"Really? Valencio told me there were people over here that night but that he didn't invite any of them, so they all had to be Candy's friends." He looked at Sylvia pointedly. "A little leeway."

Sylvia frowned. She hadn't even bothered asking who was over that night and who invited them. All she had cared about was that they not go in her room or tear up her stuff. She swallowed at the realization.

"So...what are you trying to say, Bryce?" Sylvia asked, not wanting to admit out loud that he had a point.

"I'm trying to say that while I think your intentions are in the right place, you're not setting the kind of foundation for Bryce that I think he should have to be an intelligent, responsible man. Right now he's resisting the stuff you're trying to push him into but it's only a matter of time before he caves and starts experimenting. I'm trying to avoid that."

"Teenagers experiment, Bryce. There's nothing we can do about that."

"I agree with that, to a degree. But it's not usually the *parents* that encourages them to do it."

"So you're saying I'm a bad mother." Sylvia looked down at her hands.

"No, Sylvia, I'm not saying that," Bryce said, moving to sit closer to her on the couch. He gently placed his hands on hers. "Like I said, I think you mean well. I just think your priorities are off. Sylvia, there's nothing wrong with wanting your kids to think you're cool and all that, but your main concern should be making sure they *respect* you first. When they get to be adults and on their own, you can worry about being their friend then. But now, they need parents. They need discipline and structure. You simply can't try to act their age one minute then try to be a disciplinarian the next. It just doesn't work like that."

That seems to be the party line, Sylvia thought. Her mother, Delta, and Bryce all seemed to take turns trying to tell her that she couldn't be her kids' friend as well as their mother. But she really only tried to be Candy's friend; the only thing she tried to do with Valencio was get him to loosen up a little bit.

"Sylvia, I'm here; let me help you," Bryce continued, looking at her sincerely. "We're in this together."

"Help how?" she asked, turning her eyes to him. "I don't need any help."

"Quit letting your pride get in the way of things, Sylvia. I'm not just some man off the street; Valencio is my son. And I want to see him more than I do now, especially since he's getting older. He needs a more constant male influence."

"You see him damn near every weekend already and he calls you every night."

"That's not enough for me. I want to be around my son everyday. Only a man can raise a man, Sylvia."

"Well, unless you're planning on moving in here, I don't see how that can happen."

Bryce knew Sylvia was being sarcastic, but he looked at her seriously. "Actually, I want y'all to move in with me."

Sylvia jumped like somebody stuck her with a pin and snatched her hand out of his grasp. "What?"

"I want y'all to move in with me."

"What about Candy? You expect her to stay here by herself? 'Cause you know her daddy ain't gonna let her stay with him."

"Of course not. I'm not trying to exclude her. She can come, too."

She frowned at him skeptically. "Why would you wanna do that?"

"Because I think Candy needs some constant positive male influence, too. I'm not trying to be her daddy but I can be there for her and help out with things."

"Her uncle does that," Sylvia protested quickly, referring to Dub.

"And that's great, but how often does he see her and spend one-on-one time with her? Do they even talk on the phone?"

Sylvia had to admit that Dub didn't really spend much alone time with Candy. Sure, he helped out with her financially and even gave her a ride somewhere when Sylvia couldn't, but that was pretty much the extent of it. Sylvia hadn't even realized that until just then.

"Okay, no..." Sylvia grudgingly admitted.

"So let me do that. Let me be there for all y'all. We can be a family, Sylvia." He took her hand again. "Don't you want that?"

"Are you proposing to me? I don't see a ring."

Bryce couldn't help but chuckle. "No, I'm not proposing. I think you and I both know we're nowhere near ready for that."

"I know we're not, 'cause I'm not in love with you, Bryce. And I know you're not in love with me."

"We don't have to be in love to live in the same house. It can be good for all of us. I have that house that I live in alone; there's plenty of room. You wouldn't have to worry about rent or anything so you wouldn't have to work so many double shifts and you could spend more time with both of them. And you and I could improve our co-parental relationship. Just…think about it, okay?"

"There ain't nothing to think about. That's nice of you to offer but we can't do that."

"You can't or you won't? Really, Sylvia, you need to check yourself and learn to put the well being of your children ahead of your stubbornness. Everything isn't all about you and what you want. I would think that you would want your children to grow up and be *about* something."

"Of course I do!"

"Why don't you start acting like it, then?" Bryce stood up and headed for the door, turning to look at her before opening it. "Think about what I said." Then he left.

• • • •

LATER ON, SYLVIA SAT in bed and contemplated Bryce's offer. She couldn't deny that it was intriguing. She didn't enjoy working double shifts most days of the week. And she certainly wanted to do better for her kids than she was doing. The kids would probably enjoy living in an actual house instead of this raggedy apartment. She had been to Bryce's house; it was really nice. He was an investment banker so it's not like he was hurting for money. And it would be nice to not have to worry about rent.

Sylvia slid down onto her back, staring up at the ceiling. She enjoyed being the cool parent that all the other kids wished they had. Just because she was thirty didn't mean that she couldn't have any fun. The last thing she wanted to be was like her mother; she had made a vow when she got pregnant with Candy that she was going to raise her kids like she wished she had been raised, and she was doing that. Valencio was doing great, but she knew that was in large part thanks to Bryce. Maybe there was something to having a positive male influence; she hadn't had one growing up, and Candy didn't have much of one now. Like Bryce pointed out, Dub might have been around but he didn't spend much time with Candy. Sylvia had never really asked him to; she had never even *thought* to ask him to.

She couldn't help but wonder if part of Bryce's motivation for inviting her and her kids to move in with him was because he still had feelings for her. Sylvia might have been attracted to Bryce at times, but she didn't want him like that. He was a good man but he bored her to tears. She knew part of her resistance to Bryce was due to her still being hung up on Dub, even though she had long since accepted that he didn't want her like she wanted him. But every man she met got automatically compared to him, and every man failed. Dub would simply always be her epitome.

• • • •

SYLVIA KNEW SOMETHING was up when she saw Deuce's name on her caller ID. He almost never called her.

"Yes?" she answered.

"Where my girl at?" Deuce slurred.

"What? What girl?"

"What you mean, what girl? My daughter!"

"Why you wanna speak to her? And are you drunk??"

"A lil' tipsy. So?"

"So you don't need to be talking to her when you're drunk, especially since you don't pay her no attention any other time. Call her back when you come down off that buzz."

"I can speak to my daughter when I want to, dammit!"

"The hell you can! Now, what?"

"Look, Sylvia," he said, calming down immediately. "I just wanna hear her voice. There's nothing wrong with that, right? She should at least know who I am."

"She knows who you are. But she ain't even here, no way."

"What? Where she at?"

"Why are you acting like you care, Deuce? You said you weren't gonna have anything to do with her and you haven't in fifteen years. You sure kept your word on that."

"Still, though, it's almost nine o'clock! She don't need to be out this time of night!"

"Don't worry about all that." Sylvia had been through all of this with Deuce more than a couple of times. He would call and act like he wanted to forge some kind of relationship with Candy only to leave her high and dry when he came off whatever temporary buzz or high he was on. Sylvia wasn't about to keep putting Candy through that, even though Candy hardly even mentioned Deuce anymore. She was used to not having a daddy around.

"Who she with?"

"Like I said, don't worry about it. Now I gotta go; I've got a pizza in the oven." She hung up the phone. Even though he had warned her back in high school that he wouldn't be and she had long since gotten used to it, she hated that Deuce wasn't there for Candy. The musing immediately made her think of Bryce and his offer to her. Candy liked Bryce okay; she had even heard her telling one of her friends once that she thought he was cute. Of course, she also heard her wonder why someone like Bryce would want someone like Sylvia. Sylvia couldn't deny that stung a little bit.

Not thirty minutes later, there was a loud knock on her door. "Sylvia!"

"No, he didn't," Sylvia whispered. She was glad that Valencio was with Bryce and Candy was still out with her friends. She didn't want them seeing Deuce acting like a drunk fool. "Deuce, what are you doing here?"

"Open the door!"

"Candy still ain't here so go on back to wherever you came from."

"Sylvia, just open the door!"

Sighing, Sylvia reluctantly eased the door open. Deuce stood there, looking fine but smelling like alcohol and smoke. "What?"

"Can I come in?"

Sylvia cocked a brow. "For what?"

"You know for what."

Sylvia sucked her teeth. Deuce was standing there looking at her hungrily, like he wanted to just tear off the baby tee and shorts she was wearing. They had slept together a few times over the years; they both knew it wasn't anything romantic and they didn't try to act like it was. They used each other to get off, and that was it.

"No, thanks," Sylvia resisted, even though she *did* think about it. Deuce might've been an asshole but he was still fine, especially when he had the scruffy five o'clock shadow thing going on like he had then. And he could certainly satisfy her. In fact, when they were in bed together was the only time he showed her a modicum of kindness.

"You sure?" he asked, reaching out and grabbing her with one hand by her waist and pulling her to him roughly. Sylvia wasn't about to admit out loud that she liked that kind of thing. "Girl, if you ain't got nothin' else, you got some *nice* titties. And a *fat* ass, too," he added, gripping it hard.

Deuce was already hard and ready; she could feel it pressing against her. But even though Sylvia was getting more and more turned on by the second, she just wasn't in the mood to deal with Deuce tonight.

She pushed against his chest. "Go home, Deuce."

"I don't know why you playin'. You know you want it." He leaned down and licked her neck.

Sylvia's eyes closed briefly. "No, I don't."

"Oh, you don't?" Deuce grabbed her breast and fondled it through her shirt. He backed her against the doorjamb and his other hand eased between her legs. She wished to high heaven she wasn't so wet. "Feels like you do."

Before she totally lost what little restraint she had, she forcefully pushed him away with both hands. "I don't care if I'm wet enough for you to bathe in, it's not happening. So go get your nut off with somebody else."

"Oh it's like that?"

"It's like that." She closed the door in his face, leaning against it and trying to calm herself down. Part of her wanted to open the door right back up, grab his shirt and lead him to the bed, but she made herself move away from the door until she heard him walk away. Sex with Deuce was good, but not really worth it. For a while afterwards he would be an even bigger asshole than he usually was and she just didn't want to deal with that this time.

She thought about calling Percy to scratch the itch she now had, but for some reason, she wanted to call Bryce. They hadn't had sex in years but Sylvia remembered well how good he was to her body. He was always so gentle and tender and took his time pleasing her. She knew he was still attracted to her so there was no real reason to turn her down; what man refused sex?

Hurrying to her phone, she dialed Bryce's number.

"What's up, Sylvia?" he answered.

"Hey, can you come back over here?"

"Why, what's wrong?"

"Nothing. I just need you to fuck me."

There was a pause. "Excuse me?"

"You heard me. Can you come? Now? I know you want it."

Bryce paused again before speaking. "I'm not your booty call, Sylvia," he said in a low but firm voice. "When you're seriously ready to talk about what I suggested about all of us being a family and get on the page I'm on, *then* you call me. But don't insult me with nonsense like this." Then he hung up the phone.

Chapter 9

• • • •

CANDY'S BODY MIGHT have been in class but her mind was off somewhere else. She was thinking about when she was going to get out of the house to see Roland next. They hadn't had sex in a few weeks and she wondered if he was talking to another girl. Even though they weren't officially girlfriend-boyfriend, she didn't like the thought of him being with anybody else. Candy didn't like to share.

She was so deep in thought that she almost didn't even realize that the bell had rung and class had ended. She quickly gathered her things and headed out into the hallway, looking for her friends Mya and China. They were supposed to walk to lunch together and China was going to give her the answers to the Algebra homework before they went to that class later. Candy wanted to be sure that she got that done because she didn't want her mother on her back again about her schoolwork. Sylvia had already been checking on that everyday since the principal had called and Candy had to sit with a tutor after school twice a week, which she hated.

"Hey, Candy," someone called out to her.

She turned around and automatically grinned to see it was Mac. Mac was an eighteen-year-old that was repeating his senior year because he had spent too much time partying the first time around and failed three of his classes. Candy had been harboring a crush on him for most of the year. Word was, after it was determined he would have to repeat the school year, his mother had sent him across town to live with his father, who was a former Marine. He had threatened Mac to either get his stuff together or he would be on the first thing smoking to military school. Mac straightened up the grades, but he still did his share of fooling around; he just had to be more slick about it.

"Hey, Mac," Candy responded flirtatiously.

"Can I holla at you for a minute?"

"Yeah." It took all of her restraint not to run over to where he was. She swung her narrow hips until she was standing right in front of him. "What's up?"

"You're looking real good today," Mac said, scanning her body with his hazel eyes that all the girls talked about. He leaned against the nearby lockers and Candy did the same.

"Thanks, I appreciate that," Candy replied smoothly, even though she was giddy on the inside. She was trying her best to stay even a little nonchalant. "So are you."

"I try," Mac said, smirking. He stepped closer to her. "So what's up with you after school? What you doin'?"

"I'm supposed to be going to my grandmama's. Why?"

"'Cause I want us to hang. Any way you can get out of that?"

Candy wanted to with everything in her, but she knew she wouldn't be able to. "I wish but I doubt it."

"Damn," Mac grunted. He reached out and poked her bellybutton through her shirt. "That's too bad."

At that moment, Candy hated both her mother and her grandmother . "Yeah, I know."

"You got a cell phone?"

"No." Candy was the only one out of her friends without one.

"For real? Just about everybody has a cell phone now."

"Yeah, I know," Candy said, mildly embarrassed. She felt like a lame for having to admit she was one of the few people that didn't have a cell phone. "Just haven't gotten one yet."

"So you think you can get one?"

"Probably."

"Make sure I'm the first one to get the number when you do. Then we can send each other some pictures when we can't hang out."

Feeling her body heating up, Candy's new goal in life became getting a cell phone as soon as possible. She could only imagine what kind of pictures Mac was talking about and she already couldn't wait to see them, even though she really would have preferred the real thing.

"Yeah, I'll do that," Candy promised.

Mac leaned in close after looking over his shoulder. "I can't wait to get at you. Word is you know how to put it *down*."

Candy just grinned, more flattered than offended. She didn't even care where he heard that from; she was just glad he had. "I try."

"So we're gonna hook up, right?" Mac asked as the bell rang.

"Most definitely," Candy replied, as happy as happy could be. She couldn't wait to tell her friends about this.

Candy was on cloud nine. She wasted no time bragging to her friends about Mac stepping to her, and she plotted on how she was going to get Sylvia to get her a cell phone so she and Mac could communicate whenever they wanted.

Her high was short-lived, though, when she got to her Spanish class and realized she had forgotten all about the test they were having that day. She hadn't prepared for it at all and since she had been doing more daydreaming than paying attention the last couple of classes, she knew her chances of acing it or even passing it were slim to none. And she couldn't take home another failing grade; Sylvia would surely try to put her on lockdown then.

She wished China was in her class, because she knew she would let her cheat off her. The only other people in that class she was kind of cool with was Yasmine and Jake. Yasmine was out because she was known for blackmailing girls into getting them to perform sexual acts on her, and Candy would rather flunk out than do that. She was willing to do a lot but messing around with girls wasn't one of them.

That left Jake. Jake was kind of a lame but Candy had seen him checking her out a few times so she figured she might as well use that to her advantage.

She tried to get his attention but he wouldn't look over at her. The teacher, Mr. O'Malley, had already looked over at her once and she had managed to play it off. Jake was sitting in the next row and all he would have to do was move his arm so she could see his paper.

Knowing she was running out of time, Candy hurriedly scribbled a note and started to pass it to him, but she didn't even realize Mr. O'Malley was coming down the row behind her.

"What do we have here?" he said, snatching the note out of Candy's hand.

"That's nothing!" Candy said, trying to snatch the note back, but he held it out of her reach.

"Doesn't look like nothing," Mr. O'Malley replied, opening the note.

"That's *my* business!" Candy exclaimed, not wanting him to read the note out loud. She was already embarrassed enough as it was.

"Well, now it's going to be everybody's business. You know I don't tolerate note-passing in my class." He held the note in front of his face and cleared his throat. 'Hey Jake, if you help me out on this test and let me cheat off you, I'll...'' Mr. O'Malley's face turned bright red as he silently read the rest of the note. He looked at Candy, whose own face was flaming, and cleared his throat. "I'm not gonna read the rest of this to the class but this is *highly* inappropriate, Ms. Jennings! What is the matter with you, bringing this smut into my class??"

Candy ducked her head in embarrassment as her classmates snickered around her. Jake's eyes were glued to her now, no doubt wondering what it was she would have let him do to her for helping her cheat.

"You and I are gonna have a serious talk about this, young lady!" Mr. O'Malley continued. "There is just no excuse for this! Maybe if you put as much effort into actually studying as you did trying to get over, you wouldn't need to resort to cheap tactics like this!"

Candy had never been more humiliated, but she wasn't about to let her teacher stand there and scold her like he was her daddy or something. Especially since her own daddy didn't even care about anything she did. She knew she was going to be the subject of gossip after this and she had to save face.

"Look, you need to back up off me!" she retorted loudly, giving him a large dose of attitude. "Just because nobody cares about your little boring, funky-ass test doesn't mean you can stand here and get onto me like that! I don't know who you think you are but I am *not* the one!"

Mr. O'Malley looked taken aback but he quickly recovered. "You need to watch your language, young lady, and have a little more respect! You are simply not going to speak to me that way in my classroom!"

"Well, maybe I don't need to *be* in your classroom, then!" Candy grabbed her book bag and stormed out, not even knowing where she was going or how she was going to explain it to her mother when she got home, because she knew the principal would probably be calling again after this.

Deciding not to worry about that right then, she tried to think of a place she could lay low until her next class. She headed out the side door towards the gym and her mood instantly brightened when she saw a few members of the basketball team standing around talking. Russell, Jermaine, and Jason were by far the cutest members of the team to Candy and they happened to be the best players, too. Just like that, the scene from Mr. O'Malley's class just minutes before was forgotten.

She hurried over to them, her mind working out what she was going to say. She hadn't had too many interactions with them before but she hoped that her reputation would precede her like it had with Mac.

"Where y'all 'bout to go?" she asked, opting for a causal approach as if she were already in with them.

They stopped walking and looked at her. Jason, who was the shortest of the three and the team's point guard, toggled the basketball he was holding in between his hands and said, "Why, you wanna go?"

Hell yeah was what Candy immediately wanted to say but she managed a cool, "Yeah, I'll go with you."

"You don't even know where we're going, though," Russell, the tallest of the three, replied amusingly.

"Doesn't matter. I know y'all will take care of me," Candy replied flirtatiously. She loved how dark and smooth his skin looked and wanted to reach out and touch it.

"Isn't your name Candy or something like that?" Jermaine asked.

Excitement shot through Candy like a rocket. Jermaine was, in her opinion, the cutest one of the three and the fact that he recognized her simply made her day. "Yeah, that's me. So what's up? Where we going?"

Before any of them could respond, they heard some laughing and talking from behind them. They turned to see a couple of popular girls coming out of the building Candy had just come out of. Candy turned back to the guys, hoping they could continue with what they were talking about, but their attention was no longer on her.

"Yo, there's Adrienne," Jason said in a hushed voice, tapping Russell on the arm. "That girl fine as *hell*."

"Yeah, she's something serious," Russell concurred.

"Both of 'em are," Jermaine added, his eyes glued to the girls.

Candy cleared her throat, but they ignored her.

"Hey, where y'all going?" Jason called out to the girls.

The girls stopped and turned to them, smiling expectantly. "Why you wanna know?" Adrienne asked.

"You need to be hanging with us," Russell said.

"Why?" the other girl, Connie, asked flirtatiously. She slung her long braids over her shoulder.

The guys started to head over to them, leaving Candy standing there alone. She just watched as they all headed off down the walkway, talking and laughing, without her. She thought about just following them and integrating herself into their conversation, but she didn't want to risk them telling her to get lost. She was embarrassed enough for being left there like she was nothing, anyway.

Candy sulked off, opting to just sit in the bathroom until it was time for her next class. She peered at herself in the mirror, hating what she saw. She would give absolutely anything to be prettier and have a more voluptuous body. Adrienne had a booty that was so perfect it was unfair. Even Candy caught herself staring at it sometimes. And Connie had the classic hourglass figure. Candy didn't have anything like that. Her body was just like her mother's, and she hated that. The only thing she had going for her physically was her slightly-better-than-average butt and the dimples she inherited from her dad, Deuce.

Candy didn't know how she was going to do it yet, but she vowed to make Jason, Jermaine, and Russell want her and follow behind her like they had followed Adrienne and Connie.

• • • •

SYLVIA SAT ON HER COUCH, puffing on a cigarette as she waited for Candy to get home. She had gotten yet another call from the school about Candy, this time because of cheating (or at least trying to), and then leaving the class. Sylvia shook her head. Candy didn't even have enough sense not to get caught.

As soon as Candy walked through the door, Sylvia lit into her.

"What the hell is your problem this time?"

Candy looked at her in surprise. "What are you talking about?"

"Don't act like you don't know what I'm talking about. So you're cheating on tests and shit now?"

Sucking her teeth, Candy tossed her book bag onto the couch. "What's the big deal? It's only Spanish."

"That ain't the point. I'm tired of them calling me 'cause you're up there acting up at that school!"

"That teacher didn't have no business reading my personal stuff," Candy said, referring to the note she had tried to pass to Jake. "If he had just minded his own business..."

"Quit being stupid, Candy," Sylvia spat. She glared at her. "I'm sitting up here scraping money together for a tutor for your ass and you're up in there cheating. I ain't got money to waste."

"I told you I didn't need a tutor in the first place," Candy muttered.

"The hell you don't. I guess I need to remind you that you've spent most of this year either cutting class and not paying any attention when you *were* in class, and your grades are in the toilet. Keep playing and you'll be a freshman again next year. Or have you forgotten that?"

Candy did temporarily forget about that, even though the last thing she wanted to do was repeat her freshman year. Not only would it be humiliating, it would prolong her being in school. She was already counting down until she didn't have to worry about homework and lame teachers and doing assignments that nobody really cared about.

"Okay, fine. I'll do better," she mumbled, turning to head into the kitchen.

"No, you're not just gonna do *better*, 'cause as bad as you're doing now, 'better' ain't saying much," Sylvia countered, grabbing her arm and turning her back to face her. "I had to make up some story to explain your behavior so they wouldn't suspend you, so you need to take this seriously and get those damn grades up."

"Okay, okay. You don't have to worry; I got it."

Sylvia looked at her skeptically but chose to drop it for the time being. She had run out of energy for this conversation and wanted to get a quick nap in before she had to be back up at the store. She started to head back to her room when Candy stopped her.

"Can you get me a cell phone?"

Sylvia looked at her like she was crazy. "So you get caught cheating at school then gon' ask me for a cell phone in the same day?"

"This ain't got nothing to do with that. I told you I was going to get my grades up. But I need a cell phone."

"Why do you *need* a cell phone all of a sudden?"

Knowing there was no way she would tell her mother the real reason behind her wanting the phone was so that she could exchange pictures with Mac, she opted for what she figured Sylvia would probably want to hear. "If I had one, then you'd be able to call me whenever I'm out to check up on me and see where I am."

Sylvia cocked an intrigued brow.

"Or you could have me call you to check in," Candy added, even though she knew she would hate having to do that. But if it meant Sylvia gave her what she wanted, it would be worth it. "You know how you're always asking where I am and stuff."

Sylvia continued to eye her daughter silently. She knew that Candy was probably trying to run game on her, but she also knew that she could very well check up on her more if Candy had a cell phone. And Sylvia could track it if she wanted to. Plus, Sylvia never got a phone when she was Candy's age, even though she wanted one.

"Yeah, okay," Sylvia finally said. "I'll get you one. But it's not gonna be nothing expensive so if you're thinking about some kind of iPhone or something like that, you might as well get that out of your head right now."

"Aww...why not?" Candy whined.

"Girl, I'm not buying you one of those when I don't have one my damn self. You'll get a regular phone with a cheap plan I can afford."

"What *kind* of phone, though?"

"A better one than the kind you have now! Keep talking and I'll change my mind!"

Candy closed her mouth. She figured she could put up with whatever kind of phone she ended up with, as long as she was able to take pictures and text with it. Smiling excitedly, she hurried to her room, already thinking about what kind of picture she was going to send to Mac first.

· · · ·

LATER THAT EVENING, Sylvia hung out with Delta while the kids spent the night with Sandra. Sylvia enjoyed having the night to herself, having gotten off work earlier than expected.

"So have you found out what Candy is doing in her room when she's locked in there by herself?" Delta asked, tucking her feet underneath her on the couch.

"I already know what she's doing."

"What?"

"Skyping with some boy."

Delta blinked. "I thought you said you heard her in there moaning and stuff."

"Yeah," Sylvia replied with a shrug, as if it was no big deal.

"So..."

"So...what?"

"So you're saying she's cyber-sexing? Why are you acting like that's no big deal?"

"I can deal with her doing that. Can't get knocked up over the computer."

"That shouldn't be the point, Sylvia."

"So what *is* the point? I'd rather her be in there touching herself in front of the camera than having some horny little teenager in there poking his dick in her."

"So she's a virgin, then?"

"Girl please, hell no. She tries to act like she is but I know better than that."

Delta threw her hands up. "So then it doesn't matter if she's cyber-sexing or not, then, does it?"

"I think it does. Maybe if she knows I'm cool with her doing that, she won't feel the need to go out and get the real thing anymore."

"You're smarter than that, though, right? I'm *sure* you don't think that she'll be satisfied with just cyber-sexing if she knows she can get away with more than that."

"I don't know, Delta, damn," Sylvia replied, exasperated. "How come every time you come over here, all you want to do is talk about my kids?"

"I thought mothers loved talking about their children."

"Not all the damn time. I can't have some grown-woman time sometimes?"

"Sylvia, girl, I'm not trying to upset you or insult you or anything; you know that. But I'm worried about both Candy *and* you. She's starting down a dangerous path and I just don't think you see it."

"A dangerous path?"

"You're letting her be too grown too soon. She needs discipline and guidance from you, not another girlfriend."

"Here we go with this again," Sylvia mumbled with a roll of her eyes.

"Like I said, I'm not trying to insult you but if I'm any kind of friend at all, I'm gonna keep it real with you whether it's something you want to hear or not. If Candy knows you're okay with her doing stuff like cyber-sexing, then she probably thinks you're okay with her doing just about anything. Who knows what kind of stuff she's into when she's out of this house and in the streets with her friends somewhere. I'm telling you, I wouldn't be surprised if she came home tomorrow saying she was pregnant."

"Delta, you don't think I've had that talk with her already? She knows better than that."

"Like you did when you were her age, right?"

Sylvia's eyes snapped to her friend. That hit a nerve.

"I'm sure your mother had all kinds of talks with you, yet *you* still ended up knocked up at fifteen," Delta continued gently. "I'm saying, Sylvia. Candy is turning out to be just like you. And I love you, girl, but I don't mean that as a compliment."

Chapter 10

• • • •

VALENCIO DIDN'T REALLY feel right about having friends over when Sylvia wasn't home. He knew that was something Candy did all the time without a second thought, but he always asked permission before inviting anyone over. That's something his dad Bryce had always told him to do, and certainly something that was required when he was staying with him. But Valencio's friends had asked if they could come in to use the bathroom and then one of them wanted to show off one of the new games on their phone, and before Valencio knew it, an hour had gone by. Valencio had tried to call Sylvia to make sure it was okay but she hadn't answered.

"Hey, Valencio, you got any games on your phone?" his friend Walt asked.

"No, I don't have a phone."

"What? How come?"

Valencio shrugged. "My dad said I don't need one yet. And who do I have to call, anyway?"

"Um...us?"

"We have a house phone I can use if I want to call y'all."

"I had to beg my mom for a month before she bought me a phone," his other friend, Devonte, chimed in, waving his phone in his hand before stuffing it back into his pocket. "She said I'm really just supposed to use it for emergencies, though."

"It's a phone, not a credit card. Why even have it if you can't use it?" Walt asked, sucking his teeth and plopping down onto Valencio's bed with his phone in front of his face.

"I might not be able to use my phone, but I've got something *else* we can all use right now," Devonte said mischievously, digging into his other pocket.

"What?" Valencio asked warily.

"Yo, you got it?" Walt asked excitedly, dropping his phone onto the bed and sitting up.

"Got what?" Valencio asked.

Devonte pulled out a rolled-up zip-lock bag held it up. Valencio's eyes widened to twice their size. He knew he shouldn't have let his friends into the house. He might not have ever done weed before, but he knew what it was when he saw it.

"Are you crazy??" he exclaimed, standing up. "What are you doing with that??"

"I got it from my brother. He don't know it, though." Devonte chuckled.

"Man, you've gotta get that mess outta here!"

"Chill out, V., it's just a joint," Devonte said, snapping open the bag.

"You got a lighter?" Walt asked.

"I'm not playin', Devonte!" Valencio yelled, his nervousness increasing. He half expected Sylvia to come bursting through the door at any second, even though he knew she would be at work until late in the evening.

"Valencio, quit being such a lame! You act like you've never seen some weed before!"

"I'm just not trying to get in trouble 'cause of y'all."

"You not gon' get in trouble. You said your mama don't get home 'til later on. And with all the stuff I've heard about your sister, I know she won't say nothin'."

Valencio wanted to defend Candy, but didn't know how he could do that without straight lying. "Whatever. Still..."

"Your mama ain't gon' find out. By the time she gets home, the smell and stuff will be gone. Just turn on the fans and spray some air freshener or something," Walt instructed.

"Yeah, man, you need to loosen up. You never wanna do anything we wanna do," Devonte complained. "Have some fun, for once."

Valencio didn't know how doing drugs could be considered fun, but he thought about his friends' words and also what Sylvia had told him on several occasions about loosening up and being into more than just his schoolwork. She had only ever mentioned girls so he didn't know if weed fell into the category of what she was talking about, but he figured it wouldn't kill him to try it once. He could see what all the hype was about.

"Fine," Valencio relented. "But just this one joint, though."

"It's about time!" Devonte exclaimed with a grin. "You gon' be asking to light it up all the time after this. Watch what I tell ya."

"I don't know about all that."

"We'll see. Gimme a lighter."

In the next few minutes, the three friends were sitting on the floor of Valencio's bedroom, passing the joint Devonte had brought over back and forth. Valencio thought he was going to cough up a lung when he took his first drag, but after a couple of passes at it, he got the hang of it and felt himself becoming more and more relaxed. It was something he had never experienced and he had to admit, he didn't hate it.

After they smoked up the joint, they all attacked the kitchen. Valencio had never felt more ravenous in his life and figured this was 'the munchies' thing he had always heard about from people who smoked weed. They ate up all the honeybuns, chips, leftover pizza, and grapes that were in the kitchen and for some reason, Valencio found that he couldn't stop laughing.

"Hey, let's go over to Dinisha's house; she told me today she's gonna be having some of her girls over there," Devonte suggested.

"Oh yeah, Dinisha is the one with the long braids, right?" Walt asked.

"Yep."

"You down, Valencio?" Devonte asked, taking one last swig from his soda can before tossing it towards the trashcan and missing.

Valencio only hesitated for a second before responding, "Yeah, I'm down. Let's go."

His friends looked mildly surprised, but they all quickly headed for the door, anxious to get to the girls. Valencio didn't even bother calling Sylvia to ask permission to go. He figured she wouldn't have a problem with it, since she was always on him about getting a girlfriend, anyway.

· · · ·

HOURS LATER, VALENCIO was just getting back home when a car pulled up in front of his apartment building. He didn't think much of it until the door opened and Candy climbed out of the front seat, dressed in a tube top and a pair of super-short cutoff shorts. Valencio could see what looked like an older teenager in the driver's seat. Candy leaned in and said something to him before closing the door and turning towards the apartment. She was clearly surprised to see Valencio standing there.

"Where have you been?" she asked him.

"Went to a friend's house...where have *you* been?"

"Don't worry about all that," Candy evaded the question.

"Who was that that dropped you off?"

"Don't worry about that, either."

Valencio shrugged, still too high off the afternoon's activities to be worried about Candy's latest antics. "Whatever."

Candy's eyebrows shot up as she followed him to the front door of their apartment. As soon as they walked through the door, a frown marred her face. She sniffed the air, slowly turning around in a circle as if she wasn't sure where she was.

"What the hell...is that *weed* I smell??" she exclaimed, looking at Valencio incredulously.

Valencio had forgotten all about trying to get the smell out of the apartment before anybody got home. Since this wasn't something he usually did, he didn't know if he should try to deny everything or boldly admit to it. The worst thing he had done before then was put an empty milk carton back into the refrigerator.

He shrugged. "I guess it is."

Candy's mouth fell open as she stalked over to her little brother, getting right in his face, even though he was taller than her. "You smoking weed now??"

Valencio avoided her eyes. "What makes you think it's me? I'm not the only other person that stays here."

"You know good and well Mama smokes cigarettes, not weed. Don't you lie to me, Valencio. You been up in here gettin' high?"

Valencio shrugged again. "Maybe. You gonna tell on me?"

Candy couldn't believe her ears. Her little brother was smoking weed? She didn't even think Valencio knew what weed *was*.

"Who were you smoking with?" she demanded to know.

"My friends, Walt and Devonte."

"How long you been smoking?"

"Today was the first time."

"Whose weed was it?"

"Devonte brought it. He said he got it from his brother."

"Wow..." Candy marveled, looking at her brother in a new light. She always thought he was a total lame that only cared about school and trying to be a choir boy who never did anything wrong. She wondered what it was that made him want to try doing drugs. Candy had smoked weed herself a few times, but she didn't really care for it. Part of her wondered if she was starting to have an influence over Valencio at all.

"You gonna tell on me?" Valencio asked her again.

She eyed him. "You gonna tell Mama about me coming home with Brian?"

"Who's Brian?"

Hesitating slightly, she finally answered, "He's my friend China's big brother. I had gone over to see her but she wasn't there, and he offered to let me come in and wait for her. We got to talking and playing video games, then out of the blue he started kissing on me. Then we just spent the rest of the afternoon fooling around in his room."

Valencio's eyes narrowed. "Y'all had sex, didn't you?"

"No, we did not...we came close, though," Candy admitted, not believing she was having this conversation with her brother. They had never talked like this before. She looked at him, suddenly curious. "Have *you* ever had sex?"

"No," Valencio quickly responded. "But I *did* fool around with a girl."

"What?" Candy asked, clearly surprised. "When?"

"Today."

"Dang, you're just doing all kinds of stuff today, huh? Is that where you're coming from?"

"Yeah."

"Who was it? What did you do?"

"It was this girl, Madeline. We just...kissed and stuff."

"*And stuff*? What *stuff*??"

"Just...touching on each other some. That's all."

"Wow..." Candy marveled. She really felt like she was in the Twilight Zone or something. This was a side to Valencio she didn't even know existed, or *could* exist. He was smoking weed, fooling around with girls...she just didn't know what to make of all this.

"It's not a big deal," Valencio shrugged, even though internally, he felt otherwise. If he was honest with himself, he could admit that he enjoyed himself today. He had never just let loose and had fun like that before. He wasn't sure if smoking weed would become a regular thing, but he knew he didn't want what happened with Madeline to be the last time.

"Well, look...I won't tell on you if you don't tell on me," Candy offered. She was still wondering if she was in some kind of dream.

"Okay," Valencio agreed, feeling slightly relieved. He figured he would just have to take Candy at her word, since he had never been in this kind of situation before where him getting in trouble depended on whether she kept her mouth shut or not.

"Aight." Candy eyed him again. "Done anything else you want to tell me about?"

"Nope. Now how do we get this smell out of the air before Mama gets home?"

Chapter 11

• • • •

"GET THOSE CHILDREN up and dressed; I'm going to be coming to get them for church," Sandra ordered.

Sylvia groaned as she looked at her watch. "Mama, it is six o'clock in the morning!"

"I know what time it is."

"If you knew you wanted to take them to church, why didn't you call last night or something?"

"What difference does it make? They need to go to church and I want to make sure they have enough time to get ready and get something to eat. Service starts at nine."

"They ain't gon' wanna go."

"I don't care if they want to go or not. They'll go if I tell them to. That's how it *should* be with you, too."

"Uh-huh," Sylvia yawned. 'Well, *I* ain't going."

"I wasn't inviting you," Sandra said bluntly.

Even though Sylvia didn't want to go, she still felt mildly offended. "You didn't have to say it like that," she mumbled.

"I tried for years to lead you and get you on the right track and you were bound and determined to let the devil keep his hold on you," Sandra replied. "You act like you don't need God and you know everything so I don't even bother with you. But it's not too late to try to help my grandchildren."

Something about Sandra's statement bothered her, but she brushed it off. "Whatever. I'll get 'em up."

"Good. I'll be over there at eight."

Sylvia hung up the phone and let her head fall back onto the pillows for a moment before throwing the covers off her with a groan and swinging her feet to the floor. She pushed herself off her bed and headed towards Valencio's room, figuring she'd get the easiest one over with first.

"Valencio," she said softly as she entered his room. He was lying with his back to her and she could tell he was sleeping soundly. She hated to wake him up but he never really had much problem going to church with Sandra.

Sylvia reached over and shook him gently. "Valencio, wake up."

"Hmm?" He stirred and rubbed his eyes, turning over to look at her. "What time is it?"

"Something after six. I know it's early, baby, but your grandmama wants y'all to go to church with her this morning."

Valencio groaned, actually frowning. This surprised Sylvia, but figured he was just especially tired today for some reason.

"Do I have to?" he asked.

This was another first; he never asked that question before whenever he was told to do something. He just did it.

"Yeah...yeah, you have to," Sylvia responded, looking at him curiously. He seemed different, for some reason, but Sylvia couldn't really put her finger on how. "You know how your grandmama is."

"Fine," Valencio grunted.

"So go on and get up so you can get ready and get you something to eat before she gets here."

"Yeah."

Sylvia's eyes narrowed. Yeah? While Sylvia had never really required her kids to say 'yes ma'am' and 'no ma'am' to her, Valencio had always done it because of Bryce's (and Sandra's) influence. That was something Bryce demanded of their son, and Sylvia hadn't minded it, even though she hadn't required it. Valencio had been saying 'yes ma'am' ever since he could talk.

"You all right?" Sylvia asked him.

"Yeah. I just want to say 'sleep."

Yeah, something is definitely up, Sylvia thought to herself. "There's some waffles in the freezer."

"'Kay."

Sylvia looked at him for another moment before leaving the room. Valencio didn't seem like himself, and she wondered what was up. But she figured she shouldn't make a big deal out of it unless it seemed like it was a regular thing; it could very well be him just being in a bad mood. He *was* thirteen and getting into that temperamental phase.

Sylvia went and got Candy up, who of course complained but that wasn't anything new to Sylvia. She expected that kind of behavior from her.

After Sandra had come and gotten the kids, Sylvia called her cousin Andrea to come over and re-do her braids. She didn't have to go in to work and she didn't want to keep walking around with two inches of new growth.

"Girl, why didn't you take these braids out before you called me over here?" Andrea fussed as she unraveled Sylvia's four-month-old braided extensions.

"Didn't have time," Sylvia responded. "And you know you can do it faster than I can, anyway."

"That ain't the point."

"But it's still true. It'd take me all day to take these things out."

Andrea just shook her head as her hands moved feverishly through Sylvia's hair. She knew what her cousin was saying was true, though; Andrea had been doing braids for years and had gotten really fast when it came to putting them in and taking them out.

"So what's been going on with you?" Sylvia asked, casually flipping through an Ebony magazine that Andrea had brought with her.

"Girl, dealing with these bad-ass kids of mine," Andrea replied, sucking her teeth. "You know Rocky got locked up again."

"For real?" Sylvia exclaimed, turning to look at her before Andrea pushed her head back forward. "What for??"

"Trying to car-jack somebody. Can you believe that? I think he played too much of that Grand Theft Auto mess and figured he could get away with it."

"Are you serious? Wow."

"I know, right? His dumb ass gon' be in there for a while this time, and I ain't bailing him out. I did that the last two times he got locked up and he keeps messing up. So he can just sit in there."

"Girl, you know you gon' bail him out like you always do."

"The hell I am. I ain't got the money to keep puttin' up for these fools. They wanna act stupid, they're gonna be stupid by themselves. I ain't about to keep being stupid wit' 'em."

"Them?"

"Yeah, you know Natina's locked up, too. Call herself tryin' to be in some kind of gang. But didn't none of those heffahs she hung with come to help her when she got caught stealing that TV. Matter of fact, they went off and left her ass there."

"She tried to steal a TV?"

"Hell yeah. A TV, some jewelry that wasn't even real, and a couple of pairs of jeans that she tried to hide under her shirt and pass off as her being pregnant. Just stupid."

"How did she think she was going to get away with all that? Where was she trying to steal it from?"

"Girl, Wal-Mart. Now you know they got cameras some a' everywhere. But she let 'em talk her into doing it 'cause they said they'd cover her. Natina never did have any damn sense."

"Yeah, that *was* stupid."

"At least Grover doesn't give me any trouble. I still got *one* good one."

"Grover is the baby, right?"

"Nah, he's in the middle. Natina is the baby. She's nineteen."

"You having any more?"

"Please! I am in my forties; I am *not* tryin' to have any more kids! After I had Natina I told them to yank those tubes out, if they had to. I am *done.*"

"I feel ya," Sylvia concurred, choosing to keep her opinion that Andrea didn't *need* to have any more kids because she could hardly handle the ones she had to herself. Andrea was obviously doing something wrong if two of her three kids stayed in and out of jail, in Sylvia's opinion. Candy might have been a little too grown-acting and rebellious, but she never got into any serious trouble. She never did anything illegal. And Valencio was her future doctor; he kept his head on straight, though she knew that was mostly thanks to Bryce. But he was still her son and she was proud of the young man he was growing up to be, even though she admittedly didn't tell him that very much.

The way Sylvia felt, her kids might not have been perfect, but they sure weren't as bad as some other folks'. Hearing her cousin talk about the troubles she was having with her kids just validated Sylvia's belief that she was doing a pretty good job with hers.

Hours later, when Andrea had finished with Sylvia's hair, Sylvia was feeling confident and attractive and wanted some company. She knew Sandra wouldn't be back with the kids for a while, since she always either took them out to eat after church or cooked for them, and Sylvia wanted to take further advantage of the rest of the time she had to herself.

As usual, the first person she thought of was Dub. She hadn't seen him since he had come by that day to drop off the money for Candy's dental appointment, and he had his girlfriend with him. They had only talked once or twice since then, when he called to check on them. She missed hanging out with him, and as she picked up the phone to call him, she hoped to high heaven that he would have some time for her.

"Aww damn, I wish I could," Dub said regretfully when she asked him if he wanted to go to a movie. "But I'm actually not even in town right now. Jelissa and I are in Virginia for the weekend."

"Oh," Sylvia replied, disappointed. She hated the idea of him having a romantic getaway with another woman. "Having a good time?" she forced herself to ask.

"Yeah, we're enjoying ourselves. I needed to get away for a minute."

"I sure feel you on that. I don't even remember the last vacation I've been on."

"You should take one. Everybody needs a break every now and then."

"You're right."

"Well, we need to get together when I get back," Dub said, making Sylvia smile. "We'll have to work that out. I haven't seen you in a while."

"Yeah, too long. So yeah, just let me know."

"I'll do that. You and the kids all right?"

"Yeah, we're fine."

"Okay, then. I'll talk to you soon."

"Okay." Sylvia ended the call and slumped over onto the couch in disappointment. She had really wanted to see Dub but at least he seemed like he missed her too, from what he said.

She knew she couldn't call Bryce for the kind of company she wanted, and even though Percy was her designated booty call, she didn't really want to call him, either. But then again, she didn't feel like going out and trying to find somebody new; she didn't really have time for all that, anyway.

She chewed her lip as she scrolled to Percy's number in her phone, figuring he was better than nothing. She was just about to place the call when there was a loud knock on her door. Frowning slightly, she dropped her phone onto the couch and got up to see who it was.

"Who is it?" she called out.

"Your favorite baby daddy."

She groaned. "What are you doing over here, Deuce?"

"Open the door and see."

She thought about ignoring him until he left, but she figured she might as well deal with him and get it over with. At least he didn't sound drunk this time.

Swinging open the door, she said, "Look, Candy ain't he-" Her mouth fell open in shock at what she saw in front of her.

Deuce was standing there with his penis out, stroking himself and smirking at her mischievously. Sylvia's eyes seemed transfixed on the motion. "I ain't here to see Candy," he informed her in a low voice.

"Umm..." Sylvia swallowed, not being able to take her eyes off his groin. She immediately felt herself getting wet. "Why are you standing my door jacking off?"

"'Cause you shut me down the last time I came over here and I ain't taking no for an answer this time," he replied confidently.

"Oh really?"

"Yes, really."

Deuce continued to stroke himself as he looked right into her eyes, daring her to turn him down. He knew he could still get to her when he *really* wanted to, and she had never been able to resist him when he put it right in her face.

"So...you were horny and decided to come over here, of all places, huh?" Sylvia asked, stalling. She felt her resolve weakening with every second she watched him jack off and was trying her best to hold onto it.

Deuce shrugged. "Yeah, I could've gone somewhere else but it's your turn."

"What do you mean, it's *my turn*?"

"You know you miss this dick so how 'bout you just quit playin' hard to get and let's get down to business?"

"Ain't nobody playin' hard to get," Sylvia said, her resistance weakening even more when Deuce reached out and started teasing her nipple through her shirt. Her eyes fluttered closed without her being able to help it. Biting her lip, she grabbed his wrist but didn't try to stop him from what he was doing.

"You gon' let me in?" Deuce asked in a low voice, stepping closer to her and backing her against the doorjamb. He grabbed her other hand and put it on his hard shaft, which she immediately began stroking as he had been. He moaned loudly and licked his lips; Sylvia was a pro at pleasuring him, which is why he always came back to her. There might have been finer or prettier women he could call when he needed that itch scratched, but none of them could put it down like Sylvia could.

They just stood in Sylvia's doorway fondling each other, not caring that they could possibly be seen. Sylvia was trying to work up the strength to push Deuce away, and Deuce was trying not to just pick Sylvia up, throw her on the floor, and take what he wanted. Each of their breathing had increased and Deuce's lips were just inches from Sylvia's as he eased a hand between her legs. He moaned again when she gasped at the action. For whatever reason, she was trying to resist him but he was determined to make her give in, however long it took.

"You gon' let me in?" he asked her again, sticking his tongue out and tracing her lips with it before easing it into her mouth and back out again, teasing her. He wasn't big on kissing but when he was as horny as he was right then, he was willing to do almost anything.

"Fuck it," Sylvia whispered, pulling him inside. She was done trying to resist him and decided she was just going to use him to get what she wanted like he was doing to her. It was almost like he was some kind of gift from the freak heavens, the way he showed up right when she was about to settle for her third choice. Percy was good but he couldn't touch Deuce in the bedroom.

They proceeded to wildly rip each other's clothes off, kissing and grunting in sexual frustration. Now that Sylvia had given in, she couldn't wait for Deuce to get inside her. But she had to make sure of one thing, first.

"You got some condoms, right?" she asked breathlessly, gasping as he literally tore her tank top from her body, which just turned her on even more. "'Cause as horny as I am, you can kick rocks if you don't."

"I got a pocket full of 'em," Deuce replied, pushing her down onto the couch. "I know what the deal is."

"Uh-uh, not here...let's go to my room," Sylvia protested.

"Oh, we'll get there, too, believe me," Deuce assured her, ripping off his own shirt and diving on top of her.

• • • •

ABOUT AN HOUR OR SO later, Deuce grabbed his t-shirt and slipped it over his head. They were in Sylvia's bedroom and having gotten what he wanted, he was no longer paying her much attention. Sylvia just laid naked in her bed under the covers, scrolling through the missed texts on her phone, not paying him much attention, either.

"Go get me something to drink," Deuce ordered, grabbing his pants and slipping a leg into them.

Sylvia just sucked her teeth, not even bothering to look at him. "You have lost your mind," she muttered, still scrolling through her phone.

"I ain't joking."

"I ain't, either."

"You trippin," Deuce mumbled. He sat down on the bed and reached for his shoes. "After what I just put on you, you should be in there right now cooking me a four-course meal and running my bathwater."

Sylvia laughed out loud. "Yeah, right. Ain't a dick invented that'll make me do all that."

"You oughta be glad I even still want your ass," Deuce said rudely. He hated when Sylvia didn't yield to him like he wanted her to. "It's not like you the finest thing walking."

Sylvia knew he was just trying to hurt her feelings; she had been through this with him enough times to not let it bother her. "Yet you keep bringing your ass over here when you want some. So I guess I don't have to be."

Deuce just sucked his teeth, deciding he didn't want to go back and forth with her this time. He stood up and got ready to walk out when Sylvia stopped him.

"Don't tell Dub anything about this," she said before he walked out the door.

Dub snorted in amusement. "Please. He wouldn't give a damn. Dub ain't thinking about you." He walked out, laughing mockingly.

Sylvia swallowed, trying not to be bothered by his comment. Deuce knew that was the one thing he could say that would get to her.

Sandra called about an hour later to let Sylvia know she was on her way back with the kids. Sylvia was still in somewhat of a foul mood about Deuce telling her that Dub didn't think anything about her, and she hurried up to take a shower and light some incense to get rid of any residual sex scent in the air. She didn't need to hear her mother's mouth about fornication or anything else, especially today.

When they arrived, Sylvia was mindlessly flipping through the channels on the television. Ever since Deuce had left, Sylvia wondered if what he said was true; would Dub really not care if he knew that she and Deuce had been sleeping together occasionally over the years? She liked to think he would. Not really to the point of being jealous or anything (though that would be great if he was), but just bothered by the fact that she was doing it at all. Deuce was nothing more than a convenient and surefire orgasm for her, nothing more. She certainly had no feelings for him and she knew he didn't have any for her. She just wondered how Dub would *really* feel about it if he knew.

"Hello, Sylvia," Sandra greeted as they came through the door.

"Hey," Sylvia grunted, her eyes still on the TV.

"You got your hair done, I see."

"Uh-huh."

Sandra eyed her for a moment, and Sylvia hoped she wasn't about to say something smart. She had always told Sylvia her braids made her look like she was trying to look too young, but Sylvia never cared what she said. The braids were cute and saved her a lot of time on her hair everyday.

"Are you all not gonna speak?" Sandra demanded, speaking to Candy and Valencio. "Y'all know better than to come in the house without greeting your mother."

"Hey, Mama," they chorused obediently. Sylvia just looked at them, a slight frown marring her face.

"They've eaten already," Sandra said to Sylvia. "We went to Golden Corral so they should be good and full."

"Okay. Thanks," Sylvia replied dryly.

"Y'all go on and get out of those good clothes and take a shower," Sandra ordered to her grandchildren. "It's been a long day and you have school tomorrow."

"Yes, ma'am," they sang, immediately filing down the hallway to their respective bedrooms.

Sylvia glared after them, then sucked her teeth as she tossed the remote onto the couch next to her.

"What's the matter with you?" Sandra asked.

"I don't see how come they try to act like little angels when you tell 'em to do something. If I had said for them to do that, I know I would have gotten all kinds of backtalk, especially from Candy."

"'Cause they know I don't play that mess, and I never have," Sandra replied simply, sitting down next to Sylvia on the couch. She rested her large black purse on her lap. "I've always demanded they respect me, and they do. I tried telling you that you need to do that, too, but you didn't wanna listen."

"I know how to raise my own kids," Sylvia defended testily.

"Apparently you don't, or you wouldn't be sitting here pouting about them not showing you any respect," Sandra countered. "I keep telling you, you can't try to act like their friend, *then* get mad when they don't respect you as their parent. You think they do everything their *friends* tell 'em to do?"

Sylvia's frown deepened. "Yeah, well, thanks for feeding them and dropping them off and everything but you can go on home now." The last thing she was in the mood for was another lecture, especially one that she didn't want to admit had some validity to it.

Sandra just looked at her daughter knowingly and then stood up. Sylvia wouldn't look at her, but she leaned down and hugged her anyway.

"I love you, child," Sandra said, kissing her forehead. "And I'm still praying for you."

Chapter 12

• • • •

VALENCIO COULDN'T REMEMBER when he had more fun. He was hanging out with his friends away from the house more, not wanting to risk getting caught by Sylvia or Candy. He had smoked weed a couple more times and was getting more and more used to it, but what he was enjoying the most was the time he got to spend with his new girlfriend, Madeline. As many days out of the week that he could, he would head over to her house after school and make out with her until her mother got home. He didn't expect to enjoy something like that as much as he did, but he couldn't seem to get enough of her. He loved how her lips felt against his and how her body felt under his hands. And he thought he was going to faint when she first took her hands below his waist. She had brought him to his very first orgasm and he wondered how he had gone thirteen years without this pleasure.

One particular day, Madeline told him to be sure he came by right after school because she had a surprise for him. Valencio could hardly concentrate during school for wondering what it was she was going to surprise him with. He had taken extra care in getting dressed that day, putting on a black button-down shirt, his best dark jeans, and some fresh black sneakers his dad had bought him. He sprayed on some cologne and made sure to put on deodorant. Madeline wouldn't give him any hints as to what the surprise was, but he wanted to look good, whatever it may be.

He saw her a few times during school that day and every time he saw her, he got a flashback to the things they had done on her living room couch and would find himself getting aroused. There were several times he had to duck into the bathroom or walk with his books in front of his crotch because he didn't want everyone to see him walking around with an erection.

"Hey, baby," she cooed at him in between classes, smiling up at him. Valencio was thirteen but could pass for fifteen or sixteen, having gotten his height from his father, Bryce.

"Hey, wassup," he replied, not having gotten used to calling her anything other than her name.

"You still coming by today, right?" she asked in a slightly lowered voice, lightly grabbing the front of his shirt.

"Yeah, I'm coming."

"You sure will be," Madeline replied flirtatiously, leaning even closer into him.

Valencio swallowed, willing his stirring groin to stay down. He didn't even know what to say to that. "Yeah?"

"Yep."

"Still not gonna tell me what the surprise is?"

"Nope. You'll see when you get there," she said with a mischievous smile before standing on her tiptoes to give him a quick peck on the lips. "I've gotta get on to class; I can't be late again."

"Okay."

"See you later, baby," she said, sauntering off down the hall with extra twist in her hips because she knew he was watching.

Valencio certainly was watching. His eyes were transfixed on Madeline's behind, which was just as curvy and voluptuous as any grown woman's. He loved her short natural hair, her clear brown eyes, and her soft, milk chocolate brown skin. He thought they looked good together. For the rest of the day, he couldn't concentrate on anything other than what was going to happen after school when he got to her house.

Finally, school was over and it was time to go. He had already told Sylvia that he would be going to a friend's house after school, and she had been so happy that he was spending more time out instead of holed up in his room with a book in his face that she didn't even bother asking whose house he was going to; she just told him to have fun.

Madeline had just gotten home a few minutes before Valencio arrived and she had just enough time to change into a large t-shirt that stopped right at the middle of her thighs. Her feet were bare, displaying her light blue toenail polish. She pulled him inside and locked the door behind him.

"I'm so glad you're here!" she exclaimed, throwing her arms around his neck.

"Me, too," Valencio replied, hugging her back.

She grabbed his face and gave him a deep, slow kiss. Valencio loved kissing her. She had been the first girl he ever kissed so he had no point of reference, but he couldn't imagine anybody being better than she was at it.

After a few moments, she grabbed his hand and led him towards her bedroom. Valencio was immediately nervous; they usually stayed in the living room.

"We're going to your room this time?" he asked, hoping his voice wasn't shaking like his insides were.

"Yeah."

"How come?"

"You'll see," she said, pulling him into her pink and grey bedroom and closing the door behind her.

Valencio tried to be cool, but he couldn't help but be nervous. He didn't want to get caught.

"Mama isn't going to be home until late," Madeline said, seemingly reading his mind. "It's just you and me."

"Aight," Valencio said, silently telling himself to chill out.

Madeline pushed him down onto her bed and climbed on top of him, kissing him deeply. It didn't take long before Valencio's nervousness and trepidation melted away and a warming arousal took over. His hands roamed her body and he enjoyed the feeling her short body on top of his; he couldn't resist going underneath her t-shirt and gripping her behind in his hands.

After a while of kissing and rolling around on the bed, Madeline began to unbutton his shirt and unbuckle his jeans. Valencio felt some of his nervousness return. What was she about to do?

He soon found out. Madeline slid down his body and yanked his jeans down with her, and before he knew it, he felt her lips touch his manhood. His eyes fluttered closed and his body stiffened, his hips lifting off the bed as an unfamiliar but delicious feeling shot through him like a lightening bolt. Silently and repeatedly telling himself to calm down, he gritted his teeth as Madeline proceeded to give him his first blow job. His hands gripped the sheets as his hips moved against her mouth on their own. This had to be what heaven felt like.

After a while, Madeline climbed up to lay on his still-heaving chest. "You liked that?" she asked softly, her hand resting on his stomach.

"Hell yeah," Valencio said breathlessly, feeling that was the only appropriate response. It was his first time using any kind of curse word.

She grinned. "I'm glad." She sat up, pulling her t-shirt over her head. She wasn't wearing a bra and Valencio's eyebrows shot up at the sight of her bare breasts. He had felt on them before but had never seen them front and center like that.

"Take the rest of your clothes off," she ordered, looking at him lustfully.

He hesitated slightly. "Why?" he couldn't resist asking.

"I want to feel all of you."

He sat up on his elbows, figuring he might as well go ahead and be straight up. "Madeline, look...I don't think I'm ready to have sex with you yet. If that makes you mad and you want me to go home, I will."

She pursed her lips but shook her head after a moment. "No, I'm not mad."

Valencio looked at her in surprise, having been expecting her to go off on him or something. "Really?"

"Yeah. To be real, I'm not really ready for that, either; I just thought maybe you wanted to."

Relieved, Valencio responded, "I'm good on that."

Madeline smiled. "Me, too. And anyway, I don't have any condoms and I ain't trying to get pregnant."

"We're *definitely* on the same page with that. I don't have any rubbers, either."

"But I still want us to get naked and get under the covers together, though. I bet your body will feel good against mine."

Figuring it would be okay since they had both established they didn't want to have sex, Valencio proceeded to take his undershirt and socks off as Madeline shimmied out of her underwear. They climbed under the covers of her queen-sized bed and she snuggled up next to him, throwing her leg across his. Valencio just held her close, relieved that they seemed to be on the same page and he didn't have to lose the first girlfriend he ever had within two weeks.

One of the main reasons Valencio didn't want to go all the way with Madeline was because he remembered all the talks he and Bryce had about sex and losing his virginity. Valencio knew it was one thing to kiss and touch and get head, but it was quite another to have sex. And one thing he always remembered Bryce saying was that his virginity was the one thing he wouldn't be able to get back once it was gone. He might have been doing a lot of things he never used to do, but he wasn't ready to do that quite yet.

Before long, he and Madeline started kissing again and she pulled him on top of her and wrapped her legs around him. They were careful not to join together, but they spent the rest of his time there kissing and groping and grinding against each other. And Valencio couldn't wait until they could do it again.

Ever since she had given in and slept with Deuce, Sylvia had been in a funk. She didn't know what made this time so different from all the other times; she figured it was his parting shot about Dub not caring about it if he were to find out about them sleeping together. For some reason, Sylvia hadn't been able to get over that.

She just went to work and then went home and shut herself up in her room. She didn't answer her phone or want to be bothered with anyone; she let her kids pretty much fend for themselves. For the time being, she really wanted to just be left alone to mope and worry about Deuce telling Dub about them sleeping together.

This went on for a few days before she got a surprise visit from Bryce.

"What the hell is going on, Sylvia?" he asked angrily, storming past her into the living room.

"What? What are you talking about?" Sylvia asked, tightening the belt on her bathrobe as she closed the door behind him.

"Valencio's school called me today," he informed her, crossing his arms over his chest and looking at her accusingly. "Apparently, he's been cutting class and his grades are suffering because of it."

Sylvia's mouth fell open. "What?"

"And his basketball coach said his performance has been slipping in practice too, when he's bothered to go. So apparently he's been skipping that, too." Bryce shook his head and paced to the other side of the room, as if he couldn't stand to be close to Sylvia anymore. "I don't suppose you knew anything about this?"

"Of course I didn't!" Sylvia exclaimed, still reeling. This didn't sound like her Valencio at all.

"Well, I guess I shouldn't be surprised; they said they had been trying to call you over the last couple of days but could never reach you. Your phone turned off or something?"

Sylvia looked down sheepishly. "No..."

"Then why the hell haven't you been answering it??"

"I've just had some things on my mind, Bryce. But I had *no* idea all this was going on!"

"Yeah, I bet you didn't," Bryce spat. "I knew something was up when he stopped calling me like he used to. And whenever I called him, he tried to rush off the phone."

"I didn't know that."

"What *do* you know, Sylvia??" Bryce asked, exasperated. "Do you know anything about your own damn son? Have you even noticed that he's been acting differently?"

Sylvia recalled how Valencio had seemed different the last Sunday Sandra had come to get him and Candy for church, but she had brushed it off, blaming it on teenage hormones. She never would have imagined that he was cutting school and slacking off. He had always taken it so seriously, wanting to get the best grades he could so he could fulfill his lifelong dream of becoming a doctor. When had all of this started? Sylvia liked to think that because she had done so much in her own youth, she could recognize it a mile away when her kids were up to something. But she had always focused all her attention on Candy since Valencio had never given her any trouble. Had she taken it for granted that he never would?

"I guess he *has* been acting a little different recently but I think you're overreacting. Most teenagers do stuff like this at some point, Bryce."

"Just because most teenagers do it doesn't mean *Valencio* has to do it! I do *not* accept that excuse, Sylvia!"

"Why are you yelling at me??"

"Because you're not taking this seriously enough! And really, if you want me to be all the way real with it, I think some of this is your fault!"

Sylvia frowned. "How the hell is it *my* fault??"

"*You're* the one whose been telling him to quit being so serious and to get girlfriends and hang out with his friends more," Bryce reminded her with disdain. "I *told* you that after a while, he was going to finally give in and listen to you, and then the floodgates would open. There's no telling *what* he's been doing when he was supposed to be at school, or when he's out with his friends somewhere. Do you even ask?"

Sylvia didn't want to admit that she didn't; she had just been glad he was going out at all. "Bryce, look, you need to calm down-"

"No, *you* need to check yourself, Sylvia!" Bryce yelled, stepping closer to her. Sylvia didn't think she had ever seen him this angry. "You wanna let your daughter do as she pleases, that's your business; there's nothing I can say about that 'cause she's not my child. But Valencio *is*. And if this is how you're going to be raising him, then maybe he just needs to come and live with me full time."

Sylvia's eyebrows shot up. "Excuse me?"

"You heard what I said. You are *not* going to derail our son's future with your lackadaisical parenting. I refuse to let you jack him up like you've jacked Candy up!"

Sylvia gasped, surprised at how hurt she was at his statement. "How dare you, Bryce!"

"How dare I, what?"

"How dare you say some shit like that to me!"

"You can stay in denial all you want to, Sylvia, but I don't have time for that! I'm going to nip this mess with my son in the bud *before* he gets too out of control with it! I love him and care about his future too much not to!"

"Oh, what you tryin' to say? That I don't love him and care about his future?"

"I think you care more about trying to be *cool* and shit than you care about anything else."

Sylvia didn't cry often, but she felt tears come to her eyes at his words. "I *do* love my son, Bryce!"

"Act like it then, Sylvia," Bryce retorted, unmoved by her tears. "Being a parent, a *good* parent, means disciplining your children, even if it means you come out looking like the bad guy. *That's* how you show you love them; not by letting them do whatever they want. That only blows up in your face later."

Sylvia just wiped the streaming tears from her face and jammed her hands under her armpits.

"I meant what I said, Sylvia," Bryce warned, heading for the door. "Valencio *will* be coming to live with me if you don't get it together. Quickly." He stalked out.

Sylvia just stood in the middle of the living room for several moments, not quite believing what just happened. If someone would have told her that Valencio would be cutting school and skipping basketball practice and letting his grades slip, she wouldn't have believed it in a million years. Valencio had always been her golden child. She never had to worry about him doing the right thing and keeping his head on straight. Sure, she had encouraged him to loosen up and have some more fun, but she never said or meant for him to do all that.

Now she wondered what she was going to do about it. It would make her look stupid if she turned around and told him to straighten up and get back into the books after spending all that time telling him to get out of them. Of course she wondered what Valencio was doing and where he was going when he cut class, but she couldn't imagine that he would do anything stupid like drugs or humping on some girl. Not her baby; he had too much sense for that.

While she knew Bryce was dead serious about what he said about having Valencio come live with him full time if this kind of behavior continued, Sylvia decided to let all this go for now and not say anything to Valencio about it. He was just experimenting; just about all teenagers did it at one time or another. It was nothing to freak out about. And it wasn't like Bryce was always a choir boy, either.

Sylvia figured she would just keep a little closer eye on Valencio but let things ride for the time being.

About a half hour later, neither Valencio nor Candy was home and it was going on seven o'clock. Sylvia wasn't worried, but she was admittedly now curious about where her son was when she hadn't been before.

The phone rang and she picked it up without glancing at it. "Hello?"

"Is Valencio there?"

Sylvia was pleasantly surprised to hear it was a girl. It was the first time a girl had ever called for him; at least, that she knew of. "He's not here. Who is this?"

"Pamela."

"Oh. Well, try him back later on."

"Okay."

Sylvia hung up the phone and couldn't resist a smile. While she wasn't crazy about Valencio slacking off in school and everything, she couldn't help but be happy that he was finally coming out of his shell.

Chapter 13

· · · ·

CANDY HAD LOST TRACK of how long she had been in the bathroom stall. She finally had her new phone and wasted no time trying to take just the right picture to send to Mac.

She had removed her top and her bra and tried to get the hang of holding the camera to where she got a good shot of her breasts and her face. Pouting her lips, she tried to push her modest breasts together with her free arm to make them look more luscious and appealing while gazing lustfully into the camera. After what felt like a hundred shots, she finally got one that she was satisfied with. Grinning with excitement, she hurriedly sent the picture to Mac, put her clothes back on and grabbed her book bag, rushing out of the bathroom. She was especially anxious to send Mac the picture after seeing him talking to Connie earlier. She had already stolen attention from Candy one time when Jermaine, Jason, and Russell had gone running after her and Adrienne that day and left Candy standing by herself like an abandoned puppy. Those guys hadn't paid her any more attention since. Candy didn't want Mac doing her that way, too. She had to do something to get his mind back on her like it had been before.

In fact, Candy had been putting more effort towards getting more attention from boys, in general. Always aware of her average looks, she began overcompensating even more by wearing more makeup and the tightest, most revealing clothes she could get away with at school. Her second-cousin Andrea had put some wet and wavy-style micro braids into her hair, and it made her feel even more mature and sexy, like someone in a movie. Thankfully, she didn't have to try to sneak and wear any of these things since Sylvia had been letting her wear makeup since she was twelve.

To her delight, this brought the attention from boys that Candy sought. They had paid some attention to her before, but now even more were looking and whispering and catcalling and propositioning, and Candy loved every second of it. It felt great to be desired and she milked it as much as she could. To her, a boy wanting her, in *any* way, was the much-needed validation she needed that she was attractive and desirable.

It didn't take long after she had sent the topless picture to Mac that he began sending her sexually suggestive messages in return. He talked about how he wanted to suck her breasts, sex her in the backseat of his car, and various things he wanted her to do to him. With every message he sent, Candy got more and more excited. She was more than willing to do everything Mac had suggested in those messages, and more.

Before the end of the day, several boys had approached her with a comment about the picture she had sent to Mac. Apparently he had been showing it off, which thrilled Candy more than it offended her. She loved hearing the comments about how good her breasts looked to them, which to Candy, equated to compliments. She didn't even mind when one boy whose name she didn't even know came up and grabbed her from behind, his hand grabbing and squeezing her right breast possessively. Candy didn't care who all had seen the picture; the more the better, to her. She didn't even care if girls had seen it; maybe then they would know they had some competition for all the boys' attention.

After the last class had let out, Candy was approached by Russell, Jermaine, and Jason.

"Hey, Candy," Jason called out.

Candy turned and grinned, thrilled to see who it was. "Hey, handsome," she flirted.

"What's up with you? Where you about to go?"

"Why you wanna know?"

"'Cause we thought you might wanna roll with us today," Russell chimed in, eying her up and down openly.

"Roll with you where?"

"I thought it didn't matter 'cause you knew we'd take care of you," Jermaine chimed in, reminding her of what she had said the first time she tried to hang with them.

"That's right," Candy concurred, turning towards them fully. "So let's go."

The three boys followed Candy out the side door of the school, smirking at each other behind her back. Candy was so caught up in the excitement of being asked to hang with them, she didn't even hear them whispering amongst themselves.

"So whose house are we going to this time?" Jermaine whispered.

"Can't be mine; I need to lay low after that last one. We almost got caught, remember?" Russell reminded them.

"Let's just go to my spot; you know I live with my big brother and he's hardly ever there, anyway," Jason said.

"You really think she's gonna be down for this?" Jermaine asked, eying Candy as she sauntered ahead of them.

"Hell yeah, she's gonna be down. She's thirsty; she'll do anything we want her to do," Jason replied confidently.

"Yeah, you've heard about her, man...we won't even have to run any game on her. This gonna be the easiest train ever," Russell added, actually rubbing his hands together.

Jermaine hesitated slightly as he continued to watch Candy. "You got some rubbers, right?"

"Yeah, most definitely," Jason replied. He chuckled as they followed Candy down the street. "She's not even asking where to go; she's just walkin'. We could be trying to take her to the crack house, for all she knows. Yeah, she's down for whatever."

Something about this didn't quite feel right to Jermaine, but he kept his mouth shut. This certainly wasn't the first time they had run trains on girls, but usually the girls knew about it up front; they weren't ambushed with it at the last minute.

They all walked for a few more yards with Jason and Russell continuing to whisper and plot amongst themselves, and Jermaine just listening. Candy would occasionally glance back at them and smile, almost as if she was making sure they were still behind her. She was actually trying to contain her giddiness and excitement. She couldn't believe she had three of the cutest members of the basketball team all to herself. And they had actually approached her! She never bothered to ask where it was they were going or why they were all walking behind her, even though she didn't know the destination; she was just looking forward to getting there, wherever it was. Her friends were going to be so jealous!

All of a sudden, a black Camaro screeched to a stop next to them. All four of the teenagers jumped, not being able to see who it was through the tinted windows. Candy couldn't believe it when she saw who was getting out of the driver's seat.

"Get in the car, Candy," Dub ordered.

"What?"

"You heard me."

"I'm good," she said, trying to continue walking. She was sure her face was red from embarrassment and was trying to be cool about it, but Dub easily caught up with her and grabbed her arm.

"The hell you are. I'm not playing with you, girl; get in the car!" He opened his passenger door and practically pushed her inside, slamming it behind her. "And I *dare* you to try to get out!"

"Hey, what's up with that, man?" Russell protested with his arms out.

"Yeah, we weren't gonna do nothin' bad to her," Jason added. Jermaine stayed silent, internally relieved that their plan was being foiled. He would have gone through with it, but he wouldn't have felt right about it. And he knew his friends wouldn't have listened to him if he had protested.

Dub walked right over to them with a look on his face that was clear he meant business. "Y'all might have been able to fool her but I *know* what the deal is; I was young and stupid just like y'all are. If you think you're gonna run a train on my niece, you've got another thing coming."

All three of the boys' jaws fell open. Jason spoke up first. "W-what you talking 'bout? Nobody was gonna-"

"Yeah, save that," Dub cut him off. "Like I said, I ain't stupid. Now, consider this your one and only warning: stay the hell away from my niece. And I *promise* you, you don't wanna try me on this."

Russell started to protest again, but Jermaine finally spoke up. "Don't worry about it, man; we won't mess with her no more."

His friends looked at him like he was crazy, but Dub just nodded. "Good." He shot them one last warning glare before getting into his car and driving off.

"Man, what are you doing??" Jason exclaimed to Jermaine.

"That's not even worth it," Jermaine replied, still trying to mask his relief. "We can get with somebody else. And anyway, didn't y'all recognize who that was?"

Russell opened his mouth to speak, then closed it in thought. "He *did* look kinda familiar, now that you say that..."

"Who was it?" Jason asked.

"Man, haven't you heard about those twins, Deuce and Dub?" Jermaine asked. "That's wild that Candy's related to them."

"Oh snap, yeah!" Russell exclaimed. "I heard they were something serious...which one was that, though?"

"I don't know, but from the stories I've heard, it doesn't even matter. I wouldn't wanna piss either *one* of them off. Let's go, man...the dance team practice should still be going on," Jermaine said, turning to head back towards the school. Russell and Jason followed with renewed excitement, already forgetting about Candy and talking about who on the dance team they could get with.

Meanwhile, Candy was in Dub's car, fuming.

"Why did you embarrass me like that?!" she demanded angrily. "Now they won't want to mess with me no more!"

"That's a good thing, Candy," Dub replied, his eyes on the road.

"No, it's not! They're probably gonna go around telling everybody about this now and nobody will give me any play! This wasn't any of your business; I knew what I was doing!"

Dub just glanced at her before pulling his car into a Wendy's parking lot. He cut the engine and turned to his fuming niece. "Do you not realize what would have happened if you had gone with them wherever you all were going? They probably would have tried to run a train on you, or worse. I'm willing to bet just about anything I have on that."

"So?"

Slightly taken aback, Dub blinked. "What do you mean, *so?*"

"So what you tryin' to say, that they would've raped me or something if I hadn't wanted to do what they wanted?"

"Yeah, that's exactly what I'm saying, Candy."

"Well, they wouldn't have *had* to rape me 'cause I would've *gladly* given it up to all of 'em!"

Dub couldn't believe his ears. He didn't know his niece very well, but he certainly hadn't expected her to say that. She was just fifteen and so easily willing to share herself with multiple boys at once? He had done some things back when he was her age, but he was always a one-at-a-time kind of guy. Running trains was something that Deuce would do.

Wanting to lecture her but feeling it wasn't quite his place to since this was the most one-on-one time they had ever spent together, Dub started his engine back up. He'd just have to let Sylvia know what was going on and let her deal with it as she saw fit.

"Let me get you home," he said, steering his car out of the parking lot. Candy just sat in the passenger's seat with her arms folded, looking out the window. She was still fuming over having missed an opportunity to be with Jason, Jermaine, and Russell. Dub glanced at her occasionally, his expression concerned.

Sylvia was just getting home from work when Dub arrived with Candy. She was surprised to see him drop her off, especially since Candy had an obvious and major attitude.

"What's going on?" Sylvia asked as Candy stomped towards her room in a huff.

"I was headed home earlier when I happened to see Candy walking with three guys behind her," Dub informed her, wincing slightly when he heard Candy forcefully slam the door to her bedroom. "The way they were looking and talking amongst themselves, they were plotting something. I know that look. If I hadn't caught them, they'd probably be still running a train on her right now."

Sylvia gasped. In all the things she had experienced, having a train run on her was on the short list of things that wasn't on it. "Are you serious?"

"Very. Unfortunately."

"Why is she so mad, though?"

Dub chuckled, only because of the ridiculousness of the entire situation; not because anything about this was funny. "Because apparently, Candy doesn't mind riding the train."

Sylvia hoped she did a good enough job acting like this surprised her; she already knew her daughter was fast. "She said that?"

"What she said was, when I had told her that they could've run a train or worse, '*they wouldn't have had to rape me 'cause I would have gladly given it up to all of them*.' Those were her exact words."

Even though Sylvia had known Candy was no virgin, it was a jolt to hear a recounting of her daughter saying how easily she would give it up to three boys at once. It was a little too familiar to Sylvia; she had been the exact same way when she was Candy's age. She had been pretty much willing to sleep with anybody, just to ensure boys would like her.

"Wow," Sylvia marveled, feeling like her head was spinning. She eased down onto the sofa, suddenly embarrassed and not wanting to look at Dub. What he must think of her now, having had a firsthand look at how her daughter really is? Did he think Sylvia was a terrible mother? His opinion mattered to her, and she hated that it was now marred by something like this.

"You okay?" Dub asked, taking a seat next to her and placing a comforting hand on her back.

"I don't even know *what* to think right now, to be honest," Sylvia admitted, still looking away.

"I bet."

"Look, Dub, I really, really appreciate you being there for Candy like that," Sylvia said after a few thoughtful moments, forcing herself to turn and look at him. She saw no traces of judgment in his expression; just genuine concern. It only made her love him more; most people would be pointing the finger at her for all this. "I'm so glad you were there."

"Yeah, me too. Though she wasn't too happy about it."

"Yeah, well. I'm sure one day she'll appreciate you being there for her. Especially since if it had been Deuce that had seen her, he probably would've kept on driving, if he even recognized her at all."

"Come on, Sylvia..."

"You know I'm tellin' the truth. Deuce doesn't care anything about Candy."

"I wouldn't say that. Deuce might act like he doesn't care...really, *really* convincingly...and I'm not trying to defend him not being a part of Candy's life all these years, but I just want you to understand that he's really messed up about family and stuff thanks to how our dad did us. Our dad left our mom as soon as he got her pregnant with us without a word. He never tried to see how we were doing or anything. That made me fiercely loyal to my family but it had the opposite effect on Deuce; other than me and our mom, he's never been able to bring himself to really care about anyone 'cause he just doesn't trust that they'll stay. So he'd rather not be a part of his children's' lives at all; in his mind, he's doing them a favor but he doesn't seem to get that he's just doing the exact same thing our father did to us."

"Aww, man..." Sylvia exhaled, leaning back onto the couch. She had never known that about the twins' father; she knew she had never seen or heard anything about him, but she thought their situation was something like hers; that their father had split up from their mother and had another family somewhere, and made the occasional obligatory phone call or visit to ease their guilty conscience. Hearing how things really were made Sylvia understand Deuce and the way he was a little better. Really, her heart broke a little for both Deuce and Dub but especially for Deuce; he had apparently been hurt by their father abandoning them, even though she knew he would never admit to that.

"I had no idea," she said, looking at Dub with empathy. "I'm so sorry to hear that, Dub."

He shrugged. "Thanks but I've made my peace with it a long time ago. It is what it is. I just know whenever I *do* have children of my own, there's no way I'm going to leave them hanging like our dad did to us and like Deuce does to his. There's no way in hell."

For the millionth time, Sylvia wished she had gotten pregnant by Dub instead of Deuce. If she could have one wish, it would be that. But she kept that sentiment to herself. "Those are gonna be some lucky kids."

"That's just what man is supposed to do; you lay down and make a child, you take care of it, regardless of your relationship with the mother. But if I have my way, I won't be making any children with anybody but my wife."

Sylvia smiled tightly, wishing with every fiber in her body that she could be the woman Dub married. She wanted that so bad it almost hurt. She would gladly have as many of his babies as he wanted, and do her best to be the best wife to him he could ever pray for. But she knew that the only way this was going to happen would be in her dreams; Dub didn't want her like that and she had accepted it, even though she couldn't help but wish for him to have a change of heart.

"You're a good man, Dub," she said quietly, looking down at her hands.

"I appreciate that, thanks," Dub replied, taking note of how thoughtful she had become all of a sudden. He grabbed her hands, covering her twiddling thumbs. "And you're a good woman."

"Humph," Sylvia scoffed immediately, surprised at the tear that threatened to escape from her eye. She looked in the other direction as she tried to blink it away. "But I'm a bad mother."

"Why would you say that?"

"I know I am. Look at Candy and how she acts. That's my fault."

Dub slid an arm around her shoulders and pulled her to him. She closed her eyes and relished the feeling, surprisingly more appreciative of the comfort more than the fact that it was Dub holding her. "No parent is perfect, Sylvia. You can't blame yourself for every little thing your kids do. After a while, you just have to trust you've taught them right and pray for the best."

"That's the thing, though, Dub; I *haven't* taught her right," Sylvia admitted, realizing that was the first time she had ever admitted that. The realization only made her eyes sting with more tears. "I haven't been a very good example and what happened today really just made that hit home for me. Damn it!" she muttered, hastily wiping the tears from her cheeks.

Dub just held her close to him, letting her cry. He wanted to say something to make her feel better, but didn't know what that would be. So he just kissed the top of her head and held her for the next few minutes.

Sylvia eventually gently eased away from him, not wanting to keep acting like a crybaby. She was already embarrassed enough as it was. "I better go talk to Candy," she said in a low voice, sniffling. She stood up.

"Okay," Dub said, standing along with her. He headed towards the door and turned to her, placing warm hands on her shoulders. He noticed her averted eyes and could tell she was embarrassed, and he wanted to put her at least somewhat at ease. "Look at me, Sylvia."

Eventually, she turned her eyes to him.

"Maybe you're not the perfect mother, but you obviously care...that's a good start right there," he assured her. "Let today be the day you try to do better by Candy. And if you need me, for *anything*, I'm here. All you have to do is call. Okay?"

Sylvia sniffed again and nodded appreciatively. "Okay. Thank you so much, Dub. Damn, I feel like I'm always thanking you for something."

"You're family, Sylvia. And I love you." He wiped her tears with his thumbs and planted a warm kiss on her forehead. Sylvia was thankful her knees didn't buckle; it wasn't the first time Dub had told her he loved her but it made her insides melt every time he did.

"I love you too, Dub," she replied, daring to look up into his eyes.

She was saying she loved him in a different way than he loved her, and they both knew it. But by now, there was no point in commenting on it. They both knew what the deal was.

"I'll talk to you later," he said, tweaking her chin before opening the door.

"All right."

After Dub left, Sylvia took a few moments to gather herself. She went to the bathroom, washed her face, and took a few deep breaths before heading to Candy's room, still not even sure what she was going to say.

"Open this door, Candy," she ordered, not surprised to find it locked.

After a few moments, Candy opened the door before stomping back to her bed without a word, flopping dramatically down onto it in a huff.

Sylvia's first instinct was to go off and lay into her, but she decided to take a different approach. She didn't want Candy automatically going on the defensive; Sylvia knew she'd never get anywhere, then.

"So what happened today?" Sylvia asked calmly, taking a seat in the folding chair in front of Candy's hand-me-down vanity.

"Nothing, thanks to Uncle Dub," Candy grumbled, sucking her teeth.

"Okay...what was *going* to happen today?"

"I was just going to hang out with some guys on the basketball team," Candy said, playing with her braids.

"And do what?"

"I don't know. Whatever."

"If we're gonna talk, let's keep it one hundred. Be straight up. You were gonna have sex with 'em, weren't you?"

Sucking her teeth again, Candy threw an arm over her eyes. She didn't feel like trying to pretend like she usually did that she didn't have sex. "If they wanted me to, I would have."

Sylvia had known this, but now she felt differently upon hearing it. She didn't feel proud of her daughter essentially being a chip off the old block; she felt ashamed.

"And you think that would've been a good thing to do, huh?" she asked, casually glancing around the slightly messy bedroom.

"Yeah. Why not? They're all on the basketball team, and they're cute."

"How do you know that it would've just been the three of 'em, though?"

Candy removed her arm from her eyes. "Huh?"

"I'm sayin'...for all you know, Candy, there could have been a bunch of other dudes waiting wherever it was they were gonna take you. And even if you *were* willing to do whatever, they could have taken it to another level and gotten rough with you, just because they could. Ain't nothing sexy about being gang-banged."

That hadn't even occurred to Candy, and the thought sent a chill through her. She had heard about that happening to another girl at school who ended up in the hospital. Her parents had put her in counseling and made her change schools.

"That wouldn't have happened to me," she still said stubbornly.

"Oh, so you special, huh?" Sylvia said with a shake of her head. She figured Candy wasn't going to see her point of view, or admit it if she did. "You think that stuff can happen to everybody but you?"

"I didn't say all that, but-"

"I'm just gonna put it to you like this," Sylvia interrupted, growing tired of the calm approach. "You need to quit being stupid, quit being naïve, and get it in your head that these little boys out here don't care nothing about you except what's between your damn legs. And you put it out there and make it so easy for 'em to get so even if one of 'em *wanted* to like you for you, they probably wouldn't want to bother since you've been around the block more times than Marta."

Candy looked taken aback for a second, then her face hardened. "Look, I don't even know why you tryin' to lecture me now when I *got* all this from you in the first place."

That jolted Sylvia. "Excuse me?"

"You're the one that gave me all those tips and stuff on how to have sex and all that," Candy reminded her snidely. "And you let me go out and stay out late. What do you think I'm gonna be out doing;

studying the Bible? I'm getting my freak-on just like you *taught* me to do."

There wasn't anything Sylvia could say to that, and she knew it. She had all but given Candy step-by-step instructions on how to give head, how to ride, and just about everything else. They sat right on the living room couch and Sylvia had essentially coached her on what to do and what not to do. Not once did she ever tell her to abstain. That had never even occurred to Sylvia before then, and the realization made her earlier embarrassment return full force. Candy was right; what did Sylvia expect?

"I think I hear my phone ringing," Sylvia muttered, suddenly needing to get out of there. She quickly walked out of the room, closing the door behind her.

Mindlessly going into her own room and plopping onto her bed, she considered Candy's words. It was really hitting her just what kind of influence she had been on Candy all these years. She had always thought she was being the cool mom and homegirl that she wished Sandra had been to her when she was growing up, but now she was seeing that that approach to parenting had the opposite effect that she had hoped. She thought she and Candy would be close, like best friends, but they clearly weren't. Candy didn't want to hang with her like Sylvia had always envisioned; they didn't spend quality time together. Candy usually tried to spend as much time away from Sylvia as possible.

For the first time, Sylvia began to wonder if she had been doing things wrong all this time.

Chapter 14

• • • •

OVER THE NEXT COUPLE of weeks, things with Candy and Valencio would get worse before they got better. Each of them got into trouble at school; Candy had mouthed off to her teachers again and Valencio had flunked two tests, which was totally unlike him. His teachers had called Sylvia, highly concerned about his grades that had taken a severe nosedive in the past weeks. Sylvia wasn't used to getting these kinds of calls about Valencio; if anything, they would call about how he was exceeding in class. Bryce was going to flip out when he heard about this, especially since Sylvia knew he had already had a talk with Valencio about straightening up and getting back on track. Clearly, though, Valenicio hadn't listened and Sylvia wondered what it was that had him so off his game.

Sylvia found herself growing weary of dealing with Candy's behavior and now having Valencio's added onto it, she started to feel overwhelmed. Candy's grades were doing better, which was a relief, but she was still being disrespectful to her teachers, staying out past the time Sylvia told her to be home, and God knows what else. Things couldn't continue like this, and Sylvia knew it.

After a lot of hesitation and contemplation, she broke down and called her mother, Sandra, for advice.

"You're actually asking me for my opinion?" Sandra asked.

Sylvia could sense the mild sarcasm in the question, but she figured it was warranted. Sylvia had always worked overtime to shun her mother's advice and do the opposite of what she thought she should do.

"Yes," Sylvia replied, silently telling herself not to get an attitude. She was the one who had been rejecting Sandra's parenting advice for years and had it backfire on her, so she had to remind herself that she was in no position to get defensive.

"I'm glad to see you're finally swallowing your pride in regards to those children and trying to do the right thing," Sandra commended. "I'm not gonna bother asking what happened to bring this on, but my prayers are finally getting answered."

Sylvia didn't know how to respond that. "Thanks." There was a slightly awkward pause. "So what should I do?"

"Well, it's like I've been telling you for years; those children need discipline. You have to *make* them respect you as their mother. Set rules...*sensible* rules, not just ones that you think they won't get mad at you for...and stick to them. You have to quit worrying about being their friend and focus on being their parent. That's what they need; that's what they've *been* needing."

"So just like that, I'm supposed to just start being all tough and stuff?"

"What are you waiting for?"

"I'm sayin', are they gonna listen to me?"

"You have to *make* them listen, Sylvia."

"*How*, though??"

"Show them you mean business! Start holding them accountable for the things they do, and don't let them talk you out of punishing them! Give them some responsibilities around there; I bet they don't even have any chores you make them do."

Sylvia didn't want to admit they didn't, even though she was sure her mother probably knew that.

"You're going to have to make a lot of changes, Sylvia, with yourself and how you raise those children, and it needs to start right now. And one part of that is you're gonna have to start being a better example. You can't be acting like a teenager right along with them; you have to behave like an adult. Watch how you talk, how you dress, how you act...and you can't keep bringing men all up in through there for them to see you with. They're never gonna take you seriously if you keep doing the stuff you're doing now."

Sylvia was starting to feel overwhelmed again. She knew she had to do some things differently but she hadn't expected to have to do a complete overhaul of herself.

"If you're serious about being a better mother and making a change, all of this is necessary," Sandra continued, sensing Sylvia's trepidation. "They have to see you've changed, and you have to be consistent with it. You can't be one way today and then another way tomorrow. They'll just think you're a joke and never listen to another thing you say."

"Great," Sylvia grunted, her head starting to hurt.

"I will tell you one more thing, though," Sandra said.

"And that is?" Sylvia almost didn't want to hear it.

"Don't be surprised if it takes a while for them to listen to you and change their ways. Candy is fifteen and Valencio is thirteen; before you blink, they'll be grown. I'm not saying you shouldn't try, but it's a little late to be trying to be something you should've been from the beginning."

Sylvia threw her hands up in frustration. "Well why the hell should I even bother, then?? Let you tell it, I'm damned if I don't and damn near damned if I do."

Sandra was quiet for a moment before answering. "You should bother because you love your children and want to be the best mother you can be for them," she said in a calm voice. "Even if it took you all this time to realize that you needed to, you don't want it to be said that you didn't put forth the effort."

Sylvia did want to put forth the effort. She just didn't know if her efforts would be good enough to make any difference.

Hesitating slightly, Sylvia wondered if she should voice her main concern and what had *been* her main concern since she found out she was pregnant with Candy years ago. "I hear you, Mama. Really. But...I can't help but want my kids to like me."

"Do they like you now?"

That question jarred Sylvia. "Umm..."

"Obviously, child, the way you've been doing things hasn't worked. You have to decide if trying to get them to like you is more important than having them respect you."

"I *do* want their respect."

"Well, you gon' have to earn it. Worry about being their friend and all that when they're grown; for now, they need a mother."

"Aight," Sylvia said, taking a deep breath. "I appreciate you talking to me about all this."

"It's my pleasure," Sandra sincerely replied. "Anytime. I just hope you actually *take* the advice."

Sylvia ended the call, hoping she did, too.

Later on that evening, Sylvia heated up a frozen lasagna, popped open a can of crescent rolls, and nervously sat down to dinner with her kids. It was the first time in a little while that both Candy and Valencio were both home for dinner; she could usually always count on eating with Valencio but now he was gone just about as much as Candy was. The three of them ate in relative silence; Candy was glued to her cell phone, Valencio was eating as if he hadn't done so in days, and Sylvia was eyeing both of them, wondering how she was going to break the ice.

"So..." she hedged, surprised at how nervous she actually was, "What went on at school today?"

No response. It was like they hadn't even heard her.

Clearing her throat, Sylvia asked again. "How was school today, y'all?"

"Huh? Oh, it was okay," Valencio replied distractedly as he helped himself to his third serving of lasagna.

"And what about you, Candy?" Sylvia asked her daughter.

Candy was engrossed in the text conversation she was having with Mac and almost didn't hear her again. "Fine," she answered with a distracted shrug.

"Did either of you have any tests or anything today?"

"No," both grunted.

Silently telling herself not to get frustrated, Sylvia continued on, determined. "It's nice that we're all here eating together like this, huh? It's been a while."

Candy giggled, obviously at something on her phone, and Valencio was munching on his fourth crescent roll. Sylvia wondered if she should've made him his own personal batch, the way he was going through them.

"Those things are good, huh?" she asked him, referring to the rolls.

"Mmm-hmm," Valencio replied, his mouth full. He eyed her plate. "You gonna eat yours?"

Sylvia eyed him strangely but handed him her roll, which he scarfed down in two bites. She wondered what was up with him lately; his appetite had gone from zero to sixty and he had been eating up all the groceries faster than she could buy them. He had never before been so ravenous. It was one time Sylvia was thankful she worked in a grocery store.

"Everything all right, baby?" she asked him.

"Yep," he replied, not even looking at her. He had barely looked at her since he sat down.

"How are you doing with getting your grades and stuff back up? You know your dad was pretty pissed at you for letting them slip, but I told him it happens sometimes."

"Can we not talk about that?" Valencio asked with a slight edge in his voice. "I'm not trying to talk about school right now."

Sylvia blinked, surprised. What was up with the attitude? He wasn't usually disrespectful, and any other time she had asked him about school, he gladly told her everything.

"Well I know I'm proud of Candy for getting *her* grades together," Sylvia complemented. "That tutor is a real big help."

"He's a lame," Candy said with a suck of her teeth, still texting.

"Lame or not, he's doing what I'm paying him to do, which is help you get those grades up."

"Uh-huh."

Sylvia was growing a little tired of her children's dismissive attitudes. Their bodies were there but their minds were clearly in other places.

"Maybe you could help your brother out, since you've been doing so well," she continued, still trying.

Valencio snorted. "Yeah, right."

Candy's eyes snapped up at him. "What you tryin' to say?"

"That I don't need your help."

"Uh, *you're* the one who's flunking. You obviously need *somebody's* help."

"I sure don't need *yours*."

"I don't wanna help your punk behind, anyway. You can fail every class you got, for all I care."

"I'm not gon' fail anything."

"Yeah, 'cause your dad will ship you off to military school, if you do," Candy joked, glancing up from her phone. "You know Mr. Bryce don't play."

Sylvia hated that they couldn't say that about her.

"You don't have to worry about all that," Valencio said, getting another helping of lasagna.

"Dang, why you eatin' so much? You must have the mun-"

"Candy!" Valencio cut her off, frowning at her. "Shut up!"

"Don't be telling me to shut up just because you-"

"Candy!"

"What is wrong with y'all?" Sylvia asked, tired of them arguing.

"Candy talks too much!" Valencio practically yelled.

"Don't be yelling at me!" Candy yelled back, temporarily putting her phone down.

"Y'all need to chill the hell out! What is it you don't want her to say?" Sylvia asked Valencio.

He glared at her, then stuffed his mouth full of lasagna. "Nothing," he grumbled.

Sylvia looked at Candy.

"Don't look at me," Candy said, picking her phone back up.

"Look, I don't know what the beef is here but y'all need to put it on a bun and swallow it, 'cause I'm sick of all this fussing!" Sylvia said strongly.

They both just looked at her and rolled their eyes, but said nothing in response.

Trying her best to keep her growing anger and frustration in check, Sylvia said, "There's gon' have to be some changes around here. Y'all ain't gon' be able to keep doing all the stuff you been doing."

"Like what?" Candy eyed her warily.

"Like coming and going as you please, staying in your room with the door locked when you *are* here, and most importantly, not taking your schoolwork seriously," Sylvia responded forcefully. "All this cutting school crap needs to stop and it needs to stop *now*. I better not hear about either one of you doing that mess no more."

"Uh-huh," Candy dismissed, clearly not believing her.

"You think I'm playin'??"

"Can I go spend the night at Devonte's?" Valencio asked, as if he hadn't even heard her.

"Hell no, you can't go spend the night at...look. I'm serious about what I said. Y'all need to be a little more respectful around here. I'm gon' give you some chores-"

"Chores??" Candy scoffed. "I ain't doin' no chores!"

"You'll do 'em if I *tell* you to!"

"I already have to do chores when I go to my dad's," Valencio whined.

"Well, you gon' do 'em here, too. You should be used to it."

"I don't want any more chores, though."

"Too bad! This is not a negotiation! You're gonna do what I say or *else*!"

"Or else what?" Candy challenged.

"Why are we getting all these rules and stuff all of a sudden?" Valencio asked.

"'Cause you need 'em, that's why. And I'll kick your ass; *that's* 'or else what,'" Sylvia added, answering Candy's question.

Candy just sucked her teeth and turned her attention back to her phone. "Whatever."

Sylvia couldn't believe how they were brushing her off as if what she was saying meant nothing. The fact that they were dismissing her like they were made her more and more angry, at them but also at herself for letting things get to this point.

"I *suggest* y'all start taking me seriously," she said angrily.

"Can I go to my room now?" Valencio asked, again as if he hadn't even heard her. He pushed his empty plate away and started to get up, as if he was going to go without waiting on her answer.

"Sit your ass down!" Sylvia ordered. Valencio looked at her in mild surprise, and sat back in his chair. "I'm about tired of y'all! You not just gon' disrespect me and get away with it no more! Both of y'all are on punishment!"

Both Candy and Valencio's eyes snapped to her. "What? What punishment? For how long?" Valencio asked.

"Until you both start straightening up your act or until I feel like taking you off of it, whichever comes first. You're grounded!"

Candy just rolled her eyes and scooted her chair back. "Yeah, okay," she said dismissively, standing up.

"Where the hell you going?" Sylvia screeched.

"I'm grounded, remember?" Candy said mockingly, sauntering back to her room. A few seconds later, her door closed and locked.

Sylvia's blood was boiling. She couldn't believe how her own kids were disrespecting her like they were. It didn't even occur to her right then that she had done her own mother Sandra the same way.

She stood up so fast that she knocked her chair over. "Clean up these dishes," she ordered to Valencio, not even wanting to look at him. "Then go to bed." She stormed back to her room and slammed her own door.

Her head was pounding. She didn't know what she had been expecting when she sat down to talk to her kids, but she hadn't been expecting them to so blatantly brush her off like they had. Maybe Candy, but not Valencio, despite the way he had been acting lately.

He might have been slacking off in some things, but he still showed her respect. But even *that* was over with, and Sylvia didn't know what happened. She was willing to bet he wouldn't have done the same thing to Bryce.

Sylvia couldn't remember the last time she had issued any kind of punishment; that kind of thing had never really been necessary for Valencio, and Candy had always been used to doing pretty much what she wanted, and Sylvia had foolishly let her in an effort to be cool with her. The few times Sylvia *had* tried to restrict her from something, like using the phone or something like that, it only lasted a day or so before Sylvia either caved in and rescinded it or forgot about it altogether. Sylvia had never been much of a disciplinarian, and she knew that was because her mother had been so much of one and she was trying to be the opposite of her. But that clearly hadn't worked.

She remembered Sandra's words about how it might take a while before Candy and Valencio started listening to her. As frustrated as she already was, Sylvia knew that she was going to have to stay the course and be consistent with it if she was ever going to get anywhere. Even if both Candy and Valencio got mad at her, she couldn't let that sway her like it had in the past.

Sylvia was going to have to grow up right along with her children.

To clear her head, Sylvia called her friend Delta to get another perspective.

"I'm proud of you, girl!" Delta praised. "I'm so glad you're finally getting on the ball about being a mother instead of a homegirl to your kids."

"It sure ain't easy, though," Sylvia muttered.

"It'll be worth it, though," Delta assured her. "This is what they need. You're just gonna have to show them that you mean business. And you do that with your actions more than your words."

"Girl..." Sylvia sighed, running a hand through her braids. "You should've seen how they were acting at dinner tonight. Candy was being her usual self, pretty much, but I think something is up with Valencio."

"Something like what?"

"His grades have been slipping, he's been cutting class and skipping basketball practice, he's gone off with his friends more than he's home, and he's been eating damn near everything in the kitchen for the past few weeks. He used to help me out around here without me having to ask but now I have to stay on him like I do Candy."

"Wow, really? That doesn't sound like him at all."

"I know. I had told him to loosen up and have some more fun, but this wasn't what I meant when I said that. He's just gone all the way to the left with it."

"Girl, you give some kids an inch and they take a mile."

"Yeah. That's what Bryce said," Sylvia admitted somewhat grudgingly. "But Valencio just went from zero to sixty almost overnight. If I didn't know better, I'd think he was on something."

"On something? Like drugs?"

"Either that or he done got his first whiff of the punanny."

Delta gasped. "You think he's having sex?"

"Honestly, girl, nothing would surprise me at this point. But I remember one day a while back when I came home and could swear

I smelled weed in the air, but I figured it was from Candy. It didn't even cross my mind that it would be Valencio. That would explain all the damn eating, though."

"Just curious; when you thought it was Candy smoking the weed, what did you do about it?"

Sylvia was quiet for a moment. "Nothing," she admitted in a low voice.

Delta was quiet herself for a moment, and Sylvia could only imagine what she was thinking about her.

"Well, girl, at least you're trying to do better now, and that's what's important," Delta finally said.

Sylvia appreciated her friend not judging her; at least, not out loud. "Yeah."

"What are they doing now?"

"Candy's in her room again. I told Valencio to clean up the kitchen. They're both on punishment."

"Do you think confining Candy to her room is the best punishment, though? She spends all her time in there when she's at home, anyway."

"I really just said it before I thought it through. I'll admit I haven't given out many punishments over the years."

"Well, I know I don't have any kids but I've been around plenty of 'em, and I'll just suggest to you that if you're going to ground them, especially Candy, you're gonna need to clear out all that stuff they have in their rooms. Take away their computers, their phones, TVs, and anything else that they could use as entertainment or a way to communicate with their friends. Otherwise it's not much of a punishment."

Sylvia hadn't even thought of that. "That's a good point." Though she knew Candy would raise hell if she did that.

"And I'll make another suggestion to you," Delta continued. "You need to search their rooms."

"What? Why?"

"Because you never have. You need to see what they have in there. And you have every right to do that, Sylvia; you're the one paying for that apartment and everything in it."

"Yeah, but I've never been a big fan of parents searching their kids' rooms. Seems shady or something."

Delta sucked her teeth. "I thought you were trying to change your way of thinking when it came to parenting."

"I am, but-"

"Then you need to get over this whole notion of 'violating your kids' privacy.' They shouldn't *have* any privacy. You hear all the time about how kids build explosives or hide weapons in their rooms that they end up using to shoot up a school or something like that, and the parents had no clue about any of it because they didn't want to check their rooms and *invade their privacy*. They can get privacy when they move out and get their own places."

Sylvia hadn't thought about it like that. And if she was honest, she always thought the parents of those kids that did things like shoot up a school or blow up stuff were idiots for not knowing anything about what their kids had been planning. It hadn't even occurred to her she would be right in the same boat as them if Candy or Valencio decided to do something horrible like that.

"I see your point," she admitted. She slid off her bed and headed to the kitchen to get her some water.

"Good. Just remember, you're not doing it to be nosy; you're just trying to stay on top of what your kids are into because you love and care about them."

"Yeah. You're right. I appreciate..." Her words trailed off when she got to the kitchen and saw it was still in a mess with Valencio nowhere to be found. He had washed his own plate and put it in the dish rack, but left all the others sitting on the table, along with the little bit of lasagna that he hadn't gobbled up. Valencio had outright defied her, almost as if he were daring her to do anything about it. Her sweet, respectful son had turned into a disobedient slacker and it pained Sylvia to admit that it was most likely her own fault.

"Sylvia? What's wrong?" Delta asked.

With a heavy sigh, Sylvia slumped against the nearest wall. She felt defeated already, but knew she couldn't let herself feel that way for more than a minute. Otherwise, she'd renege on everything she said she was going to do.

"I'm just...being tested, that's all," Sylvia replied, silently telling herself not to cry.

· · · ·

IT WAS ABOUT THREE o'clock the following morning when Sylvia's phone rang. She eased her head from under her covers where she had buried herself after the emotionally draining night she had. After finding that Valencio hadn't cleaned up the kitchen like she had told him to, she practically dragged him from his room and stood there watching while he got it done. He was moving really slowly, as if trying to frustrate her to the point where she got tired of waiting and either left him alone or went ahead and did it herself, but she didn't. She had stood right there with her arms folded and waited until every dinner dish had been washed and put away. When he finally finished, she lit into him for being disobedient and dragged herself to the bed, wondering how long things were going to be as hard as they were.

"Who the hell is this?" she muttered, reaching for her phone. When she saw it was Deuce, she sucked her teeth and sent the call to voicemail. But he called right back, and he kept calling until Sylvia finally answered.

"What the hell are you doing calling me this time of night?" she demanded.

"I got something for you," Deuce said.

"If this is some kind of booty call, you can keep it. I'm not fooling with you tonight."

"No, it's not a booty call, but it has something to do with our last one," Deuce said teasingly.

Sylvia sat up a little bit. "What about it?" She hoped he wasn't about to tell her he found out he had some kind of sexually transmitted disease or something.

"I told Dub about it."

Sylvia's stomach dropped and her heart started pounding so hard it made her chest hurt. Her hand clutched her t-shirt over her chest. "Wh-what?"

"I told him we got down."

Right at that moment, Sylvia hated Deuce and hated herself for ever giving in to him. "Why would you do that??"

"He's my brother. We share things," Deuce joked with a chuckle.

"Oh, you think this is funny? What did he say??"

"Don't worry about what he said. And yeah, I *do* think it's funny."

Squeezing her eyes shut, Sylvia flopped back down onto the bed, not believing this was happening. She had no idea that Deuce was lying. He hadn't said anything to Dub about sleeping with Sylvia; he just wanted to mess with her. He was well aware of the crush Sylvia still had on Dub and simply felt like making her sweat a little bit.

"I could kill you for this, Deuce," she hissed.

"Yeah. I know," Deuce said lightly. He was really enjoying this. "You should be happy, though, 'cause I let him know how good you are. If you can't do nothin' else, you can fuck."

Actually feeling like she couldn't breathe, Sylvia hung up the phone, her blood boiling at the sound of Deuce's laughter as she did so. Her head was spinning.

Temporarily forgetting about the late hour, Sylvia immediately dialed Dub's number. It temporarily jarred her when she heard a woman answer.

"Yes, Sylvia?" Jelissa asked calmly.

"Oh," Sylvia's mouth fell open. It was then that she remembered what time it was. She wanted to just hang up but what's done was done. "I'm sorry...I needed to speak to Dub about something important and didn't think about what time it was. My bad...I'll, um, I'll just talk to him later."

"Sylvia," Jelissa called out before Sylvia could hang up.

Sylvia warily returned the phone to her ear. "Yeah?"

"Dub is asleep but I'll let him know you called. In the meantime, though, I think you and I need to talk."

• • • •

CHAPTER 15

• • • •

THE LAST PLACE SYLVIA wanted to be was at work. She didn't feel like dealing with customers or co-workers or anybody else; after the talk she had with Jelissa that morning, she just wanted to go somewhere dark and stay there.

Jelissa had basically told her that she needed to back off and stop depending on Dub for so much. She reminded Sylvia that Dub was *her* man and she didn't appreciate Sylvia calling him when she needed things. Jelissa seemed to think that Dub was too nice to say this, so she was saying it for him. Sylvia wondered if Dub shared Jelissa's feelings; if he thought that she called and depended on him too much. The thought hurt her, especially since he was the one that always told her to call him if she needed anything and that he was there for her and that they were family. Had he just been saying all that? Would he tell her to call him and then complain to Jelissa when she did? Sylvia couldn't bring herself to believe that; Dub had always been a stand-up guy. But there had to be a reason Jelissa felt the need to confront her.

The day went on in a blur; Sylvia was just going through the motions, her mind on Deuce, Dub, and Jelissa. Sylvia would have given anything to know what Dub was thinking of her right then, having found out about her and Deuce sleeping together. Would he call her and ask her about it? Or would he act like he didn't know? Did he even care? Sylvia's mind was full of thoughts and she wasn't in the best mood when her mother, Sandra, called asking about how things were going with the kids.

"Things are fine," Sylvia replied distractedly.

"Fine? So you've started doing what we talked about?"

"What? Oh, yeah."

"What's wrong with you?"

"Nothing. I just...have some other stuff on my mind, is all."

"Anything you wanna talk about?"

"No," Sylvia quickly responded. "No, I don't."

"I just hope that you haven't changed your mind and gone back to your old ways, in regards to those children," Sandra said. "Lord knows they're way overdue for some good parenting."

Sighing, Sylvia knew it was time to get off the phone. "Look, don't worry about all that; I haven't changed my mind about anything. I've got some good kids; they ain't out killin' or robbing anybody so I'm doing better than a lot of parents. So I appreciate your advice and everything but I've got it from here."

Sandra was quiet for a moment before speaking. "Still being stubborn, I see," she muttered. "You still got about as much to learn as they do. But I'll leave you alone for now, since you think you know everything."

"Uh-huh. Bye." Sylvia hung up the phone, wishing she had a drink.

Unfortunately, Sylvia's day didn't get any better when she got a call about one of her kids shoplifting.

"Are you freakin' kidding me?!" Sylvia exclaimed, as she headed to the mall. She had just been about to go home for the day, now she had to deal with this. It seemed like Candy would just never learn. And Sylvia was especially incensed because she had just told her mother hours before that her kids didn't steal.

Sylvia stormed into the security office at the mall, ready to light into Candy for adding shoplifting to her list of transgressions, but she got the shock of her life when she saw it was her son sitting there and not her daughter.

"What the hell?" she asked, looking around as if she was being pranked. She hadn't even bothered to ask which child it was that had been caught; she just told them she'd be right there and hung up the phone, assuming it was Candy. The thought of it being Valencio had never even crossed her mind. "Valencio?"

He looked up at her sheepishly but stayed quiet; he was too embarrassed to speak.

"This is your son, ma'am?" the security guard asked.

"Yeah," Sylvia replied, still glaring at Valencio. "What did he do?"

"We caught him trying to steal a watch from the jewelry department."

"A watch?"

"Yes, ma'am. There were some other teens with him but they all ran off. We have your son on tape trying to sneak the watch into his pants."

Immediately Sylvia was reminded of her cousin Andrea telling her about her daughter Natina getting caught stealing and her friends running off and leaving her. Sylvia had faulted Andrea for that, internally accusing her of not being a good mother. Now she was in the same situation.

Starting to become embarrassed herself, Sylvia shook her head. "I'm so sorry about this," she said humbly. "He's never done anything like this before. I...I don't even know what to say."

"Well, since this is his first offense and he was willing to cooperate with us, and you're here to vouch for him, we're willing to let him go with a warning this time," the security guard said. "But he won't get off so easily if this happens again."

"Thank you so much," Sylvia said gratefully. "I really, really appreciate this, thank you. And I'm sorry for the trouble."

"Yes, thank you, sir," Valencio said in a low voice, sounding almost like his old, respectful self. "And I apologize, too."

Sylvia quickly led Valencio out to her car, wondering if she was in some kind of bad dream. She simply couldn't believe Valencio had been caught stealing. Things were just going from bad to worse.

Valencio looked at his mother sheepishly once they got in the car. "Mama-"

"You know what? I don't think I want to hear what you have to say right now," Sylvia cut him off with a hand up. "There is just no excuse for this, Valencio. You know better than to be stealing."

"I know. I'm sorry, Mama."

"Uh-huh. You just better be thankful they didn't really punish you for this like they could have."

"I am."

"Part of me wants to ask what in the world compelled you to try to steal a watch, but the other part of me doesn't really want to hear it 'cause whatever your reason is, it's stupid. You know just about every store nowadays got cameras in it. What made you think you could steal something and get away with it is beyond me."

Valencio just looked down at his hands.

"Not that it matters, but who were you with when you did this?"

"Walt and Devonte," Valencio replied.

"Should've damn known," Sylvia muttered, taking out her cell phone. "Got me using up the little bit of gas I got to come get you for stealing. You know, Valencio, you were always the one that had some damn sense. I don't know what's happened to you lately, but you're getting about as bad as your sister."

Valencio looked at her in surprise, but remained silent.

"You know we're gonna have to call your dad about this."

His eyes widened in fear. Valencio hadn't even thought about what his dad was going to do to him and the realization made his heart drop. "Mama, please don't!"

"Why shouldn't I?"

"Because he'll kill me!"

"Well, you should've thought about that before-"

"Mama, please! I'll do anything you say! I'll do all the chores, I won't cut class or anything, I'll stay in my room until I'm sixteen, but *please* don't tell my dad about this!"

Sylvia looked at her son, and could see traces of when he was still her golden child. Being a delinquent wasn't in his blood; he was too fearful of the repercussions. Candy sure never begged like this when she was caught doing something. But then again, she didn't have a father like Bryce to worry about.

"I can't *not* tell him about this, Valencio, and you know it."

They drove home in silence. A tear ran down Valencio's cheek as he sat staring out the passenger window, dreading his father's reaction to this latest transgression. He had already lit into Valencio about cutting class and skipping basketball practice, and had warned him that he would put him on serious lockdown if he didn't straighten up and get his act together. And Valencio knew he meant it. Bryce called every night at a certain time to check on him, and Valencio always made sure he was home by that time so he could tell his father what he wanted to hear. But Valencio hadn't changed anything like his father had demanded; he was having too much fun. He was now seeing Madeline *and* Pamela, and it was actually thrilling for him trying to keep each of them from finding out about the other. Pamela was more low-key than Madeline so all they really did was hang out and hold hands and talk on the phone; Madeline, on the other hand, was just as freaky as she had always been. Several times they had come close to having sex, but they stopped themselves. They were doing just about everything else, though, and Valencio didn't want to give that up any time soon.

As soon as they got home, Sylvia told Valencio to stay on the couch in the living room while she called Bryce. Truth be told, she didn't really want to call him any more than Valencio wanted her to, but she knew she had to. If he were to mess around and find out about all this some other way and Sylvia hadn't told him, it would just cause another problem and Sylvia didn't need any more. And really, she wanted Bryce's help with Valencio more than she was worried about him blaming her. She really felt like she was in over her head with her own kids.

Needless to say, Bryce was absolutely furious. He demanded Sylvia put Valencio on the phone and Sylvia could hear him yelling from across the room. Valencio was actually cringing as he held the phone to his ear, wincing at his father yelling at him. Sylvia hadn't seen him look so scared since he was a child and one of the neighbors' pit bulls got loose and chased him down the street.

After about ten minutes, Valencio hung up the phone, tears running down his face. "He said he's gonna be by here later," he mumbled.

"Okay. Well you just sit out here until he gets here. And don't even think about turning that TV on or touching that telephone," Sylvia ordered.

"Yes, ma'am."

Oh, so now we're back to the manners now that he just got his ass chewed off, Sylvia thought dryly to herself. She shook her head, looking forward to Bryce's arrival 'cause she just didn't know what else to say to Valencio right then.

Heading down the hall, she paused when she passed by Candy's room. With everything that was going on, she hadn't even thought about what her daughter was up to; she figured she was out somewhere. But she could've sworn she heard moaning coming from behind Candy's closed door. Starting to automatically dismiss it like she always did, this time she thought she heard a voice other than Candy's, and it didn't sound like it was coming from the computer. It sounded like somebody was in there with her.

Knowing her daughter wasn't stupid enough to have a boy in her room with her, Sylvia put her hand on the doorknob and was surprised to find it wasn't locked like it usually was. She opened the door and her jaw fell open at the sight of her daughter naked in bed with some boy on top of her, grinding like his life depended on it. They were both so into what they were doing that they didn't even notice Sylvia standing there. Sylvia just stood and watched them for a few moments, as if transfixed. She just couldn't believe the gall of these teenagers to have sex up in her house like they were doing.

"Shit, you feel good," the boy whispered to Candy, still pumping into her. "You like this? Huh?"

"Yes, Mac," Candy concurred, throwing it back at him. *Just like I taught her to*, Sylvia thought shamefully. "I *love* it!"

"Whose is it?"

"It's yours..."

"Whose pussy is it??"

"It's yours!"

"Damn, I thought it was mine," Sylvia finally said, coming fully into the room.

"*Oh shit!*" both Candy and Mac exclaimed, trying to cover themselves with the bed sheets.

"Mama, what are you doing in here??!?" Candy screeched. "I thought you said you locked the door!" she hissed at Mac.

"I thought I did!" he hissed back, trying to get up off of her and still cover himself. His clothes were across the room on the floor. "You said she wasn't gonna be home until later on!"

Candy just glared at Sylvia accusingly, and in that moment Sylvia felt something snap. She lost any cool she had left. Before she knew it, she was lunging for Mac.

"*Mama*!" Candy screamed as Sylvia's hands closed around Mac's throat.

With strength she didn't even know she had, Sylvia dragged Mac out of Candy's room and towards the front door, with him trying to pry her hands off of him.

"Get her off me!" he yelled.

"Valencio, get the door!" Sylvia ordered. Her startled son jumped off the couch and opened the front door, and Sylvia threw Mac out, naked as the day he was born, and slammed the door behind him. Then she told Valencio to get back on the couch as she stormed back to Candy's room, slamming it shut behind her.

"What the hell were you doing bringing some boy up in here like that!" she yelled, getting right in Candy's face.

"I can't believe you just embarrassed me like that!" Candy exclaimed, holding her sheet around her. "You could've at least let him get his clothes! He is gonna be *so* mad at me for this!"

"I don't give a damn if he gets mad at you or not! I ain't even worried about him; this is about *your* slutty ass! I done *told* you not to bring boys here but you thought you could try me, huh?"

"You could've at least let me get my nut if you were just gonna throw him out anyway! And you aren't even supposed to be home this early!"

"Excuse me??"

"You heard me!"

Sylvia's hand slapped her daughter almost all on its own. It was the first time she had hit Candy in years, but she wasn't sorry for it. In fact, she felt it was long overdue. She glared at her daughter, daring her to do something about it.

Candy held the cheek where Sylvia had hit her in shock. Her face turned bright red and she actually started to tremble, as if she was going to explode. "*Get out*!" she screamed.

"You can yell until your face turns green. You don't tell me what to do and where to go in my own damn house!" Sylvia yelled. "I'm about sick of your triflin' ass! You can keep thinking I'm playin' if you want to but I can show you better than I can tell you! You better start getting your little fast ass in check, and *quick*! Now get your damn clothes on!"

Sylvia hurried out of the room before she lost it and hauled off and punched Candy like she really wanted to do. She couldn't remember the last time she was so angry. Between Candy and Valencio, Sylvia was feeling like she was about to lose her mind.

She slammed the door to her room and fell against it, crying hysterically.

Chapter 16

• • • •

THERE WAS JUST TOO much going on.

Bryce had come and gotten Valencio to stay with him for a while, and Sylvia didn't even have the energy to protest. Maybe that's what Valencio needed, 'cause Sylvia obviously wasn't doing things right.

As soon as Bryce had walked through Sylvia's door that night, he was on Valencio's case like an ambulance chaser on a car accident. Even Sylvia felt a little nervous, the way Bryce was going off.

"You will go to school. You will come *straight* home. You will do your homework, your chores, eat, and go to bed, and *nothing* else," Bryce informed him angrily, getting right in his face. "I hope you enjoyed your time of being stupid 'cause it's *over* with now. I'm gonna be on you like a *rash*. Every time you get up to *pee*, you better check in with me first. And if I have to go so far as to follow you around that school to make sure you're doing what you're supposed to do, I'll do it. And I *know* you don't want me to do that!"

Valencio gulped, too afraid to speak.

"You are going to go to every one of your teachers and apologize for your behavior," Bryce continued menacingly. "*And* your basketball coach, too, even though as of this second, *your* season is over. Anything even *remotely* extracurricular is over with until *I* say so. You got that?"

"Yes, sir," Valencio replied timidly.

"You will not touch a computer, television, iPad, telephone, cell phone, video game, or even your damn *dick* until you earn every bit of trust that you've ruined back. And I can tell you right now, homie, that's gonna take a *long* while. So unless you're talking to your mother, your grandparents, or God, your contact with the outside world is cut *off*."

Part of Sylvia felt a little sorry for Valencio, even though she knew he was getting what he deserved. But she appreciated Bryce, because she knew she wouldn't have the nerve to issue or implement such a strict punishment. And she had no doubt that Bryce would see it all the way through and back up every single thing he said. She wished she had been the one to do it herself, but she was glad that Bryce was there to get Valencio in line. When she watched them leave her apartment that night, something in her gut told her that her son was going to turn things around and be all right. Bryce was going to make sure of that.

If only she had someone to bail her out when it came to Candy.

Sylvia left Candy alone for the rest of that evening, but the next day, she tried talking to her. Even though the visual she couldn't shake of Mac banging her daughter made her anger reignite, she knew at some point they were both going to have to stop being stubborn and start talking, otherwise they were never going to get anywhere.

Only problem with that was, Candy didn't want to talk to Sylvia. Every time Sylvia tried to start a conversation, Candy would ignore her. As frustrating as it was, Sylvia tried to keep her patience in place. But even though Candy was still walking around with an attitude, Sylvia still didn't allow her to stay in her room with the door closed. Sylvia had even gone so far as to grab her screwdriver and take the door off the hinges, which infuriated Candy.

"What the hell?!" she screamed when she came home from school and saw her door missing. "Where is my door??"

"Somewhere you can't close it and hide behind it," Sylvia replied calmly. "And since you don't pay one bill up in here, it's *my* door. I can take it off if I want to."

"This is so lame!"

"I don't care what you call it. But I meant what I said about you not closing yourself up in there."

"Just because Valencio is gone doesn't mean you need to be all up in my business!"

"You don't have any business. I'd be surprised if you could even spell the word. Now get in there and do your homework; I know you got some."

Candy stomped to her room and plopped down onto the bed, giving Sylvia the evil eye as she yanked her books from her bookbag. Sylvia just shook her head and went to the kitchen to fix dinner, occasionally going back to peek in on Candy, which was something she had never done and something Candy hated.

The next day, Sylvia had the morning off from the store and while Candy was at school, she remembered Delta's suggestion about checking the kids' rooms. Sylvia had always been against that, but now she didn't think it was such a bad idea. Jumping out of bed, she rushed to Valencio's room, opting to check his out first. Most of his things were gone with him to Bryce's house, but a good bit of his clothes and items were still there. Not quite sure where to start, Sylvia began looking through drawers, checking underneath the clothes and rummaging through the various items in his desk. Finding nothing out of the ordinary, she moved on to the closet. She checked any and everything on the top shelf, then dropped to her knees and rummaged through the things on the bottom. Just as she was about to write it off as another dead end, she found an empty box of Black and Milds and a lighter inside one of his shoes. The sight of these things made her fall onto her behind in shock. She had suspected Valencio had been smoking something but now she had proof of it. Now the question was if he was smoking the Blacks straight up or if he was scraping the insides out and replacing it with weed. Neither way made her feel any better.

Almost not wanting to continue, Sylvia made herself move on to the bed. She checked underneath, inside the pillowcase, and between the sheets and found nothing. But when she lifted the mattress, she saw a Black Erotica magazine, a tube of lotion, and an opened box of condoms. She dropped the mattress in shock, but after taking a moment to gather herself, she looked underneath it again. She counted the condoms and none were missing, which was a mild relief, but she began to wonder if Valencio had had a girl in his room before and just hadn't gotten caught. Was her son having sex? What did he need condoms for if he wasn't? How long had this been going on? There were so many questions that she knew she probably wouldn't get the answers to any time soon, if ever. She almost didn't want to know. Seeing her daughter having sex live and up close was enough; she didn't need to know about her son getting his freak-on, too.

Making a mental note to call Bryce and let him know about these findings, Sylvia moved on to Candy's room. She stood in the door-less doorway and wondered if she really had the mental energy to do this. If she found condoms and cigars and porn magazines in Valencio's room, there was no telling what she'd find in Candy's.

Forging ahead, Sylvia went ahead and began her search. She tried to be as thorough as she could, putting herself in the mind of how she was when she was Candy's age. Sylvia had hidden things in her room back then, although it was mostly things like makeup and clothing that Sandra had forbidden her from wearing. But as she searched through Candy's room, finding sex toys, lubricant, porn DVDs, condoms, a small phone book with a bunch of boys' phone numbers in it, among other things, she knew she hadn't had anything on her daughter when it came to that. Sylvia surely had sex as a teenager, but she hadn't been bold enough to do it at home or keep anything *suggesting* she did it at home. But Candy didn't care, probably because she didn't believe Sylvia would really do anything about it even if she *did* find it. And Sylvia couldn't really be mad at her for that because there was a time she most likely wouldn't have. Sylvia had more encouraged Candy when it came to having sex than she had discouraged her. It was no wonder Candy had all these things in her room.

Sylvia had to go find a box to carry all the things she found in Candy's room, but she took everything incriminating and inappropriate that she found after searching the room from top to bottom and put it in her own closet. She knew Candy was probably going to flip when she realized what Sylvia had done, but Sylvia would just have to cross that bridge when she got to it.

Everything in Sylvia wanted to call Dub for some insight, but she hadn't forgotten about the talk she had with Jelissa when she told

Sylvia to back off. Sylvia wasn't in the least scared of or intimidated by Jelissa, she just didn't want to upset Dub. And since she still didn't know if Dub had anything to do with that little talk Jelissa felt the need to have with her, she didn't want to cause any waves until she needed to. Part of her thought about calling Deuce, figuring he might give a damn if he knew how dire things had gotten, but she didn't really want to bother. It was a toss-up with Deuce as to what she was going to get on any given day, and she was still mad at him for telling Dub about them sexing, anyway.

She picked up the phone to call Sandra, but after the way she had spoken to her mother the last time she had called to check in on things, Sylvia was actually embarrassed to admit everything that had happened since then. She went to fix herself some cereal but as soon as she was finished eating, she found herself dialing her mother's number. She was going to have to swallow her pride right along with her Cheerios.

"Well, look who it is," Sandra greeted after a few rings.

"Hey, Mama."

"What's the matter now?"

Not even feeling like pretending that she didn't know what Sandra was talking about, Sylvia dove into the reason for the call. "Things have really hit the fan. Valencio was caught shoplifting at the mall and Bryce came and took him home with him; Valencio is probably gonna be on lockdown until Jesus comes back."

"Oh, my lord," Sandra whispered. "My Valencio was stealing? Stealing what?"

"A watch. I'm willing to bet that his little friends put him up to it but of course none of them stuck around when he got caught."

"Of course they didn't. Hopefully he's learned a lesson about who is really his friend and who isn't."

"Hopefully. But that's not even the worst thing that's gone down."

"Oh, goodness. What else?"

Sylvia had to take a deep breath before continuing. "When we got home, I caught Candy in her room having sex."

Sandra's gasp would have been funny if the situation was anything other than what it was. "Having sex??"

"Yep."

"With a boy?"

"Yeah, with a boy. As far as I know, Candy only swings one way."

"Well, part of me isn't even surprised, I hate to say," Sandra admitted. "I wouldn't have been surprised if you were calling to tell me that Candy was pregnant."

"I hope to high heaven she's not. The last thing that girl needs is a baby."

"You mean the last thing *you* need is a baby, 'cause you and I both know you'd be the main one raising it," Sandra corrected.

"I guess you have a point with that."

"So what happened after that? After you caught her having sex?"

"I threw the boy out then slapped her. She actually had the nerve to tell me I had no business being home so early."

"No she didn't!"

"She sure did. It was all I could do not to throw her ass out right behind that boy."

"I told you that you were going to have a task on your hands," Sandra said. "Thank the Lord you've got Bryce to help you get Valencio in line, but that Candy is going to be a handful. She's rebellious and defiant and she's not going to change any time soon, I can tell you that right now."

"Oh, I know. I went and searched their rooms this morning and found all kinds of stuff, mostly in Candy's. The girl has more sex toys than I do."

"Sex toys?!"

"I just don't know what I'm gonna do with that girl," Sylvia sighed wearily. "I'm trying to stay the course here, but I'm just really getting fed up with her."

"You don't have a choice, Sylvia; that's *your* child. You had her and chose to raise her like you did, and now you have to deal with the result of it. She acts like that with you because you allowed her to all these years. She's just testing you to see how long it takes for you to cave in. You can't let yourself do that."

Sylvia didn't exactly like hearing that all of this was pretty much her fault, but she knew she couldn't very well dispute it. "I know."

"I'm here if you need me, and I'm praying for you," Sandra continued.

"I appreciate it."

"And I'm proud of you for doing what you're doing."

Sylvia smiled; she couldn't remember the last time her mother had said that to her. But Sylvia knew she hadn't done much for her mother to be proud of. "Thanks, Mama. That actually means a lot."

• • • •

ANOTHER COUPLE OF DAYS passed with Sylvia trying to talk to Candy and Candy avoiding Sylvia. Sylvia had to constantly remind herself to stay determined and not get fed up. She knew Candy was just trying to see how far Sylvia would go with all this newfound discipline. Sylvia had to stay consistent and prove to her that she was serious about everything she was trying to do.

One day, though, Candy finally said something to her.

"Can I go to a party at my friend's house tonight?"

Sylvia looked at her like she was crazy. "Is that a joke?"

"No..."

"So you're seriously asking me if you can go to a party on a Wednesday night after you've been stomping around here with an attitude for the past couple of weeks?"

Candy shrugged. "At least I'm asking you and not sneaking out or somethin.'"

She actually said this as if it was something Sylvia should be proud of. Sylvia just looked at her as if she were waiting for the punchline.

"And you always let me go before," Candy added.

"Yeah, well, those days are over with," Sylvia informed her. "You're not about to be going out to a party in the middle of the week. And you're still on punishment, anyway."

"Punishment?"

"Yeah, punishment. I told you I wasn't playing about that."

"But a *senior* invited me to this party," Candy persisted. "I can't *not* show up!"

"Yes, you can. 'Cause you ain't."

Candy's jaw dropped. She really thought Sylvia was going to cave in like she always had, especially after she told her she had been invited to the party by a senior. "You're seriously saying no??"

"I'm seriously saying no."

Candy just stood staring at her for a moment before sucking her teeth and stomping off to her room.

Sylvia shook her head at her daughter's audacity but she was proud of herself. There was a time she would have let Candy go to the party without question; she wouldn't have even had to hear the part about a senior extending the invitation. But things were different now; they had to be. And even though Sylvia understood the significance of being invited to a party by a senior when you were a freshman, she couldn't renege on all that she had been saying and let Candy go. She would never be taken seriously if she did, just like Sandra said.

Candy stayed in her room while Sylvia fixed herself something to eat and watched a movie. Candy was pouting and didn't want any dinner, and Sylvia left her alone. She wasn't going to entertain Candy acting like a baby.

The phone rang and Sylvia groaned when she saw her job on her Caller ID.

"What, Lance?" she greeted her cousin dryly.

"Sylvia, can you please come in tonight?"

Sylvia sighed heavily. "Damn, Lance! I can't have a day off?? What you need me to come in for? Who called in?"

"Toni. Her father just passed."

"Oh," Sylvia felt bad for fussing; she knew how much Toni loved her father. She still didn't want to go in to work, but also knew there was no way she would say no. "Yeah, of course I'll come in. I guess you need me to come right now?

"Within the hour. Marie is getting ready to take Toni home 'cause she's way too hysterical to drive."

"Yeah, she doesn't need to be driving. I'll get there as soon as I can."

"Thanks, Sylvia. You're saving me yet again."

"Uh-huh." Sylvia didn't want to say anything about how this was going to have to be time and a half, since he was calling her in on her day off. He already knew. And nobody else got that in such situations but her.

She leaned her head onto the back of the couch momentarily before pushing herself up and going back to her room, looking at her watch. She paused when she got to Candy's room.

"Hey," she said.

Candy just grunted. She was laying on her bed with her back to the door.

"I have to go in to work for a while," Sylvia informed her. "You need to stay here until I get back."

Candy's head lifted slightly. "How long you gonna be gone?"

Sylvia's eyes narrowed. "Why you askin'?"

"I just wanna know."

"Yeah, well, don't worry about all that. Just know I could come back at any time."

Candy's head dropped back down onto her pillow.

"I'm trusting you to stay here, *alone*, and don't try anything you know you're not supposed to be doing while I'm gone," Sylvia continued. "You got that?"

Candy just grunted again.

"Candy."

"Yeah, I got it."

Sylvia paused. "Is that what you would say if your grandmama asked you?"

Candy turned over slightly. "Huh?"

"How come you don't say 'yes ma'am' and stuff to me like you do to her?"

"That's what she makes us say. You never told us to."

Sylvia knew the answer was true and kind of obvious, and she wanted to say how she felt that her being the mother should automatically garner her some respect, but she didn't have time to go into all that right then. She just shook her head and went to her room to get ready for work.

When Sylvia rushed out a little while later, she hoped Candy heeded her instructions and didn't try anything while she was gone. After that whole incident with Mac, she hoped Candy had at least learned a little bit of a lesson, and saw that Sylvia would actually punish her and not just brush it off if she found out. This would be Candy's first test to see if she could earn Sylvia's trust.

Sylvia thought (and hoped) that she would only be working for a couple of hours, but she ended up working practically a full-time shift. The store was busier than usual and they needed all the help they could get. Sylvia called home to check in on Candy, and Candy assured her she was still sitting in her room, bored. She wasn't even on her computer, which she hadn't seemed to have as much interest in ever since Sylvia had removed her door for her to hide behind. Sylvia commended her and told her to keep that up, since she wasn't sure how much longer she was going to have to stay at work.

By the time Sylvia dragged herself home, it was almost one in the morning. She could hardly keep her eyes open as she trudged back to her room, not even looking in on Candy. There was music coming from her room, so Sylvia figured she was asleep. She just kicked her shoes off and fell onto her bed, falling to sleep immediately.

It was a couple of hours later that she was awakened by the loud banging on the front door. She glanced at her watch groggily, and immediately thought it might be Deuce coming over to bother her again. She laid her head back down, snuggling into the nook she had settle into between her pillows, but when the knocking persisted, she cursed under her breath and pushed herself off the bed, immediately angry from being officially awake and having to move from her comfortable position.

She didn't bother looking through the peephole before yanking the door open. Her jaw fell when she saw a policeman standing there, and her frown deepened when she saw her daughter standing next to him.

"Are you Sylvia Jennings?" the officer, whose name tag read DaCosta, asked her.

"Yeah," Sylvia rubbed the residual sleep from her eyes. "What's going on?"

"This is your daughter?" he asked, referring to Candy.

"Yeah..."

"A noise disturbance was reported due to a loud party a couple of streets over," Officer DaCosta informed her. "Your daughter here was there and about to get into a fight with another girl when we arrived and broke things up. She said she's only fifteen but she was there smoking cigarettes, and we smelled alcohol on her breath."

Sylvia felt her face flame with an almost equal mix of anger and embarrassment. It almost amazed her just how much she wanted to reach out and rip her own daughter's face off. And Candy knew full well she was wrong; she wouldn't even look at her.

"I apologize, officer," Sylvia said, wondering just how many times she was going to have to say that to someone about either of her children. "Thank you for bringing her home."

"Were you aware that your daughter was out this time of night?"

"No...I just got in from work a little while ago," Sylvia lied. She had certainly been home long enough to know if her daughter was home or not, but she hadn't looked. But there was no way she was going to admit that to the police. It was embarrassing enough to admit to herself.

The officer eyed her skeptically, but Sylvia was thankful that he just let it go with a warning and left. Sylvia felt like her head was swimming as she closed the door behind Candy after she inched into the apartment.

"You're just on a roll, ain't ya?" Sylvia commented.

Candy just glanced at her, then looked back down at her nails.

"So you're just determined not to take me seriously, huh? You just gon' do whatever the hell you wanna do regardless of what I say, right?"

Sucking her teeth lightly, Candy said, "It ain't nothin' like that. I was gonna stay here like you told me to but when China said that Mac was at the party, I just wanted to go over there and tell him I was sorry for what went down here. You know, when you threw him out without any clothes?" she added accusingly.

"You don't have the boy's phone number?"

"I wanted to see him in person."

Sylvia glared at her defiant daughter, but she was immediately reminded of when her mother left her home alone for the first time after the time she had left the house and stayed gone for three days.

Sylvia had snuck out to a party at her friend Moni's house, and that's the night she and Deuce conceived Candy on the bathroom sink. The situations were so similar it was scary. Sandra had tried to trust Sylvia and she had betrayed that trust, just like Candy had betrayed Sylvia's now.

"Who'd you fuck?" Sylvia asked bluntly.

Candy blinked. "What?"

"You heard what I said."

"I didn't...nobody!"

"You might as well tell the truth about it. It's not like I could think much less of you right now."

Candy looked hurt for a split second, then went right back to her usual dismissive, defiant stance. "I'm tellin' the truth. I didn't do that."

"Uh-huh. I wouldn't be surprised if you came in here next week talking 'bout you're pregnant."

Candy sucked her teeth again, and Sylvia wondered if she did that as much when she was a teenager and how Sandra managed to deal with it, because it absolutely irked Sylvia now.

"I am *not* pregnant," Candy insisted.

"I guess we'll see," Sylvia said. She suddenly felt extremely tired.

"Can I go to my room now?" Candy asked, looking like she was about to walk off regardless.

"Yeah, you can go; I'm too tired to deal with you and your mess right now, anyway. But don't think that this is over."

Sylvia wasn't kidding. After that night, Sylvia watched Candy like a hawk. She made Candy stay in the room with her when they were home together, she made Candy text her between every class at school (and send selfies by the classroom clocks, which Candy felt silly doing), and when she had to work nights and couldn't get either Sandra or Delta to watch her, she made Candy call her from the house phone every half hour. Sometimes, she even made Candy go to work with her and do homework in the break room, which Candy absolutely hated. And she even finally took Delta's advice and took Candy's computer out of her room, and wasn't even surprised at all the porn and things she found on there. Candy was part of seemingly every social network known to man and seemed very active in several chat rooms, as well. Most of the things in her browser history had to do with celebrity gossip, sex, or shopping sites.

Candy hated being under such a close watch, but Sylvia wasn't letting up. It was rare that she left Candy unsupervised, because she had proven she couldn't be trusted to stay by herself. Whenever Sylvia would go pick her up from Delta or Sandra's or come home while one of them was at her apartment with Candy, she would always note the respect that Candy showed for both of them. Candy considered Delta her aunt, even though she had only known her a few years, and it rubbed Sylvia the wrong way that Candy showed her more respect in that short time than she had ever shown Sylvia. But Sylvia remembered what both of them had always tried to tell her about demanding respect, and Sylvia simply hadn't done that. Even though she knew that was true, that didn't mean she wasn't a little resentful of her daughter being so drastically different with her than she was with seemingly everybody else.

After a few weeks of constant supervision, Candy finally lashed out.

"I'm tired of this!" she exclaimed one night when she was getting ready to go to work with Sylvia. "You ain't gotta watch me all the time, you know. I'm not a baby!"

"You might not be a baby but you've already proven you're not mature enough to stay here by yourself," Sylvia replied casually as she pulled her braids into a ponytail. "I tried trusting you and you blew that, remember?"

"This is some bullshit!"

Sylvia's head snapped to her, her eyes blazing. "What did you just say??"

"You heard me! This is some bull-*shit*! I'm tired of you doing me like this! And you better not slap me again, either, or I'll call somebody to come lock your ass up!"

"Heffah, you gotta get to the phone first! I don't know who you think you talkin' to like that but you won't be able to call *nobody* once I break both your damn hands off!"

"I'm tellin'-"

"Nah, I think you've got it twisted!" Sylvia said, immediately getting in her face and actually putting a finger between her eyes. "I don't care what you *feel* like you're supposed to be able to do, I am your damn mother whether you like it or not! And you better *watch* yourself up in here and get it out your head that you can talk to me any kind of way! It's about time you get some *respect* for me, dammit!"

"Why? You ain't *been* tryin' to act like a mother! All this time you've been letting me pretty much do whatever I want; why you tryin' to get all hard now? It's a little late to be trying to be something you should've been from the beginning!"

Sylvia's hand dropped. There wasn't anything she could say to that, and both of them knew it.

$\bullet \bullet \bullet \bullet$

CHAPTER 17

$\bullet \bullet \bullet \bullet$

SYLVIA COULDN'T GET Candy's words out of her mind a few days later.

When she got pregnant with Candy at fifteen, she just knew she had the perfect solution to the resentment she felt towards her parents, the loneliness from her friends abandoning her and the embarrassment of getting knocked up by the wrong twin; she would raise her daughter as her best friend and always have somebody in her corner. She would give Candy the kind of leeway and trust and freedom that she wished she had when she was coming up, and in return, Candy would confide in her and love her and appreciate her. But that's not how everything went down. Nothing had gone like Sylvia had envisioned, and instead of having a daughter who wanted to be close to her, she had a daughter that tried to get away from her every chance she got. Candy was entitled, selfish, disrespectful, rebellious...just like Sylvia had been. For the life of her, Sylvia didn't know how her intentions had backfired like they had.

This was heavy on her mind while she was at work. Sandra was home with Candy, and Sylvia was grateful for the reprieve because she didn't feel like being bothered with her daughter right then. After Candy had called her out and basically told her it was too late for her to try to act like the mother she should have been all along, the two of them hadn't had much to say to each other. Sylvia hadn't let up on what she had been doing as far as supervising Candy, but she only said anything to her when she had to. And thankfully Candy had chilled out some; she wasn't complaining about having to constantly be watched like she had been. She didn't say much of anything at all. Sylvia didn't know if this was because she was simply getting used to the punishment or because she was quietly plotting some way to get out of it, but she chose to just cross whatever bridge when she came to it.

When Dub walked into the store, Sylvia almost didn't even notice him, she was so lost in her own thoughts. Thankfully Lance had her stocking shelves instead of being on the register, because she really wasn't in the mood to deal with any customers.

"Hey, Sylvia," Dub greeted her.

Sylvia looked up distractedly. "Oh...Dub. Hey."

"You okay? Haven't heard from you in a while."

Sylvia wondered why he was acting like she hadn't heard from him because of the little discussion his girlfriend Jelissa felt the need to have with her. Or maybe he didn't know about that. Either way, Sylvia didn't need any more drama.

"Yeah, well...I've had a lot going on," she muttered, not even looking at him.

"Everything okay? Talk to me."

"It's nothing for you to worry about, Dub."

Dub frowned, noticing Sylvia's dismissive attitude. Usually she was glad to see him, but now she was acting like he was bothering her or something.

"Sylvia," he said, trying to get her to look at him. When she didn't after a few moments, he tried again. "Sylvia!"

"What?" she finally glanced at him.

"What is going on with you? Is there something going on with you or the kids? How's Candy doing?"

The question only reminded her of the issues she had going on at home, and she felt herself getting frustrated and exhausted all at the same time.

"Dub, you know what? How 'bout you just let me worry about my own kids, and you worry about...your stuff," she said, going back to putting the boxes of pancake mix on the shelf.

Dub's frown deepened. Sylvia had never talked to him like this, or brushed him off like she was trying to do. She had always been grateful for his concern about her and her kids. Something had to be going on, and he had no idea what it could be. The last time they spoke, the day he stopped Candy from going with those boys on the street, they were fine. He hadn't spoken with her much lately because he had been so busy with work; he wondered if she was upset with him about that.

"Sylvia, *something* is going on with you," he persisted. "I wish you would talk to me. We've always been able to talk about anything before; nothing has to change that now. I know I've been a little scarce lately but it's only because of work, that's all. I'm still here for you just like I've always been."

"Hmph," Sylvia scoffed before she could stop herself. "Things are *not* just like they've always been. Look, thanks for your concern and everything, but like I said, you don't have to worry about it. I gotta go." She rushed off towards the back of the store, leaving the still-unpacked boxes in the middle of the aisle.

Dub just looked after her, wondering what just happened.

· · · ·

LATER ON, DUB WAS STILL thinking about what happened in the store with Sylvia. She would barely even look at him, let alone really tell him anything about what was going on with her, and he knew something was wrong. There had to be some reason she was acting like that. Dub never tried to take advantage of the feelings he knew Sylvia had for him, but he couldn't imagine that they had dissipated in a matter of weeks, and for no reason. They hadn't argued or fallen out about anything; this was completely throwing him for a loop. He genuinely loved and cared about Sylvia, and her behavior concerned him.

When Deuce called him a little later, Dub figured he'd try something and hope for the best.

"What's goin' on, man?" Deuce asked him.

"Dude, I've got some things on my mind," Dub informed him.

"Like what? Something going on with your girl, Jessica?"

"Her name is Jelissa, but no, it's got nothing to do with her. I'm worried about Sylvia."

Deuce sucked his teeth. "What you worried about her for?"

"I think something's wrong with her."

"I know it is," Deuce chuckled.

"Man, I'm serious. Some stuff went down with Candy a couple months ago and she was really bummed about it; I'm wondering if it has anything to do with that. Maybe you oughta check on them, namely your daughter, and make sure everything's good."

"You still tryin' that, huh? When are you gonna leave this alone? That girl don't want nothing to do with me."

"Maybe if you acted like you gave a damn about her, she would."

"You always over there, so they're good."

"I'm not her dad, Deuce. And the main reason I'm always checking on them is because you won't. Candy is my niece and I love her and would be there for her regardless, but *you're* her dad. And there's nothing you can do to change that, no matter how stubborn you wanna be."

Deuce got quiet for a moment. "This ain't about being stubborn," he muttered.

"Then please tell me what it's about. You can't really be this heartless, can you? To not care at all what happens to your own children?"

"I never said I didn't care," Deuce quickly protested.

"You didn't have to say it. Almost sixteen years of not being there proves it."

Deuce sighed. "You don't get it," he muttered.

"No, I don't. Your daughter stays fifteen minutes from you but I bet you can't even remember the last time you saw her. That's inexcusable, man."

"Look, I just ain't father material."

"Then you didn't have any business making *eight* damn kids!" Dub felt himself becoming exasperated. Men like Deuce made him sick. "What is the *matter* with you?? Do you not see how you're doing them like our dad did us? And have you never heard of *condoms*??"

"Man-"

"Nah, nah, there's *nothing* you can say that could possibly justify that! You wanna be a ho and bone a bunch of chicks who are delusional enough to let you do it, fine. Whatever. But don't bring innocent kids into it! You've got all these kids within no more than an hour of you and you're just sitting on your ass trying to pretend you don't."

Deuce was quiet.

"Man, regardless of what our dad did, that's wrong," Dub continued, calming down some. "Think how you felt when you learned what the real deal was about how he left. You might not ever wanna admit it out loud, but that hurt you. You really wanna do that to them?"

A few thoughtful moments went by, and Dub wondered what was going through his twin's mind. He wouldn't have been surprised if Deuce brushed him off like he usually did but he hoped that wouldn't be the case this time.

Finally, Deuce spoke. "I'll think about it," he said in a low voice.

Dub had to be satisfied with that; it was the most he had ever gotten out of Deuce in regards to his children. "Good."

• • • •

SYLVIA WAS MISSING her son.

He had been gone to Bryce's for almost a month and Sylvia missed him something terrible. Before he started all of his bad behavior, he was one of the few bright spots she had to look forward to everyday. He always respected her, helped her, gave her hugs for no reason, even though Sylvia had never been all that affectionate...she never realized just how good of a son she had until he started acting differently. Because of her.

She still couldn't believe that she hadn't noticed all the things he was doing. Cutting class, skipping basketball practice, letting his grades slip, smoking weed, looking at porn...Sylvia still couldn't wrap her head around it all. And she had no evidence of this, but she wouldn't have been surprised if he had started having sex, too. After all, she *had* pushed him to get a girlfriend. There was no telling what else he had been doing when he was out of her house that she still didn't know about. The fact that he probably started all that because of her urging, and her telling him he worried too much about school almost made her sick to her stomach. She would give just about anything to have her sweet Valencio back.

Sylvia really felt she was slipping; she always thought she would be able to anticipate everything her kids would do, since she had done so much herself when she was their ages. They wouldn't be able to get anything over on her, she thought. But she also figured that giving them so much leeway and freedom would make them not *want* to keep anything from her and they wouldn't have to sneak around. But obviously, that's not how it went. It was just another reminder of how she had drastically failed as a mother.

Since Bryce had Valencio on such strict lockdown, Sylvia had only spoken to him a couple of times since he had gone to stay with him. Having the sudden urge to talk to her son, she grabbed her cell phone and called Bryce's house, hoping they had gotten home already.

"Hello," Bryce answered.

"Hey, Bryce. Where's Valencio?"

"In his room doing his homework. We just got home a few minutes ago."

"Can I speak to him?"

"Yeah, just keep in mind he's on a schedule. Hold on."

Sylvia heard him call for Valencio to come to the phone, and a few moments later, Valencio came on the line. "Hey, Mama."

"Hey, baby!" Sylvia was surprised at just how happy she was to talk to her son. "How you doin' over there?"

"I'm okay. How are you?"

"Oh...I'm good." Sylvia wasn't about to get into everything that was going on at home with Candy. "How's school? You getting everything back on track with your grades and all?"

"Yes, ma'am. Dad is checking everything I do and talks to my teachers every week. I'm getting A's on everything again."

"That's great, baby," Sylvia praised, mindful that she hadn't always been as encouraging towards him as she should have been when it came to school. There were times when he was growing up that he would run to her with a test or assignment he had aced and she would act like it wasn't all that big a deal. She felt bad about that now. "I'm proud of you."

"Thanks, Mama," Valencio replied gratefully. There was a pause while Bryce said something to him in the background, then he came back on the line. "Dad says I have to go ahead and finish my homework so I can have dinner and go to bed. I'll talk to you later."

"Okay," Sylvia said disappointedly. She wasn't ready to get off the phone with him yet but she knew she couldn't have him defying Bryce's rules. "I'll call you tomorrow."

"Okay."

"I love you," Sylvia said hurriedly, surprising both of them. That wasn't something she said much, to anyone.

There was a slight pause before Valencio replied, "Love you, too."

"Let me speak back to your dad."

"Yes, ma'am."

A second later, Bryce said, "Hey."

"Hey, Bryce...so Valencio is doing a lot better, huh?"

"Yeah, he's getting there. His teachers say he's pretty much back to how he was before he started wildin'."

"But you still have him on punishment?"

"Yeah."

"Why?"

"Because I'm teaching him a lesson. If all he had to do was get his grades back on track before I let him go back to how things were before, it wouldn't be much of a punishment. He needs to learn that the things he chooses to do have consequences. I'm making it so that he won't even want to *think* about doing all that mess again 'cause it won't be worth what he's going to get."

"So...how much longer are you planning on keeping this up? School will be out in a couple of months."

"Until I feel he's *really* learned his lesson and isn't just going through the motions of what I'm telling him to do. He needs to understand the seriousness of what he did."

"You don't think he does?"

"I think he's getting there. But he still hasn't even apologized to me for all this, or to you, for that matter. I'm curious as to how long it's going to take him to realize he should."

"He's thirteen, Bryce."

"I know how old he is."

"I'm saying, maybe he doesn't *realize* he needs to apologize to us. You just gonna keep him on lockdown forever?"

"Nah, not forever. But long enough."

At that moment, Candy came into the living room where Sylvia was sitting and joined her on the couch. "Mama."

Sylvia waved her away, pointing to the phone she had to her ear. To Bryce she said, "I just don't want you to overdo it with the tough love. You know he's a good kid."

"I know he is. And I'm trying to make sure he *stays* that way."

"Mama, I need to talk to you," Candy persisted.

"You can't see I'm on the phone?" Sylvia hissed at her.

"It's important, though."

"All these days you've been ignoring me up in here, then when I get on a phone call, you wanna decide to talk."

"I know, but-"

"You just gon' have to wait," Sylvia cut her off, turning away from her on the couch. Candy just looked at her.

"Sylvia, its cool; talk to your daughter," Bryce said, having overheard them. "I need to go in here and get dinner started, anyway."

"Hold up...when are you gonna let Valencio come back home?"

"I don't know. Not any time soon."

Sylvia frowned. "Why the hell not?"

"Because to be blunt, Sylvia, you're the reason all this mess started and I'm not trying to have you derail the progress we've made. I've been telling you for years that I wasn't crazy about how you were raising our son and you chose to do it your way anyway, so now, I'm doing it *my* way."

Sylvia was hurt by Bryce's words, even though she knew there was truth to them. "So you're blaming me for all this?"

"I told you that when you give kids an inch they often take a mile. You might not be responsible for every little thing he did but you certainly got the ball rolling on it."

"I wasn't trying to, though..."

"I understand that, but you did. And you can't even say you didn't know any better 'cause you had people trying to tell you otherwise, and you wouldn't listen. So hopefully this is a lesson for you, too."

Sylvia couldn't deny that. Bryce, Sandra, and Delta had all tried to tell her that how she was raising her kids was going to blow up in her face and she wasn't trying to hear it. She just knew she knew better than all of them.

"Now I have to go," Bryce said. "I'll bring Valencio by to see you soon. Know that this isn't about me trying to keep him away from you or anything like that. But this is a time in his life where he needs a male influence the most. I'm teaching him how to be a man; that's not something you can do. Rest assured that he loves you, though."

That made Sylvia smile a little bit. "That's good to know."

They ended the call and Sylvia played with the phone for a second before sighing and turning to Candy, who was still sitting there watching her. "Okay. Now what did you want?"

"Can you please take me off punishment?" Candy asked without preamble. Her voice was surprisingly pleasant and with no traces of her usual attitude. Still, Sylvia wasn't swayed.

"And why would I do that?" she asked with a slightly raised brow.

"Because I've learned my lesson. I'm gonna start acting better. You don't have to worry about me doing that stuff I used to do anymore."

Sylvia's eyes narrowed. "So...just like that, I'm supposed to believe you're gonna be some kind of angel now, huh?"

"Maybe not an *angel*, but-"

"You know what? I'm not falling for that. You're gonna have to try to run that game on somebody that doesn't already have a medal in it."

"I'm serious! Grandmama and Auntie Delta have been talking to me a lot when they're babysitting me-"

"They're not *babysitting* you, Candy. You're damn near sixteen."

"Well, watching me, then. And they told me how the stuff I've been doing is wrong and how I'm supposed to act and all that."

"But you don't wanna listen to me when *I* say it, huh?"

Candy sighed. "You never talked to me like they do," she said in a low voice.

"But you respect them more."

"They told me I need to respect you, too. So that's what I'm trying to do."

It burned Sylvia that her daughter only tried to show her respect because somebody else told her to. Even though she knew she had nobody to blame but herself, she still couldn't help getting upset at the thought. And as sincere as Candy seemed right then, Sylvia wasn't about to make the mistake of being a fool again.

"Well excuse me if I don't jump for joy because you finally decided to start acting like you've got some sense. But you're still on punishment, though."

Candy released an exasperated sigh. "Why??"

"Because I don't think you've learned anything. I think you're just tired of being in trouble."

"I'm not tryin' to play you!"

"Yes, you are. And I ain't falling for it again."

"I want to go live with my dad!" Candy exclaimed.

"Please; your dad don't care nothin' *about* you! You haven't figured that out by now?"

As soon as the words were out of her mouth, Sylvia regretted it. Candy's face crumbled and Sylvia felt her heart crumble right along with it.

"Aww, damn," she muttered, reaching for her daughter. "Candy, I didn't mean-"

"Leave me alone!" Candy yelled, pushing her away. She got up and ran to the bathroom, slamming the door.

"Great job, Sylvia," Sylvia sarcastically admonished herself, squeezing her eyes shut as she fell against the back of the couch.

Chapter 18

• • • •

IT HAD BEEN TWO DAYS and Candy hadn't spoken one word to Sylvia. Sylvia felt bad about what she had said to her about Deuce not caring about her, even though it wasn't much of a lie. Deuce had made it perfectly clear that he didn't want anything to do with Candy or any of his other kids. It was once every blue moon that he would proactively ask anything about Candy, and he had never given her any money or provided for her in any way. That kind of thing always came from his brother, Dub. Candy had asked about Deuce a few times over the years, and she had seen him a few times, but they didn't have any kind of relationship. She had only said she wanted to go live with him because she was mad at Sylvia. But Sylvia knew she still shouldn't have said what she said. She had never seen Candy look so hurt.

Now, Sylvia didn't know how to fix things. She didn't know what to say to her own daughter to make her feel better. Every time she started to go to Candy's room to talk to her, she drew a blank as to what to say and ended up turning to walk in the other direction in defeat. Between Candy and Valencio, she really felt like a failure as a mother.

• • • •

AFTER A COUPLE MORE days of the silent treatment, Sylvia was at her wits end. Once again, she found herself calling Sandra for advice.

"What's wrong now?" Sandra asked as soon as she picked up the phone.

"I think I've really stepped in it this time," Sylvia admitted immediately.

"What? What did you do?"

Sylvia told her mother about the latest incident with Candy, as well as everything Bryce had told her about Valencio and why he wouldn't let him come back to live with her.

"Well as far as Valencio goes, I can't disagree with Bryce on that," Sandra said when Sylvia finished. "He *does* need to be around his father now, especially after those things he was doing. Bryce will get him back in line."

"Yeah, well, apparently being around me will mess all that up, let Bryce tell it," Sylvia sulked.

"Stop that. You know good and well Bryce was right in what he said to you. You were the one that got Valencio to start doing all that nonsense."

"I didn't...oh, never mind," Sylvia said, not even feeling like trying to defend herself again.

"And why in the world would you tell Candy her daddy doesn't care about her?"

"He doesn't! He hasn't done one thing for her since he knocked me up."

"That may be, but you don't *tell* a child that."

"I didn't mean to say that; it just slipped out. I was upset about Valencio and then she came at me trying to get me to take her off punishment..."

"Well, why *won't* you consider taking her off punishment? Or at least loosening it up some? You've been keeping her under your thumb for weeks, you took her computer and her phone, you searched her room...all that's good, but at some point you've gotta start letting her prove she's learned the lesson you put her on punishment to teach."

Sylvia could admit to herself that she hadn't even considered that. She had been so focused on sticking to the punishment she had administered and making sure Candy adhered to it, that she didn't think about at what point she would start letting Candy out from under it.

"I figured she was just trying to tell me what she thought I wanted to hear," Sylvia admitted.

"So you don't trust her."

"Hell no I don't- I mean...absolutely not. Why should I? As much crap as she's tried to pull on me?"

"Remember, child, a lot of that is *your* doing," Sandra reminded her. "You encouraged it. And I know you're probably tired of hearing that-"

"I *am*," Sylvia muttered.

"But you need to remember it when you call yourself getting frustrated with her about how she is. That doesn't mean let it go, but it does mean that you can't blame it *all* on her. Children need guidance and you guided her right to where she is. Now, you're gonna have to take the time to guide her out of it. But at some point, you're gonna have to let her start walking or you'll never get anywhere, or know *she's* getting anywhere."

Sylvia paused, thinking about her mother's words. "I see your point."

"Good," Sandra replied. "I'm glad you're not trying to be stubborn. Listen...you and the children oughta come over for dinner one night soon. Then we can all talk about some things and get stuff out on the table."

"You think that'll help anything?"

"Couldn't hurt anything."

"If I'm involved, it could."

"Look here, child, you're gonna have to stop being pitiful and pouting all the time," Sandra admonished. "Yes, you've made a bunch of mistakes, and you're probably gonna make some more, but you're trying to do better now. Learn how to forgive yourself and move on."

"Forgive myself, huh?" The notion had never even occurred to Sylvia; she figured she'd just keep blaming herself (and getting blamed) forever. "I guess I can try that. 'Cause I *am* trying to do better, Mama."

The smile in Sandra's voice was evident when she said, "I know you are."

· · · ·

BRYCE AGREED TO LET Valencio go with Sylvia to Sandra's for dinner that following weekend. Candy still wasn't saying much to Sylvia but instead of seeming angry during this latest round of the silent treatment, she seemed hurt. Sylvia had tried to apologize to her, but Candy acted like she didn't hear her.

"Look, I'm sorry about what I said," Sylvia had said, standing the doorway of Candy's room. Sylvia still hadn't put the door back on. "It was a messed up thing to say; I was just mad, but that's no excuse."

Candy just kept painting her toenails like she had been doing, not even acknowledging her mother.

"I know I've never talked to you much about your dad, and I realize that was wrong," Sylvia continued, determined. "Regardless of what's happened in the past between me and him or what he chooses to do now, you still deserved to know *something*. I...I guess I just didn't know how to talk about it."

Candy just kept stroking the hot pink polish onto her small toenails, not even looking up.

"I don't blame you for being mad at me for this," Sylvia said. "But at some point we're gonna have to talk about it. I'll tell you whatever you wanna know."

Candy finally glanced up at her when she said this, but then went right back to what she was doing. Sylvia decided to leave it alone for the time being.

Now, Sandra, Sylvia, Candy, and Valencio were all sitting around Sandra's kitchen table. Sandra had cooked a meal of spareribs, baked beans, potato salad, collard greens, and crackling cornbread. Usually Sylvia would be tearing up such a spread, but she was too nervous to eat. She had been worrying about how this dinner was going to turn out ever since she had agreed to it. As positively as she tried to think, she hoped this didn't turn into some kind of Sylvia-bashing session.

"I'm so glad y'all could make it over tonight," Sandra said, mostly to her grandchildren. She smiled at them. "After you eat, I made some of that lemon pound cake you like so much."

"Oooh, good!" Valencio exclaimed. Even Candy smiled excitedly.

"But before we get to that, though, we need to get something else taken care of, first."

Here we go, Sylvia thought pensively.

"I'm gonna ask y'all a question and I want you to be honest when you answer me. You hear?"

"Yes, ma'am," Candy and Valencio chorused. Sylvia just eyed them.

"I want you two to truly say how you feel about your mother."

Candy and Valencio glanced at each other, as if it was some kind of trick question.

"You can be honest," Sandra encouraged. "Your mama is really trying to be a better mother to you all and in order to do that, she needs to know what she's been doing wrong. This is to help all of you so don't be shy; speak your minds. Be honest, but be respectful."

The two teenagers glanced at each other again before Valencio cleared his throat. "Umm..."

"Go ahead, baby," Sandra urged gently.

Valencio glanced at Sylvia before looking down at his plate. "Well, um...sometimes you...you kinda embarrass me, Ma."

Sylvia stiffened automatically. "I embarrass you?"

"Yes, ma'am. Like when you came to my basketball games and had on all those clothes that showed everything, and you kept yelling the whole time you were there. My teammates kept teasing me about that."

"Oh." Sylvia looked down at her own plate.

"You embarrass me, too," Candy eagerly chimed in. "I've always hated how you try to dress like you're still in high school or something, or try to make me talk to you like Auntie Delta talks to you. Like you're trying to force me to be your friend or something."

Sandra glanced at Sylvia, who could feel her face getting redder by the second. "I see."

"Anything else?" Sandra asked her grandchildren.

"Well," Valencio hedged, "I usually prefer my dad to take me places 'cause..."

"What, I *embarrass* you when I take you?" Sylvia asked, not even being able to hide her attitude.

"Sylvia," Sandra warned.

Sylvia just sat back in her chair, folding her arms across her chest.

"Dad encourages me to become a doctor like I've always wanted to," Valencio continued, dipping the tip of his fork in and out of his potato salad. "You never do that."

"I've *never* encouraged you, huh?" Sylvia challenged.

"You always told me I'm too young to be so worried about school and I should have more fun and stuff."

"So in *all* these years, I've never *once* said 'good job' or that I was proud of you, or anything like that?"

"Okay, maybe I shouldn't say *never*, but it wasn't a lot. You were more interested in me going to the NBA than me going to med school."

"And what's wrong with going to the NBA?"

"Nothing. I just want to be a doctor, not a basketball player. I just play now for fun."

Sandra was looking at her grandson proudly, but Sylvia was regretting ever agreeing to this dinner. She had told herself to keep an open mind, that she shouldn't take any of this too personally...that it was for the purpose of improving herself as a mother and also bettering the relationship with her kids, but she wasn't feeling so positively now. She hadn't expected to be so offended by her children's assessments.

"And you didn't start talking to *me* about school at all until I started flunking stuff," Candy added.

"Oh, and I guess you didn't know you're supposed to go to class and do your work, huh? You needed me to tell you that?"

"No, but it seemed like you didn't care about it so I really didn't, either."

Sylvia glared at Candy, but when she thought about it, she knew her daughter had a point. Sylvia *hadn't* emphasized how important school was until she started getting calls from Candy's principal telling her she was in danger of having to repeat her freshman year. And maybe the reason for that was because school was never a big deal to Sylvia when she was coming up, even though Sandra had tried to stay on her about her grades. Sylvia got through high school by doing just enough to get by, or just flat-out cheating. And she didn't even think about college; once she graduated from high school, she declared to be done with school forever. She never even realized what kind of example that was for her kids, being satisfied with a high school diploma that she only got by the skin of her teeth.

Sighing, Sylvia ran a frustrated hand down her face. "Okay, so...so far I'm an embarrassing, non-encouraging slacker. Anything else?"

"Sylvia!" Sandra exclaimed.

"Well, I'm sorry, but you're not the one who has to sit here and get insulted."

Valencio looked down at his plate guiltily. Candy just looked at Sandra, almost as if she expected to get reprimanded for being honest like she was told to do.

"Nobody is insulting you," Sandra insisted. "But I thought you said you wanted to do things better. You've gotta know what you're doing wrong, first."

"Okay, fine." Sylvia looked at her two teenagers. "What else am I doing wrong?"

Both Candy and Valencio looked as if they didn't want to say anything else.

"If you have something else to say, children, speak up," Sandra encouraged.

"I used to wonder about all these uncles I have that I usually only see once or twice, and that nobody else we're related to knows," Candy eventually said. "But my friend told me that folks usually just say it's an uncle to hide that it's somebody they're sleeping with."

Sylvia's jaw fell open and Sandra sat back in her chair. There had been several men that had been in and out of Sylvia's bed over the years that she had just hurriedly told Candy was an uncle whenever she hadn't been able to sneak them out before anyone saw them, but Sylvia never expected Candy to figure out what the real deal was with that.

"So I'm a slut, too," Sylvia muttered. She sat up straight in her chair and picked up her fork. "Well, I think I've had about all the *constructive criticism* I can take for one night. How 'bout we just eat now? Maybe I'll be ready for another round of critiques when I have a full stomach."

Sandra just shook her head at her but by then, Sylvia was over this whole self-improvement exercise. She stuffed a huge forkful of collard greens into her mouth and ignored the pensive looks she was getting from her children and the admonishing one she was getting from her mother. The more she chewed, the angrier she became. She knew she was far from a perfect mother, and when she agreed to this dinner she was genuinely willing to hear whatever her kids had to say, but now that she had heard it, she wished she never had.

The four of them ate in silence, with Sylvia trying her best to ignore the fact that any of them were there. She knew her mother probably wanted her to apologize for both her behavior that night as well as what her children had pointed out, but that wasn't about to happen. She was on the defensive, she was annoyed, and she was over it.

Later, after Sylvia and the kids were back home, Bryce came to pick up Valencio. Sylvia was in her room, having gone straight back there immediately after they got home and telling Candy and Valencio to leave her alone.

There was a knock on her door. Sylvia sighed in frustration.

"What?" she yelled.

"Sylvia, its Bryce."

"Yeah, and?"

"Valencio and I are about to head out."

"Bye," Sylvia spat, making no move to get up and see her son off.

There was a pause before Bryce said, "Open the door, Sylvia."

Knowing he probably wouldn't leave until she did, Sylvia sighed heavily again as she rolled off her bed and stomped over to the door, yanking it open. "What?"

"You're not gonna come say good-bye to your son?"

"Is he going off to Iraq? 'Cause otherwise there ain't no need to say good-bye."

"Okay, what's your problem?"

"I don't have a problem."

"You certainly have an attitude."

"Women get those from time to time. Especially us Black bitches, right?"

Bryce frowned. "What? When have I ever called you that??"

"I'm sure you probably have, just not to my face."

"Okay, you're trippin.'"

"Am I?" Sylvia was salty towards Bryce because she was feeling resentful towards him, too, since Valencio seemed to love him more. And he definitely respected him more.

"Yes, you are."

Sylvia brushed past him towards the living room, where Valencio was putting some books into his backpack.

"You still in here? I thought you couldn't wait to get out of here, since I *embarrass* you so much," Sylvia said to him snidely.

Valencio's eyes widened slightly. "Mama, I didn't mean-"

"Yes, the hell you did. You said exactly what you meant. But that's aight. Go on with your dad then you won't have to worry about me anymore."

Valencio looked hurt and Sylvia felt guilty for a split second, then she remembered everything he and Candy said during dinner and her angry stubbornness returned.

"Go on to the car, son," Bryce instructed Valencio, looking at Sylvia.

Grabbing his backpack and overnight bag, Valencio headed for the door. "Bye, Mama," he said, looking back at her.

"Yeah, whatever." Sylvia turned her back to him.

Hanging his head, Valencio walked out.

"What the hell is your issue? You're gonna treat your own son like that?" Bryce lit into her as soon as the door closed behind their son.

"Whatever. You didn't hear the stuff he said about me," Sylvia retorted.

"I don't care *what* he said, Sylvia, damn! You're supposed to be the *adult*. So, what, just because he hurt your feelings you have to hurt his, too? What are you, ten??"

Sucking her teeth, Sylvia waved him off. "Get out of here, Bryce!"

"So you're not gonna tell me what all this is about?"

"No! Let Mr. Perfect out there tell you."

"Wow," Bryce said, looking at her as if he was seeing her for the first time. "I can't believe you're acting this childish."

Sylvia knew she was being childish and unreasonable, but it was almost like she couldn't stop herself. "Yeah, okay. I'll be that, then."

Shaking his head, Bryce opened the door. "How 'bout you just call your son when you're ready to apologize to him."

"Apologize to *him*?? How 'bout he apologize to *me*?? How come I'm the one that has to apologize for everything all the damn time? I ain't the only one that does stuff wrong!"

Bryce peered at her for a moment before stepping outside. "You need help," he declared before closing the door behind him.

"Kiss my ass, Bryce!" Sylvia yelled as he closed the door. "*All* y'all can kiss my ass!" She hurried to her room and slammed the door behind her, locking it. Then she turned her radio on full blast, not even caring that she didn't like the Lil' Wayne song that was playing. She just wanted to drown everything out.

During this whole exchange, Candy just sat in her door-less room, listening. Sylvia hadn't even paid her any attention, and given how she was acting, she probably wouldn't. She'd had an attitude ever since they had left her Grandma Sandra's house. Candy had been glad she finally got to tell her mother the things she had been thinking over the years, but she hadn't expected Sylvia to react like this, especially towards Valencio. He was her favorite and if she was treating *him* like she was, there was no telling how she'd treat Candy, whenever she finally acknowledged she was there.

Candy decided she didn't want to stick around to find out. She quickly stuffed some clothes and things into a bag and eased out of her bedroom, even though she knew Sylvia wouldn't be able to hear her over that loud music. This was one time she was glad Sylvia had taken her phone because she wouldn't be able to call or reach her wherever she decided to go. Candy wasn't even sure *where* she was going, but she figured just about anywhere was better than being there with Sylvia and her attitude.

So while Sylvia sulked in her room, Candy snuck out.

Chapter 19

· · · ·

ALMOST A FULL DAY HAD passed since Candy had snuck out of the house. Sylvia hadn't even realized she was gone until late the next morning. She had called in to work, lying and claiming to be sick, and when she finally emerged from her room to use the bathroom at a little before noon, she realized Candy wasn't in her room or anywhere else in the apartment. It was then that she realized she hadn't paid her daughter any attention since they had gotten home from Sandra's the night before, and Candy had probably taken advantage of Sylvia's mood to sneak out. Instead of being worried or angry, Sylvia was relieved.

"Whatever," she muttered to herself, going to fix herself some eggs and bacon. "Let her stay gone for a while. She didn't wanna be here, anyway."

Actually feeling lighter, Sylvia went on about her day, enjoying being at home by herself with nothing to do. It was nice not having to be bothered and hear folks complaining all the time. She really did love her kids, but for the time being, she just pretended she didn't have any. Valencio was with his favorite parent, and Candy was probably at one of her little friends' houses. They were fine. So she decided to enjoy herself.

Feeling frisky, she decided to give Percy a call. She hoped he was still willing to be her dial-a-dick and didn't trip about the fact that she hadn't called him in a while.

"Wow, I didn't think I was gonna hear from you again," Percy said when he answered the phone.

"Well, you were wrong," Sylvia said with a smile. "You working? Can you come see a sista?"

"Nah, I'm not working today but me and my boy were about to go shoot some ball."

"Bring him, too," Sylvia offered before she could stop herself. But she didn't try to take it back.

"For real?"

"Yeah. Hurry up."

"Bet. We'll be there in about thirty."

Sylvia hung up the phone excitedly, rushing to the bathroom to take a shower and do a quick shave on her legs. She hadn't been with two men at once in years, but she was excited to be able to do it now. She hadn't gotten any since that last time with Deuce, after which he told her he had blabbed to Dub about them still sleeping together.

Speaking of Dub, she noticed he called her a couple times while she was in the shower. When she was quickly rubbing lotion on her body, he called again. She just peered at her phone and then ignored the call, something she had never done before with him. She still didn't want to be bothered with Dub, because being bothered with Dub meant being bothered with his girlfriend, Jelissa. And Sylvia had enough issues of her own.

When Percy and his friend knocked on the door, Sylvia eagerly started for the living room. When she passed by the mirror in her bedroom, she grinned devilishly and shimmied out of the rarely-used black nighty she was wearing. Then she removed the ponytail holder from her braids and shook them out, letting them fall around her face. She felt three times sexier.

Noticing she had a couple of voicemails from Dub, she turned off her phone so she wouldn't be interrupted and sauntered confidently and sexily towards the door.

"I hope this friend of his is cute," she muttered to herself.

When she opened the door wearing nothing but her ankle bracelet, both Percy and his friend's jaws fell to the floor.

"You weren't playin', huh?" Percy asked, a slow smile spreading across his face.

"Hell no," Sylvia responded, internally thrilled that the man standing next to him eying her up and down was good-looking. He looked better than Percy did, to her. She knew she was going to enjoy herself this afternoon. "What's your name?" she asked him.

"Oh, I'm Davis," the guy replied, licking his lips.

"Fine-ass Davis," Sylvia said flirtatiously, grabbing them both by the arm and pulling them into the apartment. "I'm gonna have some fun with y'all."

Once the door closed behind them, nothing else outside of it mattered for the rest of the day.

• • • •

WHILE SYLVIA WAS ENJOYING Candy being gone, Candy was equally enjoying being gone, herself. She was staying with her friend Kita, whose mother was only sixteen years older than they were and let them pretty much do whatever they wanted. Candy missed being able to have that kind of freedom.

In no time, Candy was back to her old ways of skipping school, hanging with boys, partying and drinking. She loved it. She just stopped caring about any of the progress she had made in the past few months and just wanted to enjoy being a teenager again. And it wasn't like her family was worried about her, anyway. Her mother was more worried about her brother, her brother was with his dad, and her own dad had never cared what she did one way or the other.

One night, while Kita's mother was right downstairs, Kita and Candy decided to invite some boys over. Kita invited Gerald, who was a boy in her class that she liked, and Candy invited Mac, eager to get another chance with him. She was glad he was even still talking to her after what happened when Sylvia caught them having sex in her room and threw him naked out onto the street.

Mac brought some beers in his backpack and the four of them sat in Kita's room, drinking and talking. While Kita and Gerald were on the bed, Candy and Mac lounged on the carpeted floor.

"I'm glad you came," Candy said to him, playing with her beer bottle.

"Yeah, well, it's only 'cause you're over here. I damn sure ain't going back to your house."

"I'm sorry about that."

"Yeah. You apologized already."

"You still mad at me?"

"I wasn't mad at you. It's your moms that's crazy."

"Yeah, she be trippin'," Candy agreed, not wanting to talk about her. She scooted a little closer to him and eyed him flirtatiously. "You know, we never got to finish what we were doing when she barged in on us like she did."

Mac looked at her. "Word? You wanna get down?"

"Most definitely."

Mac took one last swig of his beer before setting it down and pulling Candy onto his lap. They began to kiss deeply and sloppily, and within moments they were taking each other's clothes off.

"Turn the light off," Mac ordered between kisses.

Candy grunted, not wanting to stop what they were doing even for the few seconds it would take to do what he asked. She hurriedly got up to flick off the light switch, momentarily glancing at Kita and Gerald, who were already on the bed kissing and grinding. Candy felt herself getting turned on just watching them, and she couldn't wait for Mac to get back inside of her. She killed the lights before shimmying out of her shorts and diving back onto the floor with Mac, who had already slipped on a condom. He rolled her onto her back and quickly entered her, and Candy moaned in ecstasy. She didn't know how in the world some girls managed to save themselves when sex felt this good.

The two couples continued to enjoy each other for the rest of the night. Candy really felt like she was in heaven and figured if this was how things were going to be, she didn't ever need to go back home.

• • • •

MEANWHILE, SYLVIA ROLLED her hips against Davis', loving how he felt on top of her. Since the time he had come over with Percy, she made sure to stay in contact with him and wasted no time inviting him back over for a one-on-one session. She slid her hands through is curly hair as she matched him stroke for stroke, hissing instructions at him.

"Kiss me," she ordered, licking her lips before he obliged her. They kissed deeply and hungrily, and Sylvia tightened her legs around him as she braced herself for her second orgasm. Just when it ripped through her body, she heard a knock at the front door.

"Who is that?" Davis panted, still pumping in to her.

"Ignore it," Sylvia dismissed, rolling on top of him. Sylvia was in one of her insatiable moods and planned to put it on Davis until he needed assistance to even walk out to his car. But when the knocking persisted, she grunted in frustration. "Dammit!"

"Go ahead and answer it; I'm not going anywhere," Davis assured her, patting her bare behind.

"You better not," Sylvia said, leaning down to peck his lips before climbing off him and throwing her bathrobe around her naked and slightly sweaty body. She hurried to the front door and peered through the peephole, groaning when she saw who it was. She yanked open the door.

"I know you didn't bring your ass over here," she said to him.

Deuce eyed her, knowing she was naked under her robe but for once, not planning on trying to do anything about it. He had come there for one specific reason.

"Hey," he greeted, choosing to ignore her comment. "Is Candy here?"

"Damn, can't you call first?" Sylvia asked angrily, tightening the belt on her robe.

"I tried to call. You never answered."

Sylvia remembered her phone had been turned off for the past couple days. She hadn't wanted to be bothered while she was entertaining. "So you just show up anyway?"

"Look, I'm not trying to argue with you; I just wanted to see my daughter. Can I come in?" Deuce asked as politely as he could.

Looking at him skeptically, Sylvia crossed her arms over her chest. "No, you *can't* come in."

"Why not?"

"Because I have company and you're interrupting us. And Candy ain't here, anyway."

"Where is she?"

"I don't know."

Reminding himself that he was in no position to berate Sylvia when it came to parenting, Deuce tried to keep his patience in check. "What you mean, you don't know?"

"Exactly what I said. Now, is there anything else?"

"Do you not care where she is?"

"Look, you really don't have any business coming over here out of the blue questioning me. Candy barely even knows who you are. So you can just go on back to whatever you've been doing for the past sixteen years," Sylvia spat, starting to close the door in his face.

Deuce stopped the door from closing with his hand. "Sylvia, can you just give me a minute, please?"

"I don't have a minute, Deuce. I told you, I have company."

"Man, forget this," Deuce muttered, starting to walk off. Then he remembered the talk he had with Dub and stopped in his tracks, telling himself not to give up so easily. He turned back to Sylvia, who was looking at him as if she expected him to try something. Her stance was defensive. It was one time he wished he hadn't treated her so rudely over the years; now that he was actually being sincere and trying to come at her honestly and directly, she wasn't trying to hear it.

"You can keep on walking," she said to him.

"Sylvia," Deuce began, looking at her earnestly, "I really want to have a better relationship with my daughter, or at least try to. I know I've wasted a lot of time and that's my own fault, but can you at least work with me since I'm trying now? This isn't about you and me."

"There *ain't* no you and me. You've always made that perfectly clear ever since you tricked me and knocked me up."

Deuce sighed. "You know what I mean."

"I just find it a little hard to believe that out of the clear blue sky, you decide you want to try to be Cliff Huxtable or something after acting like she didn't exist ever since she came up outta my coochie. You act like I'm bothering you whenever I dare try to tell you anything about her or what she's doing or what she needs, and you damn sure haven't given me any money for her. That girl can count on her hands the number of times she's seen you; if it wasn't for Dub she probably wouldn't even remember what the hell you look like."

"I'm sayin', though-"

"No you ain't sayin' nothing 'cause I don't have no more time for this," Sylvia cut him off, putting her hand on the door again. "I've got something simmerin' in my room waiting for me to stir it back up."

She closed the door in his face and went back to Davis in her bedroom, removing her robe before she even made it down the hall.

• • • •

FOR THE FIRST TIME, Deuce was actually worried about Candy.

He knew he couldn't deny that he was a terrible father; not just to Candy but to all of his kids. So he really couldn't blame Sylvia for being skeptical of him. But it bothered him that she didn't know where Candy was. She could've just been saying that, but any other time he would ask where Candy was (as few and far between as that was), and she wasn't home, Sylvia might have said that it wasn't any of his business or that he didn't need to worry about it, but she never said she didn't know. The fact that she sincerely didn't know, and didn't seem to care, angered him but worried him more. Where the hell was his daughter?

Deuce never admitted out loud to anyone, even to his brother Dub, just how much their father abandoning them affected him. He grew up thinking he wasn't good enough for his own father to even see, let alone stick around for. His dad had left before he and Dub were even born; for all he knew, he had never even laid eyes on them. Their mother Traci never really talked about him and just focused on raising them herself. And while he loved his mother and appreciated her more than he could say, he hated not having a dad growing up. And over the years, his resentment grew and grew.

When he fooled Sylvia that night at Moni's party when they were teenagers and had sex with her in that bathroom, he knew there was a possibility he would impregnate her. He hadn't worn a condom, and he always wore condoms. That night had been the first night he hadn't. And when she did end up pregnant, he thought about doing the right thing unlike his father had. But he heard himself telling her that he wouldn't have anything to do with the baby other than acknowledge it was his. And once he said that, he just rolled with it. It was easier to just stay out of the picture completely than try to do something for which he had no example of, which was be a father to a child. And over the years he just kept making babies, impregnating women and then disappearing, because it was all he knew. *That* was the example he had. Even though in the very back of his mind he knew that it was wrong, he just never put forth the effort to learn any other way.

Despite what it seemed, Deuce wasn't heartless. He cared about his kids, even though he didn't act like he did. He wouldn't want anything to happen to any of them. Candy was his oldest and he often toyed with the idea of trying to broach some kind of relationship with her, but truth be told, he was afraid of her rebuffing him. He didn't know how it would feel to hear a child of his tell him they wanted nothing to do with him. Deuce always wondered what he would say to his own father after all these years if he were to ever meet him; would he even *want* a relationship with him or would he want to beat him down for never being there? He honestly didn't know, and if he felt like that about *his* dad, he imagined his kids would feel like that about him. And knowing himself, he might try to act like he wouldn't care, but he knew he would.

Before he knew it, he found himself steering his car into a nearby Kroger parking lot and pulling out his cell phone, hesitating slightly before dialing.

"Hello?" a woman answered a few moments later.

"Hey, Brenda."

There was a pause. "Deuce?"

"Yeah, I know you're probably wondering what I'm calling you for."

"Yeah..."

"Um...would it be okay if I came by to see Watson?" he asked, referring to his son.

He prepared himself to hear 'no' or to get cursed out, but to his surprise (and relief), she agreed. "I guess that'd be okay. I'm just about to go wake him up so he can eat."

"Okay, cool."

"You dying or something?"

"What?"

"You never ask to come see him so I figure maybe you only had weeks to live or something like that."

Deuce couldn't help but chuckle. "Ain't nothin' wrong with me; just wanted to see my son."

"Oh." He knew he was throwing her for a loop; they hadn't even spoken in months. "Okay."

"Thanks." He hung up the phone and glanced at his watch before pulling out of the parking lot and heading towards Decatur where Brenda lived. Watson was just three years old and his youngest child so he figured he would start with him first and work his way up. A three-year-old wouldn't have any resentment towards him, even though he wouldn't know who he was at first. Deuce was nervous but also anxious. What would he even say? He'd never played with any babies before; how would he entertain him? Deuce figured he'd just cross that bridge when he got to it.

Despite his growing excitement about his decision to go see his other kids, Deuce was still concerned about his oldest. Candy seemed to like to be in the streets a lot, and he knew how the streets could be. And if she was anything like Sylvia was at her age, there was no telling how she would end up.

Chapter 20

• • • •

SYLVIA FELT LIKE SHE was on vacation. It had been a little over a week since Candy had left and she was still enjoying having the apartment all to herself. And she had been taking full advantage of her freedom.

She went to work, but the rest of the time she was either going out, hanging out with Delta, or having men over to satisfy her seemingly endless sexual urges. Her kids being gone really seemed to increase her already high libido. She hadn't had this much fun since she was a teenager.

Of course she wondered where Candy was, but seeing as how nobody had called or showed up at her door with any bad news about her, she figured she was fine. Candy had a lot of friends and Sylvia had no doubt she was with one of them. Since she had taken Candy's phone, she couldn't call or track where she was, so she just chose to think positively that her daughter was all right.

One night, Delta came over after Sylvia got off work, bringing a couple of fried fish dinners and a gallon of sweet tea. They devoured them in front of the TV as they watched the latest episode of *Criminal Minds.*

"You gon' eat those hushpuppies?" Sylvia asked her, reaching for one.

"Yes, I am," Delta replied, moving her Styrofoam container a little ways away and lightly slapping Sylvia's hand. "I got you extra ones 'cause I know how much you love 'em. You don't need any of mine."

"They're so good, though!"

"I know they are. I'm still not sharing, though."

"Aww."

"Next time I'll get you a whole plate of 'em. How about that?"

"I guess that'll work," Sylvia said, playfully bumping her.

"Can you bring the sweet tea out of the refrigerator?"

"Girl, please, you are not a guest here. Go get it yourself."

Delta sucked her teeth and stood up from the couch, starting for the kitchen. When she saw Sylvia eyeing her hushpuppies, she quickly reached down and grabbed her plate, taking it with her.

"You ain't right," Sylvia muttered, taking a bite of the perfectly-fried piece of whiting fish.

"You want some tea?" Delta asked from the kitchen, setting her plate on the counter and reaching up into the cabinet to get some cups.

"Yeah."

Delta poured the drinks and then re-joined Sylvia on the couch. They continued to eat and enjoy the show until Delta asked the question Sylvia knew was coming sooner or later.

"Where are the kids?"

Sylvia took her time chewing the food that was in her mouth, and then took a long swallow of tea before answering with a flat-out lie. "They're at my mama's."

"Oh yeah? She wanted to spend some time with her grandbabies, huh?"

"Yep."

Sylvia hadn't planned to lie, but she didn't want to have her evening ruined by having to endure the barrage of questions and then lectures about the truth. Valencio was fine, of course; he was with Bryce. But Sylvia knew Delta would flip if she told her that she didn't know where Candy was, and that she really hadn't tried to find out. Sylvia had been behaving like she didn't have any kids, and she didn't want to think about what that said about her as a mother and as a person, especially since she was enjoying herself more than she was missing them.

So she figured that for the time being, Delta didn't need to know what the real deal was. She was just fine thinking the kids were with Sandra. Sylvia just wanted to eat her fried food, watch her show, hang out with her girl, and then get ready for her midnight booty call with Percy.

• • • •

CANDY WASN'T MISSING Sylvia any more than Sylvia was missing her.

She was still at Kita's and having the time of her life. She really felt like an adult, getting to do pretty much as she pleased. Kita's mother, Janine, was a lot like Sylvia in her parenting style but for some reason, Candy thought Janine was cooler than her mother was. Sylvia often seemed like she was trying too hard; for Janine, it seemed more natural. Candy looked at her more like a big sister than her friend's mother.

The only thing that Janine was adamant about was them going to school, so Candy did do that after the first couple of days. She hated it, but truth be told, she didn't want to have to repeat her freshman year. She had really gotten her grades up recently and she didn't want to fall back into the hole she was in again, especially this close to the end of the school year. So after she and Kita would get home and finish their homework, it was back to the fun stuff.

One night, she and Kita were in Kita's room, drinking Janine's wine coolers and playing cards with Chris Brown's latest CD playing in the background.

"Did you see Mac talking to Shauna today?" Kita asked.

Candy glanced up at her, but turned her attention back to the cards in her hand. "No."

"China told me she said they were going together now."

"Shauna's always telling stories. Remember how she tried to say that Usher walked up to her in the mall and asked her to go on tour with him as a dancer but she turned him down 'cause she wanted to pass Chemistry first? She can't even lie good."

"I don't know, though...I *have* been seeing them in the halls together a lot lately."

Candy lightly shrugged her shoulder. "Oh, well. That's their business."

Kita eyed her skeptically. "You tryin' to say you don't care?"

"I don't."

"Quit frontin'. You know you like Mac."

"I like him all right. I most definitely like what's between his legs."

They both giggled and slapped five. Candy didn't want to admit that she was bothered to hear about Mac with another girl. She wanted him to be *her* man, but she didn't have the confidence to tell him that. She had hoped that her constant flirting, always making herself available, and willingness to give it up to him whenever he wanted would be enough. But so far, it hadn't; Mac hadn't said anything to her about them being exclusive, or even hinted at it. And Candy didn't want to risk getting shot down, so she didn't want to ask him.

"But yeah, Shauna's probably full of it," Kita commented after a few moments. She took a swig of her drink. "Mac probably isn't her man any more than Michael Jackson is mine. And Michael Jackson dead."

Candy just shook her head, chuckling and taking a swig of her own drink.

Just then Kita's cell phone rang and she picked it up from where it was sitting next to her on the bed. After she answered, she looked at Candy and smiled. "Well, speak of the devil."

Candy looked at her, smiling. "Mac?" she mouthed.

Kita nodded. After a few "yeahs" and "uh-huhs" and "okays", she hung up the phone. "We're about to have some company."

"For real?" Candy excitedly replied.

"Yep. Mac and some of his boys will be here in about an hour, he said."

Squealing, Candy hopped off the bed and hurried to the corner of the room where her duffel bag was. "I'm about to go take a shower real quick. Can I use some of your Victoria's Secret body wash?"

"Go ahead, girl," Kita replied, chuckling slightly, swinging her smooth dark legs over the side of the bed.

The two friends proceeded to get ready for their guests, both excited but Candy's excitement far exceeded Kita's. Candy couldn't wait to see Mac again. She hated that she didn't have her phone so they could keep in touch like they used to, but it thrilled her that he kept coming back to where she was. It made her think he really wanted to be with her, 'cause he certainly could have been going anywhere else if he wanted to.

Once Mac and his friends arrived, they all sat around listening to music, drinking, talking and laughing. The movie *In Too Deep* was playing on Kita's television, but they were only half watching it. Mac had brought three friends with him so Candy and Kita were outnumbered by two, not that they minded at all. All the boys were cute and they were just glad they were there.

After a while, somebody suggested a game of Truth or Dare. Candy hadn't played the game in a while, and she was anxious to see what she would be asked to reveal or dared to do. But she already knew she would be down for just about anything, especially if Mac was the one to ask her to do it.

When her turn came around, she sat up straight in her seat on the floor, waiting to see what Mac's friend Malone would ask of her.

"Truth or dare?" Malone asked her.

Candy pondered for a second. "Truth."

Malone looked slightly disappointed, as if he already had a dare ready for her, but still asked, "On a scale of one to ten, how would you rate your head game?"

Candy couldn't help but smirk. She had gotten rave reviews on her fellatio ability, even though she had only been doing it a short time. She thought it would be nasty but actually found herself enjoying it, especially since it tended to leave boys putty in her hands for a while afterwards. "I'd say an eight. But give me a few months and I'll bust that ten wide open."

The boys hooted at her answer, and Mac winked at her, having personally experienced her skills. Candy didn't only watch porn for pleasure; she watched it to learn. She studied that harder than she studied for anything at school.

Now that it was Candy's turn to choose someone, she turned to her friend, Kita. "Truth or dare, girl," she said.

"Dare," Kita said confidently.

Candy grinned at the answer. "I dare you to go to whoever you think is the cutest in here and take their shirt off."

With a smirk, Kita crawled over to Mac's friend Ray and grabbed his t-shirt, pulling it over his head. She allowed her hands to roam over his chest a couple of times, which was far muscular than Candy had noticed. She didn't blame her friend for choosing him, even though she still would have chosen Mac if she had been given such a dare.

About ten more minutes passed until it became Mac's turn again. Candy felt her heart rate quicken when he looked at her.

"Truth or dare?" he asked.

"I'll do a dare," Candy replied, having chosen truth the last two times she was asked.

"Good," Mac said, a mischievous grin easing onto his face.

Candy wondered if it was too late to change her answer, even though she knew it was. She just hoped he wouldn't try to have her doing anything too crazy.

"I dare you to kiss Kita."

Automatically filling with dread, Candy glanced at her friend, then back at Mac. Part of her wished he would say he was joking, but she knew he wasn't. Kissing a girl was on the short list of things Candy never wanted to try at least once. It was something she saw plenty of times but never got into. She was interested in boys and boys only. But she knew if she refused Mac's dare, she would be clowned. And she didn't want to risk Mac not wanting to hang with her anymore because he considered her a lame for not doing as he dared. So she decided to just do it and get it over with; he could've dared her to do more to Kita than just a kiss, so she figured she should be grateful for that.

She shrugged a shoulder, feigning nonchalance. "Yeah, okay."

"And I ain't talking 'bout no little peck, either," Mac added, his hazel eyes challenging her. "I mean a *real* kiss."

"Fine," Candy said, even though she had hoped she would've been able to get away with just a quick peck.

She looked at Kita, who just looked at her before lightly shrugging her own shoulder. Candy didn't know if this was something Kita had done before or not, since she didn't protest.

At least she's cute, Candy rationalized to herself.

All the boys looked on eagerly as Candy and Kita crawled towards each other in the middle of the circle they were all sitting in. Kita was in just a bra and shorts thanks to a previous dare, and Candy couldn't help eying her breasts. They were bigger than hers. Candy had always hoped that hers would grow some more as she got older. That was one thing about Sylvia that Candy envied; that she had big breasts and a big butt.

Closing her eyes, Candy kissed a girl for the first time. It wasn't as bad as she thought; Kita's lips were soft and moist. The kiss deepened immediately and Candy heard urging to keep going from the boys watching them. She felt Kita's hands ease onto her waist as their tongues played against each other.

She could hear Mac whispering how sexy they looked and Candy felt herself becoming aroused; more due to the fact that they were being watched than what they were actually doing. They were putting on a show for the boys, and Candy knew that. So she figured since this was just going to be a one-time thing (she hoped), that she would be all in. If they wanted a show, she was going to give them one.

Reaching around and unhooking Kita's bra, she squeezed her friend's soft breasts in her hands before pushing her down onto her back and climbing on top of her.

"Oh shit!" the boys exclaimed excitedly.

"That's what I'm talkin' about!" Mac cheered.

Her adrenaline fueled, Candy proceeded to fool around with Kita for the next few minutes, hoping this would be enough to prove to Mac that she was down for whatever, and make him want her like she wanted him.

• • • •

MEANWHILE, SYLVIA TOLD Delta about Deuce's sudden interest in Candy's life.

"Girl, he came over here out of the blue asking where she was, like he cared," she recalled, leaning back onto the couch. She placed a hand on her full stomach. "I told him he could go somewhere with all that."

"Why? I thought it would be a good thing that he wants to see his daughter finally."

"He hasn't *been* wanting to see her. So I don't know why he's trying to come around now."

"That's not the point, Sylvia. Maybe he's starting to see the light now; there's no excuse for him being absent all these years but sometimes it just takes longer for some people to grow up."

Sylvia wondered if Delta was also referring to her when she said that. "Yeah, well. Still."

"Still, what?"

"He only comes over here acting like he cares when he's good and drunk."

"Was he drunk when he came this last time?"

"No," Sylvia admitted.

"Okay, then maybe it's different. He could be really serious this time. Better late than never, right?"

"It's too late for him to be trying to do all that now. Candy will be sixteen in a couple of months."

"So?"

"So she's practically grown. She's done just fine without him up until now."

"First of all, sixteen is nowhere near grown. And second, and I'm just gonna keep it real like I always do, Candy has not done *just fine*. I think even you would agree that having a positive male influence coming up would have made a difference in how she behaves now."

"Please. Deuce would not have been no *positive* influence."

"You don't know. Maybe if he had at least shown he gave a damn about her, she wouldn't be like she is. He could have ended up being like his brother. Speaking of Dub, how is he? Have you talked to him lately?"

The question made Sylvia remember that she *hadn't* talked to Dub lately; the last few times he had called, she ignored it. She hadn't even thought to return the calls until now. She wondered what it was he wanted.

"Nah, not in a little while," she answered, looking down at her bare wiggling feet.

"I'm surprised. I thought y'all kept in touch more than that."

"Yeah, well...there's just been a lot going on, is all. Plus, he has that girlfriend and I know she doesn't like me all that much."

"Why would she not like you? What did you do? Try to kiss Dub or something and she found out about it?"

"I didn't do anything. She just doesn't like that Dub helps me out so much; thinks I depend on him more than I need to."

"Really? But you don't even ask for much of anything from him, do you? He just offers it."

"I know. But that doesn't matter to her."

"Damn. What does Dub have to say about that, though?"

Sylvia shrugged, even though she knew she hadn't even talked to him about Jelissa confronting her. "I've got other stuff to worry about besides that. She's the one with the problem."

"Well," Delta said, closing her empty food container, "I guess she's not going anywhere any time soon. Dub must really love her."

"I guess."

"You still want him, though, don't you?"

"Yeah," Sylvia answered honestly. "But I know by now it's probably not going to happen. The closest thing I can get to him is Deuce."

"Oh gosh," Delta scoffed, looking at her. "Please tell me you're not still messing around with him like that."

"Hell, why not? I can't stand his ass but he damn sure knows how to scratch the itch. But I doubt I'll go there with him anymore now, though."

"'Cause of this stuff with Candy?"

Sylvia didn't want to admit it was because she thought Deuce had told Dub about them sleeping together; the fact that he was such a lousy father apparently hadn't been reason enough not to sleep with him all these years. "I just don't think it's worth it anymore, that's all. He becomes twice the asshole afterwards."

"Good."

"I've got other folks I can call when I need some attention," Sylvia said, glancing at her watch. "Matter of fact, one will be coming over here in about three hours."

"Girl, you're a mess," Delta chuckled, shaking her head.

You have no idea, Sylvia thought to herself.

• • • •

AT KITA'S, CANDY WAS hoping what she had just done with Kita wouldn't come back to bite her in some way. It was a little hard for her to look Kita in the eyes for a while afterwards; she wondered if things would be weird between them now, even though Kita seemed to be unaffected by it. Candy already knew it would probably be around school by Monday, but she couldn't worry about it. People talked about her a lot already, anyway. Mac was pleased with her, and for now that was all she cared about.

Having grown tired of Truth or Dare after a few more rounds, Kita asked her mom Janine to order them a couple of pizzas, and once they arrived, they all sat around eating and tripping out. Candy was thankful they weren't dwelling on what she and Kita had done and were talking about other things. She figured that probably wasn't the first time they had seen two girls make out. All she was thinking about was when she was going to get some alone time with Mac again.

After a while, though, things took yet another turn.

"Look what I got, y'all," Ray said, reaching into the pocket of his cargo shorts. He pulled out a baggie full of white powder and held it up with a smile.

Candy's eyes widened. She might have never used it, but she knew what that was.

"You do drugs??" Kita asked.

"I'm eighteen; I've done some of everything," Ray said smugly. "I only do this every once in a while, though; they be doing those random drug tests at the job and I need my money."

"What, to buy more drugs with?" Mac asked.

"Man...y'all want some or not?" Ray asked frustratingly, seeming to grow tired of the questions already.

Candy definitely didn't. She was willing to do a lot of things, but cocaine wasn't one of them. Weed was about as far as she was willing to go when it came to drugs, and she didn't really even like that all that much.

She suddenly remembered something Sylvia had told her a year or so earlier:

"I know you're probably out there doing only Lord knows what, but make sure that whatever you're doing, you're doing because *you* want to do it; don't let it be 'cause of somebody else," Sylvia had said. "'Cause if something goes down because of it, nine times out of ten those folks that had you doing it won't be anywhere around."

Candy had just sat there, only half-listening at the time.

"And if you're ever in a situation that doesn't feel right to you, get the hell out. Learn to trust your gut," Sylvia had continued. "That's one time you don't worry about what folks are gon' say about it. Danger doesn't discriminate."

Candy knew she had already blown the first part of that advice by fooling around with Kita, but the second part replayed in her head over and over. *Learn to trust your gut*. Sylvia's advice about most things usually went in one ear and right out the other, but she was glad that this didn't. 'Cause her gut was telling her that she needed to do exactly as her mother had said; get the hell out.

Her feeling was confirmed when a couple of the boys opted to try some of the cocaine. Kita looked like she was actually considering it, and Mac was eyeing Candy as if he expected her to try it, too.

Candy didn't know if Mac did coke or not, but she didn't care if he proposed to her, she wasn't about to do any. She had seen enough people on the street strung out on that stuff to never want to touch it. She liked him, but she didn't like the boy *that* much.

The teenagers started to get loud and rowdy, with a couple of them trying the cocaine, and Candy felt herself getting nervous. She liked to have fun, but this was quickly becoming not her scene.

"Try some, Candy," Mac ordered, holding the bag out to her with a daring eye.

Candy was sure Mac was aware that she was willing to do just about anything he asked because of her crush on him, but even though she didn't have the nerve to tell him so, he could kiss her ass on this one. And this was about to be the first time in a long time that she took her mother's advice.

Learn to trust your gut. Get the hell out.

"I'll be back," Candy said, standing.

"Where you going?" Mac asked, quickly standing with her and grabbing her arm, as if he thought she was about to go rat them out.

She instinctively yanked her arm away and noticed Mac's mild look of surprise at the action. "I think I feel my period coming. You wanna check for blood?"

He held his hands up and stepped back, and Candy hurriedly left the room and headed down the hall for the bathroom, locking herself inside. She lowered the toilet lid and sat down on top of it, nervously biting her nails as she wondered what she was going to do next. It crossed her mind to go downstairs and tell Janine what was going on, but she didn't want to be labeled a snitch. Plus, Janine might send her back home and despite the situation, Candy wasn't ready to go back home yet. But she knew she could only stay in the bathroom so long.

For the first time, Candy really felt she was in over her head.

• • • •

CHAPTER 21

. . . .

"SO YOU WENT AND TALKED to Candy, huh?" Dub asked his twin, checking the time on his phone. He was supposed to meet Jelissa in a couple of hours.

"Tried to," Deuce replied, scratching his head then leaning back on the couch. "But Sylvia wouldn't even let me in the damn door."

"She wouldn't? Why not?"

"'Cause she said I hadn't been worried about Candy all these years so I didn't need to worry about her now, basically. Plus, she had company."

"One of her homegirls or something?"

"Nah, man. She was fuckin' somebody. I interrupted them."

"Oh," Dub didn't know why he was so jarred hearing that. "Well...maybe if she hadn't been doing that she would have talked to you. Just call before you go next time."

"I did call. But it wouldn't make no difference, anyway. She's pissed at me whether she's got somebody there with her or not."

"Why you say that?"

"You know why. Years of treating her like shit and not wanting to hear anything about what Candy needed. But it don't even matter; I'm done with it."

Dub looked at him. "What do you mean, you're done with it?"

"Exactly what I said. I'll just stay in my lane. She ain't tryin' to hear me, anyway."

"Deuce, come on," Dub said. "I thought you finally wanted to try to get to know your daughter."

"Yeah, I did. But Sylvia shut me down."

"What did you expect? You haven't done a damn thing for Candy other than admit that it was your sperm that made her. And like you said, you aren't nice to Sylvia at all; you never have been."

"I have my moments," Deuce mused, thinking of the times he and Sylvia slept together.

"Yeah, well, those moments are few and far between, so you shouldn't really be surprised that Sylvia is skeptical of you right now. You're just gonna have to prove to her that you're for real."

"And how am I supposed to do that? Her mind is made up."

"Then *change* her mind, Deuce. Show her that you mean business by not giving up. Keep trying. 'Cause if you don't, it'll be like all the other sporadic times you got drunk and acted like you gave a damn then went back to your old self the next day."

"And you really think it's gonna be that easy?"

"I didn't say it's gonna be easy. But it'll be worth it."

Deuce looked thoughtful as he pondered his brother's words. He respected Dub's opinion more than he did probably anybody else's.

"I am glad you finally went to go see your other kids, though," Dub praised, slapping his brother's knee. "I hope it's not gonna just be a one-time thing."

"Yeah, well, you know some of the baby mamas are tripping about child support now."

"Well, that's what you're supposed to do, Deuce. You helped make 'em, you can at least help support 'em."

Deuce just grunted.

"But I really do hope you keep this up," Dub continued. "And you need to go try to see Candy and talk to Sylvia again."

"Maybe you can talk to her first and get her to agree to listen," Deuce suggested. "You know she'll do whatever just 'cause you want her to."

"I don't know about all that," Dub mused, playing with his phone. "But I *do* need to talk to her and see what's up with her; she hasn't returned my calls lately. Maybe I need to go by there and make sure she and the kids are good."

"Make sure you call first," Deuce said, only half-kidding. "Or else she'll leave you on the doorstep while she goes back to get her freak-on."

• • • •

THE NEXT DAY, DUB GAVE Sylvia a call to see if it would be all right for him to come by and see her for a little bit, but once again, she didn't answer his call. Frowning, he ended the call and dropped the phone into his lap, his hand cupping his chin thoughtfully. What was going on? Sylvia never ignored this many of his calls, or took this long to call him back. She usually stopped what she was doing to take his call, even when she was at work. But lately it seemed like she was avoiding him, and he had no idea why. She had been acting strangely ever since he dropped in on her at her job a few weeks back, and they really hadn't spoken since then. He didn't think he had done anything that might have upset her. Why was she avoiding him?

Dub usually was not a person to drop in at someone's house unannounced, but due to the circumstances he was about to make an exception this time. Something was going on and it concerned him. He could admit that he had probably gotten a little spoiled with Sylvia always making herself available over the years for him, but he didn't think he had started taking that for granted. He didn't *expect* that of her; he knew she had things to do and wouldn't always be able to talk when he called. But she hadn't been answering or returning his calls for a while now, and that just wasn't like her.

When he realized no one was home, he glanced at his watch and decided to wait for a while in his car. He really wanted to talk to Sylvia and figured he could wait for her for a little while; he just hoped this wasn't one of those times she was working late. If so, he'd just swing by the store and hope she didn't leave him hanging again.

He was returning some emails on his phone when he happened to glance up and see Candy coming down the street with two boys behind her. Dub frowned; he recognized the boys as two of the ones that were walking behind Candy the day he stopped them on the street and took her home. He had warned them to stay away from his niece, but he also knew that Candy was a more than willing participant, based on what she had told him when he picked her up that day. It wasn't like they were forcing her.

He watched them for a minute through his tinted windows as they all headed towards Sylvia's apartment, with Candy occasionally looking over her shoulder as if expecting Sylvia (or maybe him) to pop up at any second. They didn't even seem to notice his Camaro sitting right in front of the building.

As soon as they entered the apartment and the door closed behind them, Dub got out of his car and hurried towards the door. Something told him it would be unlocked and it was; they were so focused on what they were there to do that they hadn't even thought to lock the door behind them.

The three of them were just starting to take their shirts off when Dub burst through the door. The boys looked startled, then downright terrified once they recognized him.

"Oh, shit!" the taller one whispered, rushing to put his shirt back on.

"Don't try that now," Dub said, grabbing the shirt with one hand once Russell got his head through it and twisting, with the boy ending up flat against Dub's chest with the shirt choking him. It was a move that was lightening quick and straight out of one of those action movies. Even Candy had to admit it was kind of cool, even though she hated that her uncle was busting up her groove again.

The other boy tried to run past them to the door, but Dub stuck a foot out at the last possible second and tripped him, then when Jason was halfway to the floor, Dub kicked him hard with the bottom of his foot, causing him to bounce off the door and land flat on his back. Dub's foot was on his throat before he could even blink.

"What did I tell y'all?" he asked menacingly, still keeping a stranglehold around Russell's neck with one hand. Russell was coughing and trying to pry his hand free, but it was doing no good. Dub's grip was like a vice.

Candy hurriedly slipped her shirt back over her head and rushed over to them, trying to pry his fingers from the shirt he was holding around Russell's neck. "Let him go! You're gonna kill him!" she exclaimed.

Dub ignored her. "I thought I *told* y'all to stay away from my niece," he said to the boys, looking back and forth between them.

Both of the boys were kicking and coughing, trying to free themselves from Dub's constraints. "We're sorry!" they choked.

"You will be."

"Uncle Dub, *I* told them to come over here! Get mad at me but let them go!" Candy pleaded, genuinely afraid for the boys' lives. Both their faces were turning red and Russell was even drooling a little bit.

"Oh, I'll be getting to you in a minute," Dub promised, glaring at her. "Damn teenagers think you know everything..."

"Please let them go! Please!" Candy pleaded, starting to freak out a little bit. She hadn't spent much extended time with her uncle or her father, Deuce, but she had heard enough stories about them over the years to know they weren't to be messed with. She just *knew* when she invited Russell and Jason over that they wouldn't get caught; it was Wednesday and she knew Sylvia always worked the late shift on Wednesdays. And as for her Uncle Dub, what were the odds of him randomly catching them again? Apparently, higher than she thought.

Dub glared at her but let the boys go after a few more moments of suffering. They both coughed and gasped for air, each grabbing their throats in relief.

"Look at me," Dub ordered to both of them.

They turned their eyes to him, fear still marring their brows.

"This will be the *last* time I tell you to stay away from my niece," Dub warned, his voice sending a chill down even Candy's spine. "I get that Candy invited you, but I don't care. She is off limits. And you," he said, pointing to Russell, "How old are you?"

Russell hesitated. "Eighteen."

"So not only are you hardheaded, you're stupid. Candy is *fifteen*. So unless you want me to have your black ass thrown in jail for statutory rape, I suggest you keep your damn distance." He got in Russell's face; Candy noticed Russell flinch and swallow nervously. "Do we understand each other?"

"Yes sir," Russell answered immediately.

"And you?" Dub added, turning to Jason, who had been inching towards the door.

"Oh, you ain't gotta worry 'bout me!" Jason insisted, holding his hands up. "You couldn't *pay* me to mess with her no more!"

"That's what I wanna hear," Dub replied. "Now get your asses out."

The boys ran out of the apartment as if someone was chasing them with a knife. Dub locked the door behind them and turned to his niece, who was standing there nervously playing with the hem of her shirt.

"You're never gonna learn, huh?" Dub asked, quickly walking over to her. She flinched and stepped back, and he paused, realizing she was afraid of him. He looked into her fearful eyes before taking her into his arms and holding her to him. He wished he had spent more time with her over the years; they were family that didn't know each other all that well. He knew it wasn't really his place to discipline her, but he also couldn't *not* say anything about the direction he clearly saw she was heading in.

After a few moments, he released her and motioned for her to sit on the couch. He sat down next to her and took a moment to gather his thoughts before speaking.

"Candy, you and I don't know each other *that* well," he began. "But you're family and I care about you and what happens to you. And I can see that if you keep going in this direction, you're going to end up somewhere you really don't wanna be."

Candy looked at him cautiously. "What you mean?"

"Candy, I've seen a lot of things in my time. My brother and I spent a lot of time out on the streets when we were coming up; not because we had to or didn't have a home to go to or anything else to do, but because we thought it was the cool place to be. We were hung up on having a certain reputation. And we ended up seeing and experiencing a lot of things we shouldn't have. Regardless of what you think about your mother or even your dad, know that they love and care about you. They care what happens to you; I know I do."

"My dad doesn't care about me," Candy muttered, looking down at her hands.

Dub pursed his lips. "I can't defend him not being here for you all these years, Candy, and I'm not gonna try to. He knows that was wrong and he's gonna have to talk to you about that. Just know that him not being here wasn't because he just didn't care. Trust me on that."

Candy looked at him.

"You're trying to grow up too fast and it's going to catch up to you," Dub said, taking her hand in his. He looked sincerely into her eyes. "Have enough pride and confidence in yourself to not give it up to anybody that'll take it. The fact that boys are willing to sex you doesn't mean they like you; they just like what's between your legs and that they can get it whenever they want."

That stung Candy a little bit. "So you're saying none of the boys like me?"

"Well let me ask you this; how many of them have asked you to be their girlfriend?"

Candy's mouth fell open, but nothing came out. The answer was zero.

"How many have you had conversations with about things other than sex? How many *ask* you about anything other than sex? How many actually try to get to know you? How many have respected you enough to turn you down when you offer it up? That's the kind of stuff I'm talking about, Candy; once you establish yourself as 'easy', all boys see you as is *available*. And available girls are just the jump-offs; not the girlfriends. That's it."

Candy never realized until that moment just how much she wanted to be someone's girlfriend. But now that Dub had said it, she realized the subject had never once come up with all the boys she had talked to and been with; all they cared about was sex or sexual things. And Candy had always loved the attention. But maybe all attention wasn't good attention.

"I've been a hardheaded, stubborn teenager before, thinking I knew everything," Dub continued. "But I didn't, and you don't either, baby. You're lucky all the stuff you've been doing hasn't put you in any danger or left you with some disease, or knocked up. Your mother was your age when she got pregnant with you. Now, this is no disrespect to her, but do you want to end up like that?"

Shaking her head, Candy replied, "No. I don't."

"You can prevent that by watching yourself, and I'm not just talking about making sure the boys you get down with wrap it up. Keep your legs closed; I know you think the boys won't like you if you do that, but believe me, it'll be worth it. Those same boys sniffing up behind you 'cause they know they can get it don't care anything about you, Candy; you could die tomorrow and they wouldn't even blink."

"Well, dang," Candy muttered. "Tell me how you really feel."

"I'm just keeping it real with you. And I hope you're hearing me 'cause I would really hate to see something happen to you, Candy. I love you."

Candy looked at her uncle and saw the sincere love and concern in his eyes, and couldn't help but lean over and give him a hug. He quickly wrapped his arms around her, holding her tightly. Candy laid her head on his chest and tried to remember the last man that hugged her; she couldn't do it. Sylvia had never been all that affectionate; Valencio certainly hadn't hugged her...other than Sandra and her Aunt Delta, she didn't get much affection other than boys ramming her between the thighs. It was nice to know that someone cared about her like this; she hadn't realized how much she needed and wanted that until that moment.

The two of them just sat on the couch with Candy holding onto Dub like he would be the last person she would ever get to hug. He leaned onto the back of the couch and she went with him, her arms clasped firmly around his waist and her head glued to his chest. Dub noticed how she clung to him; it was then that he promised himself that he was going to be a bigger presence in Candy's life, regardless of what Deuce did. She needed that; she needed a man to show her how she should be treated. She needed to know a male could care about her as a person and her well-being and not just what she could do for them between the sheets.

Neither of them realized how long they had been sitting there until Sylvia walked through the door. She was genuinely surprised to see the two of them sitting there, and all hugged up. Candy had fallen asleep on Dub's chest, but she was still holding on to him tightly.

"What's going on?" Sylvia asked.

"Hey," Dub said softly, slowly sitting up. Candy's grip on him tightened and Sylvia looked at her curiously.

"Did somebody die or something?" she asked.

Dub chuckled. "No, nothing like that. Candy," he said, shaking her gently. "Candy, wake up, sweetie."

Candy stirred, then rubbed her eyes for a moment before opening them. She looked at Sylvia, then at Dub before leaning into him even more as she looked back at her mother. Dub just rubbed her back reassuringly.

"What are you doing back here?" Sylvia asked her brusquely. It was the first time they had seen each other or spoken since the night Candy had snuck out almost two weeks earlier and there was no indication that she was happy to see her daughter or glad to see she was all right.

"I just came to get some clothes," Candy mumbled, glancing up at Dub. He looked at her pointedly but didn't comment.

"Why are the two of you here together?"

"I've gotta get back to Kita's," Candy said hurriedly, jumping off the couch and rushing back to her room. She knew Dub would probably tell Sylvia the truth about what happened but she didn't want to be there when he did.

"What's going on with you two?" Dub asked, noting the obvious tension between the two of them.

"Nothing for you to worry about," Sylvia muttered, releasing her braids from their ponytail and shaking them.

Dub frowned. "Too late; I'm worried. What's with all the hostility? Towards Candy *and* towards me? You haven't been returning my calls or anything for weeks. Did I do something?"

Sylvia looked at him and could see how sincere he was; she wanted to go to him and give him a hug more than she cared to admit to herself. But she had enough drama going on.

"Dub, look," she began, trying to gather her words, "This really isn't about any problem I have with you. You haven't done anything to me. There's just so much going on right now..."

Just then Candy rushed out of her room and went right past them, a small duffel bag over her shoulder.

"Bye, Uncle Dub," she said as she rushed out the front door. She didn't acknowledge Sylvia and Sylvia didn't acknowledge her.

"Sylvia, what's going on? Where is Candy going?"

"Back to Kita's, apparently."

"You sound like this is new information to you."

Sylvia sighed. "Dub..."

"Sylvia, the reason Candy and I were here was because I caught her and two boys trying to sneak in, wanting to get down," Dub informed her. "I had come over to talk to you and happened to see them while I was sitting out in my car waiting. I caught them and threw the boys out before they had a chance to do anything."

Sylvia just shook her head and gave a sad chuckle. "Can't say I'm surprised. She knows I work late on Wednesdays, usually."

"Things haven't gotten any better between you two?"

"No," Sylvia said, putting it simply. Dub didn't know the half of how bad things had gotten.

"I'm sorry to hear that. Wanna talk about it?"

"Not really," Sylvia replied, going to drop herself tiredly onto the couch. "I don't have to energy to get into all that right now."

Dub joined her on the couch and Sylvia tried to ignore how good he smelled. "I had a talk with her myself before you got here."

"Well, apparently she listened to you more than she listens to me, with how hugged up on you she was," Sylvia replied. "I've never seen her hold on to somebody like that."

"I just told her I care about what happens to her and that I love her, and also the truth about what these boys she keeps trying to get with really think about her. I don't think it ever occurred to her that being the jump-off isn't the way to get to be somebody's girlfriend."

"You're right about that," Sylvia muttered, mindlessly scratching her head. Sylvia had never had a real boyfriend herself, even as an adult. She had men that she 'entertained' from time to time, but none had ever claimed her as their woman. Bryce was the closest she had come to that and she always kept him at arm's length because she had always considered him too straight-laced to be with. But she had probably been wrong about that, too. Bryce was a good man, and she knew it. It wasn't until right then that Sylvia wished she really had someone to call her own and not just people to scratch her sexual itches...Candy probably felt the same way. That was probably why they both acted the way they did, and also why they clashed the way they did. They were just too much alike.

"You okay?" Dub asked with concern.

To Sylvia's surprise, tears started coming to her eyes all on their own. But unlike the last time she and Dub sat on that very same couch talking about her issues, she didn't try to hide or stop them.

"My kids don't love me," she whispered.

"Sylvia," Dub replied, scooting closer to her on the couch and sliding an arm around her shoulders. "Why would you say something like that? Of course they love you."

"Nah," Sylvia insisted immediately, shaking her head. "Maybe Valencio does, and even that's just because he feels like he's supposed to. But not Candy."

"Why not Candy?"

"I'm a bad mother, Dub. And you don't have to say I'm not," she added quickly as Dub opened his mouth to do just that. "I'm not trying to get any pity here; I'm just speaking the truth. I've done a shitty job of raising my kids the way they need to be raised because I was trying so hard to be the opposite of my mama, and it backfired. There's no telling where Valencio would be if it weren't for Bryce keeping him straight. But Candy...watching her is like watching myself. And I know when I was her age, I felt like I hated my mother more often than I felt I loved her."

"But you *did* love her, though, right?"

Sylvia gave a half-shrug. "I guess. I mean, I didn't want her to die or anything like that. But I sure as hell didn't respect or appreciate her, and Candy is the same way with me. I've been trying to do better as a mother; I really have. But it doesn't seem to be doing any good. Bryce has Valencio living with him and Candy ran away. So now I'm alone."

Dub frowned; he had no idea things had gone from bad to worse since the last time they had spoken. He wondered if that had something to do with her not taking his calls recently. Was she embarrassed? Or just overwhelmed with everything that was going on?

"Sylvia," he began, almost not really even knowing what to say. "I am so sorry. But please don't ever say you're alone. You have plenty of people that care about you. This is a rough patch but we're gonna get through this; you know I'll help you in any way that I can."

Sylvia lightly shook her head but didn't comment.

"I know Valencio has Bryce but I'm more than willing to be a father figure for Candy, even though Deuce *is* finally trying to do the right thing and forge a relationship with her. He told me he tried to come see her."

"Oh. Yeah, that." Sylvia wondered if Deuce had told Dub the part about Sylvia having company that night, too.

"I'm not trying to tell you what to do because I can understand why you'd resist him, but I hope you consider letting my brother spend some time with Candy," Dub continued. "I know you probably think he isn't sincere but he is; I know my brother. He's been spending more time with his other kids and he wants to do that with Candy, too. You just have to let him."

Sylvia knew if Dub was vouching for Deuce, then it had to mean something. "I guess I can think about that. Part of me wants to tell him to just kick rocks but that's my own resentment towards him;

I guess I shouldn't try to stop him from getting to know Candy, if that's what they both want."

"I'm glad to hear you say that. That'll mean a lot to him."

"You think so, huh?"

"I know so."

"Well, I guess we'll see."

"Sylvia, I know things look kinda bleak right now but I meant it what I just said about being here for Candy, and you know I'm still here for you. Even though you haven't been trying to deal with me lately." He leaned back a little so he could get a good look at her face. "Did I do something? If I did, please tell me. It doesn't feel good being ignored."

Sylvia felt bad. She knew that feeling all too well and hated that she had inflicted that on Dub. He was her favorite person, maybe even above her own kids, if she was honest with herself. She hadn't *liked* ignoring his calls, but she hadn't wanted to deal with any drama from his girlfriend Jelissa should she find out about them talking again. But Sylvia decided she didn't care about that anymore. She needed as many encouraging people in her life as she could get, and Dub was the definition of that.

Plus she knew if it came down to it, she could beat Jelissa's ass without breaking a sweat.

"It wasn't anything you did, like I said before," Sylvia said, wiping her eyes and sitting up a little straighter.

"What was it, then? Even when I came up to the store that night, you were acting like I was the last person you wanted to see."

"I'm sorry about that; I know you didn't deserve it."

"So what's going on?"

"Well, to be blunt about it, your girl told me to step off."

Dub's frown deepened. "Excuse me?"

"She said that I depend on you too much and you're too nice to do anything about it so she's telling me for you. She doesn't like you 'coming to my rescue' all the time."

Dub couldn't believe his ears. "Jelissa said this?"

"She surely did."

"When??"

"A while back. I had called you pretty late one night and apparently you were asleep or something, and she answered your phone."

"Wow," Dub shook his head, as if trying to clear it. Jelissa of course hadn't said anything to him about any of this or given him any indication that she had talked to Sylvia directly. The fact that she had gone behind his back and confronted Sylvia like that when she knew the reason he was there for Sylvia like he was infuriated him. They'd had this conversation several times, and he thought they were on the same page; he thought she understood that he considered Sylvia family. He felt his anger grow by the second. The fact that his woman was going behind his back made him wonder what else she had been sneaky about. And he didn't appreciate Jelissa answering his phone, either.

"Sylvia, I had no idea she did that," Dub insisted, looking at her. "I am so sorry..."

"You don't have to apologize for anything; I know that was all her. I'm the one that needs to apologize for even listening to her; I guess I just didn't want to deal with any more drama with everything else that was going on. I should have just told you about all this from the jump."

What Sylvia didn't want to admit was that she was also somewhat intimidated by Jelissa for none other than the fact that she was Dub's woman. She always figured if she upset Jelissa, she automatically upset Dub. But she should have known Dub well enough to know he was his own man who had more than proven himself over the years as somebody she could trust. She should have had more faith in him that he meant everything he always said to her about being there for her.

"I can understand that but believe me, nothing has changed," Dub promised.

"That's good to know."

"So you're through ignoring me now, right? We're good?"

Sylvia gave him a small smile. "Yeah, we're good."

"That's what I wanna hear," Dub said, smiling back. He opened his arms to her and Sylvia leaned in and wrapped her arms around his waist just like Candy had done earlier. She couldn't resist smiling harder when Dub kissed the top of her head like he always did.

"And as for Jelissa," Dub said, his smile fading and his anger returning, "I'll handle that."

Later, after Sylvia had eaten and showered, she climbed into bed and thought about the day she just had. Lance had let her go early since they were really slow at the store, and the last thing Sylvia had been expecting to see was her daughter and Dub on the couch with her clinging to him like a life raft. She was glad Dub had been there yet again to stop Candy from doing something stupid (and maybe potentially dangerous, depending on their intentions) with those boys. And while Sylvia might not have shown it, she was glad to see her daughter was all right. She was just too stubborn to say it out loud. She hadn't tried to stop Candy when she left back out again, but at least now she knew where she was.

The similarities between Sylvia and Candy were so great that it often freaked Sylvia out. From the way they looked to the way they acted, they were like the same person, just fifteen years apart. Usually this might be considered a good thing, but Sylvia figured this was why they butted heads so much. Candy was insecure and had low sell-esteem and compensated for it with sex, just like Sylvia had done. Sylvia just hoped Candy wasn't in her thirties like she was to realize that wasn't the way to go. But Sylvia also could acknowledge that she hadn't done much to alter the path Candy was going down; instead of giving her positive encouragement and assuring her she was beautiful and special and deserved to be treated with respect, which was something she hadn't gotten much of herself coming up, she taught her daughter how to please the boys between the sheets. For all she knew, Candy had some boy between her legs at that very moment, thinking it was going to get him to like her.

Sylvia laid in bed well into the night, staring up at the ceiling and wondering how and when things between her and her daughter were going to improve. She didn't want Candy to end up with a daughter that ended up being the same way she and Candy were; somehow, they had to break this cycle.

Chapter 22

• • • •

SYLVIA WAS SURPRISED to get a call from Valencio a couple days later.

"Hey!" Sylvia exclaimed, very happy to hear from her son. She had been feeling bad about how she had gone off on him the night after the dinner at Sandra's, when he had told her the truth about how he felt about her as a mother. Her feelings had been hurt, but that was no excuse for how she treated him.

"Hey, Mama," Valencio said, glad that she was no longer mad at him. Bryce had a talk with him and told him why Sylvia had reacted like she had and that he shouldn't take it personally.

"How you doing over there? You still on punishment?"

"Yes, ma'am, but Dad is starting to let me do a couple more things now. I can talk on the phone for an hour but I have to stay in the room where he is."

Sylvia couldn't help but chuckle. She had to give it to Bryce; he was far and away better than she was when it came to implementing a punishment. He had stuck to everything he laid down on Valencio after finding out about him trying to steal that watch from the mall.

"I hope you've learned your lesson about all this, and you get why he came down so hard on you," Sylvia said.

"Oh, I have," Valencio insisted quickly. "I'm gonna be sure to do what I'm supposed to do from now on, 'cause I don't wanna have to go through anything like this again."

"Good. It's worth it, then."

"You doing okay, Mama?"

"As okay as I can be, I guess."

"I wanted to tell you I was sorry for how I was acting," Valencio said. "With the cutting class and being disrespectful and stuff. I know that was wrong. Dad and I did a lot of talking and I told him everything I had been doing while I was out with my friends, and he said I should tell you, too..."

"Okay..." Sylvia braced herself.

"I, um...I smoked weed a few times. And I got a girlfriend. Two, really."

Sylvia wasn't all that shocked about the weed given how much he had been eating before he left, and also remembering the time she had come home and smelled it in the air, but the part about the two girlfriends shocked her. "Two? Are you serious?"

"Yes, ma'am. But Dad told me that was wrong; that I should only have one girlfriend at a time. He told me a bunch of stuff about cheating and dishonesty and respecting girls and stuff, too."

"And do you get what he was trying to say?"

"Yes, I get it. Especially after he said to consider how I would feel if I was with someone I really liked and found out they had another boyfriend on the side."

"He's absolutely right. It's not a good feeling, being cheated on."

Valencio almost asked if that ever happened to Sylvia, but he stopped himself, not knowing how she would receive that question. "Well, I'm not gonna do that anymore."

"Good; I'm glad to hear it." She paused, sensing that Valencio had something else to say but was hesitant to do so. So she asked what she had been wondering about for months. "Have you had sex?"

Hesitating slightly, Valencio told the truth. "No, but I came close."

Sylvia was surprised at how relieved she was. At least one of her kids was still a virgin. "So what *have* you done?"

"Um..." Valencio stammered, clearly embarrassed. "We just...took our clothes off and kissed and some other stuff. She went, um..."

"Baby, relax...it's okay. I can tell you're embarrassed so we can just leave it at that. I get the gist."

"Thanks, Mama," Valencio replied, relieved. There was a time Sylvia would have forced him to tell her in detail everything he had done with Madeline, or kept asking him explicit questions. He wasn't to the point where he felt comfortable talking about those kinds of things yet, and especially with his mother. He figured Sylvia probably knew what he was talking about, anyway.

"So anyway, I'm sorry about all that," Valencio continued, eager to change the subject. "I'm gonna do better."

Sylvia smiled. She had always been proud of her son, but she was ten times more proud right then. At that moment she also realized how right Bryce had been about Valencio needing to be around him more at this stage in his life. "I know you will. And I accept your apology. I'm sorry about what I said to you the last time you were here, and any other time I've embarrassed you. I never meant to do that."

Valencio hadn't expected a return apology; Sylvia had never been big on admitting she was wrong. But he appreciated it nonetheless. "It's okay, Mama. I accept your apology, too."

Tears came to Sylvia's eyes. She was surprised at how emotional she had become lately; she never used to cry this much. "Good."

"I have to go clean out the garage. Dad wants to talk to you."

"Okay." Sylvia wiped her eyes.

Bryce came onto the line a few moments later. "Hey, Sylvia."

"Hey."

"Everything okay?"

Just like that, the tears started back up again. She didn't know why and she didn't try to stop them. "Yeah."

"Are you crying?" Bryce asked with concern. "What's wrong?"

The fact that he was being so nice to her after how she last spoke to him only sent the tears coming faster. "I'm just...realizing some things about myself, that's all."

"What do you mean?"

"Bryce, I need to let you know how much I appreciate you. You are a great father to Valencio, damn sure better than I am a mother to him. There's no telling what shape he would be in if it wasn't for you."

"I appreciate that, Sylvia, but why are you saying this?"

"'Cause I need to say it. I need to let you know. You deserve a lot of credit for that."

"It's just what I'm supposed to do, Sylvia. Valencio is my son. But I thank you for telling me that."

"I acted like an ass the last time I saw you. You didn't deserve that. I've been trying to be a better mother to my kids and be a better person, but I already know I'm not doing a very good job. I'm just glad Valencio has you. I'm a mess and I know it. I don't even deserve to have any kids."

"Come on, Sylvia, don't say that. You shouldn't be so hard on yourself."

"Why shouldn't I?"

"At least you're trying to do better. Some people wouldn't even bother, especially when their kids are already teenagers. I've seen a lot of parents who make the mistake of being stubborn and thinking they're always right just because they're the parent. Some refuse to ever apologize to their kids, even when they *know* they're wrong. Once upon a time, *you* were like that. But you're not now. That's a good thing. You've made some mistakes but one thing I've never doubted is the fact that you love your kids; not all parents do. So give yourself some credit."

Sylvia smiled at Bryce's encouragement. He really was a good man. "I guess I'm growing up, huh?"

Bryce chuckled. "It had to happen sometime."

• • • •

"HEY, BABY," JELISSA greeted Dub happily when she got to his townhouse. She was holding a plastic grocery bag.

"Hey," Dub replied evenly, taking a swig of his beer. He eyed her as she set the bag on the coffee table and quickly walked over to him with her arms out for a hug. She wrapped her arms around his neck, sighing in contentment.

"I missed you today," she whispered, leaning up to kiss his neck.

"Yeah?"

"You know I did," Jelissa replied, taking his face in her hands and planting a loving kiss on him.

Dub kissed her back, but he didn't return her sentiment. He was still upset with her about confronting Sylvia behind his back, and he fully intended to talk to her about it and set her straight.

"What's in the bag?" he asked when their kiss ended.

"Oh, I brought you some stuff I saw you needed; dish detergent, fabric softener...and I got you some more sponges and a couple of dish towels. Those in the kitchen look like they've seen some better days."

"Thanks."

"I'll go put this stuff up and then we can go get something to eat; I didn't have time to get any lunch today and I'm starving. Or did you want to order in?" she verified, picking up the bag.

"That all depends."

Jelissa looked at him in surprise. "On what?"

"On your explanation for going behind my back and telling Sylvia to step off."

Her jaw dropping briefly, she returned the bag to the coffee table. "Well, she certainly didn't waste any time tattling to you, did she? I should've known..."

"Not that it matters, but she wasn't going to tell me anything; I'm the one that dragged it out of her when I finally got her to talk to me. She had been ignoring my calls for weeks. Now, I'm still waiting on that explanation."

Sighing, Jelissa took a seat on Dub's chocolate brown suede couch. "You should know why. I've told you how I felt about her calling you all the time."

"And I've told *you* why she calls me and why I take her calls. And I thought we were on the same page with that, but apparently not. I don't see what your problem is and what part of this you don't understand."

"So you're upset with me?"

"No. I'm pissed at you."

"Just because I talked to Sylvia??"

"Because you went behind my back. You didn't even tell me you talked to her. Are you threatened by Sylvia or something?"

"Please," Jelissa scoffed.

"Then what's the damn problem?"

Jelissa sighed again. "It's just...maybe it's a woman thing. You wouldn't like it if some man was calling me all the time. She depends on you too much, Dub; you're *my* man, not hers."

"That can change, you know."

Jelissa's eyes widened in shock. "What?? You're going to break up with me over this?"

"I'm not gonna waste time with a woman I can't trust. And when you do shit like answer my phone and confront my family the way you did and then not even tell me you did it, that makes me think I can't trust you. I'm tired of arguing with you about this. I love you, Jelissa, but please believe my life will go on if you're not in it. And if this is gonna keep being an issue, you won't be."

Jelissa couldn't believe her ears. She figured Dub would eventually find out about her conversation with Sylvia, and even be a little upset, but she certainly hadn't expected him to threaten to leave her over this. She didn't want to lose Dub, especially not because of Sylvia.

"I'm sorry," she said, looking up at him.

"Don't bullshit me. 'Cause I'm willing to bet you never would have told me about this on your own so I don't know how sorry you could be about it."

"Dub!"

"What?"

"Are you serious with all this?"

"Very."

"You know I love you. You're willing to throw our relationship away just because I said something to this woman?"

"I've explained this to you already. I'm not doing it again."

"Fine." Jelissa shot up off the couch and grabbed her purse before stalking towards the door. "I'm damn sure not gonna beg you. If I don't mean any more to you than this, then maybe I need to just leave."

Dub just sipped his beer as he watched her, not saying a word.

Jelissa turned when she got to the doorknob and looked at him. She had expected him to have tried to stop her by now, if for nothing else so they could talk about it some more. "You don't have anything to say before I go?"

"Leave the key."

Jelissa's mouth fell open. "Dub!"

"Oh, were you expecting me to beg you to stay? You've got the wrong dude for that."

Figuring she better humble herself before she lost the only man she ever really loved, she dropped her purse. "Okay, okay...can we please talk?"

"If we're going to sincerely discuss this, yes. If it's gonna just be more bullshit, keep walking."

Jelissa walked over to him and grabbed his hand, leading him over to the couch. "I want to sincerely talk about it."

Dub sat his beer bottle on the coffee table and looked at her. "All right."

"I was wrong to answer your phone and talk to Sylvia behind your back. I know you've told me why you're there for her the way you are. And I'm not jealous, it just...makes me feel some kind of way when you go running to her rescue all the time."

"I don't run to her rescue all the time. Don't exaggerate, Jelissa."

"I'm not. She *does* call you a lot."

"And I call *her* a lot. I've known Sylvia for over fifteen years, and was friends with her when Deuce tricked her into thinking he was me and then knocked her up. She's the mother to my niece, and Deuce hasn't been helping her. I've said it before and I'll say it again for the last time; I consider her family."

"I get that..."

"And she's going through a lot right now and needs support from people that love her, and that's me. You know I'm not in love with her, and so does she. I'm in love with *you*. But for some reason you can't be secure in that."

"I am..."

"Do you not trust me?"

"Of course I do."

"Act like it, then. I wouldn't disrespect you by doing anything with Sylvia or anybody else. And for the record, Sylvia has not once made any kind of move on me or even said anything about how she feels about me. I know she has a crush on me, and she knows I know. But she also knows that while I love her and I have her back, my feelings for her aren't romantic and never have been. Sylvia is not the one with the problem here; that's you."

Jelissa hated to admit it, but she knew he was right. "I know."

"And also for the record, nine times out of ten when Sylvia calls me, she's not asking for anything. Most of the time when I do things for her it's because I offer to. She's been respectful of my relationship with you; I need you to be respectful of my relationship with her."

Not being able to resist, Jelissa threw her arms around Dub's neck. She hated when he was upset with her, and the thought of him not being in her life made her sick.

"I'm sorry, baby," she said sincerely, burying her face in the crook of his neck. "Really. Please know that I *do* trust you. You're a good man, and I need to be proud of how you want to be there for her and her daughter instead of being upset over it, 'cause it really does say a lot about you." She leaned back and looked at him. "Forgive me?"

Dub just cupped her chin in his hand and brought her face to his for a kiss. She eagerly kissed him back, glad to be back on his good side again. They kissed deeply for several moments before Dub pulled back and looked at her.

"I meant it when I said I'm in love with you," he said, looking right into her eyes. "You're the one I'm devoted to; you're the one I kiss on and make love to and plan on making my wife one day."

Jelissa's eyes brightened with excitement.

"What you did not only pissed me off but it hurt me, Jelissa; I'm just being straight up about it. I'm willing to go ahead and move past this but I want you to remember that I meant *everything* I said earlier, so I hope this won't be an issue again."

"It won't...I promise. And again, I'm sorry; you've always been so good to me and I hate to think that I've hurt you."

"All right, then." He pulled her to him, rubbed her back and sighed, hoping this would be one particular headache he wouldn't have to have anymore.

• • • •

CANDY WAS HAVING THE time of her life. It was Saturday night and she and Kita were dancing the night away at Club Bounce, which they only got into because of fake IDs and skillfully-applied makeup. Kita was in a short black strapless dress and Candy was in a hot pink one that left little to the imagination. She had borrowed (stolen) a strapless push-up bra from Kita's mother to get some assistance with her mediocre cleavage, and she loved it when she saw someone looking at them. Since this wasn't high school and she was among plenty of other beautiful women who were older than her, she felt she had to try that much harder to be noticeable. But her main goal was just to have a good time with her friends and take her mind off all the drama that had been going on the past couple weeks.

She still hadn't forgotten about what happened at Kita's when Mac tried to get her to try cocaine. The only reason she got out of it was because Mac's father had texted him to come home, and his friends were riding with him. Candy had stayed in that bathroom for over thirty minutes contemplating how she was going to get out of that situation without ruining her reputation completely, but thankfully it had worked itself out on its own. Mac hadn't said anything to her about it since, and she was grateful for that.

And then there was the episode with her Uncle Dub and Russell and Jason. She had wanted to redeem herself from when they had been stopped on the street after school that day, and invited the boys over after school when she knew Sylvia wouldn't be at home. She hadn't even noticed Dub's car outside her apartment building, and when he busted through the front door like he did, she thought she was going to have a heart attack. She really thought he was going to kill Russell and Jason, and since that day they hadn't even looked at her. Candy wasn't exactly thrilled about that, but surprisingly, she wasn't as concerned about it as she thought she would be. That might've been because of the talk she and Dub had after he had kicked the boys out.

That had been on Candy's mind a lot. Dub really seemed like he cared about her, and when he pointed out that the boys she had slept with really didn't, it made her realize that maybe she had been doing something wrong. Apparently what she had been doing wasn't working, because nobody had asked her to be their girlfriend. She knew she was good in bed, so obviously that wasn't all it took. Maybe it really was like Dub said; nobody wanted the jump-off as their girlfriend.

But now, the problem was that Candy didn't know how to go about getting the boys to see her as anything *but* the jump-off. That was what she was used to and had even taken pride in, but now, not so much. She didn't even know who to ask for advice about this; she didn't want to call her Aunt Delta, because she would then call Sylvia, and she was the last person Candy wanted to deal with. She wished she had gotten her Uncle Dub's number before she ran out of the house that day after Sylvia came home, because she really wanted to see what he thought about it. He could tell her what to do.

But in the meantime, Candy just wanted to have a good time and enjoy herself with her homegirl. She and Kita hadn't spoken on what they had done during the game of Truth or Dare, and Candy was glad about that; she had hoped that things wouldn't be awkward and that Kita might even ask her to leave because of it. Candy wasn't ready to go back home yet; going home meant having to deal with her mama.

"I want a drink," Jamie, their friend who had driven them there, said over the music.

"Me too. But I don't have any money," Candy replied.

"I have a few dollars but I don't want to spend it on that," Kita said.

"Yeah, those few dollars are going in my gas tank," Jamie said, nudging her playfully.

"And anyway, we're supposed to get someone to buy drinks *for* us," Candy advised. "Not spend our own money. And Jamie, you don't need to be drinking, anyway. I'm not trying to die on the way home."

"Girl please, one drink won't do anything. But fine, I won't have any."

"Good. Kita and I can have yours, then," Candy quipped, linking her arm through Kita's and swinging her hips to the music.

"Yeah, okay. Good luck getting any; these dudes in here look kinda broke down," Jamie observed, glancing around the club.

"Don't worry about all that. *Somebody* will," Candy said confidently.

"Just be careful who you take them from; dudes try to slip you stuff," Jamie advised.

"Oh please believe, I'm not drinking anything unless I'm right there when it's made and it's going from the bartender's hand to mine," Kita insisted.

"Me, too," Candy added.

The three friends continued to dance and have a good time together before they began to veer off on their own. Candy was dancing to 'Fancy' by Iggy Azalea when someone approached her.

"You wanna dance?" A tall guy with a gold chain asked her.

Candy grinned, showing her dimples. "Most definitely."

They danced to the next couple of songs, with Candy forgetting about everything else and just enjoying the moment. When Candy had last seen Kita and Jamie, they were both dancing with guys and looking like they were in worlds of their own. They had already all agreed that they would all leave together so she wasn't worried too much about keeping track of where they were. She knew she would catch up with them before the night was over.

When the man she was dancing with finally offered Candy a drink, she didn't decline it. Having forgotten about Jamie's advice, she waited for the man to bring the drinks to her as she kept grooving on the dance floor. She threw back the Fuzzy Navels like they were water, feeling more and more liquid with each one. After a while, Candy felt like she was floating on air. So when the guy took her hand and led her towards the back of the club, she let him. When he took her to a dark hallway and immediately pressed her against the wall, grabbing her pushed-up breasts, she didn't protest. And when he yanked his pants down, her dress up, and then lifted her up against the wall, sliding into her without protection, she just matched his thrusts with her own, almost as if she was on auto-pilot. She actually giggled, the alcohol fogging her mind and clouding her already-questionable judgment.

Candy didn't say a word as this man whose name she didn't even know sexed her hard against the wall, the loud music causing it to thump against her back. Her legs clamped around his waist and she clung to his shoulders, wondering if she was somehow dreaming all this.

· · · ·

"CANDY, COME DOWN HERE for a minute," Kita's mother Janine called up the stairs the next day.

Groaning, Candy pushed herself off Kita's bed and rubbed her eyes. She had been asleep most of the day, having gotten in late from clubbing the night before with Kita and Jamie. Her head was still pounding, and for the life of her she couldn't seem to remember much about what happened last night. Everything was fuzzy; for some reason she remembered being on the floor in a hallway, but she couldn't remember how she got there.

She trudged down the stairs and went into the kitchen, where Janine was cooking dinner.

"Sit down," Janine instructed, turning over the fried pork chops in the iron skillet.

Candy took a seat at the kitchen table and rested her chin in her hand.

"Is there something you need to tell me?" Janine asked.

Candy was immediately nervous, wondering if she knew something about them going to Club Bounce. Janine was cool but Candy didn't know how she would feel about them lying their way into a club full of grown men.

"No..." she replied hesitantly.

"So there's no reason you've been staying here so long? Is something going on at home I need to know about?"

Slightly relieved, Candy shook her head. "Nope. I wasn't being abused or anything like that. Mama knows where I am. We just...needed some time apart, that's all."

Janine eyed her. "Well, you've always been cool with me and since you and Kita are such good friends, I haven't minded you being here. Plus, you're kinda like the second child my messed-up insides won't let me have. But you've been staying here for a while now. And if you want to *keep* staying here, you're gonna have to start contributing."

"Contributing?" Candy asked, confused.

"You need to get a job, girl. Having an extra mouth to feed is getting to be a little much. It's not like I'm rolling in the dough over here."

"Oh," Candy grunted. The last thing she wanted to do was get a job, but she also didn't want to leave just yet, either. She didn't want to go home and deal with her mother, especially with Valencio gone. "I'm only fifteen, though."

"I know the manager over at Taco Bell; he'll hire you as a favor to me. And it's right down the street so you can walk there."

Knowing she wasn't in a position to refuse, Candy grudgingly agreed.

But it didn't take long before Candy butted heads with her supervisor, Faye. Even though Candy was an employee, she didn't like being told what to do.

"Candy, go on back there and wash those dishes," Faye ordered.

Rolling her eyes, Candy let the mop she had been using fall to the floor. "You already gave me something to do."

"And now I'm giving you something else. You're about done with the floor."

"How come I can't learn the cash register or something? All you've had me doing is cleaning stuff."

"You're not old enough to be on the register."

"Well I'm tired of all this cleaning crap. I'm not a maid."

"Lil' girl, you ain't no better than anybody else up in here," Faye said, stepping closer to her. She towered over Candy by six inches and outweighed her by at least a hundred pounds. Her huge breasts strained against her work shirt. "*Everybody* has to help keep this place clean. Your young behind needs to be glad you're here at all."

"What, I'm supposed to *thank* you for letting me come up in here so you can order me around and have me doing all the stuff you don't want to do?"

Faye shook her head and threw her hands up. "I don't have to put up with this shit. You're fired; get outta here."

Candy just shrugged her shoulder and stalked out in a huff, but she was immediately worried about what Janine would say about her getting herself fired on her second day.

Thankfully, Janine wasn't home from work yet when Candy made it back to their house. That gave her a little time to figure out how she was going to handle this.

"Why are you back so early?" Kita asked her.

"I got fired," Candy mumbled, tossing her work visor to the floor.

"Already? What did you do??"

"They were trying to make me do all this cleaning stuff like I was the maid or something," Candy complained. "Every time I turned around it was 'Candy, mop the floor'...'Candy, wash the dishes'...'Candy, pick up the trash in the parking lot'..."

"So? That's what they hired you for, isn't it?"

"I don't wanna do that mess. I thought they were gonna have me on the cash register or making the tacos or something."

"You can't pick and choose what you want to do when you first get hired, Candy."

"I don't see why I can't."

"Yeah, well, Mama is gonna be pissed at you when she finds out you got canned. What are you gonna tell her?"

"I don't know," Candy sighed, her nervousness returning. "Maybe I can make something up..."

"You know Mama knows the manager over there. All she'll have to do is ask him what happened. That's if he hasn't called her already and told her."

Candy hadn't even considered that. Now she was really worried.

"Maybe I can get another job," Candy suggested.

"In the next couple of hours?" Kita said skeptically. "I doubt it."

"Damn," Candy whispered, dropping down onto the bed. She looked at her friend and sighed before standing up and going over to the closet to get her duffle bags. She began gathering her things and stuffing them into it.

"You're leaving?" Kita asked, watching her.

"I might as well. Your mama is just gonna put me out when she gets here, anyway."

"So you're gonna go back home?"

"I don't want to. I'm not trying to hear my mama's mouth, either."

"So where are you going, then?"

Candy ran down her friends in her head, wondering which of them might let her crash for a few nights. But she knew while her friends might have been willing to let her do that, their parents would eventually call Sylvia, and that's what Candy was trying to avoid. The main reason she had chosen to stay with Kita in the first place was because her mother was so laid back and just took her word for it that Sylvia was fine with her being there. But none of her other friends' parents were like that.

"Not sure," Candy replied, zipping up one of the bags.

"So you're just gonna wander around the streets? It's getting dark, Candy."

"I'll find somewhere to go," Candy said confidently, even though she wasn't quite so sure about that. She stood up and hoisted her bags over her shoulders.

"Candy, why don't you just go home? Your mama can't be that bad. It's not like she hits you or anything."

"That ain't the point. You just don't know the crap I have to deal with with her. I'd rather sleep on the street than have to go home to all that."

And that's exactly what she ended up doing. Knowing her grandmother and Aunt Delta stayed too far away to walk, and not knowing where her dad Deuce lived or how to get in touch with her Uncle Dub, Candy spent the night by the dumpster at the back of the Taco Bell she had just gotten fired from hours before.

Chapter 23

• • • •

SYLVIA HESITATED BEFORE she answered Sandra's call on Sunday morning.

"I'm gonna be coming to get the children for church today," Sandra announced.

"You know Valenico is still at Bryce's," Sylvia yawned.

"Oh, that's right. Well, I'll come get Candy, then."

Sylvia had been dreading this; she didn't know how she could keep putting off Sandra seeing Candy. Every time she called to come get her or speak to her, Sylvia had managed to make up an excuse. But she knew that wasn't going to be able to fly forever.

"You can't," Sylvia replied somewhat hesitantly.

"Why not?"

"She's..."

Sandra paused. "She's what?"

Sylvia started to say that Candy was sick, but knowing Sandra, she would just want to come over and see about her.

"She's...not here."

"Where is she?"

"At a friend's house." At least that much wasn't a lie.

"What friend?"

"Mama, come on...it's not like you would know who I was talking about if I told you that, anyway."

"I feel in my spirit that something isn't right over there," Sandra said after a moment. "I've felt it for a while now. When are you going to finally be honest with me and tell me what's going on?"

Sylvia felt her resolve weakening. She was getting tired of making up excuses as to why her daughter wasn't there. "Mama..."

"This isn't about me trying to be nosy; I'm concerned. We won't be able to fix anything until you're up front about what's wrong."

"This will take a lot of fixing," Sylvia mumbled.

"My God is an awesome God. *Nothing* is too hard for Him."

Surprisingly encouraged by this, Sylvia decided to come clean. If she was honest with herself, she wanted Candy to come home, despite having been initially glad about her not being there and having the apartment to herself. Even though she now knew where Candy was, it would put her mind at ease being able to see her every day. Sylvia hadn't wanted to admit to anyone that Candy had run away, and especially that she hadn't done anything to find her. What kind of mother did that?

"Mama...this is gonna sound really bad but you asked for me to be straight up so here it is," Sylvia began. "Candy ran away."

"What?!?" Sandra shrieked. "When? How long ago??"

"A few weeks now."

Sylvia thought Sandra would have a heart attack. "*A few weeks!!??* Have you called the police?? You said she was at a friend's house!!"

"Well, she is...but I can admit that I didn't know that at first."

"Help me, Lord Jesus," Sandra whispered, breathing deeply. She took a few moments to calm herself before speaking again. "Start from the beginning and tell me everything."

"Well...she left the night of that dinner we had at your house."

"It's been that long?!?"

"Yes, it's been that long. There had been some drama over here after we got back and she snuck out while I was in my room. I didn't even notice it until the next morning."

"Well what did you do when you *did* notice she was gone??"

"See, this is the bad part...I didn't do anything."

"So...let me get this right," Sandra said, her voice going from frantic to angry. "Your fifteen-year-old daughter runs away from home in the middle of the night, and you did nothing?"

"I wouldn't say it was the middle of the night..."

"Whatever! You didn't even try to find her??"

"To be honest, Mama, I was glad she was gone. I know that says a lot about me as a person and a mother, but she and I had been butting heads nonstop before then despite my efforts to do better by her and all that, and I was just tired of it. For the time being I just wanted to enjoy having the place to myself and not constantly having to hear complaining. She has a lot of friends so I figured she was with one of them."

"But what if she wasn't?? And how did you find out where she was? Or were you lying again when you said she was at a friend's house?"

"No, I wasn't lying. I had come home early one day and she was here getting some more clothes; before she left back out she said where she was staying." Sylvia left out the part about Dub catching Candy there with two boys about to have some kind of threesome. What they were talking about was bad enough.

"And you didn't try to stop her??"

"No."

"I can't believe what I'm hearing!"

"Mama..."

"I always knew you had a lot to learn when it came to being a parent and an example but one thing I always gave you credit for was loving your kids and having *somewhat* good intentions," Sandra forged ahead. "But to not even care when your daughter runs away? To not even lift one finger to look for her and to even let yourself say that you were *glad she was gone*?? That just hurts my heart."

Sylvia swallowed, surprised at how her mother's words affected her.

"Do you even love your daughter, Sylvia?"

"Of course!"

"How can you say you love her when you obviously don't care what happens to her?"

"Yes, I care what happens to her. But you just don't know how things have been around here, Mama."

"I don't care *how* things have been! There is nothing you can say to justify not looking for your daughter after she runs away! *Nothing!*"

Sylvia got quiet, knowing she couldn't defend herself.

"What if I had done that to you, huh? The time you defied me and ran out of here then stayed gone for three days, what if I had just thrown my hands up and said 'good riddance'? Every second you were gone, I was worried out of my mind, and calling any and everybody I could call to try and find you. Even with all the trouble you gave me back then, and you gave me a *lot* of it, those three days you were gone were the scariest of my life, not a vacation."

"It's not like I didn't care at all. And I was relieved when she came home that day."

"Yet you let her leave right back out so you could keep acting like you didn't have any kids. Instead of dealing with the problems you were having with *your* child, maybe seeking some counseling that the both of you clearly need, you take the easy way out and just let her go back to wherever she had run off to, letting somebody else deal with her so you wouldn't have to."

Sylvia had never thought about it like that but she couldn't deny anything her mother said. So she didn't try to.

"For all you knew, she could have gotten hit by a car or kidnapped or raped or anything else. And you wouldn't even have known. I'm just so ashamed; so very, very ashamed."

Hearing this brought tears to Sylvia's eyes. She had never really sought her mother's approval before but actually hearing that she didn't have it now caused a pang in her chest that she hadn't been expecting.

"I know I'm an awful mother," she admitted, tears running down her face. "Candy might be better off wherever she is. She hates me and I know it, even with everything I've been trying to do. I know she's my child and she's my responsibility, but I just got tired. I admit it; I was just tired of fighting with her."

Sandra got quiet for a moment, listening to her daughter cry softly. She couldn't remember the last time she had seen or heard Sylvia cry. And even though she didn't agree with how Sylvia handled it, she could somewhat relate to what she was saying, because she certainly got weary of dealing with all of Sylvia's shenanigans when she was Candy's age.

"I'm coming over there," Sandra announced after a few moments.

Sylvia sniffled, wiping her eyes with the back of her hand. "Okay."

Sandra was knocking on the door less than a half hour later. She immediately hugged her daughter, then sat down and prayed over her, talked to her, and encouraged her for the next hour. She was disappointed in Sylvia and what she had done (and hadn't done), but she could also see Sylvia was hurting. It had been clear that Sylvia had been sincerely trying to improve herself as a mother, and while it appears to have had some positive effect on Valencio, it didn't seem to have done any good with Candy. That was discouraging for Sylvia, and Sandra could see that. She wasn't going to beat Sylvia down too much about it; she had already made it perfectly clear what she thought. The important thing was what to do from here to get Candy back home.

"I think we need to call the police," Sandra suggested, holding Sylvia's hands in hers.

Sylvia shook her head. "She wasn't kidnapped. She said where she was going when she left here that day."

"So let's go get her."

Sylvia hesitated, wondering how to say what was on her mind. "I don't know, Mama..."

Sandra frowned. "What do you mean, you don't know?"

"Who's to say she won't run right back outta here as soon as she gets a chance to? I've tried, but I can't watch that girl twenty-four seven. I'm not saying I don't want her to come back; I just need to get myself together first."

Sandra pursed her lips, eying her daughter.

"I know Candy and I aren't as close as a lot of mothers and daughters, but I feel in my gut she's okay," Sylvia continued, looking at her mother earnestly. "Now that I've come out with all this, I just want to take a minute to figure out what I'm going to do once she gets back here, 'cause things just can't go back to how they were. They just can't. Something has to change."

Sandra smiled at her daughter, reaching out and running a hand through her braids. "You're growing up," she commented.

"I'm trying to."

"I want my grandbaby home but she's your child, and if this is how you want to handle it, I'll support you," Sandra said. "Just don't let too much time pass because you just never know what can happen from one day to the next. She might have been going to that friend's house but there's no guarantee she'll stay there."

"True. Believe me, this isn't about wasting time. I just want to try to make sure that when she *does* get home, she stays here."

A couple more days passed and Sylvia did a lot of soul searching, thinking, and even praying on how she should handle this situation with Candy. She felt lighter now that she had admitted to her mother what had really happened, and she sincerely wanted to make sure things were better when her daughter came back home. Things had been going okay until the dinner at Sandra's, when Sylvia had gotten defensive about the things Candy and Valencio had said about her, and she had lashed out at Valencio and closed herself off, giving Candy the opportunity to sneak out. Sylvia really felt like if it hadn't been for that, she and Candy would have made significant progress in their relationship by now. Candy might have been stubborn but eventually would have realized that Sylvia only meant her well, not harm. At least, that's what Sylvia liked to think; Candy was just as stubborn as Sylvia had been at her age, and Sylvia hadn't come to that realization about her own mother until she was an adult.

Sylvia understood she would have to become stronger and more confident in herself if she was going to withstand whatever Candy might come back with when she got home. Chances were, Candy wasn't going to be some angel all of a sudden; Sylvia would probably be suspicious of her if she was. When Sylvia had resolved to try to do better as a mother, she wasn't strong enough; she let things her kids said or did discourage her too easily. Candy especially knew there were certain buttons she could push to knock the wind out of Sylvia's sails, like reminding her of how she coached her in sex or calling her out about trying to discipline her now when she should have been doing it all along. Those things got to Sylvia, and she had made that too obvious to Candy. Sylvia knew that she was the adult; if anything was going to improve, it had to start with her, and for real, this time.

Sylvia had never been one for praying, but she did it for the first time without Sandra, asking for God to keep Candy safe and for their relationship to get better. She wasn't even sure she was doing it right; she just talked to God like she had heard Sandra do it all these years. But when she was done, she was surprised at how much better she felt; like everything would work itself out some kind of way. Maybe not immediately, but eventually.

Taking a deep breath, Sylvia retrieved Candy's cell phone from her dresser drawer and scrolled through the many contacts for Kita's number.

"Candy?"

"Actually Kita, this is Sylvia...I mean, Ms. Jennings. Candy's mama."

"Oh...hey, Ms. Jennings."

"Is Candy near you? I really need to talk to her."

There was a pause. "Um..."

Sylvia's worry antenna immediately went up. "*Um* what? What's wrong?"

"Candy isn't here. That's why I thought it might've been her when I saw her number come up."

"Where is she?"

"She left here a few days ago. I thought she might've went home, even though she said she didn't want to. I don't know where she is, if she's not there."

Sylvia started to panic, then told herself to calm down; losing her head wasn't going to do any good. "You don't have *any* idea where she might be??"

"I'm sorry, I don't. I told her she needed to just go home but I guess she was still being stubborn."

Yeah, that was Candy, all right. Stubborn as stubborn could be.

"Damn," Sylvia whispered, clamping a hand to her forehead. "Kita, if you hear from her, make sure you call me, just in case she doesn't. I've gotta find her."

"I will."

Sylvia hung up the phone and tried to get her rapid breathing under control. Her head was spinning and she had to grope for her bed because she really felt like she was about to fall over. At least she knew Candy hadn't been lying about where she had been staying, but where was she now? Why did she leave there? And more importantly, why didn't she come home when she did? Did she hate Sylvia that much?

Telling herself that Candy was probably just at another friend's house, Sylvia told herself again not to freak out and think the worst. She grabbed her phone again and started making calls, the first one surprisingly being to Deuce. She hoped that his delayed paternal urge hadn't faded 'cause she already knew she was going to need all the reinforcement she could get.

Meanwhile, Candy hated being on the street.

One of her bags had already been stolen. She had been sleeping in a little corner near the nearby Dollar General, after her first night of sleeping by the Taco Bell dumpster. She was tired, she was hungry, and she would've given anything for a shower. She didn't have any money so she couldn't buy anything to eat, and she was too proud to beg anybody for any. She spent a lot of her time trying to keep her face hidden so no one would recognize her. Unfortunately, though, someone did.

"Candy??"

Looking up, Candy couldn't believe her eyes when she saw Mac standing over her. She wished that a big hole would just open up and suck her in at that very moment; she had never been so embarrassed, but she was also relieved. Mac was her friend, if not more; they had slept together a bunch of times and he cared about her. He wouldn't leave her out there like this.

"Hey, Mac," she said as casually as she could manage, scratching her dirty skin.

"Looks like somebody decided to try those drugs after all," Mac teased, looking her over. "Though I didn't think folks got strung out this quick."

Candy frowned. "I am not on drugs."

"What you doing out here? I thought you were staying at Kita's."

"Long story."

"Uh-huh." Mac pulled out his phone and started typing, a smirk on his face. "How long you been out here?"

"A few days, I guess." She slapped at what felt like a bug crawling on her neck. "Um, can you help me out?"

Mac looked at her, his expression twisted. "Help you out, how? That was Ray that had the coke, not me."

"I told you, I'm not on drugs!"

"You damn sure look like you are."

With a sigh, Candy continued, "I just meant can you give me a few dollars or something so I can get me something to eat. Or maybe I could come stay with you. You think your dad would let me?"

"Yeah right!" Mac actually laughed, which was like a kick in Candy's gut. "Why don't you just go home? Your crazy-ass mama kick you out or something?"

Candy looked away. "No."

"So you're just sleeping in front of the Dollar General just because? Can't be a school experiment 'cause school was out a couple of weeks ago," Mac joked, actually seeming like he was enjoying this. Candy was wondering when he was going to stop playing around and offer to help her.

"I'm really not trying to get into all that right now," Candy said, trying to keep her frustration in check. She noticed he was still typing away on his phone. "What are you doing?"

"Nothing," Mac quickly replied, the mischievous smirk still on his face.

"Look, it's getting cold out here," Candy complained, pulling the shirt she had draped around her shoulders tighter around her. "Can you help me or not?"

In the next second, there was a click, like a picture had been taken. Candy's jaw dropped.

"Did you just take a picture of me??" she shrieked.

"Maybe," Mac said smugly, still typing. She knew he was probably posting it on Facebook, Instagram, and anywhere else he could, not to mention sending it to all his friends. Candy's face flamed in embarrassment, not believing he had done that. At least school was out so she wouldn't have to worry about facing people in the hallway any time soon.

"Mac!"

"What? I don't know what you expect me to do. My dad is not gonna let you stay with us; its not like your folks put you out or something. You have somewhere you can go."

Candy didn't want to admit that he was right. She was just holding on to her stubbornness with both hands. "Can you just get me something to eat? Or some water or something?"

Mac just looked at her and went into the store without another word. Candy exhaled, trying to forget that he had most likely just put her on blast via social media and focus on the fact that he was going to give her some much-needed food. Her stomach growled in anticipation. She didn't even care what it was; chips, bread, snack cakes, whatever; as long as she could eat it without getting sick, she'd take it.

A little later, Mac emerged from the store with two bags full of stuff. Candy got excited when she saw the bags; it looked like he had gotten her enough to last the next couple of days. By then, she would have figured out her next move.

But instead of handing her the bags, he reached into one and pulled out a fifty cent bag of peppermints, tossing it into her lap.

"There you go," he said, as if he had given her a feast. "I bet you need those right about now. Oh, and you can have this, too." He reached into the pocket of his cargo shorts and pulled out a half-full bottle of Dasani water. He tossed it at her, then went on to his car, got in, and drove off, not giving her another look.

"That did not just happen," Candy whispered to herself. But it had. Mac had just dissed her, leaving her out on the street like some common trash. He probably thought he had done her a favor by giving her peppermints and a half-empty bottle of water. And then to make matters worse, he had taken a picture of her and sent or posted it all over the place. She of course had no proof of that, but she knew Mac. He loved gossip just as much as most girls did. She could just imagine what he had texted or posted about her. She was embarrassed, but she was hurt more than anything. Mac didn't care about her. After all the times they had hung out and talked and she had shared her body with him, when he saw she needed help, he left her hanging. And mocked her, to boot. Her Uncle Dub's words about how the boys didn't care about her and just wanted her for sex rang in her ears. He had been spot on. She wished he would just show up out of the blue now like he had the last two times she saw him, but something told her that her luck wasn't that good.

Someone was kind enough to give her a box of Saltines and a full bottle of water, and Candy munched down a whole sleeve of the crackers without stopping like it was a steak dinner with all the trimmings. Then she curled up in her corner, using the one duffel bag she had left as a pillow, and wondered what her mother was doing. They might not have gotten along all the time, but things weren't all *that* bad. If nothing else, Sylvia provided a nice enough home for her. Candy always had food to eat, she had a warm bed to sleep in, a good amount of clothes to wear, a phone, a computer...she had it good. It was a shame that it took her being out on the street to realize it, but she did.

So why couldn't she just get up and go home?

• • • •

DEUCE AND DUB HAD BEEN in their cars ever since Sylvia had called and let them know that Candy was missing. They also had a lot of their friends out combing the streets.

Deuce couldn't remember the last time he had been so worried. When Sylvia had called him and told him Candy had run away and wasn't at the friend's house she had initially went to, she wasn't even finished talking before he had grabbed his keys and hurried out to his car. He could tell Sylvia had been a little wary about how he was going to take the news, probably not sure if he would actually care or not, but he absolutely did. His desire to get closer to Candy hadn't waned; he hadn't wanted to push too hard so he was kind of waiting on her to reach out to him. Whenever he had called, Sylvia said Candy wasn't home. Now he wondered if Candy had been missing all that time and Sylvia just hadn't told him.

But he couldn't worry about that right now; he just wanted to find his daughter.

Dub was pleasantly surprised at how concerned Deuce was about Candy being missing. Part of him really expected his brother to brush the whole thing off, but that's not what happened. When he called Deuce to check in, he could hear the worry in his twin's voice.

"I've gotta find her, man," Deuce had said, sounding more sincere than Dub had ever heard him sound. "These streets can eat you up if you don't know how to handle it. She don't need to be out here by herself."

"I know, man. We're gonna find her," Dub encouraged. He was extremely worried himself, trying his best not to think the worst. He had left a message for Jelissa, letting her know what was going on.

"Dub, man...I'm know I'm late, but I want to be a better father to her than our dad was to us," Deuce confessed. "But I can't do that if...she's..."

"Don't even say it, man," Dub cut him off. "Don't even think that. Man, you have got to think positively. We've got a lot of people looking; one of us will find her. You've gotta believe that."

"I'm trying," Deuce said.

He cruised the streets of Atlanta, his eyes looking everywhere a teenage girl might be wedged into. He roamed parking garages, checking every car that was still there; he looked in every store that was within a ten mile radius of Sylvia's apartment, going up and down every aisle, going around the back of and sides of the stores, showing all the clerks and cashiers Candy's Facebook picture and asking if they had seen her. He was getting discouraged until he stopped at the Dollar General and was told that they recognized Candy.

"You do?? Where is she?" Deuce asked urgently.

"She was sleeping out in front of the store, but she must have left a while ago," the cashier said. "I noticed she was gone when I last went outside to take a smoke."

Dub felt relieved, discouraged, and angry all at once. "So y'all saw a teenage girl sleeping outside your damn store and you didn't do anything about it??"

The young cashier turned red. "Um..."

"You didn't call the police or nothin'?? What if your daughter or sister ran away from home and nobody tried to help her when they saw her? How would you feel about that??"

"I really couldn't tell how old she was. But I gave her some crackers," the girl said weakly, taking a step back. She looked like she was afraid Deuce would dive over the counter at her. "And some water."

"You gave her some crackers and some water," Deuce repeated, eying the scared cashier. "Thanks." The sarcasm in his voice was evident.

Deciding he didn't have any more time to waste there, he stormed out of the store and back to his car, calling Sylvia to tell her what had just happened.

Sylvia was at her apartment, going through Candy's phone and computer and calling every friend she could find in each. None of them had seen or heard from Candy. When she got to a boy named Mac, he just scoffed and hung up on her. It took Sylvia a minute to recall that he was the one that she had caught having sex with Candy in her room that time. Seeing as how she had thrown him out on his ass, literally, she wasn't surprised he wasn't willing to help her, even though she had a feeling he knew something.

She hoped to high heaven that Deuce or Dub would find her; they knew the Atlanta streets way better than Sylvia did. If they didn't come back with any good news for her that night, she was calling the police. She could admit to herself, though, that she had more faith in the twins than she did in Atlanta's finest.

Delta had come over to give her encouragement and keep her calm, as had Sandra. After calling everyone in Candy's contacts and coming up with nothing, Sylvia dropped between her friend and her mother on the couch, emotionally exhausted.

"Sylvia, girl, can I get you anything? You need to eat something," Delta suggested, rubbing her back.

"Not right now, thanks," Sylvia answered, rubbing her eyes.

"What did Candy's friends say?" Sandra asked.

"None of them knows where she is." Sylvia didn't have the energy to tell them about Mac right then; she'd bring it up if Deuce and Dub came back empty-handed.

"Deuce and Dub haven't called?" Delta asked.

"Not in the last hour or so. But they will...they said they'd check in every hour or when they heard or found anything concrete."

Right at that moment, Sylvia's cell phone rang in her hand. She immediately answered when she saw it was Deuce.

"Deuce, what's up?" Her eyes widened as she listened to Deuce tell her that Candy had been seen sleeping outside the Dollar

General, but she had apparently left there and no one knew where she had gone.

"We're still out here," he assured her, his voice tight. Sylvia couldn't tell if he was upset or concerned or both. "We're still looking. She couldn't have gone too far."

Sylvia hoped he was right and that someone hadn't snatched Candy from the side of the road and driven off with her to God knows where. Just the thought had her breaking down in tears, the phone falling from her hand to the floor as if she didn't have the energy to hold it anymore.

Sandra immediately put her arms around her daughter, trying to keep her own tears at bay, and prayed to God for the millionth time to bring Candy home safe.

Chapter 24

• • • •

AFTER THE ENCOUNTER with Mac, Candy had decided to move. She was sure he had told people where he had seen her and she didn't want folks coming by to see her camped out there like it was some kind of side show. The humiliation of Mac seeing her out there and not helping her was enough; she didn't need anybody else piling on.

There was a car that had been parked in a plaza a few blocks down the street for a while, and Candy decided to camp out in there. Compared to sleeping on the street the past few nights, it was like a four-star hotel. At least she would have a cushioned place to lay down and stay warm. She climbed into the backseat, locked all the doors, and settled in for the night, her mind racing as to what her next move would be the following morning.

She didn't know how much time had passed when she had to use the bathroom. Checking her surroundings, she hurried into one of the stores in the plaza, taking her bag with her. She relieved herself, washed her face, and took a quick bird bath, changing into some of the other clothes she had in her bag. She looked at herself, noticing the dark circles under her eyes and her sunken cheeks. She didn't even want to waste any of her makeup on herself, not thinking it would help any. Thankfully her braids helped her to not look totally horrid, but Candy still hated the sight of herself, even more than she used to. She turned away from the mirror, wondering again why it was she couldn't just swallow her pride and go home.

"Maybe I'll try to call her tomorrow," she said to herself, referring to Sylvia. "Just to let her know I'm okay."

There were only a couple of cars left in the parking lot by the time Candy emerged from the store. Looking around her, she quickly headed back towards the abandoned car, but for some reason she had the eerie feeling she was being watched. She hated that she didn't have anything she could really use as a weapon on her, and she prayed to high heaven that it was just the paranoia of her situation making her imagine stuff that wasn't really there.

"I don't remember the car being way back here," she muttered to herself.

In the next second, someone grabbed her from behind, clamping a hand over her mouth. Candy immediately screamed as her body went cold with fear.

"I got yo' ass now," a gruff voice growled in her ear, pulling her in the opposite direction.

Candy screamed and fought, clawing at the man's hands and kicking and thrashing, trying to pry herself loose. She had never been more scared in her life, and in that very moment, she was sorry for any and every time she had mouthed off to her mother, because she would have given anything to be home with her right then.

"Shut up!" the man ordered, his hold on her tightening despite her kicking and screaming. It seemed like he was trying to drag her around to the alley behind the plaza, and Candy knew that there was no telling what would happen to her if he got her back there. For all she knew, there were other men waiting on this guy to bring them some fresh meat. Tears squeezed from Candy's eyes, praying for something or someone to see them and help her.

For once, Candy's prayers were answered.

"Let her go!" a woman yelled from the distance. Candy could hear footsteps running towards them; it sounded like she was running in heels. "Hey! Let her go!"

"Mind your own business, bitch, before I fuck you up, too! Ouch!" the man yelled when Candy reached up and scratched his face. She wasn't able to turn and see what he looked like, but she felt a scruffy beard, and his face was sweaty.

"I *said*, let her go!" the woman repeated strongly. She sounded like she was closer to them.

"Look bitch-"

"No, *you* look, *bitch*!" There was a gun cock and the man stopped moving, his hold on Candy loosening immediately. "Let the girl go, and I *might* not shoot your pitiful-excuse-for-a-man ass. Keep trying me, though, and that 'maybe' will turn into a *definite*."

"Aight, aight," the man quickly conceded, pushing Candy away. "You got it..."

Candy stumbled and fell to her knees, the realization that she could have just been raped or murdered making her shake and dry heave as she cried uncontrollably.

"Get the hell outta here," the woman ordered the man. There was a familiar click, as if a picture had been taken. "And I suggest you don't try doing this shit to anybody else! Remember, I know what your ass looks like!"

Candy could hear the man run off, and hands immediately touch her shoulders. She jumped, shrieking again in fear.

"It's okay, baby...he's gone," the woman assured soothingly. She rubbed Candy's trembling arms, trying to calm her down. Candy fell against her, and the woman immediately wrapped her arms around the traumatized teenager, letting her cry while being sure to keep an eye out around her. A white man walked up and asked if she needed him to call the police and she nodded, showing him the picture she had taken of the attacker on her phone.

"Are you hurt? Did he hurt you?" the woman asked Candy after a few moments.

"No," Candy whimpered, hiccupping. She finally looked up at her rescuer and frowned slightly, having the sense she had seen her before somewhere.

"Candy?" the woman said. Apparently she knew her, too.

"I know you?" Candy asked, still trying to place her.

"Not really, but I kinda know your mother...and you look *just* like her," the woman said, looking at Candy as if in amazement. "I'm Jelissa, your Uncle Dub's girlfriend. Come sit in my car; after we deal with the police, I'm gonna take you home. There are quite a few people that are gonna be glad to see you."

Bryce and Valencio had come over, wanting to help in any way they could. Sylvia had called over there in a desperate last-ditch effort to find Candy, even though she knew the odds of Candy winding up at Bryce's house were probably slim. They didn't have much of a relationship, and Sylvia knew that was thanks to her. Bryce had offered more than once to be there for Candy as if she were his own daughter, but Sylvia had shut him down for her own selfish reasons. Yet another mistake she had made.

Sylvia was a mess. Sandra had cooked dinner but Sylvia was too worried to eat anything. Delta was keeping an eye on the news to see if anything happened to come up there, and Sylvia had to leave the room because she couldn't stand to watch it. She paced around her bedroom, her phone in her hand, praying that it would ring with someone telling her they had found her daughter. It was getting late; she hated to think about her daughter out on the streets by herself at night. Young people were getting abducted and raped, or worse, every day. There had just been a report on the news Delta was watching about a teenager attacked while they were heading home from a friend's house, just blocks away from their home. Sylvia remembered all the times she had let Candy go out by herself at night and shuddered at how foolish that had been.

There was a soft knock on her door and Bryce poked his head in. "Can I come in, Sylvia?"

"Yeah," Sylvia said, not even looking at him. She continued pacing around the room.

Bryce entered the room fully and closed the door behind him. "I'm not even gonna bother asking how you're holding up. I'm so sorry...I can't even imagine what you must be going through right now. Please tell me if there's anything I can do for you."

"The only thing anybody can do for me right now is to bring my child back here," Sylvia responded.

"And I so wish I could," Bryce replied sincerely. "I'd be a wreck if Valencio was missing. He's out there crying, by the way, which surprised me. I never knew him and Candy were that close."

"That makes two of us," Sylvia said, surprised to hear that, as well. She looked down at her phone again, as if willing it to ring. When it didn't after a few moments, she dropped down onto her bed, exhausted. She hung her head, her braids falling over her face.

Bryce gently sat down next to her, placing a comforting hand on her back.

"Thank you for coming, Bryce," Sylvia muttered, her head still down.

"You don't have to thank me, Sylvia," Bryce replied. "I care about Candy. And you, too. There's no way I could know you were going through this and not come see about you."

Feeling tears come to her eyes for the hundredth time, Sylvia fell against Bryce's chest, crying quietly. Bryce just wrapped his strong arms around her and held her to him, letting her cry as he buried his face in the top of her head. The two of them just sat like that for a while, Bryce not knowing what he could possibly say to comfort her at a time like this. He felt so helpless. But as soon as he heard that Candy was missing, he and Valencio rushed right over; if nothing else, he could offer moral support.

"Sylvia," Bryce said softly after a while.

She looked up at him.

"This might not be the best time for this, but I hope you reconsider my offer," he said, looking into her eyes. "You don't have to go through everything by yourself. Valencio shouldn't just see either one of us on the weekends or whatever; we should both be in the same house. He needs you just like he needs me. I can be there to help you with Candy, if she needs anything...I just want to be here for you. I always have."

Sylvia eyed Bryce, and saw a good man staring back at her. A good man that many women would scratch her eyes out for, and he was offering something that would relieve her stress level (after they found Candy, at least) by a thousand percent. Maybe she wouldn't be going through what she was going through if she had taken him up on it when he offered it the first time.

Too tired to say no, Sylvia accepted. The tears continued when Bryce gently pressed his lips against hers; he had no idea how much Sylvia needed that right then.

My first boyfriend, she thought to herself.

• • • •

SYLVIA WAS STILL RESTING against Bryce's chest when her phone rang twenty minutes later. She immediately snatched it up without looking at the Caller ID. "Deuce?"

"Sylvia..." A familiar voice replied. "It's Jelissa."

Sighing with disappointment as her defenses shot back up, she held up a hand and said, "Look, I'm not in the mood for no drama right now. If you still got a problem with me talking to Dub then you need to-"

"This isn't about that," Jelissa interrupted her.

"Then what the hell you want?"

"I found your daughter."

Sylvia fainted.

By the time Jelissa showed up with Candy, Sylvia had come to and was anxiously awaiting their arrival. She, Sandra, Delta, Valencio, and Bryce were all watching the door like children waiting on Santa Claus. Sylvia was still trying to wrap her head around the fact that Jelissa, of all people, had been the one to find Candy. She had fully expected Dub or Deuce to call her with the good news; not Dub's girlfriend. She didn't even know she had been out looking for her. Maybe Jelissa wasn't all bad like Sylvia thought.

As soon as Candy walked through the door, everyone was on her, hugging and kissing her like they hadn't seen her in years. Candy was a little surprised by this reception; this certainly wasn't anything she was used to. Her family wasn't usually very loving and the affection was always minimal. But they all went on and on about how worried they were and how they had prayed for her safety and how glad they were to have her home safe, and Candy couldn't help but love all the attention. She had never been happier to see her family in her life. She even hugged Valencio, which was probably their first time hugging since they were toddlers.

Sylvia hugged Candy the longest, not wanting to let her go. And what surprised her the most was that Candy was actually hugging her back.

Jelissa had told Sylvia how she had stopped at the store on her way home and saw a young girl come out as she was walking to her car. She looked away and in the next moment, the girl was screaming and being dragged away by some scruffy-looking man. Jelissa, who to Sylvia's surprise was a former soldier, immediately pulled her gun and went to help her. She hadn't even known who Candy was until she got up close to her; Dub had told her that they were out looking for his niece, and Jelissa was sincerely hoping they found her, but she hadn't been particularly looking for her with everyone else. Sylvia couldn't believe how that worked out but she was glad it had, and didn't mind swallowing her pride and thanking Jelissa for saving her daughter's life. She even gave her a hug, and Jelissa hugged her back. Sylvia figured she wasn't doing any of this for show, since Dub hadn't gotten there yet. She didn't expect for her and Jelissa to become friends but she hoped they could at least be cool with each other, since apparently Jelissa wasn't going anywhere and Sylvia certainly had her fill of drama for a long while.

After everything had died down some, Delta, Dub, Jelissa, Bryce, and Valencio went home while Sylvia, Sandra, and Deuce stayed and talked to Candy after letting her take a shower and eat two helpings of the dinner Sandra cooked.

"Candy, baby, I need you to agree to be totally honest with us," Sandra said.

"Yes, ma'am," Candy agreed. She was sitting between Deuce and Sylvia on the couch, while Sandra sat in the armchair facing them.

"Where have you been all this time?"

"I was at Kita's up until a few days ago. Then her mama told me I had to get a job if I was gonna stay there, and she got me a job at Taco Bell. But I got fired on my second day, and I just left Kita's since I figured her mama would put me out, anyway."

"Why didn't you come home then?" Sylvia asked her.

Candy glanced at her, then down at her lap. "I...I didn't want to since you were here."

That hurt Sylvia and she had to turn her head and blink away the tears threatening to fall. The fact that her daughter would rather sleep on the street than come home to her was like a knife in her heart.

"Why didn't you call somebody?" Sandra asked, reaching over to rub Sylvia's knee and glancing at her sympathetically.

"I didn't have my phone. And I don't know anybody's number by heart."

"So you willingly chose to sleep on the street. Do you know what could have happened to you out there, Candy? Do have *any* idea how dangerous it is nowadays?"

"If I didn't before, I sure do now after what happened tonight."

"Yeah, you need to thank God every day that that Jelissa woman was there and was willing to come to your aid," Sandra said. "A lot of people would have went on about their business."

"These streets are no joke, Candy," Deuce chimed in, internally reminding himself not to lecture. "I've seen people get shot, strangled, beaten down...it's no place for a fifteen-year-old girl. Especially if she doesn't have to be there. You had somewhere you could've gone. Most people out there don't."

Candy looked at him, then just nodded and looked back at her hands in her lap. "I know."

"Baby, you have got to work out whatever issues you have with your mama," Sandra said. "Y'all butt heads so much because you're so much alike; I had to put up with a lot of the same things she's dealing with from you. Regardless of whether you agree with her and how she does things or not, she's your mother and you need to learn to respect her regardless. She's never done you any harm, has she?"

"No, ma'am," Candy admitted.

"Be thankful for that. Because not all kids can say that. Some parents don't care anything about their own children, but Sylvia loves you. And from what I can see, so does your father," Sandra added, winking at Deuce.

Surprised, Deuce looked at her and gave her a small smile. "Yeah, I do," he said, turning to face Candy fully. She looked up at him. "Look...I haven't been here for you all these years, and yeah, I had my reasons, but none of them excuse that. Hopefully you'll forgive me, though, 'cause I'm ready to be here for you now. I want us to start getting to know each other. What you think about that?"

Candy glanced at both Sandra and Sylvia before looking at her dad and nodding, a small smile coming to her face. Truth be told, she had always wished she had a father in her life; there were times she felt jealous of Valencio for having Bryce when she didn't have anyone. Part of her was mad at Deuce for not coming around before now, but after what she had just experienced, she knew she better be thankful instead of being stubborn.

"That sounds good," she said.

Deuce grinned, something that Sylvia had never seen him do in all her years of knowing him. He and Candy just sat there smiling and looking at each other somewhat awkwardly, each looking like they wanted to hug the other but not really knowing how to make the first move. Finally, Candy just lunged over and grabbed Deuce around the waist, placing her head against his chest; it was just like she had done with Dub. Deuce put his arms around her, somewhat hesitantly at first before he seemed to melt into it and rest his cheek on the top of her head, closing his eyes.

"Thank you, Jesus," Sandra praised softly, smiling at them.

Sylvia was actually pretty touched by the scene, herself; she honestly had never thought she'd see the day. But for Candy's sake, she was glad that Deuce was finally ready to do the right thing by her.

Hopefully he starts paying some child support, too, she thought to herself. But she knew then wasn't the time to bring that up.

After several moments, Sylvia cleared her throat. "Candy, I really hope that you and I can improve our relationship, too. Mama's right; we are a lot alike; I mean, a *lot* alike. It really kinda freaks me out when I think about it sometimes, because watching you is like watching myself when I was your age."

Candy turned where she could look at Sylvia while still holding on to Deuce.

"After I got pregnant with you, it was a time when I really felt like I didn't have anyone because my friends had abandoned me, Mama was mad at me, and Deuce...well, me and Deuce weren't really on the best terms," Sylvia said tactfully, not wanting to say what the truth was. She didn't want to sour Candy's perception of Deuce any more than it already was when they were getting ready to start trying to forge a relationship. Maybe one day in the *very* distant future she could be real with Candy about how Deuce had said he wouldn't have anything to do with her, but not any time soon. Maybe not any time ever; Candy really didn't need to know that, when it came down to it. Especially since Deuce had clearly changed his tune.

"Anyway," Sylvia continued, as Deuce looked at her regretfully, "I had told myself that I would raise you to be my best friend; that you and I would be close like the Judds."

"The who?" Candy asked, looking confused.

"Oh. Like, um...like the Kardashians."

"Oh."

"But things didn't really go like I thought they would...we didn't end up being as close as I hoped we would be. I thought letting you pretty much do what you wanted was a good thing to do, but it wasn't. At the end of the day, I was also trying to prove a point to my mama that you didn't have to be all strict and stuff like she was with me to be a good mother. But trying to be your child's friend isn't the way, either. I finally get that there has to be a balance."

Sandra looked at her proudly.

"So I apologize to you for not being the kind of mother I should've been," Sylvia said to Candy, placing a hand on her leg. "And I'm gonna do my part to improve. But I'm gonna need you to do yours, too, Candy. You can't fight me on everything. A lot of things are gonna have to change."

With a quick glance at Sandra, Candy asked, "Like what?"

"Well first, we're gonna start with respect. Like it or not, I'm your mother and you need to respect me like I am. The past is the past; you can't hold the fact that I haven't been doing this from the beginning over my head anymore. We both have a clean slate; I don't expect things to change overnight, but they need to change quick. There are gonna be rules, I'm gonna be tougher on you, and I don't need you getting an attitude when I tell you to do something. The same way you respect your grandmama, you need to respect me."

"That's right," Sandra agreed.

Candy eyed her mother, and remembered how she wished she could've been with her when she was getting dragged across the parking lot by that sweaty man earlier. If the past few days had taught her anything, it was who was really there for her and who wasn't. And also, that being stubborn could get you in some major trouble.

"Okay," she agreed softly. She felt Deuce squeeze her shoulder in approval.

"What?" Sandra quickly asked, sitting up.

"I mean, yes, ma'am."

We'll see, Sylvia thought to herself.

Chapter 25

• • • •

SYLVIA FIGURED THINGS would go a little rocky for a while, and they were.

Candy now had several chores around the house, limited phone and computer time, and a strict curfew. She wasn't any more used to having all these rules than Sylvia was implementing them, but they both knew things couldn't go on like they were going before. Neither of them had been happy, almost without even really realizing it.

There were a few times when Sylvia would tell Candy to do something and get a little push-back or very small traces of attitude, but Sylvia didn't let those little bumps in the road derail her. She had expected that; it would have been unrealistic to expect Candy to turn into some kind of angel overnight. But she could see her daughter was trying, so Sylvia was willing to be patient. But unlike in the past when Candy got an attitude with her, Sylvia didn't just let it go without consequence.

"You better watch that eye-rolling, Candy," Sylvia warned after having told Candy to take out the trash.

"I didn't roll my eyes."

"Yes, you did."

"Okay I did, but this is usually Valencio's job."

"Valencio isn't here. And trust, he has just as many chores over at his dad's as you do over here, if not more. So it's not like he's getting away with anything."

"Fine," Candy muttered, heading to the kitchen to retrieve the trash.

"Just so you know, that little eye-roll cost you thirty minutes of phone time tonight," Sylvia called after her.

Candy whirled around. "Thirty minutes?!"

"Yep."

"Really??"

"Yes, really."

"But-"

"Wanna make it an hour? Keep talking."

Candy clamped her mouth shut.

"Now, what are you *supposed* to say when I tell you to do something?" Sylvia asked her.

"Yes, ma'am," Candy mumbled, clawing at the carpet with her toes.

"Couldn't hear you."

"Yes, ma'am," Candy repeated louder.

"Good. Now go on and get that trash out before it gets dark."

This was how it usually went when Candy would in any way revert to her old attitude, and Sylvia always handled it the same way. Candy hated when any of her privileges were revoked, so one of them was usually the first thing to go when she was being punished. Over time, Candy's attitude improved more and more, and it seemed like she was being nicer because she wanted to and not just to avoid getting in trouble. Sylvia was quick to praise her when she did things right just as quickly as she reprimanded her when she did things wrong, and she could tell Candy appreciated this. It certainly wasn't something Sylvia used to be in the habit of doing, partially just because and partially because Candy usually didn't do much to praise. But like Sylvia had said, they both had a clean slate. It was a new day. And they were both trying to take advantage of it.

Deuce had also been coming around more, spending more time with Candy. Some nights he would come eat dinner with Candy and Sylvia, or take Candy out to dinner. Sometimes he would just come hang out at Sylvia's and he and Candy would chill in the living room, talking and watching movies or something. And they spent most Saturdays together. Sylvia actually thought it was cute, how Deuce was with Candy. He was like completely different person.

The hard, seemingly heartless man that she had known for years wasn't there anymore; he still had his edge, but when it came to Candy, he was developing a soft spot that nobody really expected. And Candy looked forward to their time together, also; whenever he would come over, she would run to the door and hug him like it was the first time in years. Sylvia noticed that Candy hugged on Deuce a lot, even when they were just sitting around, and she realized how much Candy must have missed having a father in her life before then. Sylvia hated that so much time had to pass before they got to this point, but she was thankful it was happening now.

• • • •

CANDY REALLY HADN'T been feeling like herself for a few days, and something told her there was a very good reason for that.

When Sylvia got home one night, Candy ventured into her room where she was taking off her shoes. "Hey, Mama."

"Hey, Candy. Had a good day?"

"Yes. I mean, yes, ma'am. Auntie Delta came and took me to the movies and out to eat."

"Yeah, she asked me if she could do that. What did y'all see?"

"Some movie with Idris Elba. She was talking about how fine he is."

Sylvia chuckled, releasing her braids from the ponytail they were in.

Biting her lip, Candy came fully into the room and sat down on the bed. "Mama, can I ask you something?"

"You can ask me anything," Sylvia replied.

"What does it feel like to be pregnant?"

Sylvia stopped taking the studs out of her ears and looked over at her daughter. Telling herself to stay calm, she asked, "You think you're pregnant?"

"I think I might be."

Taking a deep breath, Sylvia went over and joined her on the bed. She slowly rubbed her hands together, scraping her clear fingernails against her left palm. "By who?"

"Mac. He's the last one I've been with."

Candy didn't want to admit that it could've also been the man that sexed her in the back hallway of Club Bounce when she was there with Kita and Jamie. She didn't necessarily want to be dishonest, but it was embarrassing. The details of that night were kind of fuzzy but Candy remembered having sex, even though she wouldn't have been able to recall who she had it with if you gave her a million dollars. Whether it was him or Mac would all depend on how far along she was, if she was pregnant at all.

"That's the one I caught you in your room with, right?" Sylvia confirmed.

Candy just nodded, looking down at her hands.

Sylvia exhaled a long, slow breath. Part of her wanted to be angry, but the other part quickly reminded her that she was as much to blame for it if Candy was pregnant as Candy was. It was her shotty parenting that contributed to it. Maybe if she hadn't spent so much time coaching Candy on what to do in bed to please the boys, Candy wouldn't be in this predicament.

"So we need to get you tested, then," Sylvia said after a few moments.

"Okay."

The next day, they went to the clinic and it was confirmed that Candy was indeed pregnant. Sylvia was crushed; she had been holding out hope that she wouldn't be. This was one thing that Sylvia had done at Candy's age that she hoped Candy wouldn't repeat. There was nothing fun or hot about being a teenage mother. Things had been going so well, too...now, they had to contend with a baby on the way along with everything else. Sylvia imagined this must have been how Sandra felt when Candy announced to her that day that she was knocked up.

Candy wasn't feeling any more positive than her mother was. She had been hoping that she'd just caught some kind of virus or something; she didn't want to have a baby. And when the doctor told her she was a little over a month along, she knew that Mac was the father. She didn't know how she was going to tell him about this, especially after that mess when she was sleeping in front of the Dollar General and him leaving her there when he saw her. There was a time when she probably would have been happy about being pregnant by Mac, but that wasn't the case now. She really didn't want to talk to him, but Sylvia told her she would have to tell him about this as soon as possible; something about it being the right thing to do. Hopefully he would be willing to do right by her and the baby, though something told her not to get her hopes up.

Just as much as Candy was dreading telling Mac about the pregnancy, Sylvia was dreading telling Deuce. She had no idea how he would react to this, but she knew she couldn't keep it from him. She asked him to come to the store while she was working in the next couple of days so she could tell him in person.

"Hey Deuce," she greeted when he walked in. She was just finishing stocking the paper plates.

"Hey, wassup."

"Come on, let's go outside for a minute," Sylvia suggested, leading the way towards the front door. She really didn't want to be standing in the middle of the store when she told him their daughter was knocked up. There was no telling how he would react and she didn't want him making a scene in front of people.

"Everything good?" Deuce asked her when they got outside. Sylvia was glad that not only was Deuce building a relationship with Candy, he was also being nicer to her, as well. He would actually ask her how she was doing, which was something he never used to do.

They talked some when he would come over to see Candy. And he had started giving her money without her even having to ask.

"Not really," Sylvia admitted, glancing around her as she rubbed her arms nervously.

"What's wrong?"

"Well...I guess there's no way to sugarcoat it so I'll just come out with it. Candy is pregnant."

It took Deuce a second to register what she said, but when he did, a frown immediately took over his neutral expression. "What the hell?? What?!"

"Candy's pregnant."

"By who?"

"Some boy named Mac."

"Mac? Mac what?"

"I don't know his last name."

"Well we need to find it so I'll know exactly whose ass it is I'm beatin'."

"Deuce, come on. I'm not happy about it either but we need to check ourselves. This is just us fifteen years ago."

"That don't make it right, Sylvia!"

"I know it don't. But neither of us would qualify for any awards when it comes to parenting before the past couple of weeks. We haven't been the best example. To be honest, I'm not even all that surprised. There's no telling how long ago it was that Candy lost her virginity."

"Excuse me??"

"Our child is fast, Deuce; I'm not gonna front about that. But I had hoped that somehow she wouldn't end up like me, in that regard. But that's not how it went. She's knocked up and we just have to deal with it."

Deuce glared at her then took a few steps away, running a hand down his face. He tried to calm himself down and consider Sylvia's words. As much as he hated to admit it, she was right. While he had gotten significantly closer to Candy, he didn't really think he was in any position to be reprimanding her about getting pregnant when he had fathered eight kids before the age of thirty, himself.

"Has she told the boy yet? What does he say?" Deuce asked after a few moments.

"Nah, she hasn't told him yet. I told her she needs to go ahead and do it, though. He needs to know."

"How's Candy doing?"

"As okay as she can be doing. We just really found this out a couple of days ago."

"She didn't make sure he was using any rubbers?"

Sylvia's arched a brow at his question. "She said that he was wearing one but it broke. This happened when she was staying at her friend's house after she ran away. Apparently she had called him over one day when she was bored and they got down."

"That's all she could think of to do when she was bored?"

Sylvia shrugged. "You'd have to talk to her about that. She had a big crush on this boy and probably gave it up to him whenever he smiled at her."

"Damn," Deuce muttered. "So...what do we do now?"

"I'm gonna sit and have a talk with her tonight. I don't think she's really processed what all this really means yet."

"How far along is she?"

"About a month and a half."

"Wow." He looked at Sylvia. "Are *you* okay with all this?"

"I better act like I am, if I ain't. 'Cause it's coming either way."

Deuce shook his head.

"What?" Sylvia asked.

"I just can't believe I'm gonna be a fuckin' granddad at thirty-two."

Later on that evening, Sylvia sat Candy down so they could have a real talk about Candy's pregnancy and what she wanted to do.

"Have you thought about any of this yet?" Sylvia asked her. "Your life is about to change, big-time. Hell, mine too, really."

"It's all I've been able to think about," Candy admitted, rubbing a hand across her stomach.

"And?"

"Would it be wrong to say I might not wanna keep it?"

"You can say whatever you want. But I'm not really with killing no innocent babies just because you don't want to deal with the result of what you laid down and did."

Sylvia knew it was pretty ironic that she was saying this, considering that she had asked Sandra if she could get an abortion when she was pregnant with Candy, after Deuce had told he wouldn't have anything to with the baby except admit it was his. Sandra had flat-out refused; there was no discussion. Sylvia at least wanted Candy to be able to say what she was feeling about it before shutting anything down.

"I don't want to do that but I'm too young to be a mother."

"But you're not too young to have sex, though, right?"

Candy glanced at her, then looked down at the floor.

"Look, Candy. It's not like I can say too much, 'cause I was knockin' boots when I was your age, too. Obviously. And I know I didn't teach you any better. But abortion isn't the *only* option, here. Have you thought about maybe giving it up for adoption? There are a lot of families who can't have kids that would appreciate it."

Candy actually hadn't thought of that. "Yeah, that's not a bad idea. But isn't pregnancy a pain? I'd have to go through all that and not even get to keep the baby?"

"That's just a decision you have to make, Candy. None of the options are gonna be easy ones. A life is at stake, here."

Candy just nodded.

"Look, I'll give you a day or so to think about all this," Sylvia said, standing from her seat at the kitchen table. "Take some time and think about what you really want to do. This is your life, but also mine, too, 'cause I'm the one that's gon' have to help you raise it. I'm not saying we'll automatically go with whatever you decide, but I'll listen to you. Aight?"

Candy nodded again, this time with a smile. "Aight."

Sylvia headed back to her bedroom, hoping she wasn't giving Candy too much leniency again. Maybe she should have done like Sandra did and made the decision for Candy. Sylvia wasn't exactly looking forward to being a grandmother, but she didn't want to kill an innocent baby. If Candy didn't want to keep the baby, adoption was the best option, in Sylvia's opinion. But she'd see what Candy said.

Candy was seriously going back and forth about what would be the best option for her. She was not excited about this pregnancy, but she could agree with Sylvia that there were plenty of families that would appreciate being able to adopt her baby. But then she'd have to gain all that weight and go through the pain of labor and have nothing to show for it; she'd just be giving the baby away as soon as it was born.

There was a tiny part of herself that was curious about what her and Mac's baby would look like. Would it have Mac's hazel eyes? His height? Or would it take after Candy? She could admit to herself that there was a certain intrigue to having Mac's baby. It would certainly make her look good (in her mind), getting pregnant by the finest boy in school. Other girls would surely be jealous of her. That reason alone made Candy reconsider the adoption option.

As much as she wasn't looking forward to it, she knew she needed to talk to Mac. He wasn't her favorite person after leaving her hanging on the street, but she *was* carrying his child. Regardless, he needed to know that.

Taking a deep breath, she picked up her phone and scrolled to his number, looking at the smug smile in his contact picture. She hit the dial button and put the phone up to her ear, telling herself to think positively.

"Hello? Who is this?" Mac answered suspiciously.

"It's Candy."

"Oh," Mac said, sounding slightly relieved. "I thought it was your mama calling me looking for you again."

His statement just reminded Candy of the last time they had seen each other; apparently Sylvia had called Mac from Candy's phone when Candy was missing. "No..."

"So wassup? You must've wised up and gone on home."

"Yeah," Candy was already tired of the little slick comments and decided to get right to the point of her call. "Look, there's something I need to tell you."

"What? Oh, you wanna get down again? You can come over here if you hurry up; my dad will be home in a couple of hours-"

"Mac, that is *not* what I'm calling you for," Candy interjected. As much as she used to love having sex with Mac, she wasn't even the least bit tempted by his offer. He had really broken it with her when he left her hanging after she had asked him for help.

"Then what you want?"

"I'm curious what your dad would say if you told him you were about to have a baby."

There was a pause. "He'd probably be mad as hell. He used to tell me about...wait, why you askin'??"

"Because you are."

"What?!"

"I'm pregnant, Mac. And it's yours."

Mac got quiet for so long that Candy had to check to make sure they were still connected. "Uh...hello?? You don't have anything to say?"

"Uhh..." Mac stammered, exhaling a long breath. "Umm..."

"Look, I don't even know what I'm gonna do yet," Candy said, running out of patience. "Mama told me I should go ahead and tell you."

Clearing his throat, Mac finally spoke. "So...you think you might keep it?"

"Don't know."

"Well," Mac cleared his throat again, "If you do...I got you. My Pops is gonna kill me, but I'll do what I'm supposed to do."

Not expecting to hear that, Candy smiled a little to herself. She was pleasantly surprised; she had expected Mac to tell her it was her problem and hang up in her face.

"Really?"

In the next second, Mac burst out laughing. "*Hell* no!"

"What?"

"You think I want to have a damn baby? I'm about to go to college and then I'll be in the NBA, and I'll be damned if I have to deal with giving you part of my bread for years; you're just trying to tie yourself to me for life. Matter of fact, that's probably why you did this!"

Candy couldn't believe her ears. "Why *I* did it??"

"Yes, you! 'Cause you were always tryin' to get me inside you; now I know why!"

"You think I did this on purpose?? I don't want to have a baby, either!"

"Yeah, you do. No wonder you were always down for it whenever. You probably poked a hole in the damn condom or something!"

Angry tears stung Candy's eyes. "You sound real stupid right now, Mac! First of all, *you* stepped to *me*, I didn't step to you. *You* started talking about having sex, not me. And third, you always brought your own damn condoms so how would I poke holes in 'em, asshole? Why don't you grow up?!"

Mac got quiet again and Candy wondered if he was considering what she said. Then he replied in a low voice, "Man, even if all that's true, that don't mean I want to have a baby with somebody that looks like you. I ain't gon' be embarrassed by having to tell folks you my baby mama. Maybe if you were a dime, I'd claim it. But you ain't. So I ain't."

Candy hadn't thought Mac could hurt her any more than he already had, but she was wrong. His words were like a rusty knife jabbed right into her chest. She hoped to high heaven she could hold it together and not break down while she was still on the phone with him, because she really felt close to it.

"Is that right," she managed to say.

"So I suggest you get an abortion," Mac continued. "'Cause you won't be getting *anything* from me."

Curling her lips under, Candy hastily wiped the tears from her cheeks, even though they were just quickly replaced with more. "I guess there's nothing else for us to talk about, then." She hung up the phone and let it fall to the floor as she broke down crying so hard her stomach hurt.

As soon as Sylvia got home a few hours later, Candy walked up to her and said without preamble, "I want an abortion."

Chapter 26

• • • •

WITH EVERYTHING ELSE going on, Sylvia was trying to open herself up to a relationship with Bryce.

Having never been in a real relationship before, she really didn't know what was expected of her or what she was supposed to do. She and Bryce had developed something of a dynamic over the years and it wasn't as easy for her to step outside of that as she expected it to be. They were co-parents and very, very occasional lovers. That was it. And even though she wanted a man and she knew Bryce was a good one, and her head told her she needed to give being with him her best shot, her heart still wanted Dub. She knew this was something that she would have to make herself get over, though, or else she would just be wasting Bryce's time.

One of the many things Bryce did that Sylvia wasn't used to was take her out on dates. He would call her, ask her out, come pick her up, and take her somewhere nice. He held her hand, pulled out her chair, held doors open for her...and he never tried to get in her bed afterwards. Sylvia had suspected he would, at least after the first few dates, but he didn't. He kissed her, but that was as far as he tried to take it. Sylvia wasn't used to men who wanted her for anything other than sex. But Bryce actually seemed to enjoy her company and sincerely want to continue getting to know her. For Sylvia, this was foreign territory.

"Bryce, you know if you want to have sex, all you gotta do is say so," Sylvia said one night when he was dropping her off. He had just unlocked her door for her and walked her inside her apartment.

He turned to look at her. "Excuse me?"

"Oh, my bad...I meant *make love.*"

"No, I'm saying why would you say that at all?"

"I'm just saying if you're doing all this nice stuff to get me into bed, it's not necessary. I mean, don't get me wrong; I appreciate it and everything..."

"Sylvia," Bryce said, actually chuckling as he walked over to her and took her face in his hands. Looking into her big brown eyes, he gently said, "It's a shame that that's the kind of treatment you're used to. I don't have any ulterior motives here. This is how I treat the woman I'm with. It's not about sex."

"Really?" Sylvia asked, genuinely surprised.

"Really."

"Wow."

Bryce chuckled again as he leaned down and kissed her, gathering her in his arms. She slid her arms around his neck, eagerly kissing him back. Candy was with Deuce and Sylvia found herself getting more and more turned on by the minute. The fact that Bryce wasn't trying to get into her panties only made her want to let him.

"I don't want you to get me wrong, though," Bryce said after they broke their kiss, "It's not that I don't want it. But I'm trying to get in here -" he tapped her chest, " – more than I'm trying to get in there." He pointed towards her groin.

Sylvia's panties were wet. But she wasn't about to tell him that.

"I think I like that already," she said softly.

Smiling at her, Bryce replied, "Good," before leaning down and kissing her again. Sylvia loved kissing Bryce; his lips were thick and moist and soft. And he knew what he was doing. It seemed like such a simple thing but kissing wasn't something that Sylvia got a lot of; the men she slept with tended to want to just get right to the sex; kissing ended up being more of an optional side dish, not a main course. But Sylvia could feast on Bryce's kisses all day.

Bryce left a little while later, and while Sylvia didn't want him to leave, she couldn't bring herself to beg him to stay. She wasn't trying to look desperate. It just would have been nice to cuddle with him while watching a movie or listening to some music or something. But she was still happy. Despite everything that was going on with Candy, Sylvia was starting to feel good about her budding relationship with Bryce. When Delta called a little later to ask her how everything went and how Bryce was treating her, Sylvia had a simple answer:

"Like a lady."

• • • •

A LOT OF CHANGES WERE going on at once. One big one was that Candy was no longer pregnant; Sylvia had granted her request to get an abortion. After Candy told her what Mac had said to her when she told him she was pregnant with his baby, and seeing how incredibly hurt and devastated Candy was, Sylvia just couldn't bring herself to make her go through with the pregnancy, even for adoption. Candy had said she didn't want Mac's baby inside of her at all, and Sylvia could all too well relate to how she felt. It was like her situation with Deuce all over again. Sylvia knew that pain Candy was going through, and she wasn't going to make her suffer any more than she already was. So she and Deuce took her to the abortion clinic, all deciding that they would keep this situation between the three of them.

Another change was with Sylvia; more specifically, how she dressed. She either gave all her age-inappropriate clothes to Candy or took them to the Goodwill, and she started buying more conservative (yet still cute) things to wear. It took a little getting used to; Sylvia was just thirty-one and still wanted to feel sexy (especially now that she had a man) but she now realized she didn't have to show off everything to accomplish that.

Probably the biggest change that Bryce was trying to implement was changing Sylvia's last name.

"Did you say what I think you just said??" Sylvia asked incredulously, after Bryce had suggested they get married. They were sitting in Houston's, enjoying a nice dinner when he (kind of) popped the question.

"Yeah," Bryce replied casually, sipping his water.

"Are you joking?"

"Of course not."

"So you want to marry me."

"Yes, Sylvia," Bryce answered, amused by her skepticism.

"Just like that? We've only been going together a couple of months."

"It's not like we just *met* a couple of months ago, though. We've known each other since we were teenagers. We have a son together; I know I love you...can't say I know how you feel about me, though."

Sylvia opened her mouth to respond, but nothing came out. This was uncharted territory for her; she had never been in love before. Not real love. And she certainly had never heard a man tell her he loved her. Well, Dub said it but she knew it wasn't in any romantic way. She had realized that she and Dub would probably never happen years ago, though that didn't stop her from wishing it did. But now, she had Bryce, and she realized her thoughts and fantasies of Dub were dwindling. She didn't yearn for him like she used to; those feelings were now for Bryce. But was that love?

"I – I don't know what to say," she stammered, looking down.

"Hey," Bryce reached over and took her hand, tugging on it gently until she looked at him, "It's okay. I don't want you to say it back to me unless you mean it. And when you do, you'll know. So it's all good; I'm not trying to pressure you into anything." He leaned back in his seat and winked at her, picking up his water glass again. "You know where I stand. The offer is on the table."

"The offer is on the table," Sylvia repeated.

"Yep." He played with her ring finger, eying her seductively. Or at least, that's how Sylvia interpreted it. She squirmed in her seat, both from nervousness and horniness. She had found that Bryce could turn her on to the tenth power without even trying. They still had yet to consummate their new relationship, and Sylvia wondered how much longer she was going to have to wait, because she *wanted* this man. Was he waiting on her to tell him she loved him before he slept with her?

"You're a good man, Bryce," Sylvia complimented shyly.

"I appreciate that."

"I still can't believe you actually wanna marry me. *Me*."

"Well, believe it."

"Are you sure you know what you're doing?"

"I know exactly what I'm doing."

• • • •

CANDY WAS EXPERIENCING a mix of emotions from one day to the next. She would go from being angry at Mac for dissing her to crying about him dissing her in no time flat. She'd get depressed over the abortion she had, torturing herself about what the baby probably would have looked like, and if it would have been a boy or a girl. At the end of the day, she was glad Sylvia respected her wishes and let her abort the baby; the things Mac had said to her totally emptied her of any positive thoughts about her pregnancy, or much else. He had been downright cold to her, and she didn't think she would ever forget what he said to her that day.

Her sixteenth birthday had come and gone without much celebration; it was actually *on* her birthday that she had gotten the abortion. Deuce had agreed to pay for it, and he and Sylvia took her to get it taken care of. That abortion was all Candy wanted for her birthday. She just had to get Mac's seed out of her; she didn't want any part of anyone that could be so hateful.

One thing Candy was pretty pleasantly surprised about was how well things were going at home with Sylvia. They had never gotten along as well as they were now. Sylvia was really sticking to her new parenting style, and Candy could admit she resisted it some at first, but she was pretty much on board with it now. No, she didn't always like some of the things Sylvia said to her or made her do, but what kid did? She finally realized that at the end of the day, her mother loved her and that was why she gave her rules. Candy especially appreciated this after hearing about her friend Kita's house getting robbed after she had invited some friends over. Whoever it was she invited had brought someone else with them, and they then texted a friend of *theirs* to come over while they were all upstairs, and when the guest pretended to go to the bathroom, they actually went and let their friends in so they could rob the downstairs while Kita and everyone else was upstairs. Kita's mother Janine wasn't home, and when she got there later and saw what had happened, she went crazy on Kita, beating her like she was a grown woman. Candy felt bad for them getting robbed, but she also knew that something like that was less likely to happen to her because Sylvia had implemented a rule about not having guests over when she wasn't there. Candy hadn't been too crazy about that when Sylvia first told her about it, but after hearing about what happened to Kita, she appreciated it. She had a mother that actually cared about what she did.

Candy found it a lot easier to talk to Sylvia now that Sylvia was no longer trying to be her friend and was just focusing on being her mother. Sylvia was dressing differently, acting differently...Candy wondered how much of that had to do with her being with Bryce now, but Candy liked it either way. Outside of her aborted pregnancy, things in Candy's life were going better than they had been in years, or ever. It took a traumatic event to make her start appreciating things, but she surely did.

• • • •

DUB HADN'T BEEN BY in a little while, and he called Sylvia one day to ask if he could come see her and Candy. He had been calling Candy every week or so to check on her, but since Deuce was in the picture now, he fell back a little bit. But he didn't want Candy to think he hadn't really meant all those things he had said to her in her living room that day, so he made sure to keep in touch regularly.

"How are you?" he asked Sylvia when he arrived, opening his arms to her for a hug.

Sylvia smiled and stepped to him for the hug, noticing the usual giddiness that came with being close to Dub wasn't really there. She was glad to see him, but it wasn't in the same way it was before.

"Wow, you look great," Dub observed, stepping back to look at her in her dark jeans and tank top. "You cut your hair."

"Yep," Sylvia concurred, running a hand over her new short hairdo. "It was time for a change."

"Well, it looks really, really good," Dub said again, eying her from head to toe. Sylvia started to squirm under his intense gaze and she turned towards the hallway.

"Lemme get Candy in here," she said quickly. "Candy!"

Candy emerged from her room and upon seeing Dub there, rushed over to him and gave him her usual eager hug around his waist. The three of them sat in the living room and talked for a while, with Candy and Dub doing most of the talking. At one point Bryce called, and Sylvia went to her room to talk to him. She didn't realize how long she had been in there until Candy came to her door.

"Uncle Dub said he's about to leave."

"Oh okay. Bryce, lemme call you right back, baby," she said into the phone. She paused and then giggled like a schoolgirl at Bryce's apparent response, and Candy couldn't help but smile. It was nice to see her mother so happy.

Candy went to her room while Sylvia went to say goodbye to Dub.

"I'm sorry about that," she said to him, regarding the phone call. "I wasn't trying to be rude or anything."

"Don't worry about it," Dub said. "Candy mentioned that you were seeing someone now and that's probably who you were talking to. Not trying to be nosy or anything, but was it?"

"Yeah," Sylvia replied, blushing and smiling.

Dub smiled at her. "I'm happy for you, Sylvia. You deserve someone who makes you smile like that."

"Thank you; I think I do, too," she replied, smiling harder. "How are things with you and Jelissa?"

"Things are good. I'm actually thinking about going ahead and popping the question."

"Really? That's great!" Sylvia replied sincerely. She chose not to say anything about Bryce's proposal to her just yet.

Dub eyed her, not having expected such an enthusiastically positive response. "You really think so?"

"Yeah, I do. Why not? Hey, speaking of that, can you give me her number?"

Dub paused. "*Jelissa's* number?"

"Yeah. I figured it was time we get to know each other better, since she's gonna be part of the family and everything. And I wanted to thank her again for what she did for Candy."

"I'm sure she'll appreciate that, but Sylvia, you've thanked her a million times already."

"I can't thank her enough for saving my child."

Dub just looked at her earnestly, then pulled her to him for another embrace. It was like he wasn't able to help it. There was something different about Sylvia; she was more mature, and happier. She just looked at ease. He didn't think he had ever seen her like this. It was actually pretty attractive.

After a couple of moments, he pulled back and gave her Jelissa's phone number as she requested, then said he had to get on home.

"Can I ask you one thing before you go?" Sylvia asked impulsively when he had his hand on the doorknob.

"Of course."

Before she lost her nerve, Sylvia forged ahead. "Can you tell me what it was that kept you from ever being into me romantically?"

His eyebrows shooting up in surprise, Dub's hand fell from the doorknob and he turned to face her. Sylvia almost started to retract the question, but she found that she really did want to know.

"You don't think it's because there's anything wrong with you, do you?" he asked her.

"No. I mean, not anymore. I'm just curious; it's something I've always wondered about but never had the nerve to ask you. I mean, I know I'm not the best-looking woman or anything-"

"Sylvia, stop that," Dub interrupted her. "I don't even want to hear you say that kind of stuff. It's never been about your looks. And I'm glad you don't think it's because there's anything wrong with you, even though I hate to hear you ever did." He gave her a small smile. "I've just always thought of you as a little sister, that's all. The more we hung out, the cooler I knew you were. There was just something about you I always liked."

Sylvia smiled at his response. "Thank you for answering that. I guess it just kind of stung that you seemed to be cool with me like you were but wouldn't...sleep with me like you did everybody else."

"Damn," Dub chuckled. "Truth be told, Sylvia, I respected you too much to do that. Those girls I got with back in the day were just...I don't even know how to put it. They were just something to do. I'm not proud of this but I can't say I really cared about any of 'em. You remember Paula?"

"Yeah," Sylvia grunted. Paula had gotten in her way several times when Sylvia had tried to get close to Dub back in the day.

"Well she and I got down a few times, but I couldn't have told you anything real about her back then. I never tried to get to know her. I heard she's been married like three times already and gained a whole bunch of weight. She's living over in Marietta somewhere."

"Wow," Sylvia marveled, wondering if she should feel bad for being happy to hear that.

"But yeah, that's all it was," Dub continued, referring to him and Sylvia. "And don't take this the wrong way, but I'm *glad* you and I never slept together. That kind of thing can mess up a friendship. And I wouldn't want to lose you as a friend."

Grinning, Sylvia nodded. "Yeah, I wouldn't want that, either. Thanks, Dub."

"No problem. I love you, Sylvia."

"Love you, too."

Dub left, and Sylvia just stood there for a few moments, smiling to herself. Maybe it was better that she and Dub never had sex; she certainly wasn't as close with any other man in her life that she had slept with as she was with him. And she was just grateful that he loved her as much as he did, and genuinely wanted her in his life.

Actually giggling to herself, she hurried to her room to call Bryce back.

Chapter 27

• • • •

"YOU GOT A MINUTE FOR me to come by?" Deuce asked Sylvia over the phone one Sunday evening.

"Yeah, if you're able to come on now. I'll be going out in a little over an hour." Sylvia had a date with Bryce that night.

"Okay. I'll be there in a few."

Deuce showed up about fifteen minutes later and he got right to the point of his visit.

"I think we should get married," he said with a straight face.

Sylvia blinked, that being the last thing she was expecting to hear. "What??"

"We should get married," Deuce repeated.

Sylvia actually wanted to laugh, but didn't think that would go over so well. "And why is that, Deuce?"

"For Candy's sake."

"Candy? What, she told you she wanted us to get married?"

"No, but I bet she'd like it if we did."

"As romantic as that is, Deuce-"

"Sylvia, come on. I'm for real."

"You can't be. You and I both know we would have no business trying to be married."

"Why not?"

"Well, for one, we don't even love each other."

"Who says?"

"Deuce." Sylvia looked at him pointedly.

"Okay, but that's not the most important thing you need in a marriage," he finally said.

"It's certainly at the top of the list, though."

"Sylvia-"

"Deuce, look," Sylvia interjected, turning to face him on the couch as she took his rough hands in hers. "It says a lot that you want to do this, but I think you know as well as I do that in the long run, it just wouldn't be a good idea. I want to marry someone I'm in love with, and that's in love with me." She couldn't resist a small smile when she said this. "You and I are finally getting along; I don't want to do anything to mess that up. How 'bout we just concentrate on being the best co-parents for Candy that we can be, and be happy with that?"

Deuce just looked at her for a few moments before finally nodding. "Yeah. You're probably right. I was just trying to do the right thing."

"I appreciate the thought, but getting married for the wrong reasons can't be the right thing."

"True. And really, I don't even think I'm the marrying type. But I was willing to try it, for Candy."

Sylvia gave him a small smile. "You think you're just trying to make up for all the years you haven't been there for her?"

Deuce looked at her thoughtfully, then shrugged. "Probably."

"Is that why you paid for her abortion, too?"

"Well, I can admit that was partly for me. I really wasn't crazy about being anybody's granddaddy any more than Candy wanted to be anybody's mama."

Sylvia chuckled.

"I guess I just feel like I owe her," Deuce admitted.

"Yeah. But you can't try to cram almost sixteen years of neglect into a few months, Deuce."

"Yeah."

"You're here for her now, and that's what's important. And she seems thrilled that you are."

"I'm kinda surprised by that, actually. I was fully expecting her to tell me to kick rocks or something."

"I think she always wished you were around more. And after everything that's happened to her, she's a lot more appreciative of things now. I hate to say it, but her running away and sleeping on the street and getting attacked might have been the best thing that happened to her. She's like a whole different person."

"Well, you did a good job raising her."

"I really didn't. But I'm doing better now."

Deuce looked at her then looked away. "I know I owe you an apology."

Sylvia's eyebrows shot up in surprise. She didn't think he would ever apologize for anything, whether he knew he was wrong or not. "Really?"

"Yeah. I know I was wrong for how I treated you all these years. Hell, I knew it when I was doing it. I guess I just figured I could."

"And what about tricking me into thinking you were Dub back in the day and knocking me up?"

"That, too. I was a stupid, cocky kid back then, still mad at the world 'cause my dad left us hanging. Dub was the one that pointed that out to me and made me realize what a jackass I was to everybody."

Sylvia smiled, not surprised.

"He let me know that I can't do other folks wrong just 'cause our dad did us wrong," Deuce continued. "Took me a while, but I get it now. So, sorry."

Her smile widening at his simple yet meaningful apology, Sylvia replied, "I really appreciate that, Deuce. Never thought I'd hear it, but I appreciate it."

"Hell, never thought I'd say it."

They both laughed. Sylvia wanted to pinch herself, because this couldn't have been real. Deuce had actually apologized to her? They were actually having a mature conversation without arguing or cussing each other out, and had actually shared a laugh? Sylvia honestly never thought she would see the day.

"So you really don't wanna be with me, huh?" Deuce asked her.

"Nah, I really don't," Sylvia replied, still smiling. *And I never did*, she thought to herself, not wanting to be mean by saying that part out loud.

"'Cause of Dub?"

"That might've been the reason back in the day, along with you just being an asshole," Sylvia replied, nudging him playfully, "But now it's 'cause I'm with somebody."

Deuce looked surprised. In all the years he had known Sylvia, he had never seen her in a relationship. "You are? With who?"

"It's actually my son's father, Bryce. I don't think you've met him. But he's been right in my face all along and I finally woke up and saw it. And I'm really, *really* into him."

"I see you look all different and stuff now. You love him?"

An automatic smile came to Sylvia's face. "Yeah. I do."

"Well, damn," Deuce said, giving her a small smile. "I guess I can't hate on that. Good for you."

"Thanks, Deuce."

"He treating you good?"

Grinner harder, Sylvia replied, "Good ain't the word. He treats me like a queen."

"Yeah? He hittin' it better than I did?"

"Deuce!!" she gasped, hitting him on the arm.

"What? I'm just askin.'"

"None of your damn business!"

"That's a no," Deuce joked, standing up. Sylvia just chuckled and shook her head as she stood up with him and they headed towards the door.

"Aight, well I'll see you later," she said.

"Yeah. What's Candy gonna be doing the rest of the summer? She said she was getting a job."

"Yeah, she is. She starts at McDonald's next week. It's just a couple days a week so she can make a little pocket change. I think she wants something to take her mind off Mac and the abortion and stuff. Thankfully school starts back in another month or so."

"She holding up okay?"

"As good as she can be after something like that."

"Well, if it's all right with you, I wanted to take her to spend some time with my mama for a couple of days. Now that I'm getting my act together she's all eager to spend more time with all her grandkids."

"That's cool; I don't have a problem with that."

"Cool." Deuce opened the door, then turned back to her. "Oh, one more thing."

"Yeah?"

"You gon' still let me hit it every now and then, right?"

Sylvia couldn't help bursting out laughing. "Bye, Deuce!" she answered, pushing him out the door.

Sylvia was excited about her date with Bryce that night. She was finally going to tell him how she felt about him. She hadn't been sure before but now she was absolutely sure that she was in love with him. He was the man of her dreams, and he had been right there the whole time. Part of her wanted to kick herself for wasting so much time, chasing the fantasy of her and Dub, but it was what it was. She hadn't appreciated Bryce before; she did now.

Putting on a colorful maxi dress, some sandals, hoop earrings, and just a little makeup, Sylvia checked her short hair in the mirror, feeling her nerves start to tingle her skin. Her hands were actually trembling, and she shook them vigorously, trying to calm herself down.

Candy came and stood in Sylvia's bedroom doorway, leaning against the doorjamb. "You look nice, Mama."

"Thank you!" Sylvia replied, pleasantly surprised. She couldn't remember the last time Candy gave her a compliment.

"You look nervous, though."

"I *am* nervous."

"How come?"

"Tonight is kinda a big night."

"Why? Y'all gonna have..." She stopped herself before asking if she and Bryce were gonna have sex.

Sylvia eyed her, then shook her head. There was a time she would have eagerly gone into great and explicit detail about how much she wanted to sex Bryce. But that wasn't the reason for her nervousness. "No, not because of that."

"What time is Mr. Bryce gonna get here?"

"In about another twenty minutes," Sylvia replied, checking her watch. "I might be back kinda late. Remember what I told you, now."

"I know...no guests, don't be on the phone or the computer late...I got it."

"Good."

Bryce came and picked Sylvia up a little while later. Since Valencio was spending the night with Sandra, he took her to his place, where he had cooked a dinner of steak, shrimp, baked potatoes, and salad. He actually set the dining room table and lit some candles, dimming the lights to give it a real romantic aura. Sylvia's jaw dropped when she saw the finished product. There was an actual tablecloth and real china and everything.

"You did all this for me?" she asked, looking at Bryce.

"Of course I did."

"Wow," she marveled, taking it all in with a hand on her chest. She was floored. "This is *really* nice!"

"I'm glad you like it," he said, taking her hand and leading her to her chair, which he held out for her. "You look beautiful, by the way," he added, kissing her neck as she sat down.

Blushing fiercely, Sylvia replied with a shy, "Thank you." She was still getting used to all the compliments. She eyed him as he walked around the table, noting how his muscles bulged under the Polo shirt he was wearing. "You're looking fine as hell, too, as usual."

"'Preciate that," Bryce said with a smile as he took his own seat.

They proceeded to eat dinner and talk about various things, with Sylvia not being able to take her eyes off Bryce for more than a few seconds. He simply amazed her, in every way. No man had ever treated her so well, and without expecting anything in return. He simply wanted her love and respect. And she wanted to let him know he had it.

So when they finished eating and went to sit in the living room to watch *Love and Hip Hop: Atlanta* (which Sylvia knew Bryce only watched because of her), she couldn't hold it anymore.

"Bryce, I love you," she blurted out.

He looked at her. "Really?"

"I absolutely, positively, finally do. I know it."

Smiling harder than Sylvia had ever seen him smile, Bryce grabbed her by the waist and pulled her to him, kissing her hard. He had been waiting to hear her tell him that, even though he felt in his gut that she did. But he knew that being in a relationship was new to her, and he was willing to be patient. Even though a lot of people wondered why, he had loved Sylvia ever since they were teenagers. But she hadn't been ready for him until now. There was a lot of growing up she had to do first.

"And I wanna marry you and move in with you and even have another one of your babies, if you want," Sylvia rambled on after their kiss, her hands still kneading and sliding across his shoulders. They slid up to caress the back of his neck and sides of his face as she looked into his eyes dreamily. "I just wanna be with you. For as long as you can put up with me."

She grinned when Bryce's arms squeezed around her even tighter.

"You just made my day, you know that?" He kissed her again, and she eagerly returned it. It was like she couldn't get enough of him now.

Sylvia had never imagined herself as anybody's wife or being much more than someone's booty call. She hadn't seen too many positive family examples, other than on television. She hadn't even seen her own father in years, and while she knew her mother loved her and did the best she could, Sandra hadn't been very warm to her growing up. There weren't many 'I love yous' or hugs for no reason. And while Sylvia could admit that she was far from the best daughter, it would have been nice to have a little more affection and encouragement. But Bryce provided that for her now, and she loved it. She loved *him*, and promised herself to not do anything to mess things up. Part of her still couldn't even believe all this was happening to her.

"So..." Bryce said after their kiss ended as he reached into his pocket, "Are you ready to wear this now?"

Sylvia thought she was going to faint when he pulled out a two-carat pear-shaped diamond ring. She started fanning her face furiously, just sure she was about to hyperventilate.

"Is...is that..."

"Will you marry me, baby?" Bryce asked her.

Finally finding her words, Sylvia screamed, "Yes!" at the top of her lungs and threw her arms around his neck. Bryce laughed as he hugged her back, holding her tightly. Then he pulled back and slid the ring onto her finger, making it official.

Sylvia wanted to laugh, cry, and do the Nae-Nae dance all at the same time. She was actually engaged!

They couldn't wait to tell Valencio and Candy, but they each had an even bigger urge that overtook them right then. And they didn't even try to make it to the bedroom before they satisfied it.

Meanwhile, Candy was watching a movie at home, curled up on the couch as she ate from a bag of microwave popcorn. She was surprisingly comfortable being home alone, not feeling the urge to have any company. She wasn't trying to get in trouble, and anyway, after what happened to her friend Kita, Candy was going to be real careful about who she *did* invite over, whenever she did invite anybody.

After the movie was over, she talked to her friend China for a little while before wandering into her room and turning on her computer. She was just going to check Facebook and maybe play some Candy Crush for a while when she got an incoming call on Skype. It was Austin, the upperclassman that had tutored Candy when her grades were slipping and she was in danger of having to repeat her freshman year. He was a nice enough guy that Candy had initially thought was pretty lame, but ended up finding him kinda cool over time. Plus, he was nice to her, which was something she appreciated a lot more now.

"Hey there," he greeted her when she accepted the call. It looked like he was sitting in his bedroom and she could hear faint music in the background; it sounded like Drake.

"Hey, Austin. What's up?"

"You look surprised to hear from me."

"A little, yeah. School isn't back in yet."

"I know, but we don't have to just talk when school is in, do we?"

"I guess not."

"What are you up to tonight?"

"Just chilling."

"Alone?"

"Yeah."

"You want some company?"

Candy did consider it for a split second, but she quickly shook her head. "Nah. I'm good. I'm not supposed to have any company."

"Oh, okay. I can respect that," Austin said. He ran a hand over what looked to be a fresh haircut, and Candy for the first time noticed that he was actually pretty cute. He was kind of fair-skinned like her, but his skin had a creamy golden undertone to it, and it looked really smooth. Noticing his wavy hair, high cheekbones and somewhat thin lips, Candy wondered if he was mixed with something. She liked the faint goatee he wore; she didn't remember him having that the last time she saw him.

They talked for a while longer and Candy actually found herself enjoying their conversation. Austin made her laugh, and it felt good to laugh. They talked about the upcoming school year, music, mutual friends they had, and other various things. Before she knew it, over an hour had passed. Sylvia allowed her four hours of computer time a day on the weekends, so she was well under her limit.

"You wanna hang out sometime?" Austin asked her.

She looked at him suspiciously. "What do you mean, *hang out*?"

"Like maybe go to the movies, grab something to eat or something. Just chill in the same spot."

"Oh."

"What did you think I meant?"

"Usually when dudes say that, they're just talking about sex."

"Oh. I guess I can see why you say that. But I wasn't."

"Really?" That was just unfathomable to Candy.

"Yeah."

"Oh."

"You're looking real comfortable over there," Austin commented, noting her oversized t-shirt and shorts. She was sitting Indian-style in front of the computer on her bed.

Glancing down at her outfit, Candy shrugged. "I guess."

"Nice legs."

Again, Candy glanced down at herself. "You think so?"

"Yep."

"Oh...thanks. You have...nice arms."

Austin chuckled. "You don't have to compliment me just 'cause I complimented you. If you meant that, though, thanks."

"I meant it." And she did. The more she looked at Austin, the more she liked what she saw. He wasn't as fine as Mac, but she liked his attitude even more than his looks. That made him more attractive to her. If she was honest with herself, it turned her on.

They talked for a while longer before Candy started getting tired and ended the call. Really, she felt herself getting more and more aroused and figured she better quit while she was ahead. Before she did, though, Austin asked if he could call her the next day, and she blushed as she agreed, already looking forward to it.

"Wow," she whispered when they disconnected. "He actually seems pretty cool."

Not being able to help herself, Candy's hand eased between her legs as she thought about Austin. She had long since discovered that Sylvia had cleared her room of all her sex toys, so she just had to use her imagination as she ventured to pleasure herself for the first time in a while. Right as she was really getting into it, she got another Skype call, this time from Ray, one of the boys who had come over to Kita's with Mac when Candy was staying there. She had already taken off her shirt and had answered the call in her bra, and it didn't take long before they had both stripped down and were having full-blown cyber-sex. Almost immediately afterwards, though, Candy felt guilty.

"Damn," she whispered to herself shamefully. Ray had caught her in a weak moment; if she hadn't already been masturbating when he called, that wouldn't have happened. Part of her wondered if he would tell Mac about it. She tried to cut herself a little slack, though, figuring that it was one little slip-up and at least she couldn't get pregnant from what she had done.

"I guess I still have a ways to go," she said, slipping her shirt back over her head and climbing into bed, drifting off into a satisfied sleep.

Thanks so much for reading! I know this was kind of a heavy one but I hope you enjoyed it. Please consider leaving a review and/or sharing that you read it on social media; those kinds of shout-outs are invaluable (and much appreciated!).

You can find me on Instagram and TikTok at @authorjessicaterry and on Twitter at @itsJessicaTerry. And don't forget to subscribe to my email list at jessicaterry.com.

Also by Jessica Terry

About the Author

Jessica Terry caught the writing bug at a young age and loves little more than holing up at home in Douglasville, GA, cranking out contemporary novels. And eating.

Another thing she loves is interacting with her readers. Sign up for her email list and keep up to date with new releases at www.jessicaterry.com.

Read more at https://www.jessicaterry.com/.